THE BOOK OF JOEL

By Alex Fiano

GABRIEL'S WORLD ▫ BOOK THREE

∞

IF THE PAST DOESN'T KILL YOU, THE PRESENT WILL

Troublemaker Press
Bronx NY

The Book of Joel by Alex Fiano

Third Book in the *Gabriel's World* Series
Copyright 2014, 2019
Distributed by Troublemaker Press
ISBN: 978-0-9969943-6-1

To the Gabriel's World audience: I thank those readers worldwide who have taken an interest and liking to Gabriel and Joel and the Gabriel's World stories, my supportive friends, and my unpaid intern FRO. – A.F.

∞

Gabriel's World offers a compelling community of queer and allied characters, in stories that explore the extremes and complexity of good and evil.

Welcome to our World:
Homepage: **GabrielsWorld.com**
Email the author: **gabrielsworld@outlook.com**
Twitter: @gabrielsworld
Instagram: gabriels_world_queer_fiction

Gabriel's World: It's Time for New Heroes

MYSTERY/THRILLER/QUEER FICTION

∞

Reader Extras: Gabriel's World now has recaps on the *Gabriel's World* website for the chapters of each book. The recaps offer chapter summaries, commentary, trivia and other insight & info, going into the plot and characters in-depth. Read Recaps of the chapters on the Gabriel's World website: bit.ly/2wUy6dJ

Books by Alex Fiano

The Hanged Man

Two-Faced Woman

The Book of Joel

Dead for Now

Hardcore

Previously in the *Gabriel's World* Series:

Book One: The Hanged Man
What would you sacrifice to do the right thing?

New York City private investigator Gabriel Ross faces this elemental question in the first *Gabriel's World* book. After seeing Gabriel confront a bigot in a controversial viral video, attorney Raymond Booth wants to hire him to probe a disturbing incident at Raymond's charitable foundation. As Gabriel is otherwise publicly scorned and losing clients, he's keen to take on Raymond's case. But then Raymond disappears. Raymond's sister Toni hires Gabriel to find the missing man. Gabriel turns up evidence of abduction—and then Raymond turns up dead.

Gabriel's obsession with the case pulls him into the mystery Raymond wanted him to solve. Gabriel has help from journalist Alex Barclay and Gabriel's former boyfriend Joel McFadden...leading to complications in his personal life. Gabriel begins unraveling a sinister secret connected to the foundation-a cabal tracing back to the origins of Nazism. Gabriel endeavors to uncover the conspiracy of Raymond's murder without losing his license, freedom, or life.

Book Two: Two-Faced Woman
Who Will Catch You When You're Falling?

The second book in the *Gabriel's World* series continues the story of Gabriel Ross, a strong, brilliant, intuitive private investigator in New York City.

Gabriel's cases take him to dangerous places in his inner self and in the real world. On behalf of his clients, he seeks justice in the face of true danger.

In this story, he's undergoing severe psychological trauma from events during the previous summer, while he immerses himself in the cases of two special women. Sophie Faulkner, a woman with a second self, has been falsely accused of murder. Geneva Lennon, a transgender woman, is searching for her true birth identity.

While working to help these women, Gabriel also attempts to reclaim his spirituality and deal with his turbulent relationships. His boyfriend Alex is trying to change him and make him quit his profession. But Gabriel's loyal ex-boyfriend Joel is helping and protecting Gabriel on these cases, and he may convince Gabriel he's the love of Gabriel's life.

Two-Faced Woman is set in duality: two loves, two clients, two realms (dreams and reality), and mixing the spiritual and the physical. And the danger is double-downed, with two brutal criminals who will make Gabriel face his biggest risk yet—what he has to become in order to take them on.

∞

PRELUDE

Friedrich Wilhelm Nietzsche said, "He wonders also about himself—that he cannot learn to forget, but hangs on the past: however far or fast he runs, that chain runs with him."

C.S. Lewis said, "For the present is the point at which time touches eternity."

∞

Wednesday, January 26, 2011
Hackensack, NJ 7:33 pm

CARSON SMITH ARRIVES at his apartment, his mind still on his job even after picking up some take-out dinner and having a drink at the bar of the restaurant. Carson is an auditor for the New Jersey Comptroller's Office; he's been reviewing the State Division of Development. As per protocol, he had first brought the information he discovered to the chief procurement and land use officer in the DoD. But he's still thinking of who else may need to be approached, as he's sure there's serious corruption involved in what he found. He hasn't yet discussed the matter with his supervisor.

Carson tosses his keys on an end table and brings the take-out bag to the kitchen without turning on any lights. His mind is too deep into his situation. A very small kitchen light is already on and giving some faint illumination. He leaves that one on all day to discourage housebreakers.

It's only when he comes back into the living room to check his home phone for messages that he becomes aware he's not alone.

Someone is in a chair in his apartment living room. A huge figure, blurry in the darkness. No, blurry because he's in black and has a hood on his head.

Carson freezes halfway across the room. The figure gets up slowly. It's like a mythological beast rising from a pit. Carson is 5'10 but this person is much taller. And bigger. In the faint light Carson can barely make out any eyes showing through the holes in the hood. The hood is squareish and large, and drapes over the man's shoulders.

"Ah...ah..." Carson can't think of what to say. Is this a home invasion? Does it work like that?

The figure lifts a pair of glasses to the hood and fixes them to his face. As if he's about to read something. Then from somewhere in the black clothing he produces a gun. A very large gun—it looks like two feet in length. Carson doesn't know it's a WTS .50 BMG pistol and utterly impractical to use in a home invasion or anything other than stopping a tank coming at you. He only sees it's a large, large gun pointed at him.

The man speaks slowly, in a deep rough tone. "If I shot you, you'd bleed out in 30 seconds. But most of your internal organs would be destroyed anyway."

"What do you want?" Carson tries not to sound scared or aggressive. He has no idea how to handle this.

The giant seems to stare down at him. "I like to look at them bleeding out," he says contemplatively, as if to himself more than Carson.

Carson imagines that he will in fact be shot. Something in the man's posture gives the impression that he really, really wants to do this. Carson tries to reconcile to dying. *It's okay,* he thinks to himself, trying in utter helplessness to maintain some cognitive autonomy, or just comfort.

And in a sudden burst of courage, through gritted teeth he says, "Just tell me why."

The man tilts his hooded head as if he doesn't understand what Carson is saying. Carson continues—his talking is in some way, maintaining his autonomy.

"Why are you going to kill me? I have a right to know."

The man moves the gun up and down in his hand as if thinking about it. Then he speaks again, his voice changing to a more businesslike tone; now his words have a careful variance for persuasion: "You don't have to die. Listen to this...you have one chance, one opportunity. You won't see me the next time. You'll just see the blood and brains bursting out of your mouth before you hit the sidewalk. Do you understand?"

Carson tries to keep up with the words, even more unnerved by the man's change in attitude. That first voice came from a hell-being, now he sounds like a movie thug. "Uh, uh, what? What am I supposed to *do*?"

"Stop looking into things. Stop asking questions. Just do your job like a good bureaucrat. Keep quiet. Put in your twenty and retire. That doesn't sound so bad, right?"

The man moves closer to Carson. Close up, his enormous body blocks out everything, becomes a black void. He puts the gun to Carson's head. "What do you say?"

"Yes...whatever. *Whatever.*"

"Down on your knees."

Carson sort of edges down to the floor. He looks up at the gun. The man nudges him with the large rounded end of the barrel.

An impossible time goes by with the man just touching the gun to Carson's head and staring at him. So it seems behind those glasses.

Finally, the man moves away. "Just so you know, this applies if you tell anybody, *anybody,* anything about your recent investigations. And about tonight too. I still kind of hope you fuck up. I'd like to see if this would make your head actually explode. Or your chest. The head would be better for visuals, but the chest—it would be large enough to *see* through. Yeah, you could put your hand through the hole before you die."

The man chuckles to himself. Then he moves away. Carson hears the door of the apartment open and close.

It takes him ten minutes to be able to stand. He has to use an ottoman and another chair to drag himself upright while shaking uncontrollably. Then he runs to the bathroom and throws up. He can no longer eat; the to-go bag stays unopened on the kitchen table.

Every time Carson thinks about who he might call for help, he pictures the big man coming back. And his blood exploding from him in the graphic way the man described.

At two in the morning he composes a resignation note for his supervisor.

∞

Tuesday, February 1, 2011
Wayne, NJ 1:00 pm

Gloria McFadden, a blonde in her late fifties, sits across the table from the older, taller man. Larry Meese, a longtime family friend. She's pleased to see him. Although she's an attractive woman, his demeanor towards her is nothing less than proper and respectful.

"Gloria, it's been some time. I'm glad to have a chance to talk to you."

Her smile is slightly higher on one side of her face, a quirky charm. "Larry... I hope it didn't bother you that I asked you not to tell Ken."

"Of course not."

They're interrupted by the waitperson and give him their orders. Then Gloria says, "I had a couple things I wanted to talk you about."

"Certainly."

"Ken is worrying me. He's been difficult lately. I think something is wrong at work. He won't talk to me about it...does he ever mention anything to you?"

Meese has years of experience in not letting anything show in his eyes or his face, except what he wants others to see. "No, not that I can think of, Gloria. But you know, as I know, working for the state has its pressures."

"I guess...but still, he's drinking more and that's saying something. I try not to be one of those ex-alkies who are judgmental, but he's really sunk into himself. I'm afraid he'll crash."

"Let me see if I can find out."

"Thank you, Larry. The other thing...well, it's so strange..."

"I've heard it all as a cop. I *still* hear strange things in the Sheriff's Office. Don't be worried; you can tell me."

"Well...this is another thing I can't talk to Ken about right now. You've read the stories about the dead women who were found in Union County? The serial killer?"

"That guy Mathers, yeah. Glad it's in Union County; my office doesn't have to handle him. It must be a pain."

"Larry...when I read the stories about the private investigator who found these women...Joel was involved."

Meese face changes. So subtly, Gloria can't see it. It's as if the last 17 years fell away just hearing the name. "*What?*"

His voice is off, but she doesn't notice. "He seems to be some kind of *assistant* to this New York City detective. I looked for more about it online...he was working with this man in upstate New York too. Something about an arsonist in Rochester."

Meese puts on a sympathetic expression; his mind is still reeling. "My God, Gloria. To see that after all this time..."

"It *has* to be him in the stories. Larry, since I started recovery, I've had some time to think. John Dell helped me a lot with that. I want to find Joel. His birthday just passed—he's 33 now! I want to tell him I'm sorry. Even if he doesn't care, just to tell him. Look what he's doing—he and that detective. He may have made something good out of his life."

She has a hint of a smile on her face. In her handbag is a picture from a *New York Herald-Standard* story, in which Joel is standing next to Gabriel Ross. She's been taking it out during the day and looking at it, when Ken isn't around. Thinking of the picture makes her smile.

Meese smiles too. But he's thrown. His mind clicks and whirs. He almost grabs the tablecloth in his fists. "Gloria, I know what you must feel. But now...Joel...he did that terrible thing to you and Ken back when. I didn't approve of Ken throwing him out—you know that. But he was on his way to being a criminal. And I have to warn you—private investigators are sleazy. They'll pretty much do anything to make a buck. I wouldn't think this New York PI is some kind of hero."

Gloria draws back at his tone of voice. "Larry, he's my *son*. I want to know what Joel is doing, who he is."

Meese immediately adjusts his attitude. "Sure, sure. You're being a mom. Look, I can check some of my sources, see what I can find out. Just take it slow right now. You don't want to rush into anything and get hurt."

"Okay," she accedes. "I appreciate it. I just want to move forward in life now. It's why I want to know what's going on with Ken, too."

"Of course, of course. Just—as a friend who cares, don't do anything without checking with me first, right? On either of these things."

"Yes, I'll hold off until you find something, Larry."

After lunch, which Meese rushes through, he goes back to his SUV and just sits for a while absorbing the news.

He's not sure what he feels but he knows he must, *must* get a look at Joel.

∞

ONE

Bertrand Russell said, "Man, in so far as he is not subject to natural forces, is free to work out his own destiny. The responsibility is his, and so is the opportunity."

∞

Friday, March 4, 2011
Canal Street 12:35 pm

LARRY MEESE WAS ABLE to find out where Joel lived. Law enforcement personnel have access to all kinds of databases. After talking to Gloria, he combed everything he could to find Joel. He's surprised by what he finds. He had once made an attempt to find Joel after Ken threw him out, but was unsuccessful that time. Eventually he thought maybe Joel was just dead.

Thinking of that makes him angry at Ken again like he was years ago. Ken was so fucking stupid. More than that. *He had no right to make that decision.*

Anyway...Joel was not entirely off the radar between 1993 and 2011, but he wasn't high-profile either. But Meese can figure out the basic story from information dating back to 1995, 1997, and then this year.

Meese checked out that private investigator, as well. Ross has a record. However, he seems to be on the up-and-up in the situation with the serial killer. Why Joel was working with him--who can say. Maybe because Ross is a New York boy and happened to use Joel for his Jersey knowledge. Joel was doing a good deed. That makes sense. Joel would do that. Hopefully Ross didn't take advantage of him. Ross is probably some sort of egotistical troublemaker who likes his name in the papers. Let him try that crap in Passaic County...

Meese gets even more information by checking on international travel. He finds out Joel has a passport. Law enforcement may find out passport information from the US Passport division of the State Department--if an official request is made on the enforcement agency's letterhead.

On the other hand, if you have a career's worth of contacts you can get information without having to document in the proper channels. Favors mean favors in return. He has spent many years obtaining such contacts.

Now he really has a new window to Joel's life. Joel has been traveling to Europe, South America, Asia and other areas of the globe since he was 19. At least 3-4 times a year.

With anyone else, such international travel without a known career that justifies it might raise red flags. Drugs. Smuggling. Arms sales. But the law enforcement records show Meese a more logical reason Joel travels.

Now Meese is standing across the street from the New York City apartment Joel bought. He knows what the apartment is worth. Amazing. Joel isn't around right now; he's in Australia. Maybe he's still doing what he did before. Or maybe he just has money. Joel is smart enough for that.

Of course. That's why Meese chose him in the first place, so many years ago. If Ken hadn't fucked his life up, Meese has no doubt that Joel would be eternally grateful for the mentorship. There would be benefits...

But don't things happen for a reason? This can't be coincidence. Meese goes back to New Jersey and waits until Joel returns to New York City. Since Meese has a full-time job, slipping away to NYC isn't that easy. However, he takes sick leave and spends his time watching the building until finally, the following Friday, he sees who he wants to see.

There he is.

Joel exits the building on Canal Street and walks west. Meese begins following him. He doesn't get too close. But he's close enough to take note of how Joel has so much the same build, the same presence, of what Meese remembers.

Joel's destination is an art supply store. Now Meese has to be careful, but Joel isn't paying attention to other customers. He's focused on what he wants to buy. And so, with basic disguise of cap and sunglasses Meese is able to see Joel's face for a few seconds here and there.

It's a shock. All though he knows Joel is 33, it's hard to reconcile the maturity. Joel in no way looks old. Unless you're imprinted on a 15 year-old boy.

This could be enough to just leave. *Leave him. He's not who he was.*

Meese stares at him. Almost enough to make Joel turn. Joel looks up and around, as if feeling the stare. Meese moves outside the store and across the street to be able to see him again.

Joel is back on the street now. He pauses to check his phone and his expression changes. Something pleases him and he smiles. Meese almost smiles with him. He follows again as Joel makes his way downtown to Union Square to a store called Forbidden Planet. It sells graphic novels and action figures.

He still likes that stuff.

The boy is still in him, then. Maybe he hasn't really changed.

Meese can't really see him clearly, but the hazy view through the darkened window of the store on Broadway is like his fantasy. And in some strange psychological maneuver the fantasy acts as the proverbial goggles or glasses. It takes away the maturity of Joel's build and face and replaces it with Meese's memory from 17 years ago. The one that was so wrongfully interrupted. The one Ken owes him for.

The question is what to do. How can he manipulate things to bring them together again?

∞

Monday, March 14, 2011
Canal Street 11:05 am

Isabella tells Joel: "Remember, it's a magazine cover story on hot artists in the city; it's *perfect* to talk you up. The writer is new; he'll be as scared of you as you are of him. *Don't fuck it up* or I'll castrate you."

"Good luck with that. Are they really interested in the art?"

"Yes; we talked about that. The story is about five NYC-based artists. You'll blow the rest of them away. Yeah, you're on the cover because of the press with Gabriel's cases, but so what. It's what puts asses in the exhibits. So, give him some juicy details. People who don't even like art will read the feature on you because it has the crime backstory."

That fact doesn't make Joel feel any more comfortable about the idea. When he hangs up with Isabella he can't concentrate. He just wanders around his loft studio nervously, with a feeling of dread.

Joel has an artist's insight to human nature. He has additional insight due to his past experiences. But the hardest person to use insight on is one's self. Joel has been in survival mode for so long that any other sense of being is similar to wearing a Japanese *Noh* mask between him and the world...and the survival mode impedes insight to himself.

However, he recognizes that he's in borderland between past and present, and that's why he's rattled. This borderland developed around the time he met Gabriel a few years ago and anchored in him during the last year with Jan. It's new territory. It has patches of sylvan glens but also contains landmines.

Most of the paintings on the walls of his loft are new--reflecting this borderland. The older ones are covered with drop cloths. The old stuff seems disconnected.

Six paintings are from the time he spent with Jan. All are large, at least a 12 in a French standard canvas size. He was inspired from some vintage postcards that Jan had collected and adapted those styles to some surreal images. A car on a night road with figures hiding in trees. A beautiful woman on a beach, the sun on her back, water flat and glossy. Tiny creatures approach her in reverence. A vine with symbols he'd found in old books from Jan's library.

Isabella, his agent and de facto publicist, didn't want him to hang the new ones. Like his recent foray into sculpture, the newer paintings sell better as they reflect a maturity. The older ones can sell, but to those who like a little more rawness, bluntness, and streaks of emotion. Or nudity, which is why the ones of Gabriel have found buyers. Nonetheless, he wants to see the new ones on his wall because they remind him of Jan.

When he walks over to gaze out the window at Canal Street, he hears a faint rustle. He glances over his shoulder but no one is there. He starts to look back to the window and something moves in his peripheral vision. Now he turns around. No, it's just imagination. Stress. No one's here, no ghosts. Stress from the pending interview is agitating his senses.

He wishes Gabriel was here; Gabriel handles interviews with perfect ease, good press or bad press. But Gabriel is with his therapist this morning. He's still dealing with grief. Joel deals with grief differently. But they both honor the dead.

Over the last couple days, he and Gabriel went to visit several graves. Gabriel's former clients Raymond and Toni Booth (they took Toni's son, Adam, with them) and then their friend Giselle's grave in Elizabeth, New Jersey. They met Giselle's brother there.

A few of the women whose bodies they found last year were not able to be identified or family wasn't located. Joel paid for them to be buried properly, not in a Potter's field. They go to visit those women too. Gabriel also wanted to see Leonard Mathers' grave. They took Bob Jarvey, one of Gabriel's close friends, and Edward. Edward (under the identity of his other self, Sophie Faulkner) had been arrested for Leonard's murder but Gabriel's work demonstrated Sophie's and Edward's innocence. At Leonard's grave Gabriel plays *Possente Possente* from *Aida*. Leonard would have appreciated that.

Kent Varney, a vital source for Gabriel in the Booth case, is interred in a mausoleum in Bethesda. Gabriel has flowers sent there. He has told Joel he plans to go to DC to visit Kent someday. Joel has a feeling Gabriel often talks to these dead persons, as he talks to his mother and uncle as an imaginary sounding board.

The reporter, Matt Chagall, shows up finally at the loft. He's accompanied by a freelance photographer. Joel greets them with a charm he knows how exude. Matt is a tall, sandy-haired sinewy white man around 30. The photographer, Barry Mecca, is black, a little older than Joel but about his size, with long braids in a ponytail. He is carrying a Yashica camera and various accoutrements.

Both men compliment Joel on his loft, which looks a lot nicer since he bought some furniture and fixed it up. Of course, his paintings are the most significant part of the loft, along with his various sculptures interspersed along the walls. He also has shelves overflowing with equipment for painting, sculpture, and computing.

Joel is grateful his close friends Veronica and Geneva insisted he furnish the place as soon as he and Gabriel came back from vacation.

Barry begins taking photos of the loft with Joel's permission. "Hey, Joel, can you stand by the paintings? Yeah, that looks great. The sun is hitting you just right...on your sofa now. Just casual. You look good casual."

Joel follows the directions without comment. Barry continues his patter to put Joel at ease. "These brick walls are good too. I'm going to lean one of the paintings here next to you—this one, is that okay? Great. I can see you're kind of reluctant for photos."

"No, I'm fine. I can see you're good at this. You have an eye."

"I try. You're a terrific subject, don't be reluctant—or maybe go ahead. It gives you a mysterious aura, with your arms folded like that. Ah, but there's a nice smile, there."

"I guess you've worked with kids *before*, then."

Barry laughs. "You're not that bad."

Matt, following their banter, tries to act in a similar vein but comes across like he's a little out of place. "I'm still kinda new at this for the *Herald Standard.* I used to write for the *Philadelphia Inquirer* culture section. But I love covering the New York art scene. Isabella--I mean, Ms. Karimi, is doing interesting things with you. Anything new going on right now?"

He's setting up his laptop to type while they talk. His voice is strained from trying too hard to be buddy-buddy with Joel.

Joel feels strained as well. The façade he had at first is starting to wash away as if he's standing in a rainstorm. "Off the record, there's a licensing place that wants to use some of the paintings for posters and that type of thing. I want to keep control over what I do, so I'm looking into licensing myself."

"That sounds pretty complicated."

"Isabella would seek out the buyers. I'm getting a Chromira Digital to make the prints."

Barry whistles. "That's a nice machine, at 60 grand."

"Oh yeah, Clark Ahn says to say hello," Matt adds, when they both sit on Joel's sofa to actually start the interview.

"How is he?"

"Good. He has a lot of nice things to say about you and your, ah..."

"Boyfriend."

"Yeah, I wasn't sure. I didn't mean to be offensive." Matt grins nervously, typing fast in his computer to try to cover his embarrassment.

"Takes more than that." Joel smiles.

Matt begins the interview in earnest, discussing Joel's theory of art, his themes, working with Isabella and her virtual/traveling gallery. With that, Joel becomes less self-conscious, and keeps the attention of both men in how he talks about art—intelligently and with a passion.

Matt then switches gears, and asks him about the criminal cases in which Joel was involved. "I talked to Clark about Don Mathers...looks like he might be going to trial at the end of the year."

"I believe so, yeah. Is Clark going to cover the trial?"

"Yeah, he's keeping track of everything. Does Gabriel have to testify?"

"Yes. He and I both are going to."

"Wow, I can't even imagine, knowing what he's done..."

"Oh, yeah. Whatever it takes to bring him to justice. I don't have a problem with that."

"It's a wild story, Clark says. And the Governor of New Jersey sent Gabriel something?"

"Some letter came from his office, robo-signed. The Governor does not appreciate LGBT rights, you know, and yet we helped the criminal justice system enormously, including with overseas contacts to assist the women who were released from captivity...I don't want to go off on that. But believe me, Gabriel spent tons of time, even when he was recovering from almost being burned alive, to help those women."

"Wow. And the organization where Mathers was working, they're having a public relations nightmare."

Joel nods in agreement. The Women's Freedom Network was dealt a blow from the discovery that Don Mathers, Leonard's brother, was a serial killer and trafficker. He had been working at the WFN as its assistant director, under another name. One of the WFN's senior staff, Seth Monroe, has since left to run the legal advocacy department of another anti-slavery nonprofit, Humanity Unchained.

"It happens. Eventually people will forget. That's the good thing and the bad thing. People forget. They forget the bad, so people can move on. And they forget the good, so people have to prove themselves over and over."

But Monroe didn't forget that Gabriel helped find out who killed the WFN's former director. He got Humanity Unchained to talk to Gabriel about assisting in investigating other slavery cases. Gabriel has been in discussion with them on and off about that. It's a much different use of Gabriel's skills, but he is very interested in it.

Matt says, "I'm looking forward to what Clark comes up with. He's looking into Mathers' background."

"Gabriel has helped him with that some. But a lot of Mathers' case is international."

"Because of that other guy--the professor. The one who was deported. But with the international aspect, Alex Barclay has been helping Clark on that...oh."

Matt has stopped, seeing Joel's face change again. "Do you know him? Alex Barclay? I guess I shouldn't be talking about this but when I spoke to Clark, Barclay was there--he just got back from England, I think, and he was really talking up Gabriel's skills. I got the impression..."

Joel wants to rolls his eyes, but keeps control. Barclay. Fucker can't get over the fact Gabriel broke up with him because he wanted to get back together with Joel.

"Guess he didn't talk *me* up, huh?" It's sarcasm, of course, and he's barely aware he actually said it out loud, but he's surprised when Matt answers seriously.

"Um, not in detail. He did say you had an interesting past. Oh, yeah, he said I should ask you specifically about your career before you started working with Gabriel. So what's that about?"

This time Joel smiles regardless of the anger that rises in him. Barclay would do that. He thinks it makes a difference. *Fuck you, Harry Potter...Wizard Editor, Intrepid Reporter, Sore Loser.*

"I think he has me confused with someone else."

Matt types some notes and then says, "Oh, so, about your work, you didn't sell much, or rather didn't promote much, until recently, right? Ms. Karimi said she's been trying to get you to show for years."

Joel suddenly feels guarded. Almost as if shadows were growing on the wall behind him. "Yeah," he says shortly. "I mean, she has been selling my stuff on what you'd call a casual basis. I just finally figured it was right to..."

"Go big time?"

"At least just have a show, I suppose."

"Were you always artistic?"

The change in topic from his art to himself throws him. "I guess. My childhood was...rough. I'm sure Isabella told you I lived on the street for a while."

"Yeah, that must have been a rough experience. How long were you on the street?"

"From age fifteen to eighteen, more or less."

"And then, did you find something better?"

"Odd jobs, on and off." He folds his arms, feeling the tension rise, then unfolds them. *Be calm.*

Matt nods. "Sure. Nice to have success now. I mean, I heard you have a following already."

"Is that right?" Joel smiles at the idea.

"Yeah. And people are naturally interested in knowing more about you, where you come from." Matt runs his fingers in his hair, trying to smile like Joel does. "Um, you know, I thought it would be a good part of the story, overcoming challenging circumstances, beating the odds and stuff. I wanted to get some perspective—I talked to Ms. Karimi, to a person who runs an LGBT youth center who knows you, I talked to your mom..."

"You did *what?!*" Joel jumps up, startling both the other men by his ferocity. The reaction on their faces make him sit down, and think quickly how to cover this outburst.

"I spoke to your mother this morning." Matt eyes him cautiously. "Okay, I guess you two aren't close. I mean, I'm sorry. I really wanted to write a good in-depth human-interest story about you..."

Joel gets up again and paces the room. *No wonder he was feeling like a disaster was in the making.* He digs out his cigarettes. He should quit, since Gabriel has. As much as he lectured Gabriel about it...but now they serve a purpose--to give him something to focus on. *Focus. Focus. He needs to focus.* "Yeah, yeah. I understand, I got you. No, we aren't close. It's no problem."

He stops, suddenly feeling punched in the gut and overwhelmed with a strange feeling he can't categorize. "Can you tell me what she said?"

"Uh...okay. Well, I asked if I could talk to her about you, and she said she shouldn't and she sounded like she was going to hang up. Then she asked what the story was going to be about. I told her, and asked her if she had read the other news stories about you. She said she read about when you and, uh, Gabriel found the women in New Jersey. She kinda asked me what I knew about you. Which, you know, is the bio I have from Ms. Karimi. That was it; it wasn't a long conversation. Oh, she asked if you worked with Gabriel, and you do, right?"

"Yeah. I did. I do, sometimes." Joel turns from the window. "Thanks for telling me."

"Um, sure. Did you want to talk about this or anything?"

"No, I don't. Not a big deal. This isn't part of the interview, the family thing, okay?"

"Yeah, okay." Matt seems a little shaken. "I didn't mean to upset you..."

"You just walked into something unexpected. No worries." Joel smiles, trying to look sincere about it. "Seriously, okay? You're cool."

Matt cautiously begins another line of questions, and Joel answers while his mind goes elsewhere. Tumbling, falling into space. A part of him wants to run screaming out the door.

Gabriel will be over soon. Just get a hold of yourself.

Joel asks to take a break. While Matt and Barry engage in work-related banter, leaving to grab lunch, Joel walks to his kitchen. He lights another cigarette, his hands trembling.

Then his phone buzzes with a text. Gabriel. Thinking of Gabriel triggered him to reach out. That happens between people who are very close, although when Joel calls Gabriel just before Gabriel is about to call him, Gabriel pretends it unnerves him.

--My love, you are taking confidence in what you do, who you are?

Joel writes back, *--Sure.*

A pause. *--Remember what I said the night we met? Where you should be?*

Joel thinks about it. Not too hard, as he remembers every detail of his time with Gabriel from the second they met.

--In the Winter Garden. The Winter Garden is an atrium in lower Manhattan that has a spectacular view of the Hudson, high-toned shops, and some exotic flora.

--It's a favorite place of mine. It has a beauty and grace befitting you. You are there now, metaphorically. This experience only recognizes that.

He's trying to help Joel be less anxious. After therapy, Gabriel is coming over to the loft to talk about a case Joel is helping him with tonight. But here and now, at the moment, Joel uses Gabriel's words to keep himself calm.

He picks up a black Moleskine notebook. He bought it on impulse last December. He's been hesitant to write anything, but every so often he gets an urge. So after a moment, he starts making notes of things running through his mind. He thinks about when he and Gabriel met.

∞

THE ORIGIN STORY ♦ GABRIEL AND JOEL

Albert Camus said, "Real generosity toward the future lies in giving all to the present."

∞

That's when life got different.

It is August 11, 2006.

THE AMBIANCE OF THE SMALL CLUB on West Second Street has changed suddenly. Something has disrupted the serpentine line of Goth kids on the scuffed black dance floor. Joel senses it from the bar, and turns to look over his shoulder.

A man is navigating through the patrons asking them questions. Showing them a picture. He has brown hair, a white button-down shirt, jeans, flat boots and a long leather jacket.

Although the light is not great, Joel gets enough glimpses of the man to want to see more. He's attractive. He also seems amused by his own lack of success in talking to the young persons. Their indifference does not impede his confidence. He observes everything, particularly the decor. Some pieces on the wall are actually very stylish. They happen to be pieces that Joel created at the request of Rob, the bartender and part-owner.

And as he's studying the images on the wall, absently biting on a pencil, he glances over at Joel--catching Joel by surprise. And smiles.

Like he's sharing a private joke with Joel, across the room.

Joel slowly smiles back then assumes a cool posture, turning back to his sketching. But he can no longer draw. He picks up his own pencil and dots the sketch pad, waiting to see what happens.

Finally, the man heads for the bar. Under the music, Joel can hear his boots on the floor. Then he stops, somewhere behind Joel. Joel dares to look up in the bar mirror.

The man is staring at Joel's sketch as if he's fascinated. In the mirror, Joel can see he's studying the sketch like he did the artwork on the walls. Interested.

Joel half-turns, and the man doesn't even notice at first. Then he looks at Joel. In that moment something flashes between them. It's sudden and potent. They both recognize it. The man smiles again, nodding at Joel's sketch book.

"Your style reminds me of David Lloyd."

Joel is surprised again. He takes out a cigarette, one of his cloves, to cover this. "Thank you. How familiar are you with Lloyd's work?"

"*V for Vendetta. Hellblazer.* He has his own graphic novel coming out, *Kickback.* I have the French edition. A friend sent it to me." The man's voice is baritone, melodious.

"Really? I was in Europe not too long ago. But I missed that one."

"Not only Lloyd though...the angels you're drawing also look straight out of Doré."

Before Joel can ask who Doré is, Rob has taken note of their conversation and comes up ready to interfere on Joel's behalf. The man smiles charmingly in spite of Rob's glare and orders a microbrew on tap; then he looks at Joel with a glint in his eyes and asks if he may buy him a drink. Joel nods, telling Rob he'll take a glass of burgundy.

When they're served Joel says to the man, "This isn't your scene, is it? You're here because you're searching for someone."

"And what makes you think that?"

"You're asking those kids to look at a picture." He lifts one shoulder. "Maybe I can help."

"Really...why do you want to help? You don't even know what I want." His posture changes subtly, staring into Joel's eyes.

"I think you were nice in what you said about my drawing. David Lloyd happens to be one of my favorite illustrators. And I don't think you're trying to harm anyone. Don't ask me how I know, I just go on instinct. I like your looks."

The man's eyes widen briefly. He bites his lip. "You seem to know a lot about me."

Joel laughs. "I don't know who you're looking for or why. Why don't you tell me?"

The man gives him a quick once-over and speaks softly. "Forgive me, but this doesn't look like your scene either. Sketching in a bar? I can tell you did those paintings on the walls too. I see the same style. You should have a crowd around you in the Winter Garden watching you create."

Joel takes a sip of the wine before answering. "Yeah, it's not my scene. I hang out here because they leave me alone."

The man has moved closer, frowning in concern at Joel's words. But Joel returns to his former attitude. "What's your name, pilgrim? And how did you know those were my paintings?"

"Gabriel. Gabriel Ross. I'm actually a private investigator. My uncle was an art history professor and he did his best to teach me everything he knew about art—in craft, style, theme, and meaning."

"Gabriel...I guess my drawing was revelatory. I'm Joel. I remember a friend of mine said Gabriel was the archangel of mystery, of light."

Gabriel just smiles at that. Joel has to keep cool. No one, male or female, makes him nervous. But right now, if Gabriel backed him up against the bar and started kissing him he'd be at the other man's feet.

To counter that, to stay in control, he leans over and gazes at Gabriel intensely. "You're pretty observant. You recognize that no one here wants to talk. And I'm guessing you're looking for someone who has been here before. So who are you after?"

Gabriel's mouth curls up as he pulls a photo of a girl out of his jacket. "This one. I'm trying to find out if she ever did hang out here. She has a stealing problem, we might say." He then lights a cigarette. No one obeys local laws in this club.

Joel takes the photo and studies it. "I may have seen her. I think she was kind of on the high-strung side."

He waves the bartender over. "You remember this girl, Rob?"

The bartender leans down close to look. "She's been here a couple times. Not a student; a lot of people here go to NYU, but not her. She hasn't been around for weeks."

Gabriel asks, "Any idea which of these enchanting young persons she might have known?"

Rob looks reluctant. "I don't like to talk about customers."

Joel smiles at him. "Rob, it's important. He's okay."

"Well....she seemed to like Rich Majors. He's a stoner dude who lives on 11th Street. I believe he works in a music shop on St. Marks. The one with the leather mannequin in the window."

Gabriel nods and stands up. "I know that one." Rob takes the pair of twenties Gabriel offers. Joel feels a shot of anxiety since Gabriel seems uncertain what to do next. But then Gabriel picks up his beer glass, watching Joel.

Joel smiles again, slightly higher on one side than another. A quirky charm. He boldly takes the cigarette pack out of Gabriel's hand. "Camel Light Wides. Never noticed these before. The bigger the better, huh?"

"I don't like thin cigarettes so Virginia Slims are out. Do you paint on commission? I'm looking for something."

Joel is pleasantly surprised. "Yeah, I've done that. What are you looking for?"

"Could you do a mandala?"

"What's that?"

"The short version is, it's a pattern or blueprint of a mystic palace, used for meditation. The more intricate the better. There's a longer explanation, but my friends tell me I tend to get overly explanatory too soon."

Joel nods. "That doesn't bother me; I like learning. Now that I think of it, some of those Tibetan monks were working on one downtown, in colored *sand*. An exhibition near Fulton Street. Then they just wiped it away after it was completed. That was cool. Beauty in the moment. You're Buddhist or something?"

"Yeah, when I can keep it together. I've always wanted a personal mandala but I'm not that great on design."

"I can go to the library and find some examples. How big?"

"Square. Maybe like thirty by thirty or so. I like blues, for colors."

"You have a way for me to contact you?"

Gabriel gives him a business card. "Do you have a portfolio online or anything?"

"No. I don't really try to sell my stuff that often."

He sees Gabriel considering him. He's clearly feeling their chemistry.

The same chemistry is scaring Joel right now. And though he doesn't want to, he takes further control of the situation by pushing their glasses toward the bar. "I'll call you in two weeks."

"Two weeks? Shouldn't we talk about design or price?" Gabriel's voice betrays a touch of dismay in being dismissed.

God, this is hard. Why can't he be normal? But then, he doesn't know anything about this man. Playing it safe is okay. "You can pay what you think is fair when you see it. You'll like it; the design will be mystical. You're an ethereal person so it will fit. Trust me on that, like I trusted you in getting that information."

"You *did* trust me. Thank you for that. And in turn, I'll leave the painting to your intuition and expertise. I still wouldn't mind talking about it..."

Joel keeps his gaze. "I know. But you need to find that girl. I can see you're a man of action."

Gabriel hesitates then gets up from the bar chair slowly. As if Joel might change his mind. At the last moment Joel stands as well; he can't resist. *This is different. He's different.* He touches Gabriel's jacket, seeing the other man's eyes follow his fingers.

He leans close to Gabriel's ear. "I'll call you when I have it done. I promise." He squeezes Gabriel's hand hard and slow. Gabriel squeezes back, making the most of the touch.

The two weeks go by in a rush of inner excitement Joel hasn't felt for a while. He and his best friend Chris visit three different libraries and museums to look at mandalas. He buys a book on them. He buys the canvas and paints, and sketches out what he wants to do. He works on it in furious detail to have it complete in a week so it can have at least a few days to dry properly.

On Friday afternoon he calls the number on Gabriel's business card.

Gabriel answers, sounding very professional. "Gabriel Ross."

"This is Joel. Remember, from the club?"

Joel thinks he might hear Gabriel catching his breath.

"Oh, hi. Of *course* I do. How are you doing?" Gabriel's voice changes completely to sound much more personal.

Joel's confidence returns. "So, I have your mandala."

"Oh, excellent. I've been waiting..."

"I'm glad. I think you'll like it."

"Well, do you have a studio or something?"

"No. I can bring it over to you if that's okay."

"Sure." Gabriel gives him an address across from Tompkins Square Park.

Joel decides not to waste time. He's going over to check this thing out. Adrenaline makes the trip across town go by in a blur.

Gabriel buzzes him in the building and Joel takes the elevator to the sixth floor. Gabriel already has the door open. He's standing in his doorway looking casual in t-shirt and jeans, barefoot. Watching as if he's not sure Joel will actually appear. Joel smiles flirtatiously. "Nice to see you," he says.

"Same here." Gabriel stands back to let him in.

Joel walks to the middle of the living room. Comfortable, tasteful, eclectic, and slightly in disarray. Gabriel is not the everything-in-its place type and that makes Joel relax some.

"I like this."

"A lot of what's around is my uncle's. He died in an accident and he had me on the lease. I'm lucky, 'cause it's rent-controlled."

He's observing Joel without being obnoxious about it. Joel kind of dressed for the occasion with a button-down pale blue shirt, black slacks that were tailored for him by an acquaintance in New Jersey, and black Ferragamo loafers. The fact that Gabriel is dressed by Old Navy doesn't seem to make him uncomfortable.

The contrast is appealing to Joel. He knows clothes tell a story, but only a surface one. He holds out the bag with the wrapped painting. Gabriel smiles and unpacks it. Then he spends five minutes staring at it without speaking.

Joel says finally, "What do you think?"

"It's fantastic...you have the characters done so subtly."

"Chinese. I did some reading on it. I don't read Chinese but I double-checked the meaning, not like what you get at tattoo parlors."

"I can read a couple words in Chinese characters; I studied Daoism. I recognize some of the words you have here. Strength. Beauty. Integrity. Jesus; you are incredible."

Joel hears the sincerity in Gabriel's voice.

"Seriously. This is exactly what I had wanted to have. See, I've already fixed a hook in the wall." Gabriel hangs the canvas on the wall across from the sofa. "That looks so good."

"Thanks." Joel smiles brilliantly for a moment then looks down. He should say more, but he's at a loss.

Gabriel's voice gets softer. "Why don't you sit down? Can I get you anything?"

"No, I'm all right." And then he's delighted to see a black and white tuxedo cat sauntering in to see who is visiting. "Hey, what's up, cat?"

"Meet Archie. At least he's not carrying a mouse corpse today."

Joel is already down on the rug to play with Archie, who loves every minute of the attention. "He'd fit right in with the club, wouldn't he?"

"Absolutely. Right look and everything."

"Did you find that girl?"

"I sure did, with the information your friend gave me. I appreciate your help. What do I owe you for this?"

The question bothers Joel, which is stupid. He keeps his eyes on Archie. "I said what you think is fair."

"You need to estimate better for your skill and the time put in it. Five hundred good?" Gabriel takes the cash out of a wooden box on his coffee table.

Now Joel raises his head. "Sure. You need a receipt, or something?"

"No, not necessary. You have your name on it?"

"On the back; I didn't want to interfere with the vibes."

Joel watches him look behind the painting. Joel did not sign his full name; he never does.

"'J McF'...what's that stand for?"

"My last name. I don't use it a lot."

Archie taps him for more attention and purrs loudly when Joel strokes him. Gabriel leans against the shelves that hold his stereo while he watches Joel. They look at each other silently for a minute.

Gabriel asks, "Where's *your* place?"

"Not too far."

"Yeah? I've been in that area. There's a restaurant nearby called A Couple Blocks Over."

Joel smiles again but doesn't say any more.

Gabriel walks over to sit next to him on a large ottoman, then asks, "Can I take you to dinner?"

"Sure...if you want."

"Yes, I'd like to. There's a good Chinese place down the street."

"Yeah, I'd like that." And impulsively, he reaches over and puts a hand on Gabriel's leg. He feels the energy in Gabriel. A magnetic power he sensed in the club.

Gabriel's eyes go from Joel's hand to Joel's face.

"Did you want to do anything else?" Joel tightens his grip ever so slightly.

Gabriel leans a little closer to him. "Yeah, I'd like to." And then he runs his fingers along Joel's face. "But I just want to hang out for a while first."

"Get to know me?" Joel's smile turns a little devilish.

"Yeah. You can get to know me too, actually."

Joel finds himself a little fazed. Gabriel's sensed his vulnerability. Then Archie demands more attention and distracts him. "You're a great cat. I love cats."

"You have any?"

Joel looks down at Archie. "Not at the moment. I had one at home until I was a teenager. I left at 15; they told me to get out and not come back and I took them at their word."

He's shocked he said this--told a stranger something even his friends didn't get out of him right away. Then he sees the look in Gabriel's eyes. For a second he thinks Gabriel is angry at him. *No, he's angry at them, not you.*

"I'm sorry that happened to you."

"It's okay. You don't have to feel bad about it. I guess you're pretty good about getting information out of people, because I almost never talk about them."

And then Gabriel runs a couple fingers slowly down Joel's head, from his hairline down his face to his jaw. Something in this touch gets Joel's attention, breaks his façade. Then by impulse he embraces Gabriel, burying his head in Gabriel's chest. He picks up faint scents of cologne, the Camels, incense.

Gabriel's heart beating comforts him as Gabriel's arms pull Joel in closer. They listen to each other breathing. This is something deeper. In that something deeper is a definite eroticism. Joel is aware he can feel the outline of Gabriel's crotch from his position between Gabriel's legs.

"You still want to go out?" he says, feeling Gabriel tense from the sensation of Joel leaning into him. "You don't have to."

And Gabriel confounds him again. "I think you're missing the point. It's not a have to, it's a want to."

Joel shrugs. "I'm just sayin'."

Gabriel smiles. "I know what you're saying. I'm going to change; give me a minute."

After dinner, he and Gabriel walk around Tompkins Square Park for a bit until Gabriel takes his hand and leads him back home. Inside Gabriel removes his shoes. "I don't want to seem rude but I walk around barefoot."

"You don't have to explain what you do in your own place. Walk around naked for all I care."

They both smile at that.

"Do you want me to? I mean, to take my shoes off. I know some people got a thing about that. Or neighbor worries."

"I don't have a 'thing.' But I would like you to because it gives me the indicia you're relaxed here."

"Bring on the indicia." Joel sits on the ottoman and slips off his loafers. Gabriel observes him while getting a bottle of wine and glasses and bringing those to the living room.

"Joel...are you reticent for a reason or just for me?"

"Reasons. Not what you're thinking."

"I see." Gabriel lights up a Camel, holding out the pack to him. "Give those cloves a break. I got to get used to them. What do you think I'm thinking about you?"

Joel takes one of his cigarettes. "You're thinking I'm involved in something criminal."

"Um. Well. No. I wouldn't have invited you back here. I like to keep trouble out of my home. I'm thinking you're cautious. From experience."

He knows me. How does he know me?

"Do you feel comfortable here, Joel? You can sit here with me if you want."

Joel sits next to him, putting his feet up on the coffee table as Gabriel does, and then looks at their feet together.

"Yeah. You make me comfortable. You talk about feelings a lot, don't you?"

"Yes. I'm that kind of person. Hey, I have something for you."

He surprises Joel again by taking a thin book out of a drawer in the coffee table. The American edition of *Kickback.* "It just came out. I was at Forbidden Planet this week."

"Oh." Joel flips through the book and finds himself speechless. Gabriel even bought a bookmark, one with Krazy Kat on it. "This is really..."

Gabriel smiles. "It's a good story. I don't read French but Lloyd tells more in his drawings, don't you think? In any case, that's the English edition."

Joel lights the Camel and breathes in the smoke slowly, turning the pages of the book. Gabriel watches him while he opens the wine.

Joel finally says, "Thank you. This was really nice of you to think of me."

"I thought a lot about you."

Gabriel's hand goes to the back of Joel's head, running through his hair. Joel feels pleasant butterflies from that. He stares at the book; not because of the content, but because of the momentousness of the gift--and what stirs in him from Gabriel's touch. Nervously, he looks around the room. "You have so many books, so many topics."

"People ask if I've read them all."

"You have. It's in how you talk. You said your uncle was a professor. Were the art books his?"

"That's right." Gabriel hands him a glass with a dark red wine.

Joel picks up the bottle to examine it. "Barolo? Wow. That's not a casual wine. I mean, you didn't have to open this."

"Maybe I think you're worth it for the painting and the company." And he gently tips his glass against Joel's.

"You sound like, I don't know, Laurence Olivier or something."

Gabriel smiles. "I was born in the Bronx. My background is not high-class. I was nurtured into channeling energy, developing good taste, even what one might call refinement. What I see in you."

Joel touches Gabriel's hand. He senses Gabriel has his own demons, and those revolve around class issues. "It worked with you. I guess...I was nurtured into street survival attitudes. Not that I'm saying I was born refined."

"You don't have to. Wherever you were born the refinement was already there. I see it in your work and how you hold yourself even when you try to talk like a slacker."

Joel feels a little embarrassed/flattered at that. "You're seriously interesting to me. I like intelligent men."

"I have more books in the bedrooms if you want to see them."

Joel decides to go see. The main bedroom holds another couple of full floor-to-ceiling shelves. Archie walks up to sit at his feet. He senses Gabriel coming in. "You weren't lying that you know Buddhism."

And then he walks out to see the other bedroom. It's set up like an office, with a single bed on one side. A desk and desktop computer against the window. Another couple of full bookshelves. "You like movies a lot. Crime...Conspiracies...Comics, Batman. I love Batman. Alan Moore, yeah. Spiegelman. Robert Crumb and Mapplethorpe. You like the eclectic, right? Mystery novels. *Intellectual* books about sex. Well."

"You're a reader." Gabriel sounds pleased.

"Yeah, self-educated, I guess."

"Good. I don't date anyone who doesn't read. Or is a reading snob."

That makes Joel smile. "What I learned outside of experience, I learned in books. This one on sex in art, interesting... I know a guy who wants a kind of porno mural in his apartment. I'm painting it. I pick up jobs like that here and there. Not always art. I know how to do electrical stuff, computers. It's just kind of job to job now."

Why does he say it? Because this is the final test. He could just walk out. Or he could treat this like a hook-up. But he doesn't want to. God no. God no, he wants this to be different like he felt the night in the club. For the first time he's nervous over what someone will think about his past.

It's time. Now or never. Tell him and see. "I don't know why, but I feel okay telling you things. I've had boyfriends and girlfriends and...I used to escort. Not so much now. Well, I was careful about it. I mean, sometimes...but it was just a job. It was good for a while but I saw too much and I just didn't want to stay in that game full time. I'm clean, though. I got tested every three months or so."

His voice is tense now.

Gabriel slides his arm around him. "Yeah, me too. Children of the Nineties, right?"

Joel tilts his head back to look in the other man's eyes. "None of that bothers you? Sometimes people think they're cool about it, and then they find out they can't take it."

"You're a free, autonomous human being. No one has the right to judge you."

"You should write fortune cookies or greeting cards. But I like it, because I think you mean it."

"Um, I see you as an artist more than anything. And Joel is the name of a prophet in the Hebrew Bible. A friend of mine said prophets spoke the word of God; they are *Niv Sefatayim* or *Navi*, fruit of the lips."

And then, finally, Gabriel leans in to kiss him.

Fuck. This is too much.

The chemistry is real. If it doesn't happen in a kiss, it doesn't happen. And this happens. Overwhelming him.

Really?

When they break, Joel sets down his glass. "Kissing in front of books. How decadent..."

Joel's voice is cool, but Gabriel is now beyond that pretense, drawing Joel's head back to him, kissing him mid-sentence, bringing Joel close to him...

This...this is different.

This is real.

∞

TWO

Walt Whitman said, "Each of us is inevitable."

∞

Monday, March 14 2011, Continued
Canal Street, 2:00 pm

I ANSWER MY WORK CELL PHONE. "Hello, this is Gabriel Ross."

No one says anything. I hear breathing, then the call ends. Okay. A crank, or someone scared to ask for help.

The phone never stops ringing since we got back from vacation a week ago. But then, we've been in serious hit-the-ground-running mode. One person in particular was desperate to speak to me. A woman in Brooklyn, whose 15-year-old son suddenly disappeared. The woman was herself hiding from law enforcement authorities due to several outstanding warrants. She's worked as a driver for some professional thieves. She didn't want to contact the police; my reputation as of late made her feel like she could hire me without trouble.

And true, I didn't care about her warrants; I cared about the kid who was missing. I got into that right away, and was lucky enough to track a lead on what's happening with the kid--courtesy of some street criminals who like me and think I'm a more hardcore person than I am.

This past week also involved other projects that have developed in the last couple months: talking to Bertrand Herrmann on how to frame his memoirs, having some sit-in practice with Jason and his bar band, and doing some voiceover and filming for the Frontline and Discovery ID shows on the Mathers case.

I'm not exhausted; I'm exhilarated that my talents are called upon. I'm ready to move on getting information about where David--the missing teenager--is being held.

I'm on Canal Street right now in the 200 block near Lafayette, heading for Joel's loft. Joel has been busy as well. He had a successful showing of his work last month and his friend Isabella is getting him out to meet people. The fact he worked with me on the notorious Mathers case makes him a conversation piece. Which translates into publicity, money, and so on. I agree with Isabella about using the publicity, because I want Joel to transform into an artist of note as he deserves.

We haven't said much about working together since getting back from our vacation. He used to work with me a lot by his choice, but this isn't going to happen in the future as he fulfills his potential as an artist. In fact, I've recruited his friend Geneva Lennon to help out. Geneva is now also my friend and my best friend Veronica's new roommate. Veronica and I are working together now, pooling our investigation cases successfully. Geneva is a transgender woman, former Army specialist, and has skills that make her an excellent operative. She also continues her work on the side in poster restoration and book-binding. Veronica was training her in our field while Joel and I were out of the country.

I *didn't* expect to feel a little empty-nest about the prospect of Joel not working with me anymore, or that I'd have to compete with Isabella for his company now. I like her, I really do. She's very sweet towards me. But damn, she holds on to him lately. They knew each other from a long time back, both street kids. Competing with the past is hard.

Competing with my own past is hard. I've had to face that in starting therapy again. This time for real. This time to be a better person and ensure my relationship with Joel stays strong. In doing that, I have deal with the sadness and guilt over people who have passed, but also my own temper, my own stubborn self-righteousness.

I fatefully told Joel not too long ago that I felt I had some kind of violent destiny from being in violent situations over and over again. But it doesn't have to be that way. When we were on vacation--two weeks where nothing bad happened--I saw what just being with someone you love is like for the soul.

Staring 40 in the face is both daunting (What do I have to change? Who do I want to be? What must I do *differently*?) and less daunting (because *he's with me*). I want to think about where my pattern of actions take me as I get older. I went as far as I could with Don Mathers, a man I still hate. My clash with him ended fortuitously by sheer luck.

To me, that's a chance to see the opportunity for the future despite my mentors' admonition that I'm a protector. *Don't fuck it up again. Don't be that person you would hate.* I must change for myself, because change must be for one's self, and for Joel, because anything that would diminish me in his eyes would shame me or kill me.

The phone rings again, shattering my reverie. Same number; New Jersey area code. No name.

"Gabriel Ross. Can I help you?"

The person, female, on the other end of the phone takes time to answer. "Oh. Uh, do you...um, you're the same person who had found the women in Elizabeth."

I get these calls since what happened in New Jersey; people read about the case and ask if I can find dead or missing people. Some are cranks, some are unhinged, some are desperate and serious.

"Yes I am."

"You, um, that sounded like a good thing you did."

"Thank you."

"I wanted to ask you...The man who was with you..."

"Yes?"

"He's..." She stops. "I don't know what to say."

"Could I have your name?"

"Not right now. I wanted to ask, is he...Joel, Joel McFadden, he helped you, right?"

"Helped me with what? Finding the women?"

"Yes. That whole case with the murdered women and the other women who were kidnapped...I read it in the New Jersey news..."

"Yes, he did. Ma'am, why are you asking?"

"Joel...he's your friend?"

Something in the way she says his name gives me pause. It leads me to answer when I ordinarily would hang up. "Yes."

"Oh. And you're a private investigator?"

"Yes. Would you like to tell me what's on your mind?"

"Maybe...I...I'm not sure. I have to think about it." She ends the call before I can say anything further.

That happens a lot, too. People reach out for a consultation, but are afraid to go through with it. They want to know, but are afraid to find out. It wouldn't mean anything except her asking about Joel. I make a mental note to look up the number later, and continue on.

I reach Joel's building, and go up to his loft. He's mostly at my place and uses this loft apartment on Canal Street to work in. But sometimes he stays overnight. It's his place; he has a right to. We don't have a system about sleeping over--it just depends. And because it depends, it's slightly awkward. I'm never crazy about spending the night at other people's places; just a thing I have. Plus I have my cat to think of. But Joel has said when he works late, he'd like me there. It's only fair. So I have overthought it and carefully picked out some things to leave at his loft for when that happens.

It's newly domestic. That isn't something we had opportunity to be when we were together the first time around. I didn't want to push him then, and he was scared to get too close, even over two years together. When we got back together again this last December the cases overtook our attention. And vacation is vacation--it's not how people interact every day.

Now is real life. This past weekend we went grocery shopping like a couple--my idea. It was fun, even when Joel was horrified by my playfully juggling a few cans in the middle of an aisle and catching them behind my back. We also saw Alan Cumming in a Broadway preview--Joel's idea. I did nothing there to risk us being thrown out, or he would have killed me for losing even a second of watching Alan Cumming.

I don't have to use my key; he's waiting for me outside the door when I get out the elevator, smiling. "I was watching you on the street."

"You're as bad as me."

And then he has his arms around me; tight, then tighter. I hold him and consider everything that led up to this. A thousand instances of chance happening from the very first time when a case caused me to check out a Goth bar near NYU. And he happened to be there. The last four years coalesce into this moment.

I take in his scent, his feel, the vibrations from him, his pleasure to see me. I allow myself to sink in that. His head goes in my shoulder for a moment. I feel like he needs comfort; when he puts his head on me like that, my protective instincts rise. He wants to know I love him.

To emphasize it, I put my hands on the back of his legs and pick him up, backing him against the wall next to his door. His legs go around me. It's not easy, as he's nearly the same size and height I am, but I can carry his weight. He likes that; from this position he leans down to kiss me. That triggers other feelings.

I sense something is heavy with him, and try to meet his eyes. His head goes back on my shoulder. Then right before I'm going to ask what's going on with him, he moves his head back. "Ouch. You're still letting it grow out, huh?"

Meaning the beard I've had for a week or so. He claims I'm copying Keanu Reeves, who we happened to see in Australia during our two-week vacation, and who is a major crush of my youth. Few of my friends approve of my new facial hair.

Joel usually has a goatee but it's very thinned out and I'm usually clean-shaven. But he's overdoing his disapproval and supposed discomfort to be a smartass. I know it's in part to distract me from asking questions but I go with it.

I tell him, "You're not going to win this."

He slides his legs down and turns his attention to what I brought with me. "A Macy's bag? You lose your luggage somewhere?"

"When you're ashamed to be seen with me, I'll just get the fuck out." I move past him inside, seeing where he's been working to make the loft look less like a storage facility for paintings and more like a place where one could live.

In spite of the kibitzing he's actually thrilled I'm bringing clothes over. Like grocery shopping for me, clothes for him proves something...symbolizes something. Most of what I have in the bag are t-shirts but then that sums up my clothes in general. I have good suits, but I rarely use them unless in court or for important interviews.

He's taken over the bag and now inspects everything in it, taking the items out one at a time. "Well, I get a good sense of what music and movies you like, anyway."

"You already knew. I totally stan Dr. Frank-n-Furter."

"Uh-huh. No regular shirts?"

"I don't like to iron." I pick up the stack of t-shirts and jeans from out of his hands, and set them on the dresser. "How did it go with the interview, baby?"

Joel abruptly turns away to walk to his kitchen. "They were okay. You want anything?"

"Whatever you're having. Is that it? They were *okay*?"

"It went well, honestly. I appreciate you asking. Just I don't like doing it, and consequently, I don't like talking about it. I'd rather hear about you, what you were doing."

Another subtle shift of focus to me so I'll be distracted. I take a Coke bottle from him and study one of his paintings on the wall near the door.

"Nothing much to say about me today. I updated Veronica on what we're doing tonight. I just now got another strange phone call--I suppose because of the news stories, etcetera."

"To be expected."

A minute later, there's knock at his door. I'm closer so I go over. "Are you expecting FedEx," I ask, looking out the peephole.

"Um. Maybe. I've ordered a lot of stuff."

I turn to look at him and catch him straightening up my shirts on top of the dresser.

He says, "I'm getting an armoire, so you'll have more space."

I suppose that will cover the fact I'm not very neat if everything's hidden away.

I open the door for the FedEx person. He draws back a little. "McFadden?" He asks hesitantly.

I look over his shoulder and see a large stack of boxes behind him. "Yes. Hold on please."

I let Joel take over and return to my shirts on his dresser. They had been in a state of disarray, granted. He's refolded everything. I don't know how he does it so quickly and so well.

I hear the door shut.

The stack of boxes is apparently all Joel's. He smiles at me, brushing his hair back, looking at me like he's looking in a mirror. Although we look nothing alike outside of being white men. He's blondish with blue-gray eyes; I'm dark Irish in hair and coloring. We've both let our hair grow of late. His is longer, past his jaw; mine is probably in some slight disarray like my clothes. And my beard.

He says, "You ever see how you open a door? Like you're going to go psycho on the person. You were scanning him like a TSA agent."

"He didn't hit the buzzer before coming up. What's all this, the stuff you ordered?"

"It's actually some of the inheritance from Jan's estate."

I help him move the six boxes against the wall next to the door. He has an envelope too, apparently an inventory of what was sent. He opens a couple of the boxes and looks cursorily inside. I imagine I can smell Europe in them, at least a vague scent of flowers. I see Jan's name labeled on some--*Jan Andriessen.* Jan was one of Joel clients, who later became close to him. Joel took care of Jan in Amsterdam while he was dying. Joel had told me before that Jan had left him some of his possessions. Joel doesn't own a lot of *things*; he's good with just music and computers. But he's anticipated these objects to own. Not due to their worth, but because (I think) Jan's spirit may be attached. It's giving him the sense he's allowed to have *roots*, to have his own place.

Jan has left Joel more than just some belongings. I know that. Joel isn't ready to disclose the entire legacy, which has to be money. Joel is afraid I'll think differently of him for that. Because of Alex--my short-term ex--and Alex attempting to use his money as influence on me. What Joel doesn't realize is that he's not Alex, and I'm never going to think of him that way.

I see it again now as he glances at me over the boxes. He's rather obviously thinking about what to tell me. He'll come around in time. He *already* has much more money than I do. He saved rather than spent during his years escorting. He has enough to work on his paintings and sculptures without worrying about if he's selling any. But he was a middle-class kid who was thrown out at 15, and survived on the street before gaining work as an escort.

I've gone from a poor/working class kid to a paycheck-to-paycheck professional, then to being in severe financial straits last year, to now just starting to make enough that some actually stays in the back account after the end of the month.

With regards to other people, it's not whether you have money. It's what you make others go through because you have it.

In one box I catch the scent of Joel's Djarum clove cigarettes. He doesn't smoke around me much anymore since I quit and my sense of smell has improved since I gave up my Camels.

"Something of yours is in there."

He reaches in the box and shifts things around. "Oh." He takes out a stack of Moleskine notebooks. Each are a little smaller than a legal pad. "These *are* mine. I didn't take them with me when I first came back."

Joel looks around, keeping his hand on the books protectively. He finally decides to put them on a small table next to one of his computers.

"What's in those? Sketches?"

"No, not really. I brought the sketch books with me. These are...different. I'll tell you about them soon."

But the notebooks aren't stable, and tip over to spill on the floor. One opens to a page with an outline of an angel.

"Well, that looks exactly like the kind of thing you were drawing when I met you."

He picks it up and snaps it shut, a little too quickly. In that awkward moment he smiles. "Um, it might be. It's just...private."

"Joel, you seriously think I'd go through your stuff?"

He blushes. "No. I've never been in yours, either, except to look for your hidden cigarettes."

"I know that. I let you do it. If I had a problem, I'd tell you. But I *am* going to pry into your books--get a cup of coffee and set the cup on the page and get rings on it, go back to smoking and ash in the pages, maybe drip a meatball hero on cover, let Archie use them for a scratching post, set up a review of them on Yelp..."

"Enough already." He rolls his eyes, trying not to smile. "I'll tell you about them at some point. Just, you know, it's stuff from years and years before. Never easy to look at." He carefully collects the notebooks and sets them on a high shelf.

A slight self-consciousness sets in with both of us. We've really just barely started being together again. What's strange is that before this, when he was just hanging out with me and working with me, we never felt unsettled with each other.

So I turn back to work. "Okay. We need to get a hold of Bob for tonight. Where are my phones?"

"You threw them on the chair."

"I should call to be sure." I sit in the chair and take out my personal phone, setting my work phone on the table in front of me. The screen saver on the work phone fades, showing the last number calling in.

Joel starts to sit on the arm of the chair with me, and then stares at my work phone. "Gabriel, what--what is this..."

A look I've never seen before. His body draws up. "*How did you get this?*" In a scared tone I've never heard before, either.

"How did I get what, Joel?" I put my hand on his back.

He snatches up the phone. "This is *my* number."

I look at him carefully. I see his eyes turning gray with confusion.

I tell him, "This is the number of the woman who called. Remember I told you I got a strange phone call..."

"What did she *say?*"

It hits me then, seeing it in his face.

"This is your number. You mean, this is your former home in Wayne. This was your *mother* calling."

He opens his mouth but can't respond.

I repeat carefully what the woman said to me.

As he listens, he starts breathing heavily. He looks like someone sent him spinning in a centrifugal force machine. I take the phone out of his hand and embrace him. He sinks down and stays silent in my arms a long time.

"Why now," he finally says.

"You're in the news. Actually, that has to be it--that you're in the news. If she tried before, she couldn't find you. *I* never could."

Meaning, when Joel wanted to disappear, he could do so very well. And maybe now I understand why. Why he didn't want to be found, why he was so elusive. Now he's in one place with an established public identity and a quote unquote normal life and relationship. Which means the past can catch up and call you.

"Yeah...actually, the reporter called her this morning. He just went ahead and did it, I don't know why. Then she called *you.*"

"I see why you didn't want to talk about the interview. I'm sorry you had that shock. But it also explains the why now and why me. My number is public. Yours isn't. Anyone trying to find you would have to ask me--or Isabella, I guess."

"Do you think she tried to find me before?"

I hear the child in his voice; a faint hint of being hopeful. I know next to nothing about his mother, other than she was complicit with his father in throwing him out. I can't say I hold much hope about them. They were both alcoholics, and I have some experience with that. He never spoke to me much about them before.

Thinking it over, I say, "Maybe so. But now she's found you--sort of. How do you feel about it?"

Without answering, he gets up to go to one of his computers and starts searching. First, he calls up every article that mentioned us finding the women. We've already read them, but now I get the impression he's reading them as his mother would.

He runs a Google search on himself and turns up the articles again, Isabella's website showcasing his work, the recent mentions of his show in *Time Out* and *New York* magazine, and some other websites. I'm sitting next to him by now. He glances at me while he does this. "The reporter...I don't know how he connected her to me."

"He probably used those background search databases like I have."

"Oh, yeah."

He Googles her name, which I find out is Gloria Karen McFadden. He gets pages of phone number and address information. Another site comes up; he reaches over to hold my hand while he clicks on it.

"She's in some kind of recovery group. I thought they were anonymous."

"Outside of AA, anonymity is less of a thing among people in recovery these days. Bob told me."

"She still likes flowers. She worked in a nursery. She's in some kind of meet-up about flowers." He smiles faintly. "I used to draw flowers for her. The unusual ones. Orchids. You like orchids because of Nero Wolfe. She liked them for their variety. The most varied flower in the world. I took care of Jan's collection when I was in Amsterdam."

"Maybe you should stay home tonight and see how you might want to cope with this, or process what's going on. It's a lot to weigh on you."

"I'm okay. I'm not going to leave you alone."

I don't argue with him. He won't back down, as I wouldn't.

He suddenly points to the screen on his Mac. "That's her. God, it's been so long..."

He's staring a photo in three-quarter profile. A blond woman with smooth planes in her face, blue eyes, a smile that...looks like his. Jesus, they look alike. My mom was blond too, but I look nothing like her.

In the first two years that Joel and I were together, and since he came back last summer, I've never asked him about his past. I've left it open for him to disclose what he wanted, knowing that people with histories of abuse have serious boundary and security issues. However, his compartmentalizing causes problems. And I'm suddenly overwhelmed with curiosity. The man I love is sitting beside me. I can't imagine being without him. I'd give my life to save his. And somewhere I want to know more about what created him, how he came to be.

He's hypnotized by that picture, and maybe wondering what has gone on with her in all this time. "What do you remember about her," I ask.

Too much. I can see it in his eyes.

"We both like flowers, I guess. And cats. And...I used to go behind her and straighten her clothes. See, she was always a little off. Like she couldn't make the bed quite right or get things ironed correctly, and Dad would use this as an excuse to berate her. He'd say, "*Can't you ever get these things fucking folded right?*" And I'd see her cry so I tried to cover it up. I went behind her and redid everything so he wouldn't see, and it would be one less thing to hear him yelling about."

All of this pours from him like water overflowing a bathtub. He's stunned by his own words. He glances at my shirts now neatly arranged on his dresser.

"Don't make too much of that," I tell him.

"Okay." His voice is lost.

"You took care of her. I'm not surprised. You take care of me, although not in the same way, and I'll emphasize *not in the same way.*"

"I must have written about this, in one of those notebooks. I just didn't want to relive it. But I should tell you about them. Not today."

"Sure, when you feel like you want to. What do you want to do about your mom?"

He turns in his chair to look at his paintings. "I don't know. I don't know if I can do anything. Even if she wants to see me, that's a hell of a bridge to cross. You don't know what it means to go back to Wayne."

"You don't have to go back. You can call her."

"*No.*" His voice is very firm. "If I went back, I'd have to go in person. Because..." He falls silent for a moment. "Because I'm not afraid."

I watch him looking around the loft, at the beginnings of the new life he's built. My collection of t-shirts on his dresser seem too small a part of it. Then he shrugs. "Whatever. Let it go for now."

I don't like that, but I have to respect it. "Okay. What we can do, if you still want to come along tonight, is to go over how to contact Sean and see if this leads somewhere."

"I'm ready," he says, moving out of his emotional cloud. "I have an idea you're not going to like."

∞

Tuesday, March 15
23rd Street, 1:00 am

Sean stares over his shoulder at me, breaking into a sweat at my question. "I don't know what you *want*, Gabriel," he says.

In the alley, rain looks like black oil running down the grime-streaked walls. The alley, narrow and tall, framed by old buildings, is a deep ocean trench in the city.

The cold March rain makes the area even more isolated. Some homeless people are in recessed doorways and alcoves, becoming part of the still blackness like marine animals at the bottom of the sea, hiding from predators.

Right now, I'm in the category of predator, at least to Sean. I *hope* he feels isolated and alone and scared right now.

"I *told* you what I want. Where is Andreas?"

"I can't...I don't know. I don't *do* what he does; I don't hurt *kids.*"

"Oh, you have *standards*. You just sell drugs to the people that traffic kids."

I don't actually have that much issue with individual drug dealers. They most often aren't what you see on TV. Many do have standards. I've gotten good information from a few when they were aware my own information was useful to them--they're more afraid of some customers than the cops. However, Sean is not that kind of dealer. He imagines himself more of a badass than he is, and that has led him to get involved in things other dealers stay away from.

Sean's body stretches with tension. I see cracks in his face magnified and made black by the rain.

I have Sean in a coil lock. He's on the ground, face down; my right leg is around his left shoulder, and leaning on his back. I'm holding his left arm up and away from his body. Another few degrees and his shoulder will dislocate.

Except I'm not going to break his arm. I don't do that. But I want him to think so. He knows my street reputation of late. Not true, but lurid. During a previous encounter with Sean a couple days ago he told me to fuck off, and ran away.

Sean, breathing hard, meets my eyes briefly. "You're *judging* me? You sent your boyfriend in to lure me out. You think that was noble or something?"

That was actually the idea Joel said I wouldn't like. And I didn't, but I knew it would work. And as soon as he followed Joel outside the grungy club and down here to the alley, I jumped him.

Joel is standing nearby--arms folded, staring at him. He knows I'm not going too far, and we're not overly concerned about traumatizing Sean.

I increase the pressure on his arm. "You really want to fuck with me?"

His face twists in pain. "No, I...look. I'm not really working for him. I just sell stuff."

"I don't care. Tell me where Andreas has the kid."

"All right, *all right.*"

I let go. He drags himself to sit up--almost. His other arm is handcuffed to a rusted pipe.

"Look," he says, as if trying to be helpful. "Uh, he'll...he'll go after you. He's crazy like that. He says the kid is his. The kid told me he wanted to get into music. You know, Andreas claims he has connections...I just brought him there, that's all I did. Andreas said the kid was *his* then--"

Suddenly Joel says, "You just *brought* him there. That's *all* you did."

His voices sounds a little strange--a discordant note. He's moved closer to us. I look over to him, but he's focused on Sean.

"Like I said, yeah. The kid's not my--"

He doesn't finish, because Joel kicks him in the abdomen. "That's *all* you did."

Sean screams, but has no sound from the force of the blow to his solar plexus. Joel kicks him a couple more times, like he's working up to a frenzy.

I grab Joel's shoulders and yank him back and away. I have to pull hard to make him move. Then I quickly get down in front of Sean and act like I intended this to happen. "I suggest you just give me the address, before I leave you with my partner."

He's gasping now. "Jesus! I *said* I would...East Elmhurst, Queens. 129 27th Avenue. 3J, his apartment is 3J. Please, you can't tell him I told you!"

"I won't."

I get up. I can see Joel is still hyperfocused on Sean, so I push him ahead of me to leave.

Sean's voice turns anxious. "*You gonna let me go?*" He rattles the handcuff.

"That pipe is pretty rotted through. You should be able to yank it free if you pull hard enough."

By the time we're outside the alley on the sidewalk, Joel has returned to an appearance of placidity. He struggles to light a cigarette in the rain. Bob Jarvey, a close friend of mine who has occasionally added muscle when needed, is eyeballing both of us. He was watching the alley for trouble and must have seen what happened.

I take a deep breath as we walk back to my car. "Why did you do that?"

Joel shakes his head. "Doesn't matter, for people like *him*."

In the car, the cold from the rain contrasts with the heat from the tension between us. I start to drive to the 59th Street Bridge.

I have never seen Joel lose control like that. Ever. I've lost control and he's given me hell for it; most recently when I had the fight with Don Mathers. I came close to taking it too far, and Joel thought I did take it too far. But I've never seen that with him.

I tell Joel, "I know he's the scum of the earth. But he was the method to get to Andreas. Sometimes you have to make those sacrifices."

For a second he glares at me. Then looks away. "Is that what it is? A sacrifice. So you just let him bring more kids to Andreas."

"*Let* him..." I meet Bob's eyes in the rearview mirror. I'm not even sure how to respond to that.

Bob is a counselor for former incarcerated persons in recovery. He's dealt with worse situations like this. He says gently, "Joel, this was just temporary so we can ensure we find this boy and get him back. It's not giving that asshole a pass to do what he wants."

Joel continues staring out the window as we begin to navigate Queens. Finally, he shifts around and says without looking at me, "So you'll do something about him? Sean? And Andreas."

Bob and I exchange glances again. Joel's voice is different, like he's somewhere else. *Do something.* I don't know what exactly I can do.

But I feel I have to. Figure it out later. "Yes. I'll think of something."

Bob nods. He'll help me figure this out. In the meantime, my promise seems to ease something in Joel. He faces forward again and lights one of his cigarettes.

I glance at him as I drive. He's taken out his phone, and is staring at something I can't see.

Apparently, Bob can see it. "Who is that, if you don't mind my asking?"

Joel snaps his head up and looks over his shoulder at Bob. "It's...my mother. She called Gabriel today. Out of nowhere."

"Wow. That's pretty heavy to deal with. What are you thinking--maybe to contact her?"

"I'm not sure."

I ask him, "Do you need to talk about anything else?"

"Nothing to talk about now. We need to get this kid away from the human garbage who snatched him."

He puts his phone away. I can't help but feel there's a connection between his rage at Sean and the reappearance of his mother. The expression on his face when he was looking at his phone was a cross between anger and something else. Something wistful.

∞

Tuesday March 15
Alphabet City, Avenue A, 10:07 am

Archie is gently swatting my face, playing with the beard. Even he gives me a hard time about it. And being a cat, he does not care about humans needing sleep; he wants breakfast now.

I'm about to get up, and I'm surprised when Joel gets out of bed and takes Archie with him. I wait in bed, listening. He heads for the kitchen. I hear him getting Archie's Fancy Feast. Then he makes coffee. It's not like he never does this, but I am usually Archie's morning servant.

Things are iffier than I'm comfortable with.

The three of us were wired last night after rescuing David, and we didn't go home right away. Out of nowhere Joel suggested going to a pool hall open until 3 am. That was fine with Bob and myself. He and I almost got into trouble with some fellow patrons over a game we won, but managed to avoid a fight. Joel did not join us at the table. He headed for some old school video games he was clearly familiar with. I suppose that was his way of winding down.

We stayed until closing. By the time we got back to my place, with Bob staying over, we were exhausted and went right to bed. I don't think Joel said more than a few sentences to me after we left David with his mother. And at home, I had trouble getting to sleep still. Joel stayed on his own side of the bed, lost in his mind. Tiny body language cues kept me from feeling like he was close to me. That made me restless. I kept waking up and feeling him stir at the same time. Then at some point he moved closer to me; I felt his head against my shoulder, and I could finally sleep.

I sit up and think about all this. Then he comes in the bedroom, and seems surprised I'm awake. As if nothing was going on with him at all, he lies on the bed next to me and casually runs his fingers in the band of the boxers I wore to bed.

I ask him, "You okay, baby?"

Archie has finished his meal and come back to demand attention from us. Joel scratches his head. "Um...You remember the first weekend we were together?"

He's directly avoiding my question. But the tone of his voice draws me in. "Of course. What were you thinking about?"

He smiles. "Just remembering. Back before you were all Rasputin-like."

For that remark I trace my hand across his ribs and tickle him. He's extremely ticklish but loves to provoke me to do it. I have him helpless and giggling in seconds.

He slips his leg between mine, turning this erotic in just one subtle move. I sense it's also a maneuver to deflect any more questions on my part. Maybe even to be contrite; to make up for the tension. I want to know what's going on with him, but I can't help but go along with his seduction.

I stroke my fingers lightly down his side. His breath catches and he trembles a little, under my touch. The slower I go the more he trembles. That is genuine, and enraptures me.

"What specifically did you want me to remember?"

He starts to answer and stops, as if he's unsure. For a moment, I just continue touching him gently on his face, his body. I have a theory the lightest touch can bring a reaction like the hardest, if done right. If done with the right person. And he has been the one to prove that, in how he lies watching me...breathless, time stopping.

Then Archie, who has been meowing and walking around the bed, launches himself on me--somehow missing Joel, as always--and digs all his claws in my thigh, barely missing a much more sensitive area. He then swiftly takes off in a spectacular leap, thwarting my attempt to grab him and strangle him.

Now Joel laughs out loud, in spite of the fact I'm bleeding. I curse--very bad. My phone then rings.

"Hold on." Joel gets up to go to the bathroom. "Don't use your shorts to stop the bleeding."

"I only did that once." I answer the phone.

"Hey, Gabriel. It's Clark. How are things going?"

"Pretty good. How are you?"

"Decent, overall. I'm looking forward to talking with you again, but this is actually...it's a favor."

Joel comes back with some peroxide and cotton balls. I watch him stem the bleeding while I talk.

"What's up?"

"Well, it's a little unusual. I know someone with a problem, and this person asked me to have you meet him to talk about it."

"Okay, I understand that. But he would be welcome to contact me directly."

"It's special circumstances you might say. I can't really go into it now, but any way you could meet me today?"

I run my hand through Joel's hair as he presses the cotton wads against me. "I take it this is something urgent."

"Yes, and I know him enough to believe that. And you specifically are needed. Because of your integrity."

"Playing to my ego, huh? When?"

"Soon as possible."

"Give me an hour. Is this at the *Standard's* building?"

"I'm at the Lower East Side right now. There's a coffee shop off Chrystie Street, Expensive Coffee..."

"I know it. A friend of mine lives around there."

"I really appreciate it Gabriel. He wanted to emphasize it's very important."

"I got you. See you later."

When I hang up, Joel says, "You have to go somewhere?"

"Yeah. Looks like I picked the wrong time to quit smoking."

Joel ignores the *Airplane* quote and picks up Archie, who nuzzles him. The cat turns all Regan MacNeil on me but never fucks with Joel.

"Clark Ahn needs a favor of some kind. Some guy he knows who wants help--life and death situation, etcetera."

He shrugs. "All right."

"He's in Danny's neighborhood."

I hustle to get dressed. Now Bob is up and he and Joel are talking about doing something while I'm with Clark. Bob is six feet, brown hair, around 50 and a really sweet guy unless he's in a fight. He's trying to convince Joel to visit some avant garde performance art show, because it has nude female performers doing an Annie Sprinkle kind of thing.

"Reminds me of *Hair*. Or even better, this club I read about in *Hustler* that I went to one time. You've heard of ping-pong balls. This lady did *quarters*. I mean, she made change and everything."

As amusing as that sounds, I beg off hearing details so I can meet Clark and get this taken care of. I have regular work to handle afterwards.

I leave the apartment shortly thereafter and walk downtown a few blocks to Chrystie Street in the Lower East Side. Yes, the place is really called Expensive Coffee. Welcome to New York City.

I see Clark outside the shop, smoking. He smiles at me. He's Asian American, around 30, medium height, hair in a fashionable cut.

We shake hands and he says, "Well, I guess I should tell you what's going on."

"Lay it on me."

He holds the door open for me. I go inside and wait for him, then follow him past the counter to a table by the floor to ceiling windows.

You got to be fucking kidding me.

Alex is at the table, playing with his phone.

He takes off his sunglasses and stands.

"Gabriel. Thank you for coming."

He smiles and holds out his hand.

Since Clark is here, I accept his hand rather than punch him in the face.

∞

THREE

Albert Einstein said, "People like us, who believe in physics, know that the distinction between past, present, and future is only a stubbornly persistent illusion."

Tuesday March 15, Continued

"**WHAT'S THIS ALL ABOUT,**" I ask, extracting my hand from his grip.

He meets my eyes. He can see I'm not happy, but he pretends otherwise. "Sorry about the cloak-and-dagger. This is such as sensitive situation, I didn't want to risk calling you, so I had Clark play middle man."

He keeps looking at me while saying this line of bullshit. Clark doesn't know details about Alex and me, as far as I know. Maybe not even that we had a relationship. Therefore, I'm pretty sure he doesn't know Alex and I are not on speaking terms. Since I haven't responded to any emails, voicemails or texts that Alex has periodically sent since December, this elaborate lie was apparently just to drag me down here.

Clark asks, "Can I get you coffee, Gabriel? Give you a chance to catch up."

"Sure." I give him a ten-dollar bill for himself and me and he walks away.

I sit down across from Alex. "You've got some fucking nerve."

"You never write back to me. I figured you wouldn't come if I asked you myself."

"Yeah, being told I'm welfare trash ticks me off a little."

"I'm sorry I hurt you."

I feel my anger uncoiling inside. "Hurt? You don't know. What you said was beyond decency."

"I'm apologizing, Gabriel. People say things they don't mean when they break up."

"You *meant* it; don't fucking play with me. What the hell do you want?"

"I need your help." He assumes an expression of penitence. "It's about one of my sources. Obviously, based on your temperament I wouldn't ask if I didn't really need you."

"Are you kidding me? You should know better than ask me for anything. The only reason I'm talking now is because I don't want Clark to feel bad."

"Gabriel, I'm serious. *I don't have anyone else to turn to.* A man could be in serious danger over this. Because he's trying to do the right thing."

He might be sincere in what he said. But to bring it to me...why?

Because he knew you would not be able to walk away if he said someone was in danger. This makes me even angrier. *Manipulative bastard.*

The anger isn't helped by how he's looking at me. "God, I missed you. I want to talk to you about that as well. About us."

Before I can even let my jaw drop from the audacity, Clark comes back with coffee. I turn my attention to it to calm down.

Alex says, "Actually Clark knows a little about this. He's working on an angle to the story. You could say we're both benefitting from your help."

Alex is political affairs editor at the *Herald Standard,* the city's rival to the *Times.* He's a good-looking man. British and Indian, six feet, a year older than me, very cultured and intelligent.

Last summer I met Alex on a case that turned out to be life-changing for many reasons. He was one of them, and we started to build a relationship on a fast, intense level. But two things developed at the same time. First, Alex almost immediately began pressuring me to give up my profession, to commit to some sort of ideal he thought I should be. To better myself to *his* standards. Well, fuck that. I like what I do, I'm good at it, and I don't want to do anything else.

And then, since Joel returned from whatever he was doing in the two years he was away, I discovered our bond never really died. It only lay dormant until it became obvious to me I could not be with anyone else.

Not a great situation to handle, but that's life. I told Alex the truth as soon as I realized it. Alex could not believe I would want to be with Joel rather than him, and said some terrible, horrible, no good very bad things to me. I could understand his being angry over my leaving him for Joel, but his evaluation of my character exposed a side of him I had no idea existed and left me cold.

"What's the problem?"

Alex's voice turns serious. "Thank you for listening. Here's what's going on. I'm working with a source; if a story develops, I'm giving it to Clark. The source's name is Zach Mesereau. He's a government worker in an intelligence agency—CIA. He has some devastating information. You know the current administration, like the last administration, has not been kind to whistleblowers; I remember you mentioning how that angered you. The weird thing is what Mesereau says is going on—that random citizens are being targeted by intelligence agencies for a particular type of torture. Something that's used on the mind, that's used on *brainwaves.* I know you know about these topics. Can you explain it to Clark?"

"Biomagnetic. Sprung out of MK-ULTRA. Using targeted microwaves to implant thoughts, like making someone think he was schizophrenic."

"I knew you'd understand what I was talking about."

"How bad is it," Clark asks.

"This started in the 1950s during the Cold War, but some versions of it were going on before that--in the Nazi concentration camps. Anyway, first the CIA tested LSD and other substances as a truth serum. They also had experiments to develop a Manchurian Candidate through hypnosis and other fringe science, in Project Artichoke, which developed into Project MK-ULTRA. The Defense Intelligence Agency later tried things like remote viewing for intelligence--Project Stargate. The various methods in MK-ULTRA were used for spying, offensive counterintelligence, assassination, interrogation and torture. They were searching for a substance or device to control the mind--and body. To shut down parts of the body, cause paralysis, pain, amnesia."

Clark shakes his head. "And this is true?"

"MK-ULTRA and the other programs are factual. And what I mentioned is just what's in the released information. The CIA destroyed a good deal its records before the Church Committee began investigations in the Seventies."

Alex says, "So if they were already working on this stuff since the Fifties, they could have the methods even more refined."

"They could probably deploy it in drones by now. Maybe they are. Who the fuck knows? But aside from human rights, if random citizens are being targeted on US soil that's out of the CIA's operational mission."

"I don't think it's approved as such. It's the work of a rogue group within."

"A rogue group within an organization that already spends billions in black budget."

"Yes," Alex says. "So of course, we'd want to expose it. But think how it sounds. Conspiracies aren't popular now. It'd would be laughable if no proof can be offered. Mesereau is pretty sure that he can find some evidence. But in the meantime, he needs to work on that without being caught. That's the foundation of what I wanted to tell you..."

Clark's phone buzzes. "Excuse me just a moment." He gets up and steps away from the table.

Alex smiles at me. "So..."

"Cut the crap," I tell him. "What I told you and Clark can be found on Wikipedia. It isn't secret knowledge marked 'Majestic Level Clearance.' And you know it already--we talked about it before. What do you really want?"

He rolls his eyes and leans closer to me. "All right. Someone may be on to my source now. A man has turned up in Mesereau's department recently, a visiting analyst. He's staying here in the city for a few months for a project. However, Mesereau recognized his name. That's what I wanted to talk to you about. Clark doesn't know about it and I can't tell him."

Clark comes back before he can say any more. "Sorry about that. Oh! Look who's here."

Alex and I look at the window. Joel is standing on the sidewalk, staring in at us. Bob is with him, saying something we can't hear.

Shit. I forgot I told them where I was going to meet Clark. I don't have anything to feel guilty about, and yet I feel guilty.

Joel isn't looking at me, he's looking at Alex. But then Clark stands and waves at him. "Hey! Come in and join us."

Alex mutters, almost to himself, "I don't think that's a good idea."

Joel has immediately left for the door with Bob right behind. I pray to my various Buddhist spirit guides that this doesn't end with the police being called.

"Hey, man," Clark says as they approach. He and Joel shake hands, and Joel introduces Bob to him.

"Here, sit next to Gabriel. I'll get a chair for Bob."

And there we are, Clark and Alex across from Joel and me, and Bob at the end, looking like he expects World War III any second.

Clark, unaware of the tension, asks Joel, "How did the interview with Matt go?"

"Very well. As I understand, it'll be published next week. I appreciate you giving him the update on the Mathers case."

"I was glad to help...you guys should get more press."

Joel stares at Alex again. "And I understand you tried to help Matt as well."

Alex looks away, then back at Joel. They're both trying to glare at each other without seeming to. But what Joel said catches my attention.

I say flatly, "How so?"

"I didn't mention it to you," Joel says, still fixed on Alex. "Alex suggested Matt do a real in-depth thing on my life before I met you."

That makes me crush the coffee cup in my hand. It's almost full, and floods over.

Everyone but me jumps up. I'm so angry I can't move.

Clark asks, "Are you okay?"

If it's burning me, I don't notice. Clark runs to get something—ice, water, towels, I don't know.

"What the fuck are you *doing*," I say to Alex.

Alex turns impervious again. He gestures to Joel. "He exaggerates."

I stand up. "You now have serious problems with me. *Serious.*"

Alex frowns. "You're going to believe him? I was just joking. But it's *true* about him, isn't it?"

Joel hisses, "Stay the fuck out of my business."

Alex stares down at him, using his height to intimidate--if that worked, which it doesn't. "You think you could possibly do anything to me?"

Bob moves subtly in front of Joel. Having realized what Alex did, Bob gets protective. Bob in protective mode is dangerous. I've backed him up enough times to know.

"I think you better leave, buddy." He says this to Alex in a deceptively mild voice.

The three of us give Alex pause. But he can't stop. That's one of his problems. "Look, it's going to come out anyway. I could, as a favor to Gabriel, frame it in such a way as to make people feel sorry for him--"

That's it. Ignoring Clark, who has returned to the table, I grab Alex's arm and force him to move out of the coffee shop. He goes along without resisting so as not to cause a scene.

"What's the matter," I hear Clark saying behind me.

I don't care what they tell him.

Outside on the sidewalk, Alex tries to shake my hand off his arm. "Really, Gabriel. What is this? Are you going to hit me?" His voice is incredulous, wry, condescending.

"Yes. I suggest you prepare for it."

When he sees my face, the shock on his is worth the trouble I'm about to cause. And then Joel suddenly is out the door and rushing over to me. "Gabriel, don't. *Don't.*"

"Gabriel, this is what you've *lowered* yourself to." Alex's voice is contemptuous.

I move forward towards him and gratifyingly, he jumps back. Joel gets in front of me and grabs my shoulders and says in my ear, "It doesn't matter. *It doesn't matter.* Don't do it. Please."

"I'm not going to let him--"

"Doesn't matter. It's not worth it. Let it go."

I'm looking at Alex over Joel's shoulder, and he may finally see he's gone too far, staring in my eyes, seeming shaken up for once.

Joel says without looking at him, "I told Clark you both had something extremely important and confidential to talk about, urgently. And that Gabriel has to take care of his hand. Because I know no one wants more trouble, right?"

Alex shrugs, trying to recover his imperviousness. "Well, we do need to talk. I didn't get a chance to tell you..."

"You need to leave." I'm feeling myself tremble with the effort of holding myself back. "I don't care what you want to tell me. Just leave."

Alex seems as though he may still continue, and then thinks better of it and goes back inside the coffee shop.

Joel walks me around the corner and down the block to a bus stop bench. He picks up my hand and examines it. I hear footsteps and then see Bob has caught up with us.

"It's all cool," he says. "Are you okay?"

He has a bottle of cold water and Joel opens it and pours it over my hand, which is red but not serious.

"I'll get something from drug store."

I look at Joel.

He meets my eyes. "There was a part of me that wanted you to do it. But it's not the right way to handle this."

"I *still* want to do it."

"I didn't mean to put you in that position again."

"You mean after last night with Sean?"

He sighs. "That was...I don't want to talk about it. This is different. Alex is pain in the ass, but he's not Sean. If you hit him, he'd find some way to fuck with you."

"I am not afraid of him and what he can do."

Joel just smiles and leaves for a drug store. Bob and I leave the bus stop as a bus approaches.

I ask him, "What happened in there?"

"I told him that I would go out and help if necessary; if you needed a witness to say he swung first. He said, "I can't let that happen.""

I think about the differences between Joel's reaction today and last night. That it seems like from two different worlds.

∞

After Joel sprays my hand with something, he and Bob go somewhere. I have to work. I call Veronica and we meet up with Geneva and get going on our cases.

Night falls before I'm finished. I then decide to see how Joel is doing.

Turns out Isabella is there at his loft. Talking strategy or whatever. Something about licensing. Joel's set up some kind of company under a name he likes, Smoking Dharma. He once said that phrase summed me up.

Isabella gives me a hug. "You know he sold a painting to that club on Union Square? One of *you*, Gabriel!"

"Terrific. Which one?"

"One of the nudes. You've nothing to be ashamed of. I'd love for you to break the fourth wall at one of these showings."

She puts her hand on my ass briefly. She is always nice to me, and she wanted Joel and me to get back together. But she is very familiar with him, and extends that to me more and more. I'm not sure how I feel about that. Granted, talking to Alex has clouded my perspective. Isabella may have lax boundaries but she is a decent person working hard to get Joel his deserved accolades. I just can't tell if I'm bothered by her familiarity with me or her familiarity with Joel.

"Did you hear anything else from *him*?" Joel asks.

"No."

Isabella says, "I can leave; I don't want to interfere with you two."

"You're not interfering. Gabriel got hassled by a man he used to date."

"Ugh. I hate those *ex* things. Are you okay, sweetie?"

"Yeah." Although I feel a warmth going up my neck to my head. Strange. "Nothing to it." I consider if I want to sit, or try to walk off the warm numbness. I go over to the windows, hearing Isabella's slightly gravelly voice behind me.

"Joel and *I* never had that problem."

Huh. I can't help but glance at Joel, and he frowns at her. "Iz, don't say stupid things."

"What? Gabriel knows I'm kidding." She comes over to rub my shoulder. I flinch, but not because of her. The warmth is turning to something else. Things are breaking up in my vision—little fields of gray, like TV snow. I feel nauseated. Trying to get over my jealousy, I take her hand to reassure her. And clutch it a little too hard.

She says, "Gabriel? Something wrong?"

"I don't know. This might be a migraine. But it's..."

An aura clouds over the room and I lose sensation of my legs. I can barely see Joel drop what he's doing and rush over to us.

Then the pain hits. I feel him catching me, as my legs go out. He takes me to his mattress. "Hold on, baby."

"Can I help?..." Isabella's voice gets faint.

The pain starts pounding bad enough to block out sound as well as light...

I don't know how long it lasts. I wake up suddenly. Joel puts his hand on me. "How you feeling?"

I can tell it's late, much later than when the headache came on. I'm on Joel's mattress on the floor. He hasn't gotten a bedstead yet. He was reading something on his iPad, which he puts down now.

"What time is it?" My voice doesn't sound right. His hand moves to my head. I put my hand over his.

"Nearly one in the morning."

I see his concern making his face shadowed. I try to laugh it off, sitting up slowly. "Hey look, I'm my dad: 1979 through '89."

"That isn't funny. You don't have a hangover. This is serious."

"Did I pass out?"

"Not really. You just laid here in a lot of pain but you wouldn't stop talking. Like you do in your sleep sometimes. I made Iz leave; you were freaking her out. I had you take some pain medication." He begins massaging my shoulders.

I close my eyes and let him keep on with that massaging. How he touches me isn't just healing or compassionate, it's also intimate. Not sexually intimate, but emotionally intimate.

Sex can be and often is meaningless. Knowing someone intimately is a different matter, and that's where Isabella has the jump on me, like Joel's best friend Chris. I *know* Joel very well in the context of him and me—his moods, his passions, his quirks, his strengths. And yet when they're around I sometimes feel like he and I just met. Or at least, like now, that he knows me better than I know him.

∞

Wednesday, March 16
Spring Street, 9:30 am

On the top floor of the Soho Health and Aqua Center, Joel stops to look out tall glass windows lining the length of the wall. He observes White Street, seven stories down. This floor has a pool and steam room/sauna that can be reserved for exclusive use by premium members. Once in a while Joel does this when he prefers to swim alone.

This morning they woke up locked together in each other's arms. Gabriel said he was over his headache. But he stayed on the mattress for a bit, having Joel play Miles Davis softly in the background. Joel was worried over whether Gabriel really felt better, just as he knows Gabriel is worried about him feeling better. It was a mix of emotions. He watched Gabriel lying with his eyes closed, concentrating on *Bye Bye Blackbird*.

Joel then played Billy Strayhorn, which surprised Gabriel. But Joel knows Strayhorn's work very well from a client. Gabriel was actually too low-key to get much into random trivia, but did manage some fast facts about Strayhorn and his connection to Dr. Martin Luther King. Finally, Gabriel insisted he was okay to run. He retrieved a Go-Go's t-shirt from his stack of clothes, borrowed a pair of Janji athletic pants, and took off.

Gabriel is currently on the West Side Highway, a better area to run, before he goes home to Archie. Gabriel hates running but is pushing himself to be good at it. He'll never enter a marathon; he jokes that he'd always Rosie Ruiz anything like that. Rather, his running is a single-purpose activity to build endurance. Joel saw that in action last year, when Gabriel caught up with a bigger, stronger man who had shot at them in a New Jersey park and took the other man down. At 5'9, Gabriel is slightly shorter than average, but he outshines the average man in speed, strength, fighting skill, and intelligence. Approaching 40 only makes him work harder at it.

After Gabriel had left the loft Joel started to hear things from the paintings. The leaves in the trees rustling, water hitting a shore gently. The boxes seemed to be making noise as well--demanding that Joel remove the contents and find them a home. These things were not meant to be in boxes.

Jan knew every item he owned and he chose what he wanted to give Joel with a relish Joel feels now. He must have been thinking about it as they spent time together in the sun room. Jan in a thick robe on a chaise lounge reading or taking notes. Joel painting or sketching. Jan would ask for an item to be brought to him and explain its background to Joel. He had no one else to talk to, at least anyone interested in the history of the object. Others would be interested in the value of the object, perhaps. Joel would study it, ask questions, and try to see where it was when it was first created. Jan chose the items that he saw clicked with Joel for one reason or another.

With the boxes calling to him, Joel began removing things from them. A pair of 19th Century paisley strip cashmere pillows with Indian backing and front. A 17th Century Verdure tapestry of birds in a landscape with a flute player. An Art Deco clock, bronze and set with marcasite, from pre-World War II Germany. They watched *Cabaret* after discussing the clock.

He put these on an otherwise bare table while thinking where they should go in the loft. And then he felt as though he was not alone. Maybe Gabriel was coming back, having given up on running. He checked outside the loft door. Empty.

Your mind is working you.

True that. He finally decided to leave the rest of the items but promised them they will be taken care of. Objects carry vibes and he doesn't want the vibes to be distraught.

Right now at the windows, reflecting on that strange feeling in his loft, Joel goes on to the locker room. The music in the background is baroque classical, echoing the mood and activity without overtaking it. In no hurry, he undresses and changes to Diesel swim briefs.

Alone, he approaches the white rectangular pool which contrasts strikingly with the black and red tile. Two diving boards are available and he chooses the higher one. He climbs deliberately, feeling the metaphor of rising above whatever's on earth.

In his mind he returns to what he was trained to do as a kid. How to approach the board, how to balance, how to dive. It's not really thought; it's Zen. And as in Zen, his execution is flawless. He has something extra, a propulsion borne of urgency to move from the air to underwater, from one freedom to another.

Joel stays under as long as possible. He knows that swimming requires relaxation, not tension. He didn't hyperventilate before he dived and he exhales underwater slowly and naturally getting his pulse rate down. Swimming underwater alone is discouraged as dangerous. Joel knows what he's doing but also that staff routinely check the room. He breaks the rules a little, to his breath-holding capacity of just over three minutes.

He doesn't see that behind the entrance to the pool three staff members watch him through the door windows. They've made a point of it since he joined last summer. After the pleasure of seeing him surface, they disappear before the manager catches them.

For a while, Joel is alone. Usually he swims for some time as exercise and then for leisure. His energy is subliminal and nurtured by the water.

But he suddenly has the urge to dive again. He climbs out, goes back up the ladder and stares at the water.

Then he dives. Not for show, but as if he was escaping. And swims hard, using all his muscles to their maximum, to reach the other side. His heart is pounding as he rests on the edge of the shallow end. He scans the pool behind him.

It's not the lake; the lake was cold. But after the shock of hitting the water, I didn't even feel the cold. Just the urge to get away.

He puts his head down on his arms briefly. *No, no, no. I'm not going to think about it.* He feels safe in water. It's his refuge. He can't be hurt here. Don't think about *him.* Think about Gabriel. Funny he and Gabriel are both Aquarians. It fits, as much as astrology can fit anything, with their humanitarian and intellectual similarities, and their stubbornness.

"Yet you love swimming, and you told me Gabriel won't set foot in a pool or natural body of water. Isn't that right?"

It's Jan's voice, with his barely noticeable Dutch accent. Joel is both shocked to hear it and his acceptance of it. Clearly it is stemming from his sensations in the loft...but something more. It's balancing the sudden resurgence of horrible memories. He can't tell if Jan is real, like a ghost, or if he's doing what Gabriel does—have conversations with imagined dead people. He can see Jan walking along the pool as he swims. Not Jan's wasting, pain-racked body of last year, but as he was 10 years ago when Joel first met him. Jan was about 45 then.

"He won't even get on a ferry if he doesn't have to," Joel tells Jan. "When we were in Australia, he made a point of not going in the ocean or the pools. He just watched."

Joel notes that Jan is wearing one of the V-necked thin sweaters he liked, Kiton trousers, and loafers with no socks. Jan takes out a pack of Davidoff cigarettes and lights up. "You feel unsettled about your feelings. About last night."

"I don't know why. I know how to handle things better, and yet..."

"You were stirred up. It's your memory affecting you. As it is now, I see."

Joel sees Jan's point. "I let it get to me. About Sean. I let that get out of control."

"Were you successful in what you set out to do that night?"

"Yes. We all went to the building where David was being held. Andreas' assistant Farva was the only one in the apartment keeping watch over David. We broke in through the fire escape and Gabriel tasered Farva. We got David out of the building; Andreas suddenly came back, but Bob had caught him outside and knocked him out. We got David back to Brooklyn. His mom was so happy she was crying."

"Of course. And David was about 15, right?"

"Yeah. God knows what would have happened to him."

"*You* know. It happened to you at 15."

Joel moves slowly, with Jan walking beside him as he swims. Sometimes Jan would watch him swim and time how long he was underwater, using the Tag Hauer watch Joel now has.

"Um. Yeah. It was important to get him back."

"Getting him out of that situation meant everything."

"It did. I felt that all night. I'm just..."

"*You* didn't get out, you know. You survived. Better than most. Better to an incredible degree. But you didn't get out. Maybe you're angry at that."

"Why? It isn't Gabriel's fault."

"You're not angry at him. You're angry at yourself for what happened. Abused people get angry at themselves. Or they project. You've done this before--projected your anger on Gabriel because he's conveniently there."

"That's fucked up," Joel says.

Jan says to him, "Not really. Consider this. You knew people like Sean. Bystanders who are aware a child is being hurt or exploited and do nothing; who even help the predator. But because you are who you are, you've reacted against that desire to lash out--suppressed it. Until now."

Joel sees Jan staring at him. Jan was never judgmental. If anything, he was lonely. He paid for company because at least it was a relationship upfront about money, rather than someone pretending to have love in order to get closer to money. Jan was also very intuitive about human nature. This is why it meant so much when Jan wanted Joel to be with him at the end of his life.

It's why he told Jan about what happened to him, when he told no one else about what happened to him. Not the whole story.

"Why would I have suppressed everything?"

Jan smiles slightly, as if apologetic about having to say this. "Because the predator created your identity in some ways."

"That can't possibly be true."

"It's in your books; the ones that arrived Monday. The past is over in one way, and yet not so much. You can't see it, because you can't analyze what happened to you when you're in crisis. But being forced to react to what happens to us--fight or flight--ends up framing ourselves in some way. The point is not to let it become your only identity--the victim who continues to be the victim, or the victim who runs away to avoid being a victim. You tend towards the second. And what you did later that night..."

In the pool hall; Gabriel and Bob seamlessly hustling a couple of Wall Street Patrick Bateman-types. Joel staying by himself with an arcade video game, Mortal Kombat. As a teenager, he used to play that for hours in Willowbrook Mall in New Jersey.

"You went into your crisis reaction," Jan says.

"Yeah, but...I was just...I don't know, inside myself."

"You should go through those books and see what they can tell you what you need to know *now*."

Don't I know my life already?

He can hear Jan's voice behind him. "You need to come to grips with what it's done to you. To move past it. You can do this."

"I don't know. This is too much. I just...I have to find out what my mother wants." Joel says, and is overtaken with a sense of dread. "I'm going to have to see her."

Jan turns to smile at him, sympathetically, seeing the dread. "I don't know if I can do it..."

And then Jan is gone, and Joel is saying to an empty room, "Because I'm afraid of seeing *him* again."

∞

Four

George Eliot said, "...a man's past is not simply a dead history, an outworn preparation of the present: it is not a repented error shaken loose from the life: it is a still quivering part of himself, bringing shudders and bitter flavors and the tinglings of a merited shame."

∞

Friday, March 17 2011
Alphabet City, Avenue A, 7:02 AM

I'M LOUNGING ON THE COUCH; Joel's sitting between my legs leaning back on my chest. We both have coffee on the window sill next to us. I'm watching him go through an album of photos I just updated.

Much of the past week has been 12 hours straight working, being with Joel when I can, and some extracurricular things with friends, like playing keyboards with Jason's band on a couple occasions.

Late last night, I recorded the narrative for another video to go on YouTube. This was a story I put together out of Kent Varney's notes involving some dirty business in the 1980s with political intrigue. The Tertullian Society had their Chthulu-like tentacles in the spray of assassinations, coups, torture, and civil unrest happening in that time period in Central and South America.

Kent had helped me uncover information about the Tertullian Society, a secret organization which developed from occult principles and Nazi ideology. The Society still exists as a mechanism for financial and political manipulation to benefit a privileged few, and it has no problem with destroying lives to obtain its goals. Kent was killed for his attempts to help me.

I don't want to act against them directly. They warned me off and threatened my friends. I have hopes, though, that eventually they will be exposed. I take the information I have and put it out there, leaving others to make connections. Joel will upload the video later, as he does so with a software program that prevents the origin of the user from being traced.

Today I'm off. Joel is taking the day off with me. He's feeling tense again, and doesn't respond to my hints to tell me what's wrong.

"You put in pictures of us from before." He sounds happy about that. Photos from when we were together the first time. Is our renewed relationship a separate one or one that just continued even while we were apart? It doesn't matter, the photos are good memories.

"Of course."

"There's a bunch of stuff here in the back; pictures you haven't put in."

"I don't know what to do with them. I'm surprised I put in what I did."

Joel takes out the handful of loose photographs from a fabric holder in back of the album and begins thumbing through them. "Oh, this looks serious."

I pick up my coffee as he holds up a particular photo.

Joel says, "Who's *he*? He looks like Idris Elba."

"He does, yeah, now that you mention it. That's Henri."

"Oh, the guy you were with before we met."

"He's French-Canadian. He had moved to France a few months before I met you."

Joel studies the picture. "You don't talk about him."

"I don't talk about anyone I was involved with. That's just plain stupid. No one's accused me of being stupid."

"It doesn't bother me if you do, you know. Were you in love?"

"I loved him. He was a good man. I couldn't go to Europe and it was for the best. There aren't many exes I have...what can I say...non-homicidally-inclined relations with. He's one."

His manner of studying the picture unnerves me; I wonder what he's thinking.

"He was the one who sent you the French edition of *Kickback*."

"Yeah. It was a nice gesture since he knew I liked *V for Vendetta*."

"You did the same for me."

He moves to another photo. "You were about 16 here. I can tell. This is the Bronx."

"The rooftop of Danny's mom's building." Danny Martinez is my oldest friend; we've been closer than close since we met in high school.

"And this is your mom. Your dad too, right?"

"Yeah. You never had the pleasure of meeting him." I run my hands through his hair. "Why are you studying these so hard?"

"I like seeing who you were. You always have the same expression in pictures--that you're ready to start a fight with someone-- a real 'fuck you' pose. Except the pictures with me."

"Definitely. You distract me from being angry at the world."

In that not-entirely-sure feeling, I put my arms around him. He is still a sponge for affection. No such thing as too much, just like a cat.

Joel reaches for his phone to take a picture of us like this. For a moment, I think we're both not entirely sure this is real.

I trace my finger down his face. He has his eyes closed, leaning further into me.

"Goddamn beard," he says. "Scratching my head."

"You're welcome to get the fuck out, you don't like it."

His eyes flash up at me. "It scratches all *over*."

"You're not going to win this."

He turns over and stares at me face to face. "It means something."

"It means I like to change how I look now and then."

"No, you don't. That stack of t-shirts at my loft proves otherwise."

"You're reading too much into facial hair. What's the matter, baby? Your mind is practically setting the atmosphere on fire."

He drops down into my chest. "Probably time to get ready to go."

We're driving to Paterson to see Bob.

"All right."

But he doesn't move; just speaks into my chest. "Uh...uh, I've been thinking. Since we're there, I might...see what she wants." He exhales heavily.

"Would you like me to go with you when you do that?"

"Yeah. I don't know that I could do it by myself."

He then sits up and starts messing with his phone, maybe looking at her picture again. I get up and put together some tools to take with me.

Danny calls me while I'm going through what I want to bring. I greet him. "What's up?"

"Well, I got a call just now from Alex. He wanted me to try to convince you to go outside and talk to him. I guess he's near your place. I said I wasn't going to do that. I'm not trying to, you know, *interfere* with your personal life."

I'm afraid this is going to bring on another headache. "And I appreciate that, man." I go over to the living room windows and look outside. Alex is across the street, smoking. Not looking up at my window, but obviously not doing so. It makes me sigh heavily. "Jesus. All right."

"He said it was life and death. But I didn't know what to do..."

I reassure Danny that I'm not upset with him. He liked Alex, and did not care at all for Joel back when he and I were first together. But Danny's been trying to respect the change with Joel and I being together again.

By the time I end the call, Joel is at the windows.

"I have a choice," I tell him. "I can ignore him, or go out and kick his ass."

"Or you can find out what he wants."

"Really?"

Joel turns back around. "Maybe you need to find out how much of a problem he's going to be. Either he has something he needs from you, and you can deal with it or whatever, or he's a stalker and you can start building a case against him."

"I don't have time for this."

"He's not going to give up. Just see what he wants and send him on his way."

"You're being more reasonable about this than you have to."

"I'm proving something to myself. Maybe I'd like to chuck a can out the window at him. But that's because of whatever insecurities I have. You're not going to go out and run away with him...right?"

I answer by putting my hands on his face and kissing him. "No one takes me from you."

But I still have to keep my temper as I go outside. Alex is standing casually, facing away from me, ostensibly studying the courts in the park.

I stop a few feet from him. "Well? What the fuck is it you want?"

He takes off his sunglasses. "I need your help. Did Danny tell you--"

"Don't call my friends anymore. He doesn't want to be involved."

"Gabriel, I swear I wouldn't do this, except I can trust so few people."

"And why do you trust me? Why do you think I can help you?"

"Because...I know you're not corrupted. I guess that's the way I'll put it."

"And just what is it you need?"

Alex looks around to ensure no one is listening. "All right. I told you about that analyst Mesereau is worried about. Mesereau doubts he's just an analyst. He thinks this man is trying to find the leak in the department--who is Mesereau himself. Mesereau made some discreet inquiries and if this man is who Mesereau thinks he is, he's a problem."

"Meaning if he finds out Mesereau is the leak, Mesereau ends up in a one-man car accident. Is that it? Why does he think the analyst is out to get him?"

"I'm not sure. He was vague about that, and I didn't want to push him." Alex looks at the people playing in the courts. "I imagine conversations would reveal it."

"So you want me to *wiretap* him. The analyst."

Alex looks contrite, but hopeful. A wiretap means getting in where the man lives, setting up recording devices, hacking his computer, maybe trying to hack his phone to install an app. I can do that; all it takes is the equipment, knowledge and the opportunity. Just a little matter of the consequences if I'm found out.

This kind of request is not like Alex at all. He knows breaking the law is sometimes necessary when dealing with criminals; I can list all the New York State Criminal Codes I violated in looking for David. But Alex prides himself on not putting others in legal or moral jeopardy--or so I thought.

"Who is this guy, the one Mesereau is concerned about?"

"He calls himself Aaron Comstock. He is supposed to be here from DC."

Alex opens a messenger bag he's carried with him and takes out a folder. He hands it to me. Bare bones personal and professional information on Comstock. "I obtained this from Mesereau. He took some serious risks for this information."

I look it over briefly. Alex's expression turns grim. "Of course, I want you to think carefully before taking this on."

"Why? Isn't Guantanamo closing?"

He isn't amused. "I don't want to be responsible for something happening to you."

I feel my irritation rise. "Then why are you asking? You know what this involves."

"I told you, I have no one else." He looks away again briefly, then back at me. "The paper's admin would not approve of going too far on this. I can trust Clark, but I suspect some reporters and editors have friendly relations with intelligence, if you know what I mean. I know good people, but practically none that I can say for certain aren't connected or taking pay from intelligence agencies or other contacts that could get Mesereau killed. Except you. You don't have those kinds of high-level connections."

He realizes that didn't come out so well. "I mean, I know you'd never accept such connections even if you were asked. You have integrity. Plus, you have the know-how of finding out things."

"As do you."

"Not this. I saw you in action with Ethan Nelson that time; remember when we went to Eleanor's house together? That is your element, your capabilities."

"Breaking into places, breaking the law. That's what you mean. Lowlifes like me without the connections."

He purses his mouth. "It's what you do. I'm admitting this is something that you do far better than I, and yes, the irony of my asking for it hasn't escaped me. In fact, it taught me to appreciate you."

I refrain from rolling my eyes. But he sees my cynicism.

"I need to know, Gabriel. To figure out how to protect my source."

"Ultimately you can't. Even if he isn't killed, even if he has front-page headlines, if they want him to go down he'll go down."

For a moment Alex looks troubled. "He's aware of that. But let it be under his terms, not Comstock's. If you find out anything, Mesereau can probably backtrack to rescue himself." Alex looks at me plaintively. "You told me you held Daniel Ellsberg, Jeffrey Wigand, and other whistleblowers in high regard. I know you're the only person I can trust to ask."

I glance down at the folder. "I don't know. I have to think about it."

"I'm paying you personally. Whatever you need, doesn't matter. This isn't a business expense. I don't want or need records."

"I'm not taking money from you. Bad enough you used Clark and Danny to try to talk to me. And you seem to forget what you did to Joel. Tell me why I should help you after your stunt."

"I find it strange you're willing to get violent over him."

Irritated, I hand him back the folder. "I find how *you* are acting is strange. Given that, I think I want nothing to do with this."

The look on his face is stricken. "I don't know what you mean, how I'm acting."

I sigh; this is taking more time than I want. I can see Joel watching us from my apartment window. I fold my arms and figure that if I attempt the impossible--closure--that maybe he'll leave me alone.

"Alex, I felt the way I did because you tried to harm someone I love. You don't have a problem with him, you have it with me. When we were together you didn't seem like a man who would engage in such terrible behavior. I thought you were the kind of person who understands that if a relationship ends you walk away. But then, I also thought you understood *I* didn't want to be changed."

"And I'll tell you what I saw," he says quietly. "I saw someone trying to make something better of his life and fighting odds. I admired that. I saw someone with real intelligence who started falling into a dark way of life. The abyss Nietzsche spoke of. And that coincided with Joel returning. The more he worked with you, the more I saw you fall apart. What was I supposed to think? That he was *better* for you? Maybe you're defensive because of some kind of guilt; you know you did not act right about this."

"Except I didn't call you names, or throw your past in your face, when I ended it."

He shrugs. "I went too far. Jesus Christ, I was hurt. I drove myself to say things I wouldn't otherwise. I couldn't believe I was losing you."

"Okay, I get it, but I don't understand why you won't let go."

He runs his hand through his hair and looks away. "I can't help it. Maybe we weren't together long, but I still feel for you. I was building something with you and it got taken away. I feel like that was so wrong, so unfair. I know it's not right since clearly you have moved on."

I'm uncomfortable now. Maybe guilt is still nagging at me. "It's not even moving on. I shouldn't have started anything with you."

"Why not?"

"Because I still had feelings for him."

"Oh, do you believe that? You have some irrational idea you and he are soul mates? Please. No, I'm just saying, look at it from my perspective. I know Danny didn't care for him and he never said explicitly why, but..."

That reminds me of something Alex said when we broke up. During our heated conversation he brought up the reason why I ended my previous relationship with Joel. I interrupt him. "And if Danny didn't say anything about Joel, just how did you know about him?"

"I picked up some clues. Like you, I'm good that that. I found some information that more or less confirmed it."

"What information?"

"Does it matter? I'm sorry about what I said. I'm not going to print anything or--"

"It matters. I want to know."

He's agitated now, looking around. He glances at my apartment. "Is he going to keep watching us? I suppose. Well, I ran a check on him. I have my contacts too. Don't look at me like that. If the situation was reversed and you were worried about me--well, let's put it this way--if you were worried about *him*, you'd do the same."

That hits home because I actually did that. When I suspected Joel had returned to escorting after an implicit promise to quit, I followed him. God, life is sticky.

"I found out about the man in The Netherlands who left him a fairly sizable legacy. That man was known to use escorts. I acted on an assumption and asked people I know who either knew escorts or knew someone who did, with Joel's description, until I confirmed it. You want a cigarette, don't you?"

He holds out his pack to me. I know this is terrible, but I take one. He tries to move closer but I step back.

"Are you afraid of what he's going to say if you smoke?"

I ignore that. "That still doesn't answer how you knew why I broke up with him."

"What?"

"You said something that indicated you knew why I broke up with him. On that day you and I had it out."

"When you left me, you mean. That information I did get from Danny late last year. He didn't want to tell me. But he was very angry with you, and you apparently weren't speaking to him. I tried to talk to him to find out what was going on and I brought up Joel to him. I can be very persuasive, especially as he was not in a good way. I was desperate, Gabriel. Joel has a hold on you I can't compete with. Anything I thought I could use..."

I cover my eyes. "*Uh.* Jesus. This is awful. This is all so awful."

"I agree. We're driven to do awful things. I'm not the only one. Don't be angry at Danny. I just want to know--is there any way you and I can be friends?"

I stare at him. "You can't be serious."

"I am. I am sorry...including what I said about him. I don't want to just never see you again. As adults, we could be on good terms."

"I can't see that happening."

Alex looks up at my window. "Because he wouldn't let it."

"You have it wrong. I'm only out here because he suggested it. I'm way too angry at you."

"I can be wrong." He seems truly distressed, which makes me way more uncomfortable. "I'm asking you to forgive me for that."

"For what?"

"Everything. What I said to you that day. For...trying to change you. And what I said about him. I need your help, but honestly, I am sorry."

I notice the door to my apartment building opens. Joel comes out. He has a satchel, the one I was using to put in some tools. Also he has Archie in a carrying case. Since we were going to be gone a couple of days, Veronica was going to watch him. Joel sits on the three stone steps that go up to the door.

"I have to leave."

"Do you want me to apologize to him? I will."

"I don't think that's a good idea right now.

"Let me. It can be a step, right?"

"Look, I'll think about your situation. I'm not going to tap someone. I don't need the problems going along with that. I'll think about what else could work. But just let this go for now."

I throw the cigarette in the gutter before I cross the street. I don't realize Alex is following me until I see Joel frowning.

I look over my shoulder and he's right behind me.

He says, "I'm leaving, but I wanted to show I'm sincere. So, Joel, I apologize over what I said. It wasn't right at all."

Joel stares at him intensely. He doesn't say anything. Alex turns and walks away down Avenue A, toward Houston.

"Your eyes are bloodshot," Joel says, turning his intense stare to me. "Don't get another headache. Take it easy."

I pick up Archie, and we go to where my car is parked.

I still feel bad. I feel bad that I got involved with Alex when I should have given Joel another chance; I feel bad I didn't tell Alex sooner when I knew it was over.

In the car, he reaches over and takes my hand as I drive to Chelsea where Veronica and Geneva live.

"I don't want him to get between us. Whatever you feel. You look like you want to run away and not be around either one of us."

"There's no either one of you. It's just you. You are my love. Seriously. I cannot even imagine you not being here, not being with me. The world would end."

He doesn't quite feel it. And while it's true, I still have the guilt. Does that ever go away?

After dropping Archie off, on the way to the George Washington Bridge, he asks, "What did he want?"

I briefly summarize what Alex told me.

"You aren't going to do that? Bug the guy's apartment?"

"No. It's too risky. If this source needs to go that far, he can figure out a way to get in there himself. I said I would think about how he might pick up on this Comstock's guy's motives. That's it."

"Did it help, talking to him?"

I shrug. "I don't know. Maybe. Or maybe just stirs things up."

"I *wanted* it to help. I didn't want to add drama. I didn't want you to regret..."

I reach out to hold his hand again. "Don't even think that. And don't worry about me. What's bothering you?"

He takes one of his notebooks out of a backpack. "Okay...well, I guess I understand about things being stirred up. Like, I had to travel to my past since I heard about my mother. I don't, usually. I put all of it away. I don't like talking about it. I prefer that it stay locked up somewhere, anything other than the safe things. My time with Chris and Iz I value, because with them I have safe memories. The rest is old news, or it's...bad. But even though I don't make an active effort to remember, it comes out..."

I glance over. He's frowning at the cover of the old notebook as if it was the Gutenberg Bible.

"It comes out in how I handle life. And now it's boiling up since I learned about that phone call. I wanted to tell you about these notebooks. The first one I bought when I was around 12. I was trying to figure out why my mom was the way she was--what could have went wrong with her. I had no one to ask. I tried to find answers in the library...in Wayne, and in Paterson. I told the librarians I had a school project on psychology. I would write down questions and thoughts and ideas. Seeing what I wrote now really hurts."

"What's it making you feel?"

"What I felt then. God, it's hard. It made me remember how she would go through my stuff. I had to hide this book. I put out another with drawings to fool her. I drew pictures of the times she took me to the circus. Because it had cats."

"And you both loved cats."

"All kinds. It's why we'd go to the circus. See, it wasn't bad early in my childhood. I think she loved me unconditionally then. No quid pro quo. I wanted to do things for her. I would draw for her friends, and any party I was at. Mom was so proud, she told everybody how well I could draw and stuff. Of course, when she mentioned it to him, he said 'It's a useless skill.'"

He opens the book to the first pages. "I drew in this one too. See, this was the cats at the circus, because that was the best memory I had of me and her. And then she changed into something else and dragged me along."

∞

It is 1990...

Gloria breaks down in the middle of domestic tasks, crying. "I don't know what I'm going to do. He's going to come home and say he's ashamed of us..." She runs to the kitchen and pours a giant glass of wine.

Joel, 12 at this time, is there to comfort her as she wants. She cries on him, and though he hates the smell of the wine on her breath, he stays with her because she can't be alone. And then he returns to what she had been doing--scrubbing a floor, folding or ironing clothes, even cooking. He puts off what he has to do for himself, like homework, until late night or early morning.

With her in her fugue state, as with Ken when he yells, Joel backs off internally. Finds himself hiding inside, what he thinks of as The Numbness. When he gets in that state, nothing can really bother him because he isn't really there.

Each time, Gloria emerges from her breakdown after allowing Joel to cover for her, and hugs him. He is her hero, she says. She combs his hair with her fingers, telling him they're in this together. Then Ken returns home. He perfunctorily demands to know what both of them did during the day, expecting nothing less than what was required of the quote unquote 'normal' family. The most important thing with him is that appearances are met.

He gets enormous self-pleasure regaling them with stories of how he told off someone at work, how stupid his supervisors and underlings are. Everyone is stupid, except for Ken McFadden, accountant extraordinaire. The State of New Jersey would be up Shit Creek, or at least Passaic River, without him.

The strange thing to Joel is that despite Mom cursing Ken under her breath all day, she acts like he's Indiana Jones when he comes home. She's all over him. And she repeats his mantra to Joel about not doing anything to the shame the fucking family, God forbid.

Ken usually drinks during dinner, but his serious drinking time is afterwards. More and more, Ken habitually takes his precious folder of papers into the living room and puts on some sports game. This is his extra 'work' that no one is allowed to interrupt. While he 'works' anything could happen in the house and he wouldn't notice. Gloria usually gets on the phone and talks with friends all night complaining about him like a hypocrite, or drinks half a bottle of wine while reading romance novels.

At this point, Joel leaves the house to visit his best friend Tim or bikes over to Willowbrook Mall. Anything but watch the two of them in their domestic drama. The night either ends with them screaming at each other or having sex. Or both. Joel is forgotten so long as he is a). Staunch Ally and Listening Ear (to Mom) and b). Non-Defamer of the Good Name of McFadden (to Dad).

And perhaps this could go on until he was 18 if he uses a false façade as they do. But a stronger desire to get out is eating at him. He knows he's different; he is not a copy of them or a combination of them. He's smart enough to do his homework with minimal time and not paying attention in class. Even skipping classes.

Ken finds out about the class-skipping one day and slaps the back of his head. Joel is 14 by now, and feeling the differences between him and his father stronger than ever.

"What the fuck you making me look like?"

To Joel, the words have a double-meaning, although Ken isn't aware of Joel's inner life. On the outside, disgusted by his father, Joel glares at him. "Who cares? I pass my exams. Higher than anyone else."

Ken's slightly mollified that his excellent sperm is able to demonstrate itself. "Still. Absenteeism gives people the impression you're fucking off. Straighten up, Goddammit."

"Don't do anything to make your father ashamed of us, Joel," Gloria echoes, since Ken is in the room.

Fuck you.

Joel becomes less and less thrilled with being Mom's partner in crime, listening to her recite the three-act Why Ken McFadden is a No-Good Bastard monologue, and actually pursues interests of his own.

That makes her angry. She gets handsy as well. Shaking him when he doesn't come home right after school or if he leaves during the weekends. Slapping his face. Coming up with Platitudes of Guilt. And when he cautiously says he's worried about her when she drinks, she is furious.

"Why do you have to give me such a hard time? Is this how you repay me?"

"When did you decide you were too good for me? I only gave birth to you."

"Go ahead, go to your friends. Maybe they can spend every waking moment taking care of you like I did."

"Be a little turncoat. Maybe I'll adopt another son, one who actually loves me and cares about me. I suppose you're so good at taking care of yourself, you could have done that as a baby, too. Didn't need me to nurse you or feed you or make sure you didn't die of meningitis."

And sometimes, when drunk--happening more often--a hiss, a whisper.

"You make my life hell, sometimes. You used to be cute. Now you've turned into some horrible monster."

Am I a monster, Joel asks himself. He's felt the first attractions to other people, boys and girls. Of course, children are socialized to learn that same-sex attraction is 'wrong,' and so he feels like something is wrong with him. Why did that happen...to be so different?

It's not a topic of measured discourse in the McFadden house, same-sex attraction. Ken McFadden, if encountering some odd creature known as a 'homosexual,' would mutter that the person was shaming where he/she worked, lived, the person's family and name for all time, etc. etc. for some disgusting sexual perversion, etc. etc. Gloria was only interested in who might be 'homosexual' (the vagaries of bisexuality not even on the radar) if it was something juicy to talk over with the neighbor gossip-bots.

Although once in a while his mother would, in a rare moment of clarity, suddenly be the loving person she used to be, that person is fading like a Polaroid photo left in the sun. Her new mantra is, You love me and never leave me, or I hate you.

∞

"I drew myself as a monster." Joel tries to make his voice flat. He then turns pages and points to numbers he wrote. "These were child abuse hotlines. I didn't call them. I didn't know if I could be considered abuse. I didn't understand about emotional abuse. But I read books with stories about kids who were in the foster care system or put into reform school. I just thought I'd stay with the devil I know."

"Baby, did you have any other family?"

He looks at me wide-eyed. "No one I could turn to. My dad wasn't close to his brother or his parents. He just kept up appearances and talked about how smarter he was than them. Mom has two sisters. One was very cold, my aunt Christine. She was the oldest sister. She rarely visited. Some serious problems there. She wasn't mean to me, just formal. The other sister tried hard to be there and she was much more fun to be around. Aunt Margaret. She was the youngest. I think she would have been the one to go to, but Mom cut her off long before I thought about this. Margaret once disagreed with her, and you can't do that--disagree that Mom was the most tragic, selfless, put-upon martyr in the entire universe. And so, boom. That was it. Margaret moved somewhere and I had no idea where she went."

"That was the hardest part, I imagine. Not having anyone to tell."

"Who could do any good? Tim, my best friend, knew enough. His parents were okay with me coming over. He wasn't good at math or English, and I helped him. They were in some weird religious cult and always talked in canned sayings about fate and sin. Tim hated it; that drove him crazy. He liked to get away as much as I did. It's how we found those furnaces on Caraway Road.

"You know, I did tell someone at school. You see, next to the numbers? Jeffries. The school counselor. He told me, '*Your parents are good people. They've donated money to the school. Why would you do this, Joel? You're making this stuff up for attention. Your mom told me you were having behavioral issues.*' At that point, I was 14. I felt like I could never trust an adult again. There were two other teachers I liked. My swim coach and my shop teacher. Both seemed to be good people...but after Jeffries I was afraid to try. I started skipping class more to go to Willowbrook Mall. You know Willowbrook, right?"

"Yeah, a person I knew used to steal cars from the Willowbrook parking lot."

"That old boyfriend whom you're so cagey about? No pictures of *him*, I notice. Maybe you and I were there at the same time for all I know. I took my bike there, across the Transit tracks. Had to be careful, because sometimes kids were hit by trains they didn't hear coming. But the risk was worth it; being at the mall was better than school."

"What did you do there?"

"Video games. Just like John Connor in *T2*. And I hung out at PC World. I got the people there to tell me about computers. Commodore, Apple, IBM, Tandy. The guys who worked in the store, they liked explaining things. They showed me the DEC PDP-11, the Altos 386, the Apollo and the NeXT. I got into it. They didn't care I was out of school, although some managers in other stores didn't trust me."

When I glance at him, he smiles. "They had reasons; I shoplifted some but I never got caught. From Barnes and Noble, some clothes stores and art stores. I bought the notebook, though. My mom paid me for whatever I did around the house but I found out when she was dead drunk, I could also get money from her purse. Or his wallet, for that matter, so long as I was careful to stay within a certain amount. Drunks, even genius accountant drunks saving the State of New Jersey from certain financial disaster, can't remember exactly how much is in their wallet within a twenty-dollar range or so."

He laughs when he sees me frowning. "Not like I'm proud of all this."

"It's okay. I'm not proud of helping that guy steal cars, when I think about the poor person having to come back to find it missing. And then having to collect it later fifty miles away."

Joel's smile gets deeper. "What did you *do* in those cars? You don't have to say; I can see it in your face. And would the owners have known?"

"He didn't care, but I cleaned out the condoms. What, are you judging me?"

"I'm surprised condoms were *used* based on this guy's bad habits. I suppose your DNA may still be in those cars somewhere, huh?"

"God, don't remind me."

I see his smile fade as he looks at his hands. "I think I gave myself your headache."

∞

Some minutes later.

"....coffee?"

"What?" Joel feels a rush of adrenaline. But he's in the car, Gabriel's Camry. They're just past Rutherford on NJ-3. He had zoned out after talking about his parents, and his thoughts had drifted to another person. That held him in hypnosis until he realizes Gabriel is talking to him.

"I was going to stop for a minute. You want anything?"

"Whatever you're getting."

Gabriel turns Joel's face his way, to kiss him, before he gets out.

Joel opens the notebook and stares at the stub of a ticket taped to a page in the notebook. He saved it from 1993. October in 1993.

He doesn't realize he's just staring at it until he's startled by Gabriel getting back in the car.

"Baby, are you okay?"

Gabriel is looking at him carefully. Then his eyes fall to the notebook page. Joel tries to see what's reflected in his eyes. *He can see it on me. He can see what I am.*

Gabriel asks quietly, "What are you re-living?" Then he takes Joel's hand. "You want to talk about it?"

"I'll talk about it later."

The rest of Saturday goes well. Bob is always happy for company. He lives in a two-story condo apartment in a complex on the outskirts of Paterson, near a shopping mall. He wants to do some renovation. He's not very good at it, and has been impatient for Gabriel and Joel to help. Both of them are good at carpentry jobs; adding shelves, cabinets, repairing furniture. Gabriel also changes the locks on Bob's doors and improves overall security measures for the place.

Gabriel and Bob discuss Don Mathers' upcoming trial and Bob recounts some lurid stories about his drug days.

The discussion of the past gets Joel agitated. He doesn't brood but he comes close. They're watching bad horror movies that night; Gabriel and Bob engage in *Mystery Science Theater 3000*-style kibitzing on bad acting and cheesy special effects. Joel's on the floor with his head on his knees thinking about his mother being a few miles away. Calling Gabriel and asking about him.

Joel gets up and leaves the condo with his cigarettes. He sees that Gabriel watches him go to the door. Gabriel's concerned but not judging. Joel can spot the slightest hint of judgment. Gabriel is not looking at the mark on his forehead, the taint in his blood, the sign that he's damaged goods. Just compassion.

After he lights up, he feels a hand on his arm. He jumps a little, startled. Jan is standing next to him.

"You're going tomorrow," Jan says.

"Yes. It has to be done. But I'm not alone."

"He loves you. For that, I'm grateful you two found each other."

"Um, yeah. Sometimes I don't know how to handle it."

"This is true. It's in the books you have. Each open to a part of the past. As you open parts of yourself. Open them and you can handle this. Because you want to. You want to change."

"I thought I had."

"At times. But you still need to open yourself to being loved. And that comes from what they did to you."

"I'm scared."

"You're angry, too. Remember what we talked about? Your anger. You're here to confront that. And to do so, you need to say exactly why you're angry."

"Not just being thrown out, but why I was thrown out. Because of *him*."

Joel sees that Jan is holding one of Joel's notebooks. Jan opens it. "You have a right to appreciate why you're angry. Both what they did, and what they didn't do."

"They didn't protect me." Joel scans the pages. A night in October, 1993. He had tried to write something on the page several times and crossed it out. He remembers doing that. Because there was no way to fittingly introduce or describe what happened. He had finally just written: *He does not own me.*

Bob's door opens. Gabriel comes outside. "What's going on, baby?"

For a moment, Joel can't speak. His own words on paper are stupefying him.

"I just needed to clear my mind," Jan says, to help him.

"I just needed to clear my mind," Joel says in turn.

Gabriel nods. "You can't read that in dark, can you?"

"What?"

"Your notebook. You've been reading it all day."

They look at each other in the dark, Gabriel framed by the light from Bob's bay window. For a moment, Joel feels guilty, as if he was hiding something.

Gabriel says, "If you wanted to talk about it, I guess you would. I think you should put that book away now—so whatever it is doesn't eat away at you."

Joel goes to the parking lot to grind out his cigarette. He puts the notebook in Gabriel's car and walks back. Gabriel waits for him.

As they move through the dark shadows of the condo units' lawn, Jan says, "It will be better when you tell him."

"I can't do that now."

"I understand...One thing at a time."

∞

Saturday March 19
Wayne, NJ, 8:00 am

Gabriel has stopped the car at Ryerson Street. He's pulled to the side to bring Joel out of his reverie.

Joel feels his heart pounding. The past is still skimming along the present, and for a moment, he doesn't want to be touched. Touched, taken, forced, abused, violated. He's ready to run away.

And a sudden epiphany comes to him. He lashes out through his running away. And does so because lashing out/running away against Gabriel is safe. Gabriel is not going to hurt him; but he stands in unintentionally for those who did hurt Joel.

His relationship with Gabriel is different. Support, space, no judgment. That allowed him to be angry.

"Oh, God, I'm so sorry," he says.

Gabriel doesn't ask what he's sorry about but just says, "It's okay now."

Joel pulls out the pack of cigarettes and lights one, to clear his mind. Gabriel puts his hand on the back of Joel's head, cradling him.

Finally, Joel says, "It's five blocks down."

The houses in the neighborhood known as Old Wayne are surrounded by woods, bordered by the Pompton River.

Joel points out a two-story house, the kind where the second story was added some years after the house was originally built. The first floor is off-white, the second dark blue. The house looks well-kept, yard and all. Nondescript, clean.

When the house appears, Joel starts trembling. His breathing gets loud enough for both of them to hear.

Gabriel asks in a quiet tone, "Where do you want me to park?"

He can't answer. Gabriel drives past the house and turns the car around in the middle of the street. No real curbs in the narrow streets. He parks across from the house, with the car pointing towards Route 23.

Gabriel still has his hands on the wheel, watching him.

You can still leave.

I can't run away anymore. That's the point. I have to know what she wants.

He gets out the car. Gabriel gets out as well. "Do you want me to go with you?"

Joel nods. He walks around the car, and then he and Gabriel cross the narrow street to the house. He refuses to think of anything so he's able to get to the front door.

And so he's come back to the same porch he was cast out of, like a Biblical story. While Gabriel is beside him, Joel can sense Jan is here too. But he has his back turned. Jan refuses to look at the door. "Remember why you are angry," He tells Joel. "This is the first step to moving forward."

Gabriel keeps his hand on Joel's back as Joel reaches out and rings the doorbell.

An endless moment. Then Gloria peeks through the window set in the door. They can hear her gasp.

She unlocks the door. It takes her a few seconds, as if she's nervous. Finally, she opens it and stares out at them.

Gloria McFadden is a few inches shorter than Joel, in her late fifties. Her blonde hair, the same shade as Joel's, is pulled back in a ponytail.

She opens her mouth but can't speak. For a long moment mother and son lock eyes.

"Mom," Joel says finally, the edge clear in his voice, "You were asking about me?"

"You're actually *here...*"

Gabriel feels some relief that her tone is one of hope, indicating she's glad to see him. He can't tell if Joel feels the same looking at the real woman instead of her picture.

They hear a male voice from inside the house, coming closer to the door. "Gloria! Who is it..."

Ken McFadden is also in his late fifties, medium height, getting on the soft side in the middle. His receding hair is graying, somewhat wiry. His face is pleasantly banal, somewhat puffy from heavy drinking.

He looks over his wife's shoulder. He doesn't recognize Joel, as Joel's mother does. He just glares at both of them.

"Who are you?" A trace of belligerence in his voice.

"Joel..." Gloria finally says.

Ken McFadden actually looks back and forth between Joel and Gabriel, not sure who's his son. Joel gets it. Ken has banished Joel so thoroughly from his life and his *good name* that he no longer remembers what Joel looks like.

"It's me," Joel says.

∞

M E E S E

George Orwell said, "Who controls the past controls the future: who controls the present controls the past."

∞

He does not own me.

It is September, 1993.

JOEL IS 15; he's a devoted fan of Batman in comics and movies. He has drawn the characters in the Batman stories dozens of times. He's also fascinated by Alan Moore's work; *Watchmen, V for Vendetta.* He imagines himself a hero who comes from nowhere, fighting repression, freeing people from tyranny. His well-worn copy of *Vendetta* is a constant companion, and he and his best friend Tim study *Vendetta* and other cherished graphic novels the way other people engage in Bible study.

They often do that during and after school. But when Joel has his shop class, he stays late. The teacher, Randall Rotero, encourages Joel's talents with carpentry, electrical work and appliances. He thinks Joel could be an engineer. He spends far more time than he needs to going over how to repair and build things because of Joel's interest and appreciation. Rotero is a little odd, a little androidish. Not a 'people' person, but he likes Joel.

Tim, as usual, is *done* with school, which he hates. He waits for Joel out of friendship. If Joel didn't patiently help Tim with homework he'd flunk out for sure. He's already mentally off the school yard, waiting for Joel outside while deep into his own Batman collection. Joel is spending more and more time helping other students understand Rotero's projects. He has a natural ability to tutor beyond his years.

Tim jumps up when he sees Joel finally leave the building. "Let's go to the comic store. The new *Knightfall* is out. *Who Rules the Night.*" This latest months-long series arc involves the psychologically-suffering Batman up against the monolithic but superintelligent Bane. Heady stuff.

"Yeah. Okay." Joel is ready to go, but feels eyes on him. He turns to see his father's friend, Larry Meese. Meese is a local police detective; a medium-tall husky white man in his early forties, light brown hair, ruddy complexion. Eyes in a perpetual squint, with bags developing. He's about 50 feet away, against the fence, watching them. Watching Joel, really.

"He's always staring at you," Tim says. "Are you in trouble?"

"No more than usual. Cops are always watching people. Maybe my dad asked him to spy on me. He's been around a lot."

Gloria thinks Meese is an unsung hero. *A real crime fighter, not like those comics you insist on spending time with. And he cares about kids at risk. You don't care about anyone but yourself.*

Dad actually talks to Meese with respect--someone who might just be as smart as Genius McFadden. They often spend hours talking in Dad's den during which Ken gets drunker and drunker, and Meese smokes incessantly. Occasionally, when Joel would be around, Meese stops the conversation to ask him how he's doing, how school is going.

He's always been like that, though. While Joel is reserved around adults, Meese has been the one who's attempted to serve as an alternate father figure over the years. He has done things like occasionally taken Joel to area games.

Meese seems to be pleased they're looking at him, smiles and walks over. "Hey, boys. What are you up to?"

Tim is cautiously polite. Joel is neutral. The adult world seems almost completely confusing, hostile, and indifferent. Meese is still part of that world, no matter his friendliness. Joel has taken cautious steps into the adult world no one knows about. He doesn't want his parents, his best friend, or Meese to know this.

Meese seems to want to try harder today. "So...I wanted to let you boys know this. I thought you'd be interested. I have friends in Paterson who are in the Police Athletic League. We've talked about a pilot program for a branch here. A more elite group, kinda. Boys with real *promise*. Joel, I've seen you at the swim meets this semester. You have excellent form. You look real good."

Joel barely acknowledges the compliment. "I'm not keeping up with that."

"Now, don't throw away opportunity. Not everyone is special like you."

Joel shrugs. The swim coach, Jon Lane, who Joel actually respects, strongly encourages him to continue. He had known Joel in middle school and moved on to coach his swim and diving abilities in high school.

Lane says that Joel has real talent in swimming, enough for a scholarship. That is a meaningless concept at the moment, although Joel appreciates that the coach cares. His parents have shown up at some meets, but aren't very *present*. Ken merely takes it as another sign of his--Ken's--superior genes, and Gloria resents the time not given to her, as well as Jon Lane's influence.

Joel notices persons of both genders watching him when he swims and dives, and sometimes in the locker room. Very, very furtive. He avoids looking at anyone himself lest he be found out. Even the girls. But it's becoming harder and harder. For one, just like shop class, other students want his help to learn to swim better. And some of the school staff has started to come to the meets just to watch him and the attention makes him very nervous. The attention, the decisions, even the concern from Lane makes him go to the Numbness again. It's easier.

Meese lays his hand on Joel's shoulder. "Ken giving you a hard time these days? This is a good way to hang out with other people your age, develop some skills."

When Joel doesn't change expression, Meese tries to kid him out of it. "Come on, surely kids like you can take on an old man like me in basketball, huh? Now, I know I'm practically Larry Bird, but you guys might still almost get a ball past me..."

This actually gets a smile out of Joel.

"That's it. Look, one thing I notice about you, Joel, is that you're a good influence on other boys. Right, Tim? Yeah. So you can help me with a good deed. So what about this Friday afternoon, in Morris Park? Let's see what you can do..."

Gloria is happy to hear about Meese's offer, and subsequently affectionate as a reward. So Joel decides to go ahead and try it out. Joel and Tim meet up that Friday after school with Meese in the park. A couple other kids have joined them. Tim and Joel are more interested in discussing how the events in Gotham City are turning out, but Meese encourages them to play with the other teens in practicing shooting baskets.

Meese is right. Although Joel's not into basketball, he can play it decently. He stands out in being self-sufficient, self-possessed. The attitude that makes him seem more mature. Several of the 6 or 7 boys in this PAL meet-up, from his school and other area schools, are drawn to him.

In those meet-ups, Meese is particularly solicitous of Joel. He talks to him a few minutes after each session. "You're different, Joel. That's why they like you. You're miles above your classmates in intelligence. You're nice *and* you're confident. In anyone else, I'd think it was criminal." He laughs and Joel smiles obligingly.

That self-possession, a trait admirable in adults, gets Joel targeted as being stuck-up at times. This same self-possession, given wings of freedom, education, mentorship, could be the foundation of his growth of an artist--the ability to pull back and observe with a mature perspective. Could be.

In the last days of September Joel has had some real pressure weighing on him and Meese seems to sense that, trying to encourage him to unload what's bothering him. Joel politely refuses.

After the next Friday meet-up, Meese has Joel wait until the other boys leave.

"Joel, I'd like you to meet me outside the plaza tomorrow around 12. I'll buy you lunch. We should talk some."

When Joel looks hesitant, Meese claps him on the shoulder. "Don't worry. I'll tell Ken everything's cool. This is you and me. We're friends."

The following day Joel bikes up to the plaza, and finds Meese waiting for him near a pizza place. After some innocuous conversation Meese gets serious.

"Brass tacks, Joel. What's bothering you?"

"Nothing much."

"Come on. I'm not your enemy. I'm not going to go running to Ken with what you say either, I'm not like that. I don't snitch. What I see is a good kid with a problem and no one to talk to. No one to help. I take it you don't tell Timmy Donovan much of what's on your mind. At least not this."

"No..." Joel stops. Even saying this much is too much.

"You like that comic book store, don't you? Let's take a look. I was into that when I was your age. Superman. The Green Hornet."

Reluctantly, Joel goes with him and loosens up some when inside, in his element. He shows Meese the *Alien* series he likes and Meese asks him some questions about the books, and then buys him one.

Afterwards, Meese says, "Want some lunch? I know you do. Wait here. I'll get it for us and we can go to the park."

Meese disappears into a pizza joint and comes back with a couple boxes and bags. He has Joel get in the unmarked car. Meese drives to the far side of the park. A lone picnic table is nearby; Meese points it out for them to use.

Once at the table, getting Joel to eat, Meese keeps his voice low and comforting. "Really, now Joel. I want to help you. Nothing you've done could be that bad. I *know* you. You didn't murder anyone, right?"

"No! 'Course not."

"There you go. You're a good kid. What else would you do? Not rob a store or beat up old ladies for their Social Security checks."

"No..."

Meese is watching him carefully. "So...I think someone *got* you in trouble, and you're worried about it. Maybe this person is trying to intimidate you. I can take care of that."

When Joel still doesn't speak, Meese takes his shoulders. "Joel, whatever it is, it's not that bad. Now is the time to tell me, so I can help. I'm not going to judge. I know you're...special. That's what it is, special. You can trust me about it. I'm not your father. Whatever you think he will judge you about, I wouldn't."

Joel feels obligated to relate some of the story especially as Meese had bought him the comic book. In addition, the pressure from the situation makes him want to unburden to *somebody.*

Joel had run into Scott Rhodes at the Willowbrook arcade a couple weeks ago. Rhodes teaches at the other high school in Wayne; Joel recognized him by sight. Rhodes talked to him in a friendly manner and looked at Joel's drawings in the sketch pad Joel carries around. Rhodes was interested and said he'd like to 'mentor' him, whatever that meant.

Joel had heard around school hints and whispers about a high school teacher who was gay. His instinct told him Rhodes was that teacher. Joel had become adept at climbing out his window and taking his bike to other places at night while his parents were otherwise occupied. He found Rhodes's house and watched it for some time. Eventually, Rhodes showed up late with another man. Figuring out where the bedroom window was, Joel stayed long enough to hear what was going on.

Joel looks at Meese now, and when Meese clearly shows he's not upset or disgusted, he gets into the story of the next time he talked to Rhodes, about a week ago. Rhodes invited Joel to his house. Joel's self-possession gave him the confidence and curiosity enough to do so, knowing what would happen. He wanted to do something that would make him adult, take him away from his miserable home life.

Uncertain because of his dual attractions, afraid he might be found out and ostracized, Joel's been hesitant to act on any flirtation with other teens in school. But Rhodes...it's clear what he wanted.

While Meese listens, nodding, Joel alludes to what happened in Rhodes' house without being specific and adds that Rhodes gave him money. Rhodes was dismissive to him once the sex was over, though, telling him to leave. Joel felt angry over being dismissed, being treated like...he doesn't know how to describe it. And that on impulse in that anger mode, he took extra money he saw in the house.

After spilling the story Joel is sort of relieved, although he feels like some giant hammer from the sky might come down on his head. He looks up at Meese and sees him frowning intensely.

"How much did you *do* with this man?"

"Not much, really. I don't want to talk about it."

Meese eases his expression. "Honestly Joel, is that all? I know Ken would shit himself if he heard this, but being a cop I've heard everything. You're a young man; you experiment. Rhodes saw that and took advantage of you."

Joel meets his eyes. "He caught me at the arcade and said I'd better give it back or he'd go to the police."

"I doubt that very much. You're 15, Joel. He's not going to report having sex with you and lose his job. Don't you worry about that. I'm not telling your parents. If Rhodes calls you, let me know. Now, enjoy your lunch. Everything's going to be better now."

Joel manages to relax some.

"Like I said, it's the right time for you to come to me. We should talk about how you need a future, since Ken isn't bothering."

One evening a few days later in Joel's house, when Meese is about to leave, he goes upstairs to use the bathroom and stops at Joel's door.

"I'd like you to come to my boat Friday after school. You know I live in Acquackanonk, right? Just come right to the back of the house to the dock, and come aboard. Maybe we can talk about getting you into a program for early college or something." He lowers his voice. "Get you away from home sooner, huh?"

Joel agrees, willing to listen to anything to get him out of this misery.

Joel arrives at Meese's house as instructed on Friday. Acquackanonk Lake is just north of Wayne, a slightly more remote area with a three-mile-long body of water. Some areas are almost exclusively used by the surrounding residents; houses set comfortably apart from each other, with individual docks, ring the lake.

Meese's boat is his favorite possession. Meese is divorced and doesn't have children, and Ken McFadden has suggested more than once that his boat, the *Tartarus*, a 38-foot cabin cruiser, *is* his child. Ken has been on it a few times. Meese sport-fishes when he isn't patrolling the town. He talks about fishing a good deal--the pleasure of waiting great lengths of time for the right fish. Getting the proper lure. Seducing the fish to bite, and reeling it in for a trophy. Joel tends to go on autopilot when he hears those stories.

"Come in, Joel." Meese smiles warmly at him as Joel climbs aboard the boat. He unlocks and opens a hatch, then leads Joel down a few steps to a fairly spacious lower interior area. "I'm glad, once again, you confided in me about that teacher. Rhodes. I'm keeping an eye on him."

"I wasn't trying to get him in trouble."

"I know. But I'm looking out for you. You know Gloria and Ken have their difficulties with being effective." He shakes his head.

The lower deck has a bedroom area in the fore section of the boat, with queen bed at one end and a thin folding panel as a door. Outside of that is the main room with a sofa and bench table against one wall and a galley on the other wall. He waves Joel to the couch, and turns on a small TV installed in one cabinet. "You like sports, right?"

Joel doesn't like sports so much as he likes looking at the men or women playing. But he feigns interest. He becomes aware Meese is watching him.

"Rhodes...he could get you in trouble. He'd turn on you. Get you arrested."

Joel frowns at him. "Wouldn't it be more trouble for him than me, you said?"

"I looked into it. He has friends in the Department...but I don't want you to worry about it. I'm *your* friend. I'll protect you. I just want you to understand the situation so you don't let it happen again."

Joel doesn't respond to that. He tries to be relaxed, since Meese is being nice. After a few minutes of small talk, Meese gets up and opens a mini-fridge and takes out two bottles of beer. He holds one out to Joel.

"It's okay. You're practically a grown man. I know who's mature enough to handle this. That's why I want to find a way to get you out of that house."

He's tried stuff before. Beer that other classmates have managed to obtain, some of his mother's wine that she offered as a 'secret reward,' even tasting the whiskey his father drinks. Trying the alcohol, even when it tastes awful, feels like a way of controlling the uncontrollable with his parents.

Meese seems to treat him as a peer, so he goes along with Meese's gift. Meese nods, watching Joel drink.

"You can handle it. You're my friend, right, Joel?"

"Yeah."

"Good. I like that. You're a good kid. Not like some of the punks at your school. They aren't smart as you. You're special. I've known you before you were born. You grew up practically before my eyes."

The beer is the kind of drink that seems better in TV ads than real life. Nonetheless, Meese appears pleased that he's drinking it. He moves closer to Joel and briefly places his hand on Joel's head.

"Ken doesn't appreciate what he has with you. Gloria, I don't know. They both should appreciate you. They give you a real hard time, don't they?"

Joel shrugs in affirmation.

"I saw. Like I said I've watched you your whole life."

Joel can hear a change in Meese's voice but can't place what it is.

Meese continues talking. "My father was a drunk. He used to berate me and tell me I wasn't good enough to carry his name. I know what it's like to be alone, like you're alone. I know what you're going through."

Meese rambles on about his father for a few minutes. Joel is a little sympathetic, but also impatient to see what Meese was going to tell him about getting out of his situation.

"Drink up. I'll get you another."

"I can't. They'll be able to tell I've been drinking."

"I doubt it. They won't give you trouble. I'll protect you."
Meese is at the counter next to the little fridge. He seems to have
some trouble getting caps off the bottle out of Joel's sight. "Hold on a
minute...there we go."

He turns and gives the bottle to Joel. He seems even more
expectant, waiting until Joel actually drinks from it before relaxing.
And then he starts questioning Joel about what he does in school,
what he likes to do in his off time. "You cut class sometimes, don't
you? I think you should be careful about that."

Joel wonders how Meese could know when he's in school.
How often does he go around there? Suddenly, Joel feels a jolt of
something in his system. A wave of dizziness hits him. "I need to use
the bathroom..."

"Sure. Other end of the boat, over there by the stairs. Hey,
you got to learn how to handle these beers, kiddo."

Inside the tiny bathroom, Joel tries to recover. He splashes
water on his face, but it doesn't work. When he steps back, he
stumbles. The boat isn't moving--the lake is calm--but Joel feels dizzy
like he's in a storm.

Meese opens the door. "Joel, are you okay?"

Joel struggles to pull up the zipper on his jeans. Meese takes
him by the arm and steers him back to the sofa. "Sit down now. Take
a minute."

Meese sits next to him. "Not feeling well? Maybe you should
go home. Of course, Ken and Gloria aren't going to be happy seeing
you like this."

"You just said..."

"I want to protect you. But I need to make sure we're friends
first. You're my friend, Joel?"

"Yeah..."

"You're going to prove it now." Meese takes Joel's collar and
pulls him closer, mashing his mouth against Joel's. Joel feels a surreal
dread under the dizziness, and shock. It feels like a vile parody of
anything seen on TV or the movies.

Joel tries to move back but Meese holds him in place. Joel's head is feeling almost detached from his body, but he's acutely aware of the sensation of being utterly helpless. Briefly, he flashes back on having his tonsils out at 12, and the feeling of waking from anesthesia. Somehow a connection is made in his mind--Meese put something in the second beer. Something to make him helpless.

Meese is breathing heavy. "I've been waiting for the right time...you know this." Meese's hand crawls over him like a snake, invading. It causes nerves to jump in Joel's body. He tries to twist away.

"What, you don't like it? That's not very nice." Meese's voice sounds surreal and strange. *Like a Batman villain.* A change has come over Meese in his posture. He seems bigger, more guttural. "What did you and Rhodes do? Tell me."

Joel turns red, trying to move from that awful hand on him. "I don't want to talk about it."

"No, you're going to tell me." Meese squeezes again, in a nasty way.

Joel gasps from the pain. Terrified that Meese could really hurt him, alone in this boat, Joel tries to answer. "He...wanted to..." There's no way to say it that isn't utterly embarrassing. Stuck here in this boat/interrogation room, Meese with his nostrils flaring, waiting to hear.

"Joel, you need to tell me. He wanted to go down on you, probably. Was that it?"

"Yeah."

"Did he do that?"

"Yeah."

Meese loosens his grip. He almost seems to *inhale* what Joel said. "Did you do it to him?"

"No."

Meese smiles, appearing delighted at that. "Did you, you know, get off? You can tell me."

Joel swallows, feeling humiliation now on top of the fear and dread. "Yeah."

"Did he?"

"I don't know."

"Did he do *anything else* to you?"

The question is sad a lurid sense of urgency that makes Joel feels sick all over again. "No."

Meese's posture has changed. His eyes are wild and focused at the same time. He grips harder, possessively. "Good. Good. So I'll tell you what, since we're friends. I want you to do to me what he did to you."

Joel struggles to get away again. "I can't."

"Yeah, you can. You need to prove you're my friend, Joel."

The mask of Meese the Good Cop falls and Joel sees the Monster within. "You don't want your parents to find out what happened," the Monster says. "Or the school. If we're not friends, Joel, I can't protect you. Rhodes...he filed a complaint against you. I didn't want to tell you because I didn't want you to worry. They asked me to look into it. Rhodes said you stole from him. They could take you to Juvenile in Paterson, Joel. I can't protect you there. Ken isn't going to do anything for you."

Meese moves his hand to Joel's shoulder, digging in a nerve. He makes Joel move from the couch to the floor.

Meese keeps talking. "He and Gloria will send you there because they're ashamed of you. Other boys will rape you every night; the older, bigger ones. I've seen boys like you end up in the hospital after they were gang-raped. But I can make that go away. I can make Rhodes go away. The complaint is in my desk. Your choice. Be my friend, or Juvenile."

Joel loses his balance and falls over. Meese yanks him back to his knees.

"It's time for you, Joel. You know now...you have nothing else but me in this world. I've been waiting for this for a long time—ever since I realized you were special...for you to prove you're my friend."

Staring at Joel, Meese's voice takes on a strange, intimate, surreal tone. "You're *mine* now..."

∞

Afterwards, the combination of shock from what Joel was forced to do and the drug still in his system creates overwhelming nausea. Meese waits casually while Joel is throwing up in the bathroom. Finally, Meese goes in to check on him. Joel is afraid that Meese will try something else, but Meese just leads him out with a hand on Joel's shoulder. He steers Joel back to the sofa.

And then stares at him. Joel is staring at the floor but eventually he looks up. Meese's expression is wild. He's looking at Joel and looking through him.

"It's okay. I did that too, the first time. It's just so much to handle, right? I know. You did good."

Joel wants to throw up again but tells himself it's almost over. He has to go home. Meese has to let him go home.

"I waited for you...and it was just what I wanted. What I knew you were. Yeah." Meese sits next to him. Joel tightens up inside. Meese pushes him down on the sofa.

"I have to go home," Joel says desperately.

"I know. I wish it was different. I know you want to stay here with me. I wish you could too. But not yet. They can't know about it. Just let me have a minute."

He lies down with Joel, holding on to him, muttering to himself. Joel is absolutely frozen. His body feels too heavy to fight, listening to Meese's crazy words.

"Maybe I should have tried earlier. But you know, I wanted to be careful for us. Well, the important thing is that we're together now."

Then suddenly Meese sits up. "Let's go..."

Joel gets up carefully and follows Meese up the stairs to the top deck. Whatever was in the beer has made him feel drunker than his mother or father at their worst. He can barely walk. Coming into the night air is a relief, but at the same time is like being the survivor at the end of a horror movie. The world still looks normal. *Doesn't anybody know what was going on?*

"I'll take you home so they don't notice anything," Meese says conspiratorially. He shuts and locks the hatch, then stops and digs in his pocket, taking out his wallet. "Here." He tucks three twenties in Joel's jeans pocket. "This is just the beginning. I know Ken does a crap job of seeing you get what you need. Don't you worry. Now that you're mine, I'll be looking out for you."

Meese leads Joel out of the boat and back to where his bike is on the dock. Joel would like to grab his bike and get away from Meese as fast as he can, but in his helpless state he can only watch Meese put the bike in the trunk of his Bronco. As Meese drives them to Joel's house, Joel starts to feel the Numbness, the disconnect that freezes his body further.

Meese goes in the house with Joel, whispers for Joel to go upstairs, and then moves to talk to Ken and Gloria, who are in the kitchen. Joel curls up in his bed with his cat, Freddie, dimly hearing Meese tell his parents how well Joel is doing in the "PAL," and how Joel is "worn out" today. His mother thanks Meese profusely for taking an interest in Joel and correcting his behavior problems. "Finally, someone is teaching him to not be so selfish..."

What kind of hell is this...

Later, Meese comes up to Joel's room. He puts his hand on Joel's head. "You proved yourself. That's important. You can't tell anyone else about us, right? I'm the only friend you got. But I'm the one who really cares about you. The one who really knows who special you are. You know that, right?"

To make him go away, Joel nods. Meese moves away, satisfied.

The next day Joel manages to at least look normal, if not feel normal. He shuts down inside rather than show any emotion, rather than let anyone suspect what happened. He survived but feels more trapped than ever.

He hopes this whole thing is over. But while he's with Tim in the schoolyard the following week, Meese pulls up in one of the unmarked police cars. Tim says, "He's looking at you again. What's up with him?"

Joel doesn't answer. He glances at Meese. When Meese sees him doing so, his face changes in a way that horrifies Joel. Happy. He's genuinely happy to see Joel.

"Creepy," Tim mutters.

Meese looks around authoritatively, then indicates that Joel should come over. Reluctantly, Joel walks over.

"Hey," Meese says. "Don't make it obvious."

Joel frowns at him.

"They know you're glad to see me--but we want to keep this between *us*, right?"

He's crazy. He has to be crazy.

"Anyway, I've got another book for you."

It's another *Aliens* graphic novel. Joel doesn't want to take it, but reluctantly accepts and mumbles a thank you.

"I have some projects to talk about. You want to help me with them? Your mom's okay with it."

"I don't have time."

Meese stares him down. Smiling, but his face tenses and gets redder. "That's not how friends act, Joel. I know I said not to let them know, but come on. You want to leave that house and have a better life, don't you? Who's going to help you? Or do you want me to tell Ken what you were doing with Rhodes?"

Helplessly, Joel says, "What do you want?"

"Let's just talk. Say goodbye to Tim. You can show him your book later."

The feeling of dread returns. Joel waves quickly at Tim, who stares after him and raises his hands like *what the hell?* Joel has the strange feeling of being in a completely different world, totally separate from his friend.

Meese takes him back to the house, and then around back to the boat again. Joel has a small hope Meese really does want just to talk but a part of him knows better. Meese is hustling him into the boat with an air of expectation that fills Joel with dread. He then starts up the cruiser, taking it partly out into the lake several hundred feet from the dock. Eventually, he eases the throttle, and puts the anchor down. He then indicates Joel should go downstairs.

Joel tries to keep space between them, moving back towards the bedroom which is closed. The afternoon sun is going down and the room is getting dark.

"Have a beer." Meese opens his small fridge.

"I don't want it."

"Just do as I say."

Joel feels sick inside. "You put something in it before."

Meese hands him a bottle. "Open it yourself. It's clean. We're sharing this, Goddamn it."

Joel forces himself to drink some, which makes Meese beam at him.

Meese then tugs Joel closer, taking the bottle and putting it on the sink. He brushes Joel's hair back affectionately. Joel is filled with revulsion.

"Okay, we're safe now. You've been looking forward to this, right? You know what I want you to do." Meese's fingers prod Joel's shoulders. Joel hears again the anticipation in Meese's voice.

"It will be better this time. It was for me too."

"I can't." Joel starts to back away and Meese grabs him roughly. His expression flashes between anger and affection.

"No. You're going to. Look, I know you're afraid. You're afraid you're not going to make me happy. But it's okay. You did it good, and you'll do it better. I'm very happy with you. You wouldn't want to make me *unhappy*."

Meese digs into Joel's shoulder, to a nerve that causes Joel's legs to buckle. "If I'm unhappy," Meese whispers, "You go to that jail in Paterson."

Part of Joel splits off in that moment. His mind goes elsewhere; turning in some other realm. Meese is not going to stop. His parents are not going to help. He's helpless and stuck here. *No. No. It doesn't matter what happens. There's always a way out. This can't be all that happens.*

Thinking of that keeps him from not losing his mind during and after.

Then he hears something behind him.

It's three men, all around Meese's age. Unfamiliar to him. All three are in the bedroom area which is now open--one man standing and two sitting on the bed.

One says, "He's even better than how you described..."

Joel realizes they've been there watching him being raped.

"Oh, you'll like him. He was *born* for this. But...I hate to give him up, even for a little bit," the Monster speaks in a strange tone of voice, vaguely regretful. "He's special. I like him being mine."

"You have a deal, Larry. Don't tease us and then be selfish."

Joel panics, starts to move away. Meese grabs him. "Joel. You're my friend. Now, I really, really need you to be nice my other friends. It's what's best for you. We had such a great time together-- they want to be part of that."

Joel struggles this time trying to get up, but Meese doesn't even break a sweat holding on to him. "Don't make me angry, Joel." He takes Joel's face in his hand, presses his jaw hard to hurt deliberately, staring in his eyes. "*You do not want me to be your enemy.*" The threat is very clear.

After a minute he lets Joel get up, sensing the fight has gone out of him. Meese nods. "That's my boy. You and I, we have plans. This is part of it. It will be good for you."

He turns back to the other men. "George, you might as well be the first."

One of them says, "I don't want him that way. I'd pay you more..."

"Shut up!" Meese is suddenly angry at the other man, almost vicious. He grabs the man by the collar. "He's mine, first and foremost. *I break him in.* You wait your turn. That comes later."

"Okay, okay, calm down, Larry. He's yours. I understand."

Meese stares at the other man for a minute, then releases him. He strokes Joel's head in a possessive manner that's repulsive to Joel, as well as the proclamation that he's somehow now *owned* by Meese.

"All of you should feel privileged. He isn't going to just anybody. He's mine. He'll be my protégé. I'm not going to let just any asshole off the street have him."

Joel realizes that Meese has some kind of idea that he's going to make Joel have sex with other men. Pimp him out. That's his plan. That's what Meese is waiting for.

The boat sinking and drowning them all would be relief. Being dead would be better than being here. But it doesn't happen.

"I know you love me," Meese whispers to him quickly. "But you know--favors for friends. I'll keep an eye on you. It's why I had you first."

Meese pushes him to the first man who anxiously takes him to the bedroom; he sits on the bed fumbling with his zipper, one hand on Joel's shoulder.

Meese waits to make sure Joel actually submits, then goes back to the galley. However, they all watch what happens.

Joel can hear Meese tell the one who said he wanted more, "I'll be watching *you* so you don't pull any stunts. Asshole."

The other man protests that he didn't mean to get Larry upset, he knows he's lucky to be here...

Joel still wants to die for the misery of this. But then the something in him, whatever voice it is, splits him off again and says he'll get out of it. *You are beyond them. You can survive. You can survive this.* The Numbness sets in. And helps him. As he's passed from man to man, he recognizes that they don't see him as a person, but a tool. That is a mistake. Just as it was in the graphic novel stories he knows by heart.

The best way to get past them is to pretend he's giving in, to pretend he accepts what's being done. He finds himself noting every detail of his surroundings. This little bed area has the built-in bed, cubbyholes on both sides, and not much else. A two-foot high window is on the wall fixture that holds the folding curtain, at the foot end of the bed. That window opens to the deck and lets light shine into the bed area. The sunlight seems anachronistic to the horror.

By the time the third one is finished, Meese has had a few beers and is almost lighthearted, praising him. He gives Joel another beer and tells him to wait while the three men rest and talk, because "...we have more for you to do. I want you to pay attention, because some day...Well, I won't go into that now. It'll be a surprise. But you just follow my lead for now. These men respect me. I see how other boys respect you the same way...that's part of the plan."

Joel knows now that Meese took the boat out to trap him. By the time they are finished with him he'll be too beaten down to do anything about it. Meese, respected detective, lives in the better part of town, has the authority and the connections. Joel would be forced to do anything Meese tells him to.

But worse than that is the fantasy Meese has that Joel wants this, agrees to this, *loves* him.

Joel tells himself he can still save himself. What they did to him is over now and he's still alive. He sees the idea in his head on how to get out. He recognizes that what he'll have to do will be hard, but if he dies trying so be it.

Joel sits on the floor, as if he's totally broken down, scared, obedient, almost crying. Meese buys into it, gets off on it, and strokes his head affectionately. "It was okay, right Joel? I know they weren't me, but it was okay?"

"Yes," Joel says in a small voice. "Just please...don't let them hurt me. You said you would protect me." *What else can he say to make him believe?* "You don't think of me like they do."

Meese is pleased at this. His tone gets lighter, softer, *intimate* in a way that makes Joel more ill, though he doesn't show it.

"Of course I don't! My God, we're...what's between us is so special. I'll make sure you're okay. After all, you're mine. I'm going to make sure you get something really good out of this. No one's going to treat you like a common whore. I'm going to show you how to like it--what we do next. You'll like it from me."

The other men almost ignore them, chatting and drinking in the disgusting self-assured camaraderie they have.

Joel says, "I'm going to lie down, if it's okay."

Meese nods. "That's it. Get a little rest. Since you're there on the bed, I want you to take your clothes off. I want them to see what I see."

Joel gets up and walks to the bed area, and steps behind the mostly closed curtain. He takes off his shoes and lets them on them drop on floor, so Meese will hear it.

Then he climbs on the bed. He can just reach the window. He quickly unlatches it and hauls himself up. The window and the bed squeak a little, but he doesn't hear a reaction. He pushes himself through the window to the deck.

Behind him, Meese's muffled voice says, "What are you doing?"

And then Joel dives off the side of the boat and starts swimming for the nearest shore line. As fast as he can. Using all the muscles in his body to their maximum.

Coach Lane once told him he'd like to take Joel to the ocean, to really see where Joel can use his strength. The adrenaline makes him feel it now. The water is cold in October, but he pushes himself with desperation. He hears voices behind him. A flashlight goes over the water, but doesn't find him.

An impossibly long time later he reaches another dock. His bike is still at Meese's house in Meese's car with his backpack. Shivering wildly, Joel carefully makes his way back. By this time, Meese has taken his boat back to the dock. He now seems to be driving the men somewhere. No other cars are at the house so he's probably taking them to wherever they parked their cars. Meese pulls Joel's bike and backpack out and throws them on the driveway, then gets in the Bronco and pulls away. When he's out of sight Joel collects his things and makes his way back to his house.

As he has often done before he climbs in his second-floor window from the back porch roof. He changes clothes and waits, trying to get warm and massaging his sore feet. Freddie scratches at Joel's door and Joel lets him in. Cats know when you've been through something bad. Freddie nuzzles him and settles in the bed, purring. Joel lies down with him, stroking him.

God knows what might happen. What if Meese comes by and demands to take him? The idea of telling either parent about what happened is unthinkable.

It doesn't happen. Eventually Joel falls into a rough sleep, still shaking.

Two days pass. Each day, Joel goes out of his way to avoid being caught on the street; he waits until the last minute to go in the school building and leaves before school is actually over. The second day, someone from the admin office comes by the class, telling him he's wanted in the principal's office. A police officer is looking for him. Joel stops in the boy's room and climbs out the window to run home.

That night, his mother tells him he's wanted on the phone.

When he picks it up he hears Meese's voice. "Joel. Really, I'm disappointed in you."

"Go away. Leave me alone." He whispers it so his mother won't hear. Even Meese's voice makes him sick again. He can feel Meese's sweaty hands, see his red Monster-face, re-living what Meese did.

"Joel, you have the wrong idea, and I'll tell you why. You were scared. I understand. Even with me, the idea must have scared you. I told them that. They aren't mad. But...it kinda made me look a little bad because I was so sure you were ready. So I had to promise *a lot* to get my authority back and now you're going to do what I say. That way, you'll get more good things. I got more money for you because they really liked you even though you ran away. You come back on your own, you're still in good with me. We can forgive a little mistake. Wouldn't you rather have a friend, Joel--"

Joel hangs up. He stares at the phone in case Meese calls again. But it's silent. He knows this was a risk but he can't go back to Meese. He can't be sold to these men. *Life isn't supposed to be like that.* Life isn't fair, but it can't be true that he has to give in to this...

Joel isn't sure what to do. Who can he tell? The school counselor would never believe this. He has no one. Still, somehow, he has to keep Meese away.

On Thursday he's so distracted he's not even listening to teachers, not listening to Tim's worried questions. But when he goes home after school, he knows something is terribly wrong as soon as he gets in the house. That primeval sense of trouble.

The feeling is worse when he sees his father standing in the doorway leading to the dining room. Ken McFadden looks cold.

"So you're home. What have you been doing?"

Ken has just started drinking, and is at his most combative. The way he stares at Joel has the feeling of apocalypse.

"I was at school."

"That isn't what I heard. I've been told you cut class to go out and...Larry told me he found out what you were doing. Trying to ruin my good name by being some fucking pervert. To *men*! I ought to break your Goddamn neck."

Joel backs up, on guard. Ken has worked himself in a fury, grabbing Joel's collar and shaking him. "You little son of a bitch..." Suddenly he hits Joel hard across the face knocking him to the ground.

"Meese is lying," Joel says desperately.

"He *saw you. My friend* had to see that you were *selling yourself.* You're *disgusting.*"

"He's lying...He made me..."

Ken hits him across the face again. "You don't say that about my friend, you lying little faggot."

When Joel attempts to say something further, Ken tries to hit him again. Joel manages to block him. Ken sees Joel is not as small as he once was, and is maybe as strong as him. In the bully's manner, he backs down, slightly.

But Ken has other ways to fight. He looks back over his shoulder towards the dining room. "You've destroyed her. She hates you."

"I don't believe that." Joel goes through the living room and around the other entrance to the dining room.

His mother sits at the table drunk, staring at the wall. She won't look at him.

It's been bad, so bad, for so long. He thought he had driven away any feelings he had for her. Each time she yelled at him or twisted the knife of guilt in him he hated her. But somewhere he must still have something from his childhood. A desperate wish she'd change back to the loving mom she once was. She'd be sorry for what she did. She'd love him. Protect him.

But now her face is as cold as his father's, and she's even drunker. "*You betrayed me,* you rotten little bastard. Get away from me."

"Mom, you know what kind of person Meese is, don't you? Really? Can't you see it?" He gets on his knees next to her. She glances at him then turns away.

Joel keeps talking. "He made me...Mom, please. He hurt me; molested me. He threatened me. Whatever he told you was a lie--he was the one who did things to me. *Please help me.*"

Now she stares at him with disbelief.

"Mom, you have to believe me about him. He'll make me do it again..."

He tries to will some compassion, some justice from her. Isn't that what mothers are supposed to do? But all he sees is anger. A hateful, selfish, black anger.

"*I can't believe I gave birth to something like you.*"

He feels a hand on his shoulder pulling him away. Joel yanks himself out of the grip.

Ken is saying over and over, "Get out. Get out of my house."

"You can't do this."

"I won't have you in my house, making me look like a fool. I'll kill you first."

His eyes are wild with his alcohol-fueled psychosis, and Joel tears out of his grasp.

He starts for the stairs but Ken blocks the way. "No. Get out. You're not taking anything. It doesn't belong to you anymore. I'll make her throw it out, all of it. Give me your keys."

Joel's hand goes in his pocket and when he takes the keys out he throws them at his father. McFadden ducks back then grabs the backpack from near the door. "Nothing but the fucking clothes on your back. I'm telling people you ran away. It's all you, not me. Not me. If you try to come back, I'll say you threatened to kill your mother."

Joel looks down the hallway, but his mother is not coming out to stop this. Still in shock and in a rising feeling of anger, loneliness, and fear, he moves over the threshold of the front door.

As he goes out, McFadden says, "You're not coming around again. You can fucking die of AIDS. You deserve that."

Joel looks at his father a last time. "You're an evil monster, just like him."

His father slams the door shut.

Joel is on his own.

But another voice is already telling him what to do, even as he's falling apart inside. He grabs his bike and rides, crossing the tracks to other side of town towards the library. But the library is near the police station. He keeps going and finally stops at a coffee shop and thinks for some time. He fights the urge to break down. How could his mother....no, no good now. This is survival.

He's not sure why but he goes to a pay phone and calls the police department, gets Meese on the phone.

Meese sounds like he's expecting this. "What happened, son?"

"What did you tell them?"

"Now, Joel, I was concerned about you. After what you told me about the teacher, I didn't want you to get in more trouble."

"Did you tell them what you did?"

"That's *our* secret Joel. They wouldn't understand what you feel about me. What's going on? I was worried about you cutting school. I told them not to hurt you."

"They threw me out."

Meese is silent for a moment. Then he sounds angry. "*Threw you out?* What the fuck--" He catches himself and switches back. "My God, Joel. I'm sorry. They clearly overreacted. We can take care of this. Don't you worry, I'll come get you and you can stay with me until I get this cleared up. Ken is such a dumb fuck..."

Meese's words fill in the missing parts of the story for Joel. Meese told them a lie so they'd agree to let him 'counsel' Joel. Meese didn't think his parents would go so far as to kick him out the house. Now Meese is trying to save his plan. His *plan*. "God, no," Joel whispers.

"Where are you now, Joel? I'll send a car or get you myself."

What if he can trace the call? Joel hangs up with a feeling of dread. The conversation with Meese cuts through the sorrow and sharpens his senses. Not knowing when or how Meese can send other cops, Joel has to hide now.

He spends the night in the park. In the morning, when his father leaves for work and his mother goes off to play martyr somewhere, he finds the spare key in the backyard and goes inside. In his parents' room he searches every inch and gathers all the cash he finds. His father likes to hide away cash. No time to pack much from his room but he gets his backpack and his notebook. He says goodbye to Freddie with a hug.

Then he takes his bike for a last ride, south to the Route 23 Transit Center. The Montclair-Boonton line of the New Jersey Transit system stops here, and continues to Penn Station in New York City. Joel once took this train with his mother, to visit a botanical garden in New York. He can't remember where. Now he leaves his bike for whoever wants it, and boards the train that comes close to 10 am. A little less than an hour later he's in New York City.

∞

FIVE

Percy Bysshe Shelly said, "The world is weary of the past, Oh, might it die or rest at last..."

∞

Saturday, March 19 2011, *Continued*

Remember why you are angry.

KEN MCFADDEN'S FACE turns dark, showing his years of alcoholism. It's almost like a mask with this level of alcoholics. Even when they're not drunk, they're drunk.

"I told *you* not to come back here." He tries to draw himself up to be threatening.

Joel flashes between being 15 again and now. The fear of walking up to the door is over. It's a replay of that day he was ejected from the house but in reverse. His father is paler, softer, weaker. Joel does not have to be afraid of him. He is almost shocked at how he does not have to be afraid of him. He's dealing with him as a man, not a child.

He steps forward. "What are you going to do about it?"

Ken McFadden seems to sense that Joel's not going to be intimidated but can't process it. He shakes his head. "What the hell are you doing here? What do you want?"

He glares at Gabriel as if he might have the answer.

Gabriel ignores him. Joel glances at his mother, who is still in shock mode. But her eyes are changing. Like her son, her eyes change from blue to gray. Her expression is completely different from Ken's impotent rage.

Joel matches his father's tone. "I came here to tell you what a fucking asshole you are."

Ken's face gets dark red. "You have no right--" He jerks forward as if he's going to the porch. Joel also moves forward. Gloria then stiffens her body between them, almost as a barrier.

Joel says, "I have *every* right, after what you did to me."

They lock eyes, but Ken can't keep the gaze. His eyes drop and he becomes unsure of himself. Then he suddenly turns to Gabriel. "Who the fuck are you?"

Gabriel speaks quietly. "Gabriel Ross. I'm with Joel."

"With him?" Ken frowns. "What the fuck does that mean?"

Joel's mother gasps again, staring at them both. "Oh yes, I..."

She stops. Ken frowns at her. "What is with *you?* Jesus Christ, no matter." He goes back to Joel. "You're still not welcome. Get the hell out of here."

Joel puts his hand on the doorframe to stop Ken from shutting the door. "No. You're going to hear this."

While he takes a breath, he sees his mother has a strange expression. "Oh, Joel..."

Her words hit him. Joel feels that in spite of her cruelty to him, he hasn't completely burned away all trace of feeling, longing for her. Mothers have that draw.

And then while she and Joel stare at each other she reaches out to him hesitantly, touching his hand still on the door frame. And Joel, without thinking about it, takes her hand. Automatically both of them tighten their grip.

Then Ken shoves her back in the house.

Gabriel and Joel both react to that. Joel grabs his arm. "Don't touch her again."

Ken raises his other hand as if he might hit or slap Joel in retaliation.

Gabriel tells him, "Do not try it."

"You think you can take *me*..." He stops. Gabriel is staring him down.

"Do. Not. Try. It."

Gabriel's voice and face have changed. This makes everyone freeze. Ken has triggered something in him very much like the rage Joel had with Sean, except Gabriel's is cold.

In the wake of those vibes, Ken backs down. While cautious towards the wolf staring at him on his front porch, his voice is still contemptuous. A show to his son.

"She doesn't want you either." He looks over his shoulder at his wife and smiles in triumph. But she's just frowning at him and shaking her head. "That's not true."

This pisses him off. "I don't care! Get away from my house."

Gabriel says, "He's not finished talking to you."

"Fuck that. If you don't leave right now, I'll call the police on you."

"Go ahead. Call them here. Let's all talk for the neighbors' benefit."

Angered at this bluff being called, Ken glares at Gabriel. "Who the hell you think you are..."

Joel interrupts him. "Shut up, you Goddamned psychopath."

Ken turns his glare to Joel. "What did you think you'd get coming here?"

"I don't need anything from you. You are nothing. *Nothing*. You thought you'd destroy me when you threw me out. But I survived, and I'll live long past when you die alone."

His father has the strange smile again. "But you couldn't stay away. You had to come back. Some part of you hoped for approval, didn't it? Isn't that why you're really here? If you didn't care, you wouldn't have bothered."

Joel meets him head on. "I came back because you need to know you aren't invincible. You've always thought you could do what you want. Why do you still have the door open? Why aren't you calling the police? You're scared of what me being here means. Maybe I'm smarter, I'm better than you are."

A trace of concern goes across Ken's face, because a few people are leaving their houses and glancing over at them. "Get out. You'll be damned sorry you came here."

"What are you going to do about it?"

He turns red. "You little fuck. You have no idea who you're dealing with. The people I know who could take care of you for good." He glances at Gabriel with a nasty expression. "Whereas you have to have him do your fighting for you."

Joel answers him. "I fight my battles. You want to go at it right here? I will. Come on out and try me, you fucking coward."

"What I did...all I did for you. You had no right to be in my house. You were weak, like her."

The reality of Ken McFadden strikes Joel then as almost pathetic. Whatever façade he built up to convince himself he's a good citizen...his words are meaningless. He's meaningless. As an adult, able to face his father, the fear is now gone.

"You want to come out and see how weak I am, asshole?"

They stare at each other for what seems like an endless time. Eventually Ken takes a step back, almost unconsciously. He puts his arm in front of Gloria. "No...you're not going to do this..."

Joel now directs his stare at his mother, interrupting Ken's words. "Can you stand up to him now? Do you want it to be this way?"

Ken speaks before she can answer. "Don't talk to her. You are not part of this family. If you ever come back, I'll have you arrested. I still have influence."

"*Your* influence? *You can't do anything to me.* You already tried. You let the worst happen to me. You failed in every way and for that you have no right to call yourself a parent, a man, a *human being.* But I'm still here. I survived. And I'm telling you what a worthless piece of shit you are, so you have to live with yourself knowing I know the truth about you."

His raised voice makes more people look over at the McFaddens' house.

"*Get out.*" Ken says it through gritted teeth.

"Go fuck yourself." Joel spits at his father's feet. That makes Ken jerk forward, but Gloria grabs him and clings, pulling on him.

Ken slams the door shut.

∞

I hold his hand on the way back to Paterson and Bob's apartment. He's shaking the entire time, silent.

Bob is mutedly cheerful on our return. "How'd it go?"

"He did fine."

Bob gives him a hug. I can see Joel does not know how to process what happened.

"You need anything? Want some ginseng tea? It's actually pretty soothing, even if it doesn't taste great."

"Okay."

We rest on the sofa while Bob goes into the open kitchen, keeping up innocuous patter. He's good at that. It gets people distracted. That's why he's a counselor.

Eventually Joel is able to calm down. He stays quiet the rest of the day while finishing the projects.

At one point Bob says, "What you did was brave, Joel. Facing the past is a bitch."

Joel can't answer. He seems to be staring into empty space as if he sees ghosts.

"It's all good," I tell him.

∞

John Dell is considering whether it's too early to water his shrubs. The little house on Ryerson is what you'd call unassuming. But it's his. His parents' life insurance paid off the mortgage. John is 41. He's a detective in the Wayne Police Department. He always wanted to be a cop. His staid, taciturn parents were good with that idea. They weren't so good, however, with aspects of his personal life they sensed about him. That helped him decide to volunteer for the first Iraq War. He came home eligible for the GI Bill and studied Psychology and Criminal Justice. After graduating Rutgers, New Jersey's state school, with honors, he joined the Wayne PD.

He got called up again after 9/11. Two more years in the Fertile Crescent. When he came back, he had the shock of someone waiting for him. Usually it's the parents who have the visitor to tell them the bad news. John instead found his mother's brother waiting for him. Mom and dad had been killed in a car accident. Drinking was involved. His older sister was devastated, and herself drinking heavily. Her marriage was strained pretty bad by then.

He bought out her half of the house and stayed there. She's been married twice since, not happy. He started drinking heavier. He had drank heavily in high school, in college, in the military, and periodically after. It something to do alone, and he's alone a lot. It's taken him years to be able to deal with people after the second military go around.

Gloria, who's known him since he was a kid--longer than he can really remember--reached out to him. He remembered that. When he came back after his first time in Iraq, her son had disappeared. Something about running away. Since Joel was younger, John didn't remember too much about him and she rarely spoke of him.

When Dell came back the second time, Gloria checked in on him and how he was handling the loss. Her kindness led him to talk to her on occasion.

But Dell continued his own anesthetization-by-vodka until he hit a very bad spot. One night he picked up a man in Paterson who seemed to like vodka as much as Dell did. He also said he was an Iraq War vet. They talked about being on the down low in uniform. They got drunker. Eventually went to a local hotel. Then the man found Dell's service revolver. Clearly Dell shouldn't have had it with him, but his caution had been eroding lately. John woke up from a vodka-infused haze, uncertain of who he was with and what both of them had done--until he saw the man playing with the gun. In the next four hours John worked on talking the man out of pointing it at John and then himself. He had been sure one of them or both of them would die.

Then the other man calmed down. Just like that. He put the gun on the floor of the hotel room and left.

Dell stared at the gun as an odd symbol of a second chance. This was the situation that was The End. The End is what Dell calls the mental state that puts you in recovery: accepting it, not making excuses, understanding the lack of control, and most importantly the willingness to commit.

The following week he took advantage of a recovery program specialized for vets. That was in 2005. He built his life back to a sense of peace, and it wasn't easy--to do that and maintain a career.

He recognized the symptoms of depression and alcohol in both Gloria and Ken. Despite her kindness, he avoided her to avoid being triggered. Then she had her DUI, and asked him for help. He was able to get some consideration for her but only if she agreed to really engage in recovery. He wasn't hopeful she was at her End, and Ken did nothing to help. Ken made excuses, tried to stop her from getting any treatment.

But Gloria stayed with it. And Dell acted as her sponsor to help her past the hard part--the fact that Ken would not accept his own problem, and gave her hell for assuming he had one. In addition, she had the most difficult thing in the world of realizing why she had to change...what had happened in the past that led to this point. And most especially, who was hurt by her actions. It was an emotional crash that could have triggered her drinking again.

This time he took a step in bringing himself a little further back into the world by helping her, counseling her. And that understanding of the blackness one must go through for recovery bonded them.

Lately she's worked with him in landscaping his house, using her ideas from years working at a nursery. Rather than build another floor to the small house he built out into the backyard. Built a glassed-in porch for more plants. It cut into the backyard, but hey. He tiled that over and planted more exotic shrubs. His father had the old school ones: boxwood, hydrangeas. Now Dell has Abyssinian Banana, Summersweet, Weigela, Beautybush. Lilac, Chaste tree, and Bridalwreath in the backyard—and most spectacularly, bright bi-colored Butterfly Bush. The hummingbirds and butterflies are just starting to make an appearance now. Gloria said it would work out. The blend of the shrubs with the beautiful beings the shrubs attract. He waters them a bit now, just so they stay in good shape.

He can hear Ken's voice across the street as Gloria opens the door. Ken is yelling at something. Big surprise.

He hears Gloria's shoes clattering on the street and looks over. She's pulling her sweater close to her although it's not cold.

She's near tears, he sees.

"What happened?"

She shrugs. "He's mad about something. It doesn't matter. You know what happened? Joel came by!"

Dell turns off his hose. "Really? Tell me about it."

She goes in his house. Inside, Dell had turned his parents' room into part of the glassed off area, built out his own room, and left his sister's as a guest room. The inside is painted with bright colors and contrasting edges.

Gloria tells Dell about Joel showing up with Gabriel. "He must have told Joel I called. I didn't tell him who I was but..."

"He figured it out."

"John, should I just call Gabriel Ross again, and see if I can find Joel?"

Dell, who was going to help Gloria locate Joel anyway, says, "I think you should. From how you describe it."

"Larry said not to when I told him I found Joel, but you know...something in Joel's eyes...maybe it's not hopeless."

"Larry? Larry Meese?"

"Yes. I was talking to him about Ken. He's been such a touchy bastard lately. Although was better for a little bit; not today, though. I thought Larry had talked to him like he said he would. Anyway, Larry said be careful about Joel. And yet, he showed up here, right?"

Dell doesn't know Larry Meese too well. They were on the Wayne PD at the same time until Meese retired and went to work for the Sheriff's Department. He knows Meese is a family friend to Ken in particular. Meese had a good reputation as a detective and seemed to know a lot of people, political contacts and so on. Dell mostly stayed to himself then and now, and so he and Meese did not socialize when they were in the department together. He does wonder why Meese would tell Gloria to be careful. Well, maybe Meese knew the kid. Maybe Gloria expects too much.

But he did show up here. And sure, he yelled at his father. Understandable. Gloria admitted to Dell a year ago that Joel did not run away; he was thrown out. No wonder she took an interest in John as he isn't that much older than Joel.

"I think you should. You don't have to tell Ken anything." Or Meese, Dell thinks. Not his business.

Gloria's cell phone rings. It's Ken, yelling. Dell compares the sound to Yosemite Sam. No, Yosemite Sam is more likeable.

"Touchy sonovabitch," Gloria says. "Sorry, John. I don't like to curse. I guess he isn't as better as Larry thinks he is."

"So what's going on with him, anyway?"

"I don't know." She shrugs. "Right now, it's not important. I want to think about if I'm going to call, and what I'd say."

∞

Sunday, March 20
Fulton Street, 3:05 pm

I'd been putting off thinking about Mesereau's situation, but when Alex emails to ask how I am, I figure that's his way of asking if I have any ideas.

I meet with Veronica to talk about it. We have an office in a micro-office service, the kind that has a mail drop and conference room. It's nice enough to invite clients to. But for space reasons, we keep old client files and evidence in a secure storage facility.

Veronica is about my age and height, well-built and shorter blondish hair in a bob. She likes androgynous clothes and hair. Like Joel's friend Chris, she's bisexual/genderqueer, but goes by female pronouns. She and another friend of mine, Michaela Connor, have been dating recently. After helping me out in the Mathers case last year she was fired from her part-time job with an investigations agency. It was a karmic opportunity to partner up informally and we have been working on the logistics of formality—sharing clients, cases, filling in for each other when necessary. We've worked together before and this partnership has helped both of us immeasurably.

I'm discussing Alex's request with Veronica because as my partner, what I do can affect her. I'm already bothered that Alex would try to encourage me to engage in an illegal tap.

She asks, "He never said why this guy Mesereau felt Comstock wasn't who he thought he was?"

"No. He said the man wouldn't tell him. That bothers me."

"Let's see if we can find by checking him out, then."

I tell Alex I'm doing preliminary research. He offers to pay, and I ask him to send over a retainer for any work Veronica does and other expenses. Without telling Alex, she and I spend a couple days following Mesereau. It's not very exciting. Mesereau goes to work then he goes home.

I call Alex and ask him to call me back, securely. When he does, I ask, "Can I do a sweep of Mesereau's apartment and any computers he has, to check for bugs?"

I'm surprised when he says no. "I'm afraid he's rather paranoid."

"Um...wouldn't it help his paranoia, for me to check his place out?"

"I think he's assuming that his place is tapped already."

It always annoys me when people don't act sensibly. "Well, can you ask him why he thinks this Comstock has targeted him as a leak?"

Alex hesitates. "I believe from some things Comstock has told him. Like I said before, he wasn't specific."

"And you're going ahead on some non-specific allegations from a person who doesn't want a basic security sweep? Are you sure he's not just making this all up?"

"Yes, I'm sure. Look, Gabriel, he has information and evidence on this mind-control story. The fact he's extremely cautious doesn't detract from his sincerity to me. Can you reconsider getting in Comstock's--"

"No. I'm not doing that."

"Do you have any other ideas?"

"I just offered one. To sweep his place. If he doesn't want his apartment and computer checked out, or to answer some damned questions, not much I can do."

"Please just look into it.

Okay. I'll look into it. When I end the call, I decide we'll follow Mesereau *and* Comstock.

∞

Wednesday, March 23
West Village, 6:45 pm

Veronica, Geneva and I get started on a new set of cases and make plans to do the Mesereau/Comstock job. I also have a final dental appointment for repair on broken teeth from my fight with Don Mathers. Joel has immersed himself in his own work. While he doesn't talk about how he feels, I sense the confrontation with his parents did him good. He's started placing some of the items Jan sent him around the loft. He actually rented a local Post Office box to replace the mail drop and forwarding service he had. Forging roots.

For me, today featured the final recording for the *Frontline* show on the Mathers case. After that I stopped by to see my friend Jason Evans, who owns a used books store in the West Village. He's recruited me part-time to play keyboards in his bar band No Drama. We practiced as much as possible in February and early March, and had a couple live shows at small bars. Our chemistry--also no drama-- works out well. I can't do it all the time because investigative work often involves nights. But it's been energizing when it happens.

He's also recruited me to help him with stocking and organizing. Because I love books, I like hanging out in his store and going through his inventory. Even on good days running a used book store is an economic challenge and Jason can't afford paid help. I volunteer my time. I've even rung up sales for him on occasion.

He and I discuss possible songs to work in a show.

"We may have a private gig coming up," he says. "A party in Westchester. A couple celebrating an anniversary. A lot of love songs. The women like it when you sing Cetera."

I laugh. "I guess I can handle that."

Then a man walks into the store. I recognize him. Walter Cleveland. He's a white man in his late fifties, a couple inches shorter than I, wearing three-piece vintage English tweed.

He's a well-known true crime writer, mostly for *New York* magazine but also several high-toned books on famous cases. He's a celebrity in his own right, a talk show and public radio staple. I've always liked his writing but recently he's been dogging my heels.

"I thought I'd find you here," he says dramatically. "You're a *literary* man."

A new superhero, I suppose. Literary Man.

Jason raises his eyebrows. "I'm sorry, we're closed. I forgot to lock the door."

"You don't mind, just for a moment? Mr. Ross has been difficult for me to get a hold of."

And I have my reasons for that. "How exactly did you know I'm here?"

"You told people at the film studio today; you passed out cards for this shop. And for your friend's poster business, and your boyfriend's cards for his artwork. In any case, one of those persons told me. People tell me things. I've heard that you have that same quality—people like to tell you things. This is why we should work together."

"I'm not interested."

"You were for *Frontline*."

"They seemed to approach it objectively. You, on the other hand, are going to write what you want to write. My input is meaningless."

"I want your perspective. You often work on behalf of criminals for legal matters and yet you were attacked by a criminal. Did that change your philosophy?"

"No. Could you leave me alone? You're becoming a stalker."

Cleveland looks shocked that he could possibly be anything other than a thoughtful, well-respected writer. "You resent me? But Gabriel, you make a living intruding into people's affairs."

"So what? When people don't talk to me, I don't harass them about it. Nor do I ever assume that because of my work I owe anyone in any analogous work *anything*."

"I still think we'd be good together. I'm in the *Frontline* show as well. Of course, you know that. They wanted my commentary. My expertise can help you process what happened."

"Excuse me," Jason tells him. "I believe he doesn't want to talk to you. And as I mentioned, we're closed."

"How about if I buy something?"

"You're suggesting it's okay that you trespass if you buy something?"

"I just want to make it beneficial for your time. I'd would like to set one of my book chapters here in the store. As a focal point for Gabriel to come and recharge."

Jason rolls his eyes. "I hope you don't plan to stay long. I do need to close."

"Jason, let me show him the most expensive book in this place because he's going to buy it now for the trouble he put you to. Then he's getting the fuck out." I tell Cleveland, "Say what you need to say while I show you that book."

I head up the narrow staircase to the second floor of the shop. Cleveland follows. "What's the book?"

"First edition of *Birds of America*, Volume One. It's a beautiful book. Five thousand dollars. Don't write a check; he has a credit card machine."

I see a smirk on Cleveland's face. "I like how he let you take over his shop. You have that quality too. People see you as a leader. Things happen because of you and *around* you. I can make you a hero, Gabriel."

On the landing I say, "He does it because I earned his trust, not because I'm a magician or an X-Man who clouds people's minds. You know that other writer Tom Freeman--your rival--has been pestering me too."

"Yes, my rival. He's a good writer, but not stable. No, a better way to look at it is he's not *perceptive* in some ways. Yet we *are* rivals. Two straight men are rivals for your favors, that's interesting. Tom's being sued, you know. One of his subjects felt Tom betrayed him in how Tom wrote about his story. He punched Tom in the face. You're familiar with that, yes? Someone turning on you with violence, you having to fight violence with violence. It's hard to be understood coming from a tough upbringing--what you have to do to survive."

I open the cabinet where the book is kept, and look at him stonily. "Such a poor child of the ghetto am I; I can barely write my own name. After I finished beating up the other orphans, I stepped over them to ask the headmaster, *Please sir, may I have some more?* ...I'm putting this book in a Mylar bag to keep it preserved. If you have a glass case in your Hamptons estate, this book would go in it."

"You're a little testy about your background."

"You would be too, if the scion of a famous literary family was looking at you like you were a zoo animal. A raging street-sullied blue-collar *n'er do well*, to be shown off to your audience like fucking Lord Greystoke."

Cleveland blushes. "Wow. Okay, we're from different lives, I get it. You're reading way too much into me, though. It's okay; maybe I deserve it. I wanted to meet you. Out of this whole story with Mathers, you're the most interesting person. And now you're testing me. Alpha males do that; test who's going to challenge them. You're a loner of sorts, but very alpha. That's why you draw the attention. People have probably tried to push you and come out the worse. More people should know that, Gabriel. Especially because you're gay."

Using a cloth, I carefully put the Audubon book in the Mylar bag. Then I fold my arms. "What the fuck does that have to do with *anything?*"

"How many true crime stories have a gay hero? You know standard Hollywood stories. Gays are either the victims or the perpetrator. If you were straight, the Governor of New Jersey would have met you in his office. You'd either be the straight loner with a heart of gold, or the family man he could play up. But as you are with your boyfriend--I've seen his art work, by the way--you're considered an outsider. Especially with the Governor, who's a Republican presidential hopeful. For some reason, people can't consider same-sex love as love, but as something tainted with sexual perversity."

"Oh, is *that* the problem? God, I never thought of it that way before."

He smiles at my sarcasm. "Life is unfair. Maybe it's time you had a little extra help. You and your boyfriend."

"He would not want to be part of the story."

Cleveland reaches over to pick up the book. "It would help his career. Both of you are in careers that only benefit from this. You have a reputation for being honest regardless of your pugilistic nature. You care about your people, your clients. I know what you went through because of Raymond Booth. This is...karma. As for Joel, well, he's piquant. Fascinating in his own way. I'd like to know more of his backstory."

I pause to look him in the eye. "Is that so?"

Cleveland then steps back, hugging the book to his chest, regarding me. "I saw your eyes change when I said his name, Joel's name. You're not a zoo animal, you're a *wild* animal. A wolf. A bear. A dragon. No, wolf fits you more than anything. The noblest of the beasts. The alpha male protecting his mate, making the lesser animals scatter in fear as he prowls the forest. You'd tear my throat out, wouldn't you, if I did anything to him, said anything *about* him. I promise, Gabriel. I will not say anything about Joel. You'd have total control over that. I understand."

I relock the glass case. "Just what do you want?"

Cleveland stares at me, wide-eyed. "We can work through the trial and get the picture across about Mathers. You know some people are going to consider him a victim, or fetishize him--like Bundy or Gacy or Ramirez. Women will write him, desperate for contact. He'll get marriage proposals. You know those strange people who feel that he's misunderstood or they can change him...the ones who follow brutal rapists and murderers. He'll make that trial a show trial. He made a speech at his arraignment, you saw that?"

"Yes. The judge cut him short. He claims he's going to represent himself."

"Just like Bundy, he wants his control. That's why they don't plead guilty, some of them. They want the trial even if they get the death penalty, because they can draw it out and control it. He's waiting for you on the stand, to see what he can do to you because you brought him down. He's your *nemesis*. And so, I think I can understand you and how you work by comparing you to your nemesis. Your work to his."

I more or less quote Jurassic Park: "'Yeah, but you're so preoccupied with whether or not you could compare me, you didn't stop to think if you should." Cleveland stares at me, then smiles slowly. "You have a sense of humor, good."

"It keeps me from getting pugilistic."

"We can confront this through the book."

"Really? You think I need that? The only people who need the spotlight are the women who he victimized. I'm not trying to play hero on their bodies."

"Your integrity is admirable. But this is the way the world works now. People make up their minds fast. If you don't talk about the story, something's wrong with you. The Discovery ID show and the *Frontline* piece are airing next month. That's how fast they want it out. No one can do a think piece at a slow and leisurely rate.

"I'm going to start serializing what's going on in *New York*, and I want to bring you in on it. Now Tom, my rival...I've often seen him in court covering the same stories. We sat through Scott Peterson's, Drew Peterson's and Michael Peterson's legal battles. We attended Bradley Manning's hearings. We both talked to Assange and Madoff. Polanski talked to *me* about his troubles, as Tom has some serious issues in being fair at times. That's confidential, by the way."

"Sure. God forbid I gossip with Tom Freeman."

"Is there anything I can do for you now?"

"Yeah. Don't use the term 'Gays' any more. I'm a man who happens to be gay; I'm not 'a gay.' I fucking hate that patronizing way of using words. Let's get this book paid for."

Cleveland follows me down the stairs. "I will do that. You know my books? You know I play fair. You're a book lover. We can use books as a framing device, your favorite books. From one book lover to another. We can meet on an intellectual plane."

Downstairs, Cleveland takes out a plum AMEX for Jason. What he got for his bestsellers on celebrity murder cases, high-profile white-collar crimes, and sexual salaciousness in the jet set. Good writing, victim sympathy, interesting angles. I'm the angle now. I go find some of his books on the shelves and bring them over.

"Jason, Walter says he'll autograph these."

Cleveland smiles. "Of course. If you want a picture, go ahead."

Jason, no fool, takes a photo he can put on his wall in the store. Celebrity adds credibility, as I know.

Some of what Cleveland said made sense, although I hate it. Hate it.

After I take the picture of him with Jason, I tell him, "Give me your card or whatever, to contact you."

He smiles. "My pleasure." He hands me a cream-colored business card. It feels like linen. "That's a private number. May I have yours?"

Like he hasn't been all over my website. I give him my Vistaprint special. "You think I'm interesting, Walter? You know that saying--*may you live in interesting times*. Fuck me over, and you'll find out what that means."

He laughs, picking up the book, now carefully wrapped in brown paper. "That is the first thing on my list not to do. And I love Audubon, actually. My wife will like this very much too. *You* are going to be a great book."

After he leaves, I'm shaking inside. I want to vomit. He thinks he can get in my mind; he thinks he can manipulate me. Intellectual snobbery. Him just casually mentioning Joel, saying I would tear his throat out. He has no idea what I would do to him, to anyone, who tries to hurt Joel. How far I will go.

Jason has z'ed out the cash register, and now comes from the back of the store with two acoustic guitars. "Let me teach you a few chords. Take your mind off being a literary rock star for a while." He locks the door and checks it, and pulls down the shades.

∞

On Thursday, I'm watching Comstock's place, and Geneva is watching Mesereau. Veronica is acting as back-up for either of us if something happens. Mesereau is staying in a building off Fulton Street, and Comstock is in Battery Place.

Geneva lets me know that Mesereau left his apartment and is meeting someone in a bar uptown, on Second Avenue and 63rd. Veronica takes over my watch, and I go to that bar to check it out.

Geneva is waiting for me at the bar. She's about 35, has long black hair, large black eyes and olive coloring. She's dressed in a gray pantsuit, like a businessperson anticipating the end of day martini. I walk over and act like I'm going to pick her up.

Into her martini, she says. "He's in the far-left back corner."

I glance over that way. Mesereau is a white man in his forties, and the mystery man he meets is about 10 years older. They seem to be talking formally.

"How'd they greet each other?"

"Just a quick shake. They seem to know each other; it's not a first meeting."

We get a picture of him with one of my devices; we can't get close enough to listen without drawing attention, which I don't want to do. This meeting may be about anything or nothing, but it's a start.

The next night I'm watching Comstock again. This evening, he leaves his building and heads uptown. A hotel bar near Times Square. I give him a head start and then go in.

I'm surprised to see Comstock talking to the same man Mesereau was talking to.

They are by themselves. No one is around them, so like the previous night, I can't get near without them noticing. I stay long enough to get a picture of the two and decide it's also business conversation. From the body language, it's not a pick up or friends getting together.

I have to be suspicious of this. What if Mesereau and Comstock are connected? What if the whole thing is a set-up? They could be running a con on Alex. Thinking about how journalists can be misled leaves me concerned for him.

The next morning, I call Alex. I ask him, "Did you check out Mesereau before you got into his story?"

"I know my job, Gabriel," he says, testily.

"So do I. Everyone can be fooled."

"And what makes you say this?"

"Some information I found out while following him."

"You *followed* him? I didn't authorize that."

"You authorized me to come up with information. I do that my way."

"Just drop it, then," he snaps. I hear anger in his voice. "If you have to have things *your* way, I'll take care of this."

"I don't fucking get it. It's okay with you if I break federal laws to tap Comstock, but not okay if I legally follow your source."

His voice now turns supercilious. "I didn't think you'd get caught, unless you lost your skills. Perhaps in your decision to live a more reckless life, you did lose them."

And then he hangs up on me. *He* hangs up on *me*.

I have to take a moment to calm down. He's an adult and a professional. I'm not going to chase him down about a job I didn't want in the first place. At some point I'll give him the information I found, because he should know.

∞

Saturday, March 26
Union Square, 10:00 pm

Joel wants me to go to a dance club tonight with a group of friends. I went clubbing all the time with Danny when we were younger, and then stopped around 30. I love the music. I'm not crazy about being in crowds. Nonetheless, I want to be with him.

The club, Cronos, is near Union Square. At 10pm we all meet up outside, the group now including Veronica, Mikki, Danny, and Chris. Danny is six feet, dark hair and eyes, my age, Puerto Rican. Chris Szala is taller than Danny, and thinner. Chris has unruly brown hair and big eyes, and can look remarkably sultry. Danny runs a tenants' rights organization. Chris does freelance IT and systems analysis work, and some hacking.

The women look sophisticated and hot. Chris has tight black pants and some kind of leopard print shirt with fringe.

Danny dresses flashy for clubs. He'll save up to buy Kenzo, or Gant Rugger. He shakes his head at what I'm wearing and glances at Joel. Joel dresses casually expensive--more like Alexander McQueen--and looks it. I dress. Period. I used to do more, but lately my style bible has been not giving a fuck.

"I tried with him," Joel says. "I was lucky he was even willing to join us."

Danny takes the edge of my Gap Henley between his fingers. "I'm pretty sure that's Dexter's kill outfit. At least you don't have *sneakers* on this time."

"You're all welcome to get the fuck lost if you don't like it."

Danny pretends to slam his hands into my shoulders to knock me back. I grab his arm and pull him in for good-natured fake fighting, replaying what we used to do in the school yard of John Philip Souza High. We get caught up in that for a few minutes, until Joel is yelling at us to come on. The bouncer on duty knows him and is waving us in.

"So that's why you wanted to come here," I say.

"V and I were here all the time in the fall."

"I didn't know that." But then, I was with Alex at that time. I guess this is what Joel did when he would leave my apartment for the day.

"We practically lived here."

The inside of the club, before one gets to the dance floor and bar, is all red from ceiling to floor. It's like being in the inside of an artery. Some paintings are on the walls under Plexiglas. Only few people are out in this entryway. I can see a packed crowd ahead.

A manager-type is walking by and grabs Joel, greeting him like a long-lost friend. I realize it's Rob. He was the bartender at the club where Joel and I first met. "We put it up," he tells Joel.

He points to one of the paintings. One of Joel's, in his adaptation of de Lempika's style.

Veronica and Michaela rush over to the painting to study it. So does Chris. "Oh my God. Mephisto, you sold them one of Danger Man. And he is *some* kind of naked there."

They all look at me. I shrug. "Apparently, that's *all* he sells."

"I'll have you naked across the city."

Rob frowns, finally recognizing me. I guess I look grungier than four years ago.

"Oh! Well, this is really special." He takes my hand. "Who would have thought, right? You're practically famous, Gabriel. Could I talk you into a side by side comparison?"

I smile agreeably. "Maybe for Easter Sunday."

Danny says with a smirk, "You know that beard's gone too far when you'd have to take out your dick to be recognized." He seems to think that's hilarious, and when it sparks a lot of kibitzing about my fashion sense and facial hair, I move on past them towards the dance floor. "Fuck you all very much."

I feel Joel more than see him rush to catch up with me. His arm goes around me, and mine goes around him.

He says in my ear, "No matter what you wear, you're always hot."

He purposefully navigates us through the crowd at the lower level of the floor. The club has three floors. The great unwashed and serious dancers are in the lower level. On each far side is a bar. One raised level up is a passageway for bathrooms and for lurkers to engage in voyeurism; it encircles the dance floor and has some tables. The third level has the office, which watches over the facility, and the VIP area. The DJ's booth is on a raised platform at the far edge of the dance floor.

I have the pleasure of seeing that certain magic he has in getting most men surrounding us to suddenly lock in on him. He ignores the eyefucking and focuses on me. That makes me look like something special by being with him. He stands in front of me, snaking his arms around my neck. One of the best things in the world is seeing and feeling the subtle maneuvers, expressions, and touches he has just for me. Playing into how I respond to him; the unique erotic chemistry we have.

Then after the next song, the DJ goes into his snarky patter, and then points out local celebrities.

"....And if you need protection, the East Village's resident badass Gabriel Ross is on the floor..." It takes me a moment to realize he means me. *Wait, what?*

"Mess with me, and I'll have to unleash him on you. We only want to see him knocking out the bigots who deserve it, right?"

He's referring to my tiresomely notorious incident punching out a 'preacher,' Mel Bunton, who led a protest over a funeral of a friend of mine last summer in Jersey. It got all over YouTube and caused me some bad press for a while. Raymond Booth hired me because of it, though. And later, after the Mathers case, things turned more my way.

Lights briefly flash over us. I then see a few dozen more eyes check me out. Don Mathers' evildoings got New York coverage and as Walter suggested, increased interest in me. Which makes me uncomfortable.

The DJ continues, "And so our manager tells us, if you want to see a little more of Gabriel...well, a *lot* more, check out the new painting in the foyer. This one's for you." He starts playing Billy Ocean's *When the Going Gets Tough.*

I have an urge to run the hell out of there, but Joel says in my ear, "Enjoy it; you deserve as much."

Enjoy it? I realize this is the good kind of attention. I'm not used to that but now I can see some admiration in people. And I know, even though I don't want to, professionally I have to work that. I just stay cool and apparently that's the right reaction. Several patrons make a point of saying hello to me, or say they're glad I punched Bunton; I just nod along with the kudos.

A couple of people actually know about what else happened in New Jersey, how Veronica and Joel and I found Mathers' victims. They shake my hand. A few people I stopped speaking too long ago drift by and act like we're still friends. That's okay, too.

Another person who I knew from college comes up to say hi, and tells me I look like Matt Bomer if he was playing a homeless person, or Rob Thomas on a drug binge. But this guy's always been a little weird and actually means it as a compliment.

After several more unexpected greetings, Joel says to me, "You want a threesome tonight you have your pick."

I pull him closer. "Wouldn't work. Another man tries to touch you, I'll have to kill him."

Usually Joel is the one with the really serious magnetism, the one who inspires other men to attempt to pick him up right in front of me (if I had a dollar for every time that happened in Australia, it would have paid for the vacation). But my bestowed celebrity ripples through the crowd and interest arises.

Eventually I feel it's okay to indulge in a drink of some kind, and he leads me to the bar.

Danny comes along with us and asks, "Feeling the love?"

"I feel *violated*, a half-dozen hands on my ass and a couple grabbed my dick."

This sends Danny into peals of laughter. "Send them to me. I'll tell them fucking me is the next best thing to fucking you."

"How about going upstairs?" Joel says.

"Oh, you can arrange that too?"

"I already did. I spent a *lot* of money in this place, Rob is part-owner, plus they like the painting. But I didn't ask the DJ to say anything. That was all you, Resident Badass."

We all move toward the stairs. I feel more hands on me in the darker parts of the floor. "Don't you feel the sensuality," Joel says in my ear.

"When I was younger, maybe. Now I'm just cranky. *Get off my lawn.*"

"No, I can take you there again. I got you to a sex club that one time. Even though you acted like a tourist."

"If you don't like it, you can get the fuck--"

He puts his hand over my mouth dramatically, and then pulls me upstairs to the third floor. I've never been up here before. It is somewhat quieter and much easier to get a drink.

So many people seem to know Joel, or know how much he's spent and tipped here, that he is catered to pretty nicely. We all sit down on black leather banquettes with small cocktail tables. More people drift by our group to chit chat and I see Joel leading the conversations in a way I've only seen privately.

Joel briefly steps away from the tables to go talk to Rob some more. While he's away, a man I recognize introduces himself to me; he's a software mogul billionaire, Travis Churchill. He's white, thin, around 45, tall and tan, wearing a long white shirt over gray slacks. I can see the money woven in those hand-tailored slacks, his haircut, and the casual way his jacket rests on his shoulders. We converse a bit, and then I in turn introduce him to everyone.

Joel returns, and I introduce him too. "This is my boyfriend, Joel McFadden..."

Churchill and Joel look at each other. After a brief pause, Churchill holds his hand out. "*Joel.* Joel. Yes. It's a pleasure. You're an artist, right? Gabriel told me."

The fact I know Joel so well cues me in on the faint hesitation in his eyes and smile; no one else would notice. They know each other.

"Nice to meet you. Yes, I am." Joel takes his hand. Churchill covers Joel's with both his, and holds on to Joel's hand as he speaks, which raises red flags with me.

"Are you at a gallery? No, wait, you're doing something different."

Joel brings out one of his cards with just the right amount of casualness. "At the moment, I'm at the Cultural Center." He flicks the card out sharply between his fingers.

Churchill finally lets him go and turns the card over in his hands. The only reason either of them would pretend they hadn't met is that Joel must know him from his escorting work. Which means Churchill was a client. The emphasis Churchill put on Joel's name when Churchill greeted him...I realize Joel must have used a different name when he was an escort. Strange I never thought of that before.

Churchill doesn't seem so bad, for a rich guy who bleeds thousand-dollar bills. He isn't being condescending or anything, just an entitled devil-may-care attitude. But when he says to Joel, "I'm really looking forward to checking it out," I sense that he's suggesting more than just looking at Joel's work. He puts his hand on Joel's arm and says in an overly-familiar tone, "Wouldn't you come along, for a private tour?"

In that moment I do something I don't usually like in other people, which is to act possessively. I gently tug Joel down onto my lap. To his credit, he doesn't appear to be annoyed by it. I keep my hands on him, pretending it's just due to the music.

Joel glances down at me and says to Churchill politely, "Call my gallery agent, Isabella Karimi."

Churchill grabs a chair and sits what I'd call uncomfortably close to Joel, and then remembers I'm here. "Of course, with Gabriel too...I know your reputation; it's quite impressive."

Maybe he's also heard on the street I'm a crazy bastard. Good.

He's wary of me for a second, but it doesn't last. He just inches forward and says to Joel, "Tell me more about your work, what you've done."

Mikki, who's been watching me, leans over to say to me quietly, "Take it easy."

I nod to her; I don't know how much she's picking up on this but I can't treat it casually. Churchill's getting to be a bit much.

I know this tension is making Joel uncomfortable, because the closer Churchill gets, the more likely Joel can see me breaking Churchill's fingers. *No, you're not going to be like that,* I tell myself.

I substitute one bad behavior for another. Mikki asks Churchill a question, and I use that as an excuse to get up and pull Joel a little away from the table. I bring him closer to me as I lean against the railing, kissing him, pressing my body against him. In this club, it's hardly shocking. But for me, it's bold. I might as well put Joel on the cocktail table and fuck him to prove he's with me.

Maybe because we're both a little *folie simultanée,* Joel's more than good with this dick-measuring behavior...giving in to me showing off for Churchill's sake.

After a few seconds of this, I excuse myself and find the DJ.

When I come back, I see Churchill is still standing by Joel and talking, and he has his hand on Joel's back. I guess my acting out is making him try harder.

I briefly picture tossing Churchill over the railing behind the banquette. Instead, I reach in between them and take Joel's hand. The DJ is playing *You're Still the One* at my request.

The fact the DJ is enjoying following us with a spotlight would annoy me ordinarily, but not now. Not when the lyrics apply to us, not when I can pull him close.

I can see Churchill watching us from the floor above. I try to tune him out. What makes that easier is that Joel's eyes are only on me. And I can prove to the world we are together. He is not with anyone else.

∞

Sunday, March 27
Alphabet City, Avenue A, 8:45 am

We did not participate in an orgy in the club, nor bring home a gaggle of admirers. I was not forced to hurt Churchill. We went to my apartment and it was just him and me and the remaining eroticism, and more music.

In the morning he's truly relaxed in our domesticity...we can be sweetly affectionate to each other. And this is what I wouldn't trade for anything in the world.

Life often lets you have peace for just minutes.

While Archie jumps on invisible mice, and he and I are together in the kitchen sunlight, in the kind of gentle touching that is really foreplay, my work phone rings. The call has a New Jersey area code. "Hello?"

"Is this Mr. Ross?"

I recognize the voice. "Yes, it is, Ms. McFadden."

∞

S I X

Master K'ung Fu-tzu said, "Study the past, if you would divine the future."

∞

THE ATMOSPHERE BECOMES DIFFERENT. The past from last night, the past from this morning. His body tenses against me, and his breathing changes. I feel bad about that happening.

She says, "Hello, again. I guess you know I had called you before. And you were here with him...that was nice. I'm not in my house right now. I'm calling from my cell phone for some privacy."

I open my eyes to look at Joel. He watches me intensely.

"Okay. What are you calling about?"

"I...um...can you get me in touch with him? With Joel?"

"Do you want to talk to him?"

"I...yes. Yes I do."

I touch the back of his head. "Why? I'm not letting you hurt him."

"No, no. I just want to talk."

I mute the phone. "Do you want to?"

He trembles a bit. I hate seeing that but he's going on determinedly. "Yes."

I give him the phone. I start to leave to give him privacy and he grabs my hand to stop me. He puts it on speaker. "Hello?"

"Joel...Joel. I...I don't know what to say. But I wanted to talk to you."

"Okay." His fingers dig into my hand.

"Joel? Honey...what happened then...I'm sorry."

He breathes in sharply. "Are you, Mom? Why did you let him do it? Why did *you* do it?"

She snuffles on the other end. On this side the teenager shows through the man. Emotional, vulnerable.

"It's hard for me to say. It was such a bad time."

"Bad time...you have no idea what that is. Did Dad poison you that much? Why did you stop loving me, Mom? I never..." His chest hitches. "I never understood what happened to you...

His mother's voice gets wavering. "I don't know everything that happened to me. That may sound crazy, but being an alcoholic...it turns you into another person. Some of that is fuzzy. I do know, I realized, I didn't stop loving you, ever. Some time after you were gone...I knew it was wrong, but I had no idea what to do. I told myself Ken was right. Then when I gave up drinking, I went to therapy. I had a DUI and it was dismissed on condition I go into therapy for alcoholism..."

I'd be amused that both she and I have ACD'd cases, except this situation isn't funny.

"A friend of mine, John Dell; he's a police officer here. He stood up for me, and I didn't want to let him down. He's in recovery too. I started trying real hard. Ken's made fun of me, of course, so this didn't help us. But my biggest regret is you."

"You regret having me."

"No! What are you saying? I regret abandoning you. Letting this go on for so long. John was going to try to figure out how to find you. We read those articles. Then that reporter called. I thought..."

They're both silent for the moment. Joel has the phone on the counter and is leaning on his elbows, staring at it. He looks up at me. I keep my hand on his back.

Then she says, "Did you come here that day to tell me you hate me?"

"I came to tell him what I told him. And to see what you wanted. I know I have nothing with him. He's still the same asshole he always was."

"I'm sorry what he said to you and Gabriel. I see he's your friend..." She falls silent.

"He's my boyfriend! *Boyfriend.* We sleep together. We have a relationship. Jesus fucking Christ, it's in the articles you read; is it so hard for you to deal with in Two Thousand Fucking Eleven?"

His explosion takes me by surprise. From how he described her during his childhood, I wouldn't be surprised if she hung up. But she doesn't.

"Oh, Gabriel's your boyfriend. I didn't realize that. Maybe it was in the articles. Yes, Joel, I can deal with that. I was wrong in how I treated you then, and I'm sorry how Ken treated you and Gabriel when you came by. I know you're mad, but...I don't want you to...I don't want you to hate me."

"What *do* you want?" He says it quietly, his fury disappearing like a sea monster returning to the deep.

"I want to talk to you. Please. You came to see me; can I ask you to see me again? Please? I have some of your things I can give you."

"My things?" Joel glances at me again.

"I have all your drawings..."

"I thought he threw them out."

"He left it for me to do. I put everything in the attic. He never goes up there. Can I meet you *please*?"

"I don't know if I can go back to that house."

"John lives across from me. He would let me use..."

"A *cop's* house? I don't think so."

"All right then. Where are you? I can go to where you are."

He hides in my shoulder a moment. "Hold on."

I pick up the phone and mute it.

Joel says, "Not here. Not in our...space."

"Our home, yes. Either one. I know. We can find somewhere safe. We could go to a restaurant over there or that waterfall outside Paterson. Or Willowbrook even."

"Willowbrook. Wait, no. I don't know if I can deal with other people being around. Maybe the loft is okay."

"No, give me a minute." I call Bob on my other phone. "Can we use your place today for a family meeting? I'll buy you lunch."

"You two did a bang-up job here. I just need to get banging, so to speak. But no one's available today, so sure. What's up?"

"Joel is going to speak to his mother."

"Damn. He's really going for the distance. Come on over."

I nod at Joel.

"Okay." He then gives his mother Bob's address.

∞

Joel has gone so far in his thoughts that by the time we get to Bob's place I think it's best if I wait outside for Gloria McFadden. I want to be on top of everything. Family matters are the most dangerous.

I see her Chrysler pull up in the parking lot of Bob's condo building. The building has a large grassy area with trees on the front side, and individual walks leading to the street. On the back side each apartment has a sliding glass door to a small patio, more grass and trees, and then the parking lot. She gets out and smiles hesitantly when she sees me.

"Mr. Ross." She takes a large shopping bag out the passenger side. I go over to help her. In the sunlight she seems vulnerable, frail, from her emotions.

"You can call me Gabriel."

She takes my hand gently. "Then call me Gloria. This is kind of you to be here."

"It's what we do for each other."

She nods. "I got that idea. I saw how you looked at him."

"That's how it is, Gloria. I'd protect him with my life."

"Well..." She shrugs. "I guess that's what I would ask for. For him to be taken care of. He's special, Gabriel. I know I'm talking like a mom, but he always was."

"No news to me."

She follows me up the walk to the apartment. I see her looking at me, taking it in. "You sound very sincere about that."

"I am," I tell her.

"I'm...glad. You, you...care about him."

"I love him."

She bites her lip. "And Joel with you...Gabriel, I don't have that love. I haven't for a long, long time."

She smiles again. Telling me is easier, I suppose.

"I'm sorry, Gloria. I've gotten the idea about what kind of man Ken is, although it's not my business except in how it affects Joel. I hope you aren't here to hurt him."

"Oh my God, no. I know he doesn't feel very good about me right now. But I'm trying..."

I open the door. Joel is sitting on the sofa, staring into space. He stands, politely. Bob is in the background near the kitchen. I introduce him to Gloria. He comes over to shake her hand.

She smiles more timidly at Joel. "Hello..."

He nods. "Mom."

The moment is awkward. He doesn't know what to do. She just stares at him, what he looks like. I can see him through her eyes. A stranger/not a stranger. He's staring at her too. I feel for him. I want to go over and protect him.

"Please go ahead and sit down," Bob tells her.

Gloria moves to a chair, then changes her mind and sits next to Joel on the sofa. I put the shopping bag next to her feet.

She looks down at it. "Oh." She reaches into it now, taking out a photo album and some folders. "I brought some of your things over, like I mentioned."

Joel's expression changes, completely confounded. Gloria places the items on the table in front of him, like an offering.

He's too stunned to say anything.

Bob asks, "Gloria, can I get you coffee, or tea, or something else?"

She's focused on Joel again. "Oh, coffee, I guess...black."

Bob and I get the coffee. He takes the chair, I sit on the other side of Joel. Gloria gets into a mode. I'm familiar with modes. This is hopeful, make-the-best-of-it mode. I sense she's used to figuring out how to cope with difficult circumstances. She smiles at me to include me in the mode. She then opens the album. "Gabriel, I guess...you haven't seen pictures of him when he was young."

"No, I haven't."

"Joel, remember the zoo? For your birthday?"

He's almost scared to look, frozen in his chair.

I can't help it; I want to see the pictures. "More animals? He told me about the circus."

It helps, because she can use me as a buffer. She smiles at me, at my interest and Bob's interest. He leans over from the chair to look.

"Yes, the circus. That's in here too. Joel, he loved the big cats. Lions, tigers, jaguars. We never had to go anywhere else at the zoo, really."

"That doesn't surprise me at all." I examine the photos with a sense of wonder. "Joel, you were such a cute kid; I always knew that had to be true."

"He was gorgeous. Little girls used to follow him around. And he could draw, all his friends pestered him to draw them things. You have no idea..." She laughs and then looks over to him, and his unreadable expression. "He's so very handsome now."

"He is," I say, "absolutely beautiful. Inside and out."

He has not yet said a word. He could have any reaction. He could suddenly jump up and start screaming, throw the album out the window.

But he doesn't. Each picture seems to frighten him as a snapshot of the past, but somehow my interest is helping him. Gloria explains each picture to us as his eyes dart between us nervously.

Then on one page, there's a photo is of a group of teenage boys with a tall man in a suit. On seeing that picture, Joel jumps up, inadvertently flipping the album over the edge of the coffee table. "Take it out!"

Gloria frowns up at him at Bob and I stare, wide-eyed. She says, "Joel; what on Earth?"

I see him trembling all over and I get up too. "Baby, are you okay?"

"*Take it out*, Goddamn it. What the fuck--putting him in there?"

With shaking hands, she picks up the album and removes the photo from the plastic folder and puts it in her purse. "Joel, I don't understand. Larry *wants* me to get in touch with you."

The look on his face chills me. I try to interpret it but I can't. I realize he's in an area I know nothing about; something frightening.

"You talked to *him* about me?"

"I think he still cares. He said what happened was so long ago..."

He's staring down at her. His eyes have turned dark. Bob and I look at each other, helpless.

"What happened? What he *did* to me?"

"Well, his telling us about you, I suppose. He thought we had to know what you were doing."

And at this point he draws away from her. He tries to speak and his face gets red around the edges. "What I was doing. What he told you I was doing."

"It's okay, Joel. You've changed since then."

Joel looks around without seeing us. I know that look. Anger, frustration, desperation.

He says to Gloria, "*Get out*. Get the fuck out of here."

But he's the one who turns and leaves. He doesn't shut the door; maybe he's afraid he'd slam and break it.

Bob is up now. I nod toward the door and he leaves. I turn to Gloria. "What happened?"

She's staring at me with hurt eyes. "Back then? I don't think I can..."

"Just tell me."

It amazes me how her face in pain looks like his. "Our friend Larry, Larry Meese. He used to be a police detective. He told Ken and me that Joel was...having sex with men. For pay." She gasps at her own words and seems horrified. Either at the idea or because she's telling me.

Oh, God. I doubt very much this was true. One of the few things Joel told me, and he doesn't lie, is that he did not hustle until he was in New York.

I think of Joel's reaction to the picture. "Was that Meese?" I point to her purse.

"Yes...he had a project with the boys. I took a picture of them. I don't know why..."

Joel once told me a cop hurt him, without being specific. I start to fill in the blanks.

"Gloria, did you consider Meese may have lied about that?"

She frowns. "Why would he? Maybe I can see a--what would you call it--a misidentification. But Larry said he caught him in the act. Oh, I'm sorry to say it. I hope that doesn't make you think less of Joel."

Now I have to stare at her. *Seriously?* I want to say. But she doesn't know.

"No," I say carefully. "Nothing can. I think you might have to understand that this cop may have lied to you."

"How would you know, Gabriel? I'm sorry Joel's upset; I don't know why..."

Joel is suddenly back in the condo, Bob following. He's no less in a fury. "You don't *remember* what I told you when you threw me out..."

"*He* threw you out. I didn't know until later..."

"Like that makes a difference. I was out, at fifteen fucking years old. Did you look for me?...I thought not. Do you remember what I told you or not?"

She stares at him in fear. "I was upset. I was worried about what would happen."

He grabs his head and sighs deeply. "Oh, Jesus. Jesus. Jesus. Jesus. Well, I'll tell you what *you* said. You said you were sorry you gave birth to something like me. Does *that* ring a bell?"

Gloria turns red, glancing at Bob and me. Hearing how horrible that sounds. "I don't...I don't know. I never...never meant anything like that. You have to believe me, Joel..."

He moves up right in front of her.

He doesn't touch her, but gets right in her face and says in almost a whisper, "Do you remember what I told you about Meese?"

She stares at him, a hand's breadth away. I see her trying to think.

"What was it?" she whispers. "What did you say? I don't remember."

He turns to look at Bob. "Can that happen?"

"Yes." Bob is serious. "It does something to the brain. I have whole days, weeks even, that I don't remember."

"Is she telling the truth?"

"I can't tell you that. She seems sincere. Gloria, if it meant you not seeing Joel again would you stick to that story?"

She shrugs helplessly, almost panicking. "I swear I don't remember. Yes, I was drinking that day. I was so shocked to hear what Larry told us..."

"He was lying. Do you understand that? I guess not, since you and he are such good friends. He fucking lied, and you didn't even ask *me*. You didn't give me a chance."

She bursts into tears.

He glares down at her, but when he looks over to me, he's uncertain.

I ask, "What happened, Joel?"

His expression changes at that question. I see him mentally retreat behind a wall.

"I don't want to talk about it," he mumbles.

I keep trying. "Joel, maybe it's time..."

"No." His voice is suddenly sharp enough to make me draw back. "She doesn't remember anyway."

"Tell me," Gloria says through her tears. "Tell me what happened."

He shakes his head. "Do you believe me that he lied?"

They lock eyes. Then she glances again at Bob and me.

"Do you need references," he asks sarcastically. "Or can you just believe what your son tells you?"

It's a major decision. She reaches up and takes his hand. "I believe you." The tears come again. "It was all a horrible, horrible mistake. My mistake. For letting your dad do that. For not listening."

Joel's intensity suddenly fades from his posture, and his face goes blank. He sits next to her. "Yeah. It's over now."

He starts turning pages of the album. His abrupt calmness takes us by surprise.

He says without looking at us, "You two can sit down. You think I'd hit my mother? She's trying, I guess."

We sit down. "No," I tell him. "We know better."

He lights a cigarette, locking eyes with me briefly. Gloria holds on to his hand.

I see another photo, one of the teenage Joel at a pool near a diving board, with a coach. In the background people are watching him. To change the unsettled mood I say, "You were a swimmer then too."

"He was very good, the coach encouraged him to stay with it."

"We know what happened with that, right?"

"Joel, please, just be calm."

"Be calm. I was there covering up for you every fucking day with him. You made me your substitute husband. You gave me shit for everything I wanted to do outside the house including swimming. But when I needed you, you chose him. I see you're trying, but you know what that did to me?"

"I'm sorry," she says. "I wish I could take it back, what happened to you."

I feel him trembling.

"I let the drinking take over my mind," she whispers. "I can't believe it happened. I regret that so much, every day."

He exhales, wiping a tear away quickly. "I wish I could feel empathy for you, but, you know, it's really fucking hard."

I put my hand on his back. He's still lost inside.

Her voice shakes. "I'm just glad you're talking to me. Even if you're mad."

The photo album is still open. He looks down at it and touches the photo of himself.

"Can I see it?" I ask. I reach over and take it out. "We were in Australia a few weeks ago...I finally saw him swim. I didn't know he was so good. Like, he literally took people's breath away diving."

This gets him to look at me. The men who watched him dive at the hotel pool in Australia are like the people watching him captured in the photo at whatever school event he was at. Enraptured even more because he refused to acknowledge them. I could imagine that at 15 as I saw him at 33, climbing out the pool with his shorts clinging to him, brushing his hair out of his face. Coming out the water like a mythological creature of beauty, a male Venus. Other men drifting close to try to catch him between the hot blue sky and the hot white cement.

And he ignored them and looked over at me, smiling. Just like in the club last night. He doesn't smile now but I see a tiny spark in his eyes. Hard to believe in this stress that our intimacy was only a few hours ago. But it's still inside. I can't help but draw my fingers down his face.

Gloria blushes, and then getting herself together she then opens the folders with his drawings. "I saw his work online. His paintings and sculptures. You're in some of those paintings...I realize that now, Gabriel. Well, see what he used to do? See how good he was?"

I pick through construction paper, notebook paper, and other materials where he drew animals (cats), designs, some people. His skill became sophisticated as a teen. And darker. Black suns. Frightening woods. Also some parody drawings. Sketches of celebrities as Snow White and the 7 Dwarves, Cinderella.

I study them, but Joel only glances at them as if his own work unnerves him.

Gloria picks up her coffee cup, and it rattles in its saucer. Her hands are shaking. Joel turns to her, and in an almost unconscious gesture, gently catches her hands and holds them steady, which helps her drink. "Are you all right?"

"It's...just what happens. Age and the alcohol, catching up with me. And the emotions, I guess. I was nervous about seeing you. And Ken has been trying my nerves."

"Nothing's changed, I guess."

"He's...I don't know. I talked to John about it, I talked...anyway. I've never gotten involved in his work. I just kind of live my own life. But Ken's been very aggravated lately; he's totally preoccupied and super-cranky. He won't tell me what the problem is. When I ask him about it, he tells me to leave him alone. He gets pretty vicious about it."

"How vicious?"

Gloria stops, as if afraid she's said too much.

"What does he do to you?"

"I didn't say he did anything, Joel."

"Does he hit you?"

"No. I'm not saying that. I just feel like *something's* wrong. You know what I mean?"

"I'm not surprised with him. From what I remember, he had some scheme or the other going. Because he was so much *smarter* than everyone."

She looks away. "I never asked. I didn't want to know."

"Mom, it doesn't matter if you try to be ignorant. Whatever he does illegal you might be liable for too because you're married."

"How could that happen? I didn't approve anything."

Joel looks at me helplessly.

"Let's not worry about that now," I say. "First let's figure out if he's doing something."

Joel turns to his mother. "Mom? Really, what do you know?"

"I don't know how I'd know."

"Money," Bob says. "It's always around money."

"Bob's right. Does Ken have money he shouldn't have? More than your collective income should justify?"

She thinks. "Well, he told me once he had an account...on some island, I think. He said I couldn't tell anyone."

"Cayman Islands?"

"That sounds like it."

She's probably not heartened by the fact we all roll our eyes.

"What's wrong?"

"Might as well wear a sign that says, *I'm hiding assets.* When did you realize something was wrong?"

"In January. Ken started getting very tense. He'd take calls outside, he started drinking more."

Joel says, "What, more than usual? How would you notice?"

She looks down. It's uncomfortable, the silence.

Joel catches the look from her to me. Uncertainly, he says, "What can we do for her?"

"Run a background check on him. Start looking for records."

Something clicks with Joel. I see it, but he doesn't say what it is.

Gloria asks, "Can you talk to him?"

We give her the same skeptical look.

"Well he won't tell *me*; he's always been that way. But maybe you can convince him to do something." Her eyes are on me. "You're professional. He might respect that."

I see Joel roll his eyes again.

"I will if it's okay with Joel."

She turns to him. "Would you? Please?"

He bites his lip, just like she did before. "You're here for him, to save him again. Is that it?"

Gloria draws in breath. "No, Joel, not for him. When that man from the newspaper called me, I wondered if this was a sign. If you don't want to talk to him or anything, I understand. I did want to see you but I was afraid. When you showed up, I thought maybe that sign was real. I'm here for whatever you'd be willing to give."

He shifts around nervously. "I don't know what to give you."

She looks down at her feet, her loneliness evident. At the same time, Joel is angry again. "It took me years to be able to get to a place where I felt I was a decent human being."

"I'd give anything to go back and make it different. Maybe that doesn't mean much to you now. I guess I'm just realizing what my life is. I don't know that I can live with him anymore either. My health is bad, I just wanted some peace, whatever I have to pay for it. I just...I saw your life in the articles I read, and I said to myself, my son could do something with his life. What he wanted to do. Why can't I? But it's probably too late. I have no way to start."

And although he's angry, furious with her and what happened to his life, I see him still feel that connection.

Joel finally says, "Do you want to leave him?"

"I don't have anywhere..."

"Do you want to leave him? Answer me."

Her eyes meet his. Both Joel and his mother carry the same intense emotion that turns their eyes dark blue. "So long ago I chose him over you. Something in me is weak. You have that strength I didn't. I thought I ruined your life but I didn't. You survived it. I'm not sure what I can do, but I don't want to go on another twenty years with him."

"Then you don't go on like that."

She clutches his hand like a lifeline. He's not sure about it, looking at their hands together.

But she is. In a way that's automatic to mothers, she moves closer and starts combing his hair with her fingers as if he was a child again. He closes his eyes, his breathing uneven as she touches him.

"I'll get you out of there," he says. "Doesn't matter what he's doing."

"I still want to know. I deserve to know." Now she looks angry through the tears. "I've done what he's wanted for thirty years."

∞

Sunday, March 27
Acquackanonk Lake, NJ 8:12 pm

Meese puts his phone away. He stares at his dining table for a moment, then gets up and walks out his back door to his boat. Then he turns and goes back to his garage where he keeps his fishing equipment. He's not planning to go out--it's late on Sunday, but he fingers through everything as if he was.

He had just called Gloria to put things in motion. "I think you should get in contact with Joel, see if he will come over."

"Larry, I already did."

Her voice sounds different, strained. Unlike her usual gushy self, she seems to be thinking about what to say. She describes calling Gabriel and then Gabriel and Joel showing up on the doorstep.

"Why didn't you tell me?"

"It was a very difficult thing to go through. My son and my husband yelling at each other. Joel walking away again."

Meese felt a flash of very old anger at Ken. *He's still doing it. Still interfering.*

"Well, don't panic. I think if you call him again..."

"I did. He's...we talked some."

Meese is a little ticked at her for not asking him what to do. Didn't she want his help? More importantly, her bouncing around in her nutty way doesn't help him keep to his plan.

Now Meese takes out his poles and practices casting with a smooth, expert hand.

He kept himself calm. Cops are used to unexpected things happening. It's how you handle it that counts. He thinks about what she told him.

"That PI was with him, huh? Strange Joel would take his boss along."

"Gabriel isn't his boss. He's...uh, they're close."

Remembering her saying that makes Meese's hand snap too hard. The fishing pole bounces against the wall and nearly breaks. *Who the fuck is this guy?*

"How close, Gloria? What did you see?"

"I believe they're...involved."

Meese drops the pole. He goes to look over his box of lures. Shiny, bright colored...resembling insects the fish would be searching for. Of course. This Gabriel Ross must be some kind of predator. A hustler. Not even a former cop. Probably can't hold a real job. Joel likes to do good deeds. Ross suckered him in. *Lured* him. It's what *they* do. He probably goes to one of those gay bars and has sex with a dozen men, and then plays upon Joel's sympathies to seduce him. Corrupt him. That teacher almost corrupted Joel, but Meese saved him.

Meese shakes his head. Joel has some naiveté. Of course, because Ken interrupted the training Meese was going to give Joel. Taking the time, the care, the *love,* to teach him how to handle perverts like Ross. Joel must still have the ability to draw people to him, which is good. Just that he can be taken advantage of so easily.

Meese's remaining conversation with Gloria was him giving her strict instructions to wait until he decided what she should tell Joel. To get him here without that New York City fucker. Put him at ease so Meese could drop by for a friendly chat. Meese anticipates how shocked and then happy Joel will be to see him. That will give him the idea how next to proceed. Not rush into things right away, now.

Ken can't be there, so this has to be handled carefully. Gloria's voice was very tense. Probably sorry she didn't listen to Meese in the first place. She should have called him when Joel showed up. Meese could have come over and rescued Joel. Anyway, Gloria muttered something about still having problems with Ken.

That fool. That fucking fool.

∞

Monday, March 28
Wayne, NJ, 5:35 pm

We're back at Joel's parents' house on Monday; Gloria has the day off from her job managing a nursery. She lets us in the house quickly. "He'll be back any second."

We move so fast into the house that it takes a moment for Joel to appreciate his being in it again. To me, it's a house. To him, it's making a strange return to the place where he was thrown out.

Gloria realizes that and stops.

Joel looks around and shrugs. "I can take it." But he moves carefully, as if the furniture might come to life.

The inside of the house is sort of u-shaped. A wide hall from the front door leads directly ahead to a dining room. A solid wall to the right. An entrance to the left to a living room. The staircase to the second floor is at the far side of the living room.

"You don't have any cats?"

"Oh, Freddie...he passed away a couple years ago."

Joel turns and glares at her. Then he looks down and bites his lip.

"I took care of him...I don't want you to think--"

"No...no. I'm glad you took care of him."

"It was hard to think of getting another, but maybe..."

Gloria leads us to the dining room. At right is the entrance to the kitchen. At left is another entrance to the living room.

We take chairs at the side of the table and hear the kitchen door opening. Ken McFadden calls out, "Where are you?" No greeting, charming as he was before.

"You need to come in here." She makes her voice imperative.

McFadden stomps into the dining room, impatient. "What is it?" Then he sees us. "What the fuck is this?"

"We're here to talk to you," I tell him.

"Are you fucking kidding me?" He looks at his wife contemptuously. "You're so damned weak."

"Leave her alone," Joel says.

"Get the hell out of here. You have no right to be in my house."

Gloria tells him, "It's my house too. I invited them."

He turns his glare to us. "What do you want?"

"To talk for a few minutes. Then we'll leave."

He gives us a real put-out expression, almost a pout. He sits at the opposite end of the table. Gloria brings him some kind of drink without asking. I smell whiskey. I understand why Joel doesn't drink whiskey.

McFadden sips slowly, staring at us. "Well, what is it?"

Joel and I look at each other.

"There's concerns you might be involved in something illegal."

He glares at Joel, then his wife. "What did you tell them?"

She turns and walks out without a word. His reaction confirms for me he's up to no good.

I tell him, "You're lucky she cares. Whatever you're doing, you'd better consider what happens if you're exposed."

He focuses on me. "Am I supposed to be afraid of you?"

"I'll find out what you're doing. I'm good at that; and I'd do what I can to ensure Gloria doesn't get caught in it. What happens to you, I don't care. But maybe you have a chance to get out even if you have to flip on someone."

"Fuck you."

"I applaud your bravado. But I'll tell you something I learned in my work. Drunks are sloppy. They make mistakes because they're busier thinking about how to get the next drink than covering their tracks."

His eyes get mean. "What do you know about me?"

"What I know," Joel says. "You've been scheming some kind of shit with Meese for years. You probably still are."

The two of them face off.

"You'd be surprised what I found out back then," Joel adds.

McFadden breathes heavy. "Just like her, aren't you?"

"Stay away from her. I swear, if you touch her, I will beat the shit out of you."

McFadden struggles to stay cunning. "You're awfully forgiving of her, considering everything. Well, she's the one who wanted you out of the house. You were a traitor, she said."

I feel Joel's body become rigid beside me.

Gloria suddenly rushes back into the dining room. "How dare you! I never said that, never!"

"You want to pretend you're all mother to him now?"

"*I hate you.*"

At that, Ken stands and yells, "Get the fuck out of here, you bitch!"

Joel jumps up so fast his chair falls over.

Gloria screams at Ken. "I hate you! *Hate you! Hate you!*"

Ken tries to grab at her and Joel steps between them, shoving Ken hard into the wall. "Get your hands off her."

McFadden flinches a little from Joel's expression but he still wants to provoke. "Oh, you are going to beat me up? Your father? You think that makes you *her* man now? Maybe you want to know more of what she said. What she told the neighbors about you, if you think she's so wonderful..."

Gloria reaches around Joel to smack at Ken. "Shut up! *Shut up!* You bastard!"

Ken tries to grab her hands and for a few seconds they're both fighting around Joel. I'm coming over to help stop this human tornado. But Joel is able to control the situation. He shoves both of them apart. "Stop it!"

The two of them pause. Then Ken says, "Get out of my way."

"No. You want to try me, I'll knock you the fuck out."

Ken stays still, staring at him. Gloria remains behind Joel, her hands on his shoulders. Joel turns and moves her out of the room to the kitchen. I notice how she leans into him, as if her allegiance has been transferred effortlessly. In the back of my mind I hope that's for the better.

McFadden now stares at me, angry over the exposure of their domestic bliss.

I tell him, "Seriously, whatever you're into that's illegal is going to be discovered. Even in New Jersey, eventually it's discovered. This is the time to do something about it."

"You don't know anything about me," he says.

"I know you think you're too clever to be found out. But you have others involved. In this state, entire city governments are taken away in handcuffs. Maybe the feds are already watching you. You're smart enough to know that he who talks to the FBI first gets the most immunity. And I *will* find out what you're doing. I do that for a living."

He actually thinks about what I said.

I add, "Something's going on you don't like, because it shows. I can also find the contacts for the best person for you to go to. And to protect Gloria."

I see it turning over in his mind. For a moment. But his biggest enemy is himself.

"No, no. I'm not going down as a snitch. And you. How could someone like *you* possibly be able to help me?" He gets up and heads to the hallway muttering, "Goddamned faggot telling me my business..."

Pathetic.

I go in the kitchen. Joel is by his mother on a banquette trying to convince her to leave. "...just pack something quick and go with us."

She's trying to stop her tears with a paper towel. But she's listening. In fact, both of them seem to be acting in the high emotional intensity of the moment. "What do I have now, Joel? What can I do?"

"You have me." He looks up at me. "And Gabriel."

She now looks at me. "Yes," I tell her. "Come with us. You shouldn't stay here. Not the way he is."

"But..." She looks around, making a decision. Seeing the kitchen, the home, the history, the marriage, the life. "What about him?"

Joel's eyes turn dark. "Fuck him. You did your part. It's time to change."

She stands, and then shows hesitation. Unsure of Joel's veracity. Reminding me of when he was unsure of mine.

"I'll take care of you," he says. "You don't need him anymore."

And suddenly it's as if she won the lottery. A chance at freedom. "Are you sure? We have so much pain between us."

"I can handle that. Just leave with me."

"Let me...I have to pack something."

"Just overnight. I'll make sure we get the rest of your stuff. But we can't stay here. Just get some stuff for right now."

"Ten minutes." She hustles for the back stairs.

Joel stares at me as if he now realizes the enormity of what he did. "Are you okay with this?"

I can't say I don't have doubts about this new situation. But also I can't do anything but support him, as he does me. "I'm with you all the way."

Now, in the flush of this momentous decision, he gets up and takes my hand. "Maybe we should go up and help her. Make sure she doesn't change her mind."

"She won't. What did your father do with Meese? That you know of."

He tenses up again. "This isn't the time to talk about it."

Gravel crunches outside. A car pulling up. I check out the window. "And...the police are here."

Joel's inhales sharply. He looks out the window over my shoulder. We see two uniformed cops get out of the car. And a man is walking over from across the street. He talks to the uniform cops and they all head for the front door.

"That asshole." I shake my head. "They're here to throw us out. Stay calm no matter what he says. We're leaving."

Joel goes to the foot of the back stairs. "Mom! You need to come down now."

I can hear McFadden's angry voice at the front door. A minute later the man who we saw come over from across the street enters in the kitchen and looks at us coolly. He's a little taller than I, white, around 40, medium build, brownish short hair and a trim mustache, very fit. Fairly expressive, intelligent eyes.

"Gentlemen, I'm a police detective." He shows us his badge. "Mr. McFadden says you forced your way in here."

"We were invited by Gloria McFadden. We're here with her permission."

Ken steps in the kitchen to glare at us, followed by the uniformed officers. The detective raises his eyebrows at Ken.

Ken waves his hand dismissively. "She has no idea what she's doing. They threatened me. They threatened to beat me up."

The detective turns back to us. "Who are you, please?"

I speak carefully and calmly, for Joel to pick up on my tone. "My name is Gabriel Ross. I'm a licensed investigator. This is Joel McFadden, he's their son. We were visiting with Gloria at her request. We're leaving, now, Detective...?"

"Dell. John Dell." He stares at Joel.

"*You're* John Dell," Joel says quietly, "You were helping her find me."

"Yes, I was."

"Oh for fuck's sake," Ken says.

Dell's expression has softened a little, but not much.

The younger cop steps back, using a radio to see what information he can find on us. No doubt that will be interesting. I almost sigh to myself.

Dell says, "Mr. Ross, are you armed?"

"No, I am not. I'll take my jacket off if you like. You can see."

"Joel?"

"No."

"You know what he did?" Ken points at me. "He's violent. He's hit people. My own son brought him here to *terrorize* me."

Joel's breathing changes subtly, getting angry. I make my voice soft for his benefit. "Neither of us are here to terrorize anyone. You can ask Gloria about that."

I can see Dell doesn't like something in McFadden's tone. "Ken, can you go in the other room with Officer Bellingham?"

Ken grumbles and leaves. Bellingham, the younger one, whispers in Dell's ear. Dell moves closer to me. "Would you have a problem with me searching you?"

In New York City, I would. Here, just go with it. I shrug my jacket off and lay it on the banquette. Hold my arms out.

Dell pats me down. Joel glares at him, and I tell him with my eyes it's okay. Dell briefly looks at my jacket, doesn't find guns or drugs and steps back. He looks at Joel, considering the same question. I'm not sure Joel will go with it. But then following my lead, he holds his arms out. Dell similarly pats him down. No rough stuff, he's professional. Doing his job. I don't often get along with cops but I respect doing one's job when it's professional. A domestic call is always dangerous so I want to minimize any likelihood of things getting out of control.

Afterwards he stares at Joel again. "I remember you as a kid."

Joel says, "You lived across the street. You fixed my bike once."

Dell smiles. "I still live there. By the time I came back from Iraq in the early nineties..."

"They'd thrown me out."

"She told me."

That makes Joel angry again. The thought of what she told him. Going back to the lies she believed from Meese. "Nice of her to confide my life to you."

Dell's a little taken aback by that that. I tell him, "Detective, we came here on a visit by invitation. We're leaving. Gloria is leaving with us."

He's assessing me as I speak. "Is that so?"

"She'll be down shortly. I'd like her to walk out with us, but we'll wait outside if necessary."

"Where is she now?"

"Upstairs, getting ready."

He goes to the stairs. "Gloria? It's John. Can you come down?"

Gloria runs down the stairs. "John? What's going on?"

She has a suitcase with her, and has put on a sweater coat. She looks from Dell to us. Joel takes her hand. She holds on to it, turning back to Dell.

He says, "Ken told us these men threatened him, forced their way in here."

"I invited them here, John. This is Joel, you remember Joel. Of course you do. Well he's here now, and this is his boyfriend, Gabriel Ross. Ken is being..." She shakes her head. "Please, this is ridiculous."

"We have to check it out, Gloria. Ken seems pretty serious. Mr. Ross has a reputation."

I don't respond to that.

"He's done nothing wrong. This is something I have to do, John."

"I need to make sure you're okay."

I can hear the closeness in their tone. Despite the age difference, they're bonded.

"I'm going with them. I don't care what Ken thinks."

Ken has come back into the kitchen, followed by Bellingham. "What the hell do you think you're doing?"

She turns away into Joel's arms. "We're leaving," she says.

"You can't do that. You're not doing that!" Ken's voice is angry. The cops all look carefully at him, for the indicia of domestic violence.

"Sorry," Joel says suddenly, in a voice that sounds very different than himself. "She's going with *me*."

I realize he has triumph in his voice. The tone, the words, have an entire history embedded.

And Ken's fury erupts. "You are *not* taking her away. After what you did to this family!"

He steps forward and Dell gets in front of him.

"I did nothing," Joel says. "No, wait. I did. I was the only person in this family who did something with this name. More than *you'll* ever do."

Just as Dell is subtly trying to keep Ken back, I subtly try to draw Joel away, towards the kitchen door.

Dell says, "Ken, maybe you should go back in the other room."

"What the hell? This is my house. She's my *wife*. They can't take her."

"I'm leaving on my own." Gloria says this without looking at him.

A mini-standoff. Dell says, "Let me talk to you alone, Gloria."

She sighs and goes back upstairs, with him following.

I put my jacket back on, while Ken regales the uniformed cops about the injustice of persons like myself and Joel interfering with his life. Joel now stares stonily at the floor. His outburst, if you want to call it that, is over, and he's retreated inside himself. I walk up and put my arm around him, to look at the day outside the kitchen window. The strange oppressiveness of the small neighborhood. Joel looks over my shoulder. He leans on me, but I feel the tension in his body.

Gloria returns to the kitchen, along with Dell.

"It's okay," she says to us.

Joel picks up her suitcase. He and his father exchange glances, and I can't help but see the victory rise again in Joel's face at taking his father's wife away from him.

Ken yells at her, "What the hell do you think you're doing?"

She turns back to him, her emotions rising, her face getting red.

"You can't tell me what to do anymore! You've held my life down for too long—I did what you wanted. I kept up appearances even when it cost me my son. Even when I had to live with you making fun of me for going into recovery. That's over, Ken. I'm done going along with your dirty work."

Joel opens the back door to let his mother out.

Ken turns crimson. "Stop them! I told you he threatened me-- you're going to let two Goddamned fags take my wife out of here?"

I keep my eyes on Dell to see if he'll let two Goddamned fags take Ken's wife out of here.

He meets my gaze briefly then looks back at Ken. His expression turns cold. "You need to step away, Ken. She's leaving of her own will."

"What the fuck? How can you let them..."

I follow Joel to the door, then turn back. "Thank you, Detective, officers."

Dell nods. I shut the door behind me. Heading for the Camry, we can hear Ken's voice getting louder.

He suddenly bursts out of the back door yelling at us. "You're going to be sorry for this..."

Joel's voice is contemptuous. "What are *you* going to do?"

"You think you can fuck with me now? I'll show *you*..."

Joel helpfully gives his father the finger as he gets his mother in the car.

Dell is outside now with the other cops, who drag Ken back in the house. I quietly thank Dell again for his help. Then I lose no time starting up and driving away.

Joel is agitated once in the car. "You thanked them? They had no business saying anything to us..."

"Do I look upset about it? It's just playing the system. Courtesy has a purpose."

"Fucking *cops.*"

"Joel...John is a decent man. Gabriel was very professional."

He isn't listening to that and just glares at me. "You don't like cops either."

"I've been hassled by them enough times. Nonetheless, you don't cause trouble where you don't need to. Ken came out of that worse, if you notice."

Joel's still angry. I know it's just nerves, but Gloria is anxious. She puts both her hands on his shoulders. "It's okay, honey."

I feel his anger in how he stares at me. I say, "I am still well aware of police brutality, corruption and entitlement. Nonetheless, you remember the detective in Elizabeth was a nice person who believed us on Mathers' case. Andrew Green, my NYPD friend, is also decent man."

"Exceptions to the rule."

I have to smile. "I remember when we met you wanted to be sure I wasn't a former cop."

"I had my reasons. That cop in there is going to be all in her business if he isn't already."

"Joel, John is a friend of mine. He helped me get a reduced sentence for the DUI, to get in recovery, and he stayed with me when it was tough."

I'm sure Joel's anger isn't really at me, or even these cops in particular. It's something else that has been disinterred in him.

Joel rolls his eyes at Gloria's remarks and she sees him do that in the rear-view mirror, frowning at him like a mother would at insolence. An odd interplay of visual exchanges go between them. He sees her frown and he turns petulant, defiant. She then looks hurt, and he suddenly assumes a cool, authoritative posture. I'm so fascinated by this I have a hard time keeping my eyes on the road.

Suddenly she leans up against his seat and puts her arms around him. "You are my hero," she says softly.

I risk glancing over at him. He's frowning at the words. He lights one of his cloves and rolls his window down, casually gazing outside. The authority carries into his voice. "I'm going to take you to my loft. We'll get you set up in there for now."

"That isn't putting you out, is it?"

"No, I'll stay with Gabriel. Don't worry about it."

She drops her hands and her voice changes. "Those are strange cigarettes. You shouldn't smoke; it's bad for you. You know better than that."

Just like a mother. No matter how you express your adulthood, they know how to establish their parental role to get to you. For a second he becomes infuriated, stares her down in the mirror. Then puts his cool expression back on and crosses his legs, folds his arms. "Get used to it."

Her head drops down, and she fusses with something in her purse. Conceding to him. Then she reaches over and starts combing his hair with her fingers, and straightening his shirt collar, which is already straight.

I look over at him now and he won't look back at me directly, just in his peripheral vision. All right, this is his family thing to work out. I just don't want him caught in psychodrama when he's beginning to become what he should be.

While I drive into Manhattan, in his methodical TCOB way Joel has Gloria give him a list of what she needs for the next few days to stay at his place in Chinatown. He continues avoiding catching my eye unnecessarily. I feel him building his façade. Not shutting down, but surviving. He doesn't respond much to her reaction at arriving in the city, of going to his apartment, or of seeing his paintings, which dominate the loft space.

Gloria can't stay still. Her nerves are running high. She just left her husband, she's with the son she hasn't seen in 17 years, they have a huge emotional storm between them, but she's enraptured by his work and with him. Since Joel barely nods at her comments, she uses me for a sounding board.

After a few minutes of this I ask him, "Would you like me to go shopping for her, so you two can talk?"

"I'll go." And Joel grabs his keys and cigarettes and is at the door before I can move. He flashes me a guilty/sorry look--knowing this isn't right--and leaves.

I turn back to Gloria. She's staring at the closed door. Her face has gone red. She has the exact same guilty/sorry look as he. They're practically twins.

"We have a lot to work through," she says quietly.

That's an understatement.

∞

Ken continues raging after his son and his wife have left. John Dell lets him rant.

"Why didn't you stop her?"

"She has a right to leave, Ken."

Ken growls to himself, wound up in his anger. "Right to leave...she's planning something. With him. They think they can outsmart me. Probably nosing in my business...going to ruin everything I have..."

At this point he doesn't even see Dell anymore. Dell's instincts take Ken's words and turn them over. Ken is paranoid about something. What? Does this have to do with his mysterious work problem?

Pressure can come from anywhere. Ken could be having an affair, he could be gambling and losing money. But his words spark another idea in Dell, because he just received a routine, or what seemed to be a routine, request for a criminal file check from the US Attorney's Office in New Jersey. On Ken. Ken doesn't have a record, but why would they ask? Not for a job. Ken's not going to leave for a new position at this point in his life.

Dell hears Ken wander off into the dining room. He tells the uniforms to wait for him in the car.

Ken has his cell phone out and is speaking urgently in a low voice. While Dell can't make out the exact words, he gets the impression Ken wants to meet with someone. And he hears the name "Larry." Larry Meese, no doubt.

Yesterday, Gloria had told him she had reconnected with Joel. She didn't say she had invited him and Gabriel Ross here to talk to Ken, but she explained this upstairs when she spoke to him. She said Larry Meese had lied about what Joel was doing before he was thrown out. She doesn't understand why Larry would lie like that. It was what made Ken so over-the-top angry to throw Joel out in the first place.

And it's a lie that can't really be disproven, Dell thinks. Ken is easily manipulated to anger, so maybe Larry wanted him angry at Joel. Why? Meese was known for mentoring teenage boys; but a lie is a stupid way to help someone with family problems.

Now Gloria is in an emotional free-fall with Joel taking her away. Dell is concerned for her. He has no idea what kind of person Joel is. He knows the story on Gabriel Ross, who seemed professional enough. The two of them are extremely close. He got that. He saw how protective Ross was with Joel.

As a cop he has to consider everything. Ross and Joel might be up to something. Ken might be up to something. Ken and Meese might be up to something.

Dell's own friendship with Gloria leads him to decide he's going to have to look into all of them to figure out what's going on.

∞

Meese ends the call and leans back in his office chair, rubbing his eyes. *Damn Ken, he's going to get them all...*

No, he isn't. There are options. Meese sees this now. Ken's hysterical call confirms what needs to happen. Meese leaves his office to call to another party.

The other party says, "What's going on? I need to see that auditor again?"

"No, far as I know he quit his job. We don't have to worry about him. This is about Ken. He might be a weak link."

"You sure?"

"I'm looking into it. You have a problem moving on that?"

"No. It's business."

"Good."

"I have to do it my way, you know."

Meese rolls his eyes. *This* one with his blood fetish. How he managed to contract with the Jersey families and not get whacked himself with his indulgence in bloodlust...but still. "Yeah, no problem. I'll let you know. Just be ready."

Meese's mind moves between anger at Ken and the anticipation. If Joel took his mother out of the house, that means they have a relationship again. Which means he will have good opportunity to see Joel soon. He anticipates seeing Joel's face. How happy Joel will be. It's been so long! Bittersweet at first, because Meese can't get close to him right away. Have to be careful. People don't understand what this true relationship is like.

It's indulgent, but Meese takes a personal day on Wednesday to drive to the city. He waits in his SUV outside Joel's building. While he's waiting, he's thinking, fantasizing...which makes the wait very pleasant.

And then Joel leaves the building. Meese inhales upon seeing him. But damned if that fucking PI isn't with him. What the hell? Come on, Joel.

He didn't have the chance to learn. You can't hold that against him.

True. But watching them on the street, talking to each other...it's bewildering. Ross, looking like a Sixties throwback hippie with his beard, reaches for Joel's hand and grasps it briefly. Joel smiles at him in a way he used to smile at Meese.

I understand. You have to pretend things sometime. It's okay. You won't have to do that much longer.

Ross moves closer to Joel, which makes Meese grip his steering wheel so hard his fingernails dig into the wheel. He says something in Joel's ear while putting his hand on him possessively.

It's so not right. When people like Meese have to be careful, because the world just doesn't understand what is right.

"I'll rescue you," Meese says.

When Gabriel Ross finally walks away, Meese has a clear view of Joel's face. Barely 50 feet away. Again, the maturity jars him. The vision of Joel at the high school pool, about to dive. Of Joel in his parents' house, answering questions about school and giving Meese a very private look letting him know it was time. Of Joel nervous and shaking, but only wanting to please him. The youth and beauty before it's corrupted by people like Ross.

It's hard to reconcile with the man standing on the street lighting a cigarette. *Joel doesn't smoke. His mother would kill him for that.*

For a moment, Meese feels very dull inside. The facial hair, the smoking, the clothes, the attitude. That's not his Joel.

Anger rages in him and Ken having taken it away. Leaving Joel to be manhandled by the likes of Gabriel Ross. He slams his fists against the steering wheel and makes the car shake.

Then Joel looks down at the sidewalk briefly, which changes his expression and makes him look younger. And in Meese's mind the Joel he knows, *his* Joel, is laid over this one. Like a transparency. Meese realizes that Joel's in disguise. Of course. He has to be in disguise for his own protection. My God, what Ross would do to him if he could see the *real* Joel.

It occurs to Meese that Joel just might be in danger and that he, Meese, should take steps to protect him.

∞

Thursday, March 31
Alphabet City, Avenue A, 7:39 am

Over the last couple days, I've seen Joel become two people. There's the strange role of the adult son-quasi caretaker. He doesn't want to try to reenact his role with her in his youth. Instead, he's handling this relationship with the new authoritative demeanor to control her, make her deferential to him. She accepts that role almost as a token of love or perhaps accepting as the payment she is willing to give.

It unnerves me a little and reminds me of his friendship with Isabella, who provokes him into getting authoritative with her and then seems delighted to accede to him.

Then there's how he is with me. Completely different, almost as if he's in a fantasy. When we're in my apartment he avoids talking about anything family-related as if his mother doesn't exist. He focuses on me in a flirtatious, subliminally erotic way, like he did in the club. The kind of attention that's very intoxicating to me. Although I sense he's using this side to keep the other side compartmentalized.

I want to enjoy this other side as the baser part of my nature urges. But I know he can't keep living separate lives. Not anymore. The truer he gets to himself, the more starkly conflicting these façades become.

This morning Gloria calls and has a conversation with him that makes him irritated. She's talking about personal matters here on the phone instead of waiting for him to go to Chinatown. Interfering with his fantasy.

He ends the call and lights up a cigarette. "She wants to know what we're doing about him."

"Okay, for a start where might he keep any records on his business? At the house?"

He thinks about it. "No. Not the way she noses through everything. A couple times I saw him go to a storage facility just out of town. He stopped off when driving me somewhere."

"It wasn't just for household items?"

"I asked, and he said he was holding stuff for a friend. It sounded like bullshit to me."

"Let's go check it out."

I make sure with Veronica I'm not otherwise needed, then we get some tools to take with us and head back out to Paterson and the storage unit place. It's not a building but a set of garage-like lockers on ground level. A hundred spaces of varying size in lines of 20.

His father's locker is at the back, furthest from the office and any cameras. It's locked with a standard padlock. No sweat to pick that.

Joel flips on the light uneasily. I can see he feels almost ready to run, as if an adolescent again, afraid his father will catch him.

The room is 8 x 8, with some wooden tables, plastic crates and boxes. All filled with paper.

"Not very neat, is he?"

Joel's discomfort is replaced with a disgust of his father's habits. Several empty bottles of Dewars are by one of the crates. A half-filled one is on a stack of papers. The papers themselves are piled haphazardly. Whatever these are, there's no sense of order.

"Just like at home. Shit piled everywhere. She wasn't much better when she was messed up, but always trying to cover up 'cause he blamed her for everything. Whenever I would walk by him passed out next to these..."

He picks up one of the stained, bent and ripped folders, the contents spilling on the floor, "I'd just feel contempt. And then to see her pick up after him...I suppose this is why I give you a hard time about doing the dishes."

"Don't mix one era of life with another, sweetheart."

Joel sighs, running his hands through his hair nervously. "I don't want to spend hours in here, feeling his vibes. Let's see what we can find."

I get a portable lamp to help us look. The first and best is a laptop. We don't want to take it and make Ken suspicious, so Joel starts this one up and copies what he finds, including the internet history. I go back out to the car while he's doing that, to get some water. I notice he's brought more notebooks, tucked carefully under his backpack in the back seat.

I think I hear him talking to himself in the storage room. And the sound of something dropping.

This makes me rush back inside. He's curled on the floor with the contents of a folder around him.

"What happened?" I get down with him.

His eyes are closed. "I was just going through what looked like some bank stuff...I felt like...I don't know."

"Okay." I pick up some of the papers. "Okay. These are bank documents. Looks like your father is in a partnership with a company, Tartarus. Does that sound familiar?"

The look on his face tells me the answer is yes. I put my hand on the side of his head. He turns his eyes to me.

"Tartarus is a...a...boat."

"Baby, what's wrong?"

He moves his head to my thigh. "A boat. His boat." I feel the shudder in his body.

"Your father's boat?"

He shakes his head. "No. His...Meese. He has a company named after his boat. Fucking son of a bitch."

"He and your father are in this together, maybe. You said you thought so."

"They used to talk all the time." Joel's voice gets distant. "And before they threw me out, he had..." Joel stops. "He had..."

He pauses again and I'm not sure what he's going to do. Then he puts his head on my legs, and tells me what happened with Meese.

∞

By the time he's done, he's exhausted. His head is still in my arms. I feel a rising tide of anger in me. My primal urge is to find this Meese and destroy him, utterly and completely.

I feel Joel in my arms, trembling, trying to stop crying. He's depleted by the revelation. Surrounded by the evidence of the wrongdoings of his father and a man who abused him. But not broken. But still, abuse isn't even the right word. It's only used because what really happened is too hard to say. Anger isn't going to work right now. He needs compassion. I hold him, stroking his head, for a long time.

"Do you see it on me," Joel asks, interrupting my thoughts.

I don't know what he's talking about. "See what, sweetheart?"

He looks up at me in the dim light.

"What he did. What he said."

"No...Joel, that doesn't happen. It's not you, it's them."

∞

Joel, getting to his feet, says, "I'm going out to the car for a moment."

"Okay." Gabriel is up with him, but Joel holds up his hand. "I'll be back...I just..."

Gabriel nods.

In the car Joel finds a bottle of water, and spends a moment calming down. He runs his hands through his hair, feeling the sweat.

"That was hard; perhaps the hardest," Jan says beside him. "But you've done it. That frees you to be stronger."

"I don't know if I can be stronger," Joel tells him.

What Gabriel said runs through his mind. *It's not you, it's them...*

Jan has the notebook. "You wrote, *she is my salvation because she made me stronger.*"

"Grace."

"History can repeat itself," Jan says.

∞

GRACE

Robert Louis Stevenson said, "Don't judge each day by the harvest you reap, but by the seeds you plant."

∞

She is my salvation because she made me stronger.

It is November 7, 1993.

JOEL SITS ON A BENCH in Christopher Park, a tiny park off Christopher Street, a triangle patch of green. It's just after ten pm. He supposes he looks like he's trying to score drugs. He's cold enough not to care.

A young woman surely not much older than he is watching him from another bench, smoking. She's lithe, black, tall. She has on an oversized army style jacket, high-heeled boots and a gold cloche hat with fuzzy black earmuffs over it.

He watches back, hugging his knees. The streets buzz around them. People walk by, yelling, talking.

Silence then. Everything disappears.

A hand on his head. He draws his breath in, opening his eyes. He realizes he's lying on the bench now.

"Damn, you're cold." It's the young woman. She's beside him. She has lavender lipstick and heavy mascara around her eyes. Her hand is on his forehead. "And somebody jacked you up. Baby, you're going to freeze to death out here."

"I don't have anywhere else."

"I thought not." The girl has a scent that is both smoky and exotic, like incense. "Where'd you come in from?"

He gives her a short version. In from Jersey City, a lie, and then the truth. Some kids claimed they knew a good place for him to stay, invited him to share some weed they had with them. They acted like they knew, and sympathized with him...five of them sitting with him in an alley. Then they beat him. They thought he might have money. The only thing they left was his notebook. He tells her about the man who found him on the street shortly after. Pastor Sal. Pastor Sal took him to the Community of Faith church near Gansevoort, fed him, let him clean up. Then came on to him. Despite being hurt, Joel reacted in fear--punching Pastor Sal. And taking his wallet. He's not proud of that, but it seemed like payback for everything that happened before.

The girl raises her eyebrows at Joel's story. "I've seen him around. Good to know when you're on the street. Some of us have tried the big church shelter, the famous one. But if you're gay or trans, they'll beat the shit out of you there and the priests will just ignore it."

Her voice is deep, with softness around the edges from practice. He realizes she's transgender. She picks up one of his hands. "You're pale, boy. Going to turn into a ghost."

She touches his head in such a way that is so gentle, so kind, it causes him to cry.

"What's really going on," she asks.

In spite of his trust having been violated repeatedly, and violently, Joel feels he can tell her a brief version of what happened with Meese and being thrown out. She keeps her hand on his head.

"Honey, it's not you. It's them. Their loss, their evil. My mama threw me out when my grandma died. She didn't want to set eyes on me anymore. That's her problem."

"I don't know what to do..."

"Come with me." She pulls him up. In spite of the suspicion newly driven in him from the experiences of the past couple weeks he goes with her. She puts her arm around him, taller by nearly a head. Then just shrugs off the army coat and drapes it over both their shoulders, pulling him close to her. They end up a few blocks away at an alley on West 10th Street. He pauses, wary of being abused again.

"I'm not them," she tells him. "But I've run into them. Or people like them. I know what you went through."

He follows her to the back of a nonprofit. A large metal structure like a garden shack is in back. It's locked. The woman takes a thin metal rod out of her bag and picks open the lock. "I know this place. It's clean."

"Stay, like sleep here?"

"Why not?" She slips inside.

Hesitantly, he follows her. The shack is empty except for some tarp. It has just enough room to lie flat. Since the bin has a tiny air grate, she takes out her pack of cigarettes, with the name Djarum. "You want to share one with me?"

He watches her light the cigarette. It smells of cloves. "What's your name?"

"Grace, baby." She takes a drag of the clove cigarette and hands it to him. They're curled up close against each other. "It was my grandma's name. And she used to say it over me enough times."

He's tired, so tired he can't believe it. The shocking thing is that he can't remember the last time he lied next to a person. Grace has her hand on his head again, and he has his head against her chest, on the jacket. "What do I call you?"

"Joel."

"Joel." She strokes his head.

In the morning they both wake up, hearing activity outside the building. Grace peeks out and tells Joel it's time to leave.

The cash in Pastor Sal's wallet gets them food and use of the diner bathroom to wash up. Joel looks a little beat-up, but Grace is taken with him and even gets him to smile from her teasing. She uses a pay phone to check on the credit card. It hasn't been canceled so they go to Kmart to buy some things she says they need, including a pair of sunglasses that helps hide his bruises. Grace stops in a bodega and buys a couple packs of Marlboros and a couple packs of the Djarum clove cigarettes.

By the end of the day they're close. By the end of the week, they're inseparable. Grace knows a lot of places to stay, including subway tunnels, under highways, doors, hallways, roofs. The cold is the biggest problem. Being together helps, Joel discovers. You can go through things easier when you're not alone, although the flip side is you're not willing to risk as much when you're not alone.

As the days go on, he finds out Grace occasionally hustles, to pay for hormones from street dealers. She knows a guy, Striker, who can inject her. Self-trained in needles, he also does cut-rate tattoos. He talks about having a shop someday and she talks about being a model or designer.

To Joel, neither the tattoos nor the steroid injections seem healthy.

"Better than shaving my face on the street," Grace says. Her hair is tightly braided under the hat, but she has a couple of wigs carefully wrapped in her blue canvas carry-all bag. She wears the longer wig for warmth and when she's tricking. She does not say how old she is, but he guesses around 17-18.

1993 has segued into 1994, and Joel has just turned 16. Grace has been extremely protective of him and is not happy that he thinks he should do the same thing she is to bring money for both of them.

"Less risky than stealing," he says. He's showing some of his self-possession, and even more so, taking courage from her courage.

She raises one eyebrow at his words. "Yeah, because the cops *never* bust hookers. You even carry condoms, they're writing 'intent' all over your ass. I know plenty of girls and some guys gotta choose between risking catching AIDS or risking the Tombs."

"I'm good at staying out of trouble. You're good too."

"You have no idea." She shares her cloves with him. "But you don't do it right now," she says. "You don't know enough yet. I'm not going to let you get jacked again."

They spend a lot of time wandering around Manhattan, talking to other people on the street, in essence getting Joel a primer on the non-tourist/non-Wall Street/non-yuppie/non-hipster way of life. The underground that Mayor Giuliani would prefer disappear. The homeless vets, homeless kids, homeless mentally ill. Drug dealers, addicts, predators, thieves, pretenders and prostitutes. Ways to hear the NYPD before they turn on the siren. Ways to sum up a person's character in less than 30 seconds by clothes, eyes, posture, voice. Ways to escape. Ways to defend. Who to be friends with, who not to waste time with.

When they find a place to hide from the day and be alone she's intrigued by the progress of his physicality. The facial hair coming in on him, the subtle and strong changes in his voice and musculature.

One night she rubs her hand on his face imprudently, as usual. No one else is allowed to touch him like that, just her. "Is it growing all over," she suddenly says, and runs her hand under his shirt. It's different, soothing. And something else. That makes him feel confused.

Grace senses that and takes her hand away. Inside and outside her work she has to be careful. Men might not care she's trans, might be attracted, or might be repulsed. The third category is dangerous if they take her as a threat to their masculinity.

But that isn't Joel. He is scared; he feels the fear of being violated. But Grace has proven herself to be trusted. She doesn't hurt him. And he realizes he wants the affection he wants her touch. He moves closer to her so she knows it's okay.

Seeing where his eyes are while she has her hand on his chest, she then puts one of his hands on her breasts. He's never touched a woman sexually. He knows instinctively she wants to be treated with care. Are breasts delicate? He keeps his fingers light, listening to her heart beat, and feeling her skin react, grow taut.

"You're not completely gay," she says. "I can *feel* that."

They kiss then, and that brings all the sensations together, sparks a natural heat between them. Things change as their chemistry changes. Grace unzips his pants and puts her hand in. "You got something to show here, boy," she says softly. Feeling his shaking, feeling his desire, she brings her mouth to him. At first, he's scared they'll get caught by anyone passing by. Then he forgets about that in feeling something new. New in the mutuality of it. In his wanting it to happen.

After, he's not sure what to do, feeling helpless beside her. "What do I do for you?"

"Are you willing?"

"Yes." He flushes, almost embarrassed at his vulnerability, his exposure from coming with her. She kisses him gently in their quiet niche. Eventually, he's aroused again.

Her hand on his erection, Grace breathes heavy. "You gotta know...I'm on hormones, so what's *there*...it's gotten small. That happens. I know eventually it won't work at all. But I got the boobs to make up for it."

"You have nice..." He's not sure what to say. He strokes her breasts again, and this time kisses her on her breasts. It pleases her, to see his lips on her femininity.

"Thank you, baby. Oh, keep doing that....Some trans women don't like to be touched down *there*, to be reminded of what's still there, you understand what I mean?"

"Yeah."

"I feel anything else you can touch, like you are now. And you can have me from behind. You ever done that?"

"No. Just, uh, what you did."

"Well, I have condoms. That's what I want, you to have me. I'll tell you what to do."

She tells him how to use what she has in her bag, the condoms and lube, to enter her. "Will you come," he asks breathlessly, when she arches against him.

"I don't always. But..." she stops talking, moving with him. "When I do, it's powerful. When it's the right man. You'll make me, baby."

Her voice and her sensations carry over to him. And his in turn, the desire, the want, go to her. That mutual feeling of desire reflected by desire creates the cloud of intimacy. That makes the difference. And she is right that his intimacy makes her come.

A few months with her has him feeling like a street veteran. He *is* a street veteran. Joel and Grace are never far apart unless she's working. Some men have tried for him, some street denizens have tried for him. Being realistic that he's determined to pull his weight in their relationship, she works on getting the male hustlers in the Times Square area to talk to him about their work. Some are friendly, some are hostile.

Mario is a friendly one around 18 who knows Grace well. He tells Joel about how to pick up a trick, and some to avoid. Mario introduces Joel to Orest, a kid who doesn't hustle. No one is sure what he does but everyone knows he likes knives and plays with them all the time, freaking people the fuck out. Orest likes Joel because Joel doesn't act like Orest is a freak. He gives Joel a switchblade and shows him ways to use it and tells Joel to keep it close just in case.

Joel is a draw the first couple of times he hangs around the Times Square area and the West Side Highway. He does not like turning his back on people, being vulnerable. His first incidents with the men who pay him are nerve-wrecking at first, then less so. The street rivals for tricks make him more nervous with their resentful competition, then with time less so, as his confidence develops. He has a manner that draws people to him to protect him or try to seduce him.

He expands to the East Village and the hunting grounds of the all-male peep joint under the notorious and dangerous Sahara Hotel. The hotel is officially 'closed' but that is not a barrier to those who want unofficial shelter or privacy. Mayor Law & Order is gradually sweeping people out of classic pick-up points such as Times Square and the Meatpacking District, in order to make the world safe for Disney souvenir stores and designer-addicted gentrifiers. But people still want to buy sex, and like water falling in gravity to whatever space it can find so too do the sex workers and tricks adapt to wherever they can find.

He lets Grace figure out what they should buy with the money. She knows better, and he trusts her. He doesn't care about buying anything except a decent coat from an Army/Navy store. And another notebook to draw in.

Grace recognizes that he's scared whatever he gets will be taken away. She tries to build a bubble around him, of trans friends who will watch for him in relay. Her friends give him haircuts and act as lookout when needed. He has a casual acceptance that the women appreciate and they spend time talking to him. Like Grace, they have dreams of doing something completely different. Acting, dancing, modeling. He draws them with their permission, as he draws other scenes of street life.

Grace watches him draw sometimes when they sit in the Winter Garden, buying coffee for the right to have a table for a few hours. They seem as paired as any middle-class tourist couple sitting there.

She tells him, "You're good; you need to do *this*, not hustle."

He ignores her, and she lights a cigarette. "You don't like to be told you're good. Sex is one thing, but you can't hear anything else, can you?"

Instead of answering he starts drawing her.

Early April. A strangely cold day, and rainy. The chill makes people stay off the streets. Joel is heading for the West Side. He stops at a pet store to look at the kittens in the big cage in the window. Cats, no matter where, catch his eyes. He's threatened people he's seen trying to hurt stray cats, brandishing the knife Orest gave to him. The saddest part now of being thrown out is missing Freddie. Well, even drunk, Mom loves cats and knows how to take care of one.

A thin, sinewy white man in his thirties approaches Joel while he's watching the kittens, crouched down in front of the window. The kittens vie for his attention by sticking their tiny paws through the metal strands of the cage.

"Hey, they're so cute," the man says.

Joel doesn't respond, just eyes him warily.

"I've seen you before. You're real nice." The man takes out a card. "I can get you into something better. To do some 'risqué'-type modeling. *Big* money there. You don't need to be on the street, not you. You want to check it out right now?"

"No." Joel already knows to turn everything that sounds like a too-good-to-be-true offer down flat.

The man shrugs. "My name's Art. Think about it. I have an opening for someone like you."

Joel takes the card and moves away from him.

When Joel returns to where Grace is supposed to meet him, he's concerned when she doesn't show. Mario sometimes serves as a messaging service for street people. Joel finds him in an arcade in Times Square. "She's searching for her connection with the *stuff,* you know."

"Hormones."

"Yeah. Striker's out of town, and no one's sure who else might be holding."

While waiting for her, Joel wonders if Art is on the up and up. If he is, maybe Joel can get in a better situation. Help them both.

He shows Mario the card.

Mario shakes his head "I never heard of him."

"I'm going to go talk to him. Tell Grace if you see her."

Mario protests, but Joel has made up his mind. He calls the number, and Art invites him over to an apartment on West 11th. Joel writes down the address, and gives the scrap of paper to Mario to give to Grace.

Art is waiting for him outside when he arrives. "Wow, you look even better than I remember." He seems like he's reading from a script. "You want to come in? Hang out? I have some weed. Just talk awhile, you know?"

Joel has no interest in drugs, even to escape being homeless. When some street people scrape up a toke, he will sit with them, but pass. Too much can happen when you're not in control.

Joel takes out one of Grace's cigarettes she gave him this morning. "What do you want with me?"

"I know some people who would like your looks and you can make money off of it. Nude modeling, photography. No *touching.* I don't allow that. Could I just *see* you? I'm not going to hurt you or anything."

Joel is torn between the prospect that this is real and suspicion that it's a trap.

"You shouldn't be on the street. Just talk to me. Come to the apartment."

The weather is still freezing, which prompts Joel to say, "Just the hallway."

Art unlocks the door and waits for Joel to follow. Joel stops by the mailboxes. It's a narrow, old building, with tall ceilings and peeling paint, but still some grandeur in the fixtures and banisters.

Art continues his patter. He knows people who like to photograph young men. Nude, but the faces in shadow. Joel could be very popular in this line of work. Art gets him to go up one flight to sit on the steps where it's warmer. Art puts his hands gently on Joel's arm, and then asks to touch him.

"No. I don't want that."

Art nods. "Okay. I understand. Could I just look at you though? I really want to see you out of the clothes. I have a nice shower and you can sleep here if you want. I'm kind of lonely since my friend went away, I'll admit."

"Are you alone?"

"Yeah, I don't live with nobody or nothing...Well, my *cat*. He's not much older than the ones we saw in that store."

That becomes irresistible to Joel, to see the cat. He follows Art one more flight up.

Below, they can hear the front door slam open.

"Some skells around here. Just ignore that," Art says casually.

But the sound of shoes clattering on the stairs alarms Joel. And he hears Grace's voice, calling him: "Joel! Are you in here?"

He leans over the railing. "Grace?"

She sees him from below. "Joel, get out of there."

Art now leans over. His voice suddenly takes an edge. "Who the hell are you?"

Grace runs up the rest of the way and takes Joel's arm. "Let's go. Get away from him, baby."

Art tries to step between them. "Hey, you don't own him. I'm trying to help him. Just let him alone. He can do better than this."

"Joel, come with me."

This has Joel scared from the urgency in her voice. He moves away from Art and Grace puts her arm around him.

Suddenly Art gets furious. "You fucking bitch, get out of here!" He yanks a knife from a pocket and lunges at her. Trying to move away, Grace falls backward, nearly down the steps. Joel manages to hang on to her.

In a rage, Art tries to jump on her with the knife. Joel manages to get his arm across Art's neck and pull him away as Grace keeps her arms up in defense. "Run, Joel," she gasps. "Get out of here."

But he isn't leaving her alone. "Stop," he tells Art. "Stop this!"

Art has pinned her down on the dirty floor of the hallway. The point of his knife is at Grace's throat, at the artery.

Art's voice has changed to something else, a monster. "Joel, you better go to the apartment and go in. I'll kill her if you don't."

Joel's not as strong as the bigger man but he is stronger than people think. He holds on to Art. Grace struggles underneath and the knife cuts into her, horrifying Joel.

"Joel, don't do it, just run."

"I'll kill you, you fucking trannie whore."

The knife moves desperately, cutting them all. From nowhere, really, something shifts in Joel's mind and he drops his right hand to punch Art in the ribs. As hard as possible.

This takes Art by surprise. Joel starts punching again, and allowing the anger in him to build, making him stronger than he was in fear. This blitz lets Grace crawl from under Art's hands. He drops the knife and that reminds Joel of his own. He has it out in his hand and kicks Art's knife away.

Grace doesn't run, though. Joel now has his switchblade at Art's neck, keeping him still. Art tries to reach in his jacket again and Joel rips it off of him, and then he and Joel are rolling on the hallway floor, tangled and fighting viciously.

Grace looks for a pause to jump in, like playing double-dutch, and for a moment both of them are whaling on the other man in anger--anger at everyone who ever hurt them. So much so that Art eventually crumples, arms over his head, moaning. Grace finally gets up but Joel won't let go, digging at Art, but she manages to pull him away and down the stairs with her. They run out the building and down several blocks.

They stop at a closed store and look at each other. They both have blood on them. A check shows the cuts aren't serious but the wounds hurt in the cold.

Joel is now strangely calm. "What was going on?"

"He's a bad man, Joel. When Mario showed me that card...I've heard of him. He sells people."

"Sells? Like *slaves*?"

"Yeah, what line did he give you?"

Joel tells her. She shakes her head. "You're still so much a baby."

"I'm not; I wanted to help *you.*"

Grace frowns. "Don't get mad, Joel. I mean you just don't know what's out there."

"I know. I told you I was raped."

"I've been too; more than a few times. That doesn't mean you know every danger that's in this city, though. If you went in there, he'd have knocked you out, and trapped you in that apartment. You'd be raped five times a day by men who get their shit off that way. Nobody knows what happens to those boys who goes in there, but they don't *come out.*"

Joel's face burns. He feels stupid for giving Art a chance. He also feels Grace is judging him. He has an urge to run away. And he starts to run, but she catches him. "Don't leave me, baby. You might try a thank you, since we're outta there. I see you're all filled with macho right now like I was *questioning* you. That isn't the case."

He looks back at her, and sees the blood drying on her neck and clothes. She holds him. "It's just survival. Why do you think we're together? To just let shit happen? Don't get upset. It's not you that's wrong. It's them."

It's them.

∞

SEVEN

William Shakespeare said, "What is past is prologue."

Friday, April 1
Alphabet City, Avenue A, 7:45 am

I SCANNED THE CONTENTS of the folder with a portable scanner before we left the storage place. The legal papers are for a few companies that do banking in the Caymans. Many banks in the Caymans are known to help in hiding assets, such as banks that exist only on paper, perfect for tax evasion and laundering money. Right now, I have the paper that shows Ken is partnered with a company likely owned by Meese. Hiding assets involves a four-step process: obtaining the money illegally, putting the money in the stream of commerce somehow (like a bank account), 'layering' the money (moving it to different accounts, different countries, different shell companies), and the re-integrating the money back to the original thief and co-conspirators.

I review the records carefully; they are partly blacked out and covered in scrawls in what I'm assuming is Ken's handwriting. Nonetheless, I can see transfers to other banks in Panama and the Bahamas. I'm thinking with some digging I can figure out where Ken's money has gone, and hopefully who he's in partnership with. The reason why this kind of thing goes on so long undetected is not because the transactions are so complicated, it's that an investigative agency has to have a reason to look for it in the first place. These transactions occur every day, legitimate and otherwise. Now, if the IRS thought Ken was evading taxes, they may look into his business (which worries me about Gloria being considered complicit in tax evasion). If the NJ Audit Division of the State Comptroller found some trouble in Ken's agency, they may look into Ken's business.

The question is what sort of thing is Ken doing that involves fraud? Ken is chief procurement and land use officer for the State Division of Development. It's a new office that is supposed to be corruption-free. Since it was set up in former Governor Corzine's administration, I doubt very much that goal has been met. The importance of corruption-free is due to the office making decisions about land use for the counties in New Jersey.

Ken's regional office handles Passaic, Essex, Bergen, Hudson, and Union Counties--some of the most populous in the state. Everything in eastern New Jersey is so crowded people live stacked on each other. Ken's office determines who gets first rights to bid on land and land renovation (quite often parking garages for some reason), what public facilities (like colleges) may acquire, and purchasing items relating to land the state owns. All of that from bidding to building to buying has the potential for corruption. Bribery, bid-rigging, contractors...all that's missing in Ken's case are New Jersey specialties like stolen body parts, religious law intricacies, and murder-for-hire.

I have Gloria's permission to investigate their finances. Through some preliminary work, I note that Ken is already double-dipping. He retired from the Department of the Treasury, Division of Purchase of Property to work at the new agency a few years ago. As per NJ law, he's allowed to receive a full pension while still working full time. I write some ideas down about what I might look into via public records and sunshine laws with this agency. And perhaps see if anyone in Ken's agency might have something to say about him or any odd things that may have happened lately.

What would Meese's role be? As law enforcement, he has all kinds of potential for political contacts. And contractors are involved in work bid out from the Division of Development...that means connections to organized crime are likely.

In the meantime, Joel has recovered from his revelation; at least he said he did. He does have a way of snapping back from trauma. I'm afraid that just means he's compartmentalizing it. He had stopped by his loft to take a small box with him. Gloria wanted to know what he was doing and what the box was; he ignored her questions. Back at my apartment, he spent time on my bed during the evening going through a few pictures of his own. I can tell he's not ready to really tell me about them or show them and I gave him space.

Friday morning, I wake up with Archie between us. He knows I'm awake, and he's waiting for me to stop pretending. He starts purring to let me know and adds a tiny meow.

"Ask your other dad," I tell him. "He's living here now; has to pull his weight."

I see a hint of a smile on Joel's face.

My phone buzzes. God, what now? Can't people wait until after 10am to bother a person?

I pick it up. It's a text, with an unfamiliar number.

--Gabriel. This is your friend from the Met.

"What...the...*fuck*."

Joel pushes himself up to look at the phone with me. "What is it?"

"Zest. He's back."

"Are you sure?"

Zest. If he has another name it doesn't matter. The clean-up man--the closing pitcher, if you will--of the Tertullian Society. We clashed last summer and strangely, he felt some kind of camaraderie with me even as he threatened me and everyone I care about. I first met him in the Metropolitan Museum of Art, where he explained the facts of life about those who cross the Tertullians.

I owe him nothing. The last time I saw him was when we were walking out of a warehouse in Westchester County where Joel had been taken by an evil man--Ethan Nelson. Zest, because of the imagined professional camaraderie between us, took over the situation and Nelson, and let us out. But I owe him *nothing*. He is not my friend.

--Look outside your door.

I'm out of bed and going to my second bedroom for my Sig Sauer, then to the door. I'm thinking I need a new system for my weapons to access them more quickly.

Joel is up now and watching me, following me to the front door. I look outside the peephole. Nothing. Suddenly I want new security for this entire apartment. Cameras inside and out.

I stand to the side of the door and open it without getting in front of it. Slowly, looking for traps, wires, explosives, whatever.

There's just a cell phone on the hall floor, in front of the door. I get down and look at it. The screen has a message. *--Text me back.*

I pick it up carefully and look it over. It could be rigged with anything.

I type: *-- What?*

While I'm typing I move to the living room windows and look outside. He could be around, like across the street, watching. I scan the park.

The phone beeps.

-- The job you are doing that involves following a man named Comstock. You need to drop it.

Now I feel cold. I stare at what Zest is saying. Then I type.

--*Is this connected to them?* Meaning, the Tertullians.

--*Yes. Both the persons you followed.*

--*How did you know about me?*

--*I saw you there. I was doing someone a favor. And I figured you were not aware of the situation. It's in your best interest to let it go. No one knows about you being there but me.*

I put the phone down and rub my face, to try to calm myself down. Then go back to the phone.

--*Why are you telling me?*

--*I wanted to extend you a favor.*

I get angry, but anger isn't going to serve. Some things you can't piss on.

--*Thank you.* It hurts to write that.

Joel grabs the phone out my hand to read the messages.

"What do you think? He's telling the truth?"

"Probably. The very fact that somehow, *they* are involved, it's too dangerous."

I take out some tools and dismantle the phone. I wrap it in paper and put it on a butcher block and smash it with a hammer. It's necessary but I admit a little anger goes into it that I even have to hear from Zest again.

Archie hides in the bedroom while I do this. The sound is muffled by the paper but still rattles the counter.

Joel says wryly, "Feel better?"

"No. I'll be back." I pull on some pants and a jacket. "Going to throw it away."

He waits while I take it downstairs, across the street, and dump bits of it in three different trash cans.

Then I come back inside. During this time, I'm thinking, thinking, thinking. I'll make a temporary acquiescence that Zest is being helpful. Why, I can't say.

Joel has fed Archie and is trying to make the kitchen seem normal. I wish for a cigarette, but just lean on the counter from the living room side and watch him. Then I walk around the apartment checking all the rooms, looking for trouble. I have a new device that is supposed to detect bugs. Nothing in the apartment sets it off.

Joel says, "Are you going to tell him? Alex?"

"I don't know. He should be told. But it's risky." Alex knows who the Tertullians are, but doesn't know about Zest, the notes I have from Kent Varney, or what happened in Westchester. He also doesn't know that I never gave up my investigations of them.

"Any electronic communication must be assumed to be unsafe. But meeting him in person is as bad."

"Would they kill him? I don't want him dead, I'm not like that."

"I don't either. So I'll have to tell him." But I know of too many stories, stories Kent Varney had given me, of journalists who had been on to a story and suddenly turned up dead in car accidents or by 'self-inflicted' gunshot. Always with the wrong hand or shot twice, sending a message.

"And he'd listen to you?"

"He would. Wouldn't you, under the circumstances?"

"Yeah...because it's you." Now he's thinking, while drinking coffee. "We can get you to him without anyone following and back without anyone following. You might be seen talking to him, depending."

"Or recorded."

"I have a couple of audio jammers I made. I figured you'd want one. We can test it. And you can go in disguise. Shave, for instance."

"The beard helps. He has a routine, he likes routine. That's good and bad."

"This isn't hard. Do what Zest did. Buy a burner phone. Leave it for him, tell him to come out without his own phone. Wear a basic cover-up. Keep your meeting to five minutes while you're doing something else, like in that park across from his office building."

"And getting the phone to him?"

"Messenger service. I'm your messenger boy. I have an ID somewhere I created. I tested it out a few times."

"Why?"

"Just 'cause. All right, a few times on the street I did stuff like that for people. Simple IDs. It brought me some money. It comes in handy for this work, right?"

"It does now. He should be at the *Herald-Standard*. Let's get this started, then. Get it the fuck over with."

We get moving and shortly thereafter Joel goes into the *Herald-Standard* building with a package addressed to Alex for immediate delivery. Inside is a burner cell with a texted message to go to the park now without his phone. However, I have the audio jammer anyway.

I'm in the small park, which has six benches and several trees, and is sort of an oasis in the middle of a business street. I have on more downgraded, beat-up clothes than usual, including a watch cap under a hooded sweatshirt and dark sunglasses, and I'm pretending to fix a bicycle. It's Joel's, since I don't ride one. I'm just trying not to break it.

It might not work but journalists are as nosy as investigators. A half-hour later, I see him leaving the building for the park. The best part is he doesn't recognize me and is looking around for whoever sent the phone.

He walks by me toward the benches and I say, "It's me."

He stops. I continue looking at the bike through my sunglasses, not at him.

Alex is not stupid, even if he's an idiot. He knows immediately I have a reason for this. He takes out cigarettes and says quietly, "What's going on?"

"You don't have your phone, do you?"

"I'm not worried about..."

"You need to be. Give it to him."

I glance up carefully. Joel, who has changed clothes some, is now next to him with a big dog. The dog is Isabella's. She had come over to meet us and wait with the dog. I'll give her that. She makes a point to help and not ask questions.

Alex frowns. "I'm not..."

"You are. You need to."

Showing some sense, he takes out his cell and hands it to Joel without looking at him. Joel covers that by pretending the dog is giving him trouble. It's a Husky, and *is* giving him some trouble, barking. Joel then walks the dog closer to the people around, who admire the beautiful animal.

I tell Alex, "I'm out of this investigation with your source. And I strongly suggest you drop it as well."

"What makes you say that?"

"I just know."

"Jesus, Gabriel. You just tell me to drop it? Without a reason?"

"I can't tell you why. I can only say that it's deeper than you think. You don't have to listen; that's your choice. But you should."

"Come on. You can trust me to tell me. I have to know."

"Alex, I don't back out of things easily. You know that. I'm saying this isn't something you want to get involved in."

"I find this so strange. Maybe we can work together to find out..."

"I'm out of it. I was never here. I was never anywhere near you. I don't know anything about this."

"What if I--"

"No." I nod at Joel. He comes back with the phone and drops it near Alex's feet, then lets the dog lead him away.

"Are you in danger, Gabriel? Can I help?"

"No; I'm fine. I have to leave."

He starts to reach out to me and stops, bending down to get his phone and grinding out his cigarette. He says while looking at his phone. "How bad is it? Could we meet again to talk about this?"

"Assume the worst. Nothing else to talk about."

"Are you sure you can trust *him*?"

I walk away with the bike without answering.

∞

The rest of the week and weekend was much better. On Monday, I go over to Joel's loft in the afternoon. Danny is with me; he took off today. We had spent some time together like we used to. I don't hold it against him what he said to Alex. We make mistakes, and I know he wouldn't do it again.

He hasn't been to Joel's loft before. They never used to get along, but something went down between them after Joel and I reunited and they are now fairly cordial to each other. That is important to me with regards to both of them.

Isabella and Chris are there. Gloria isn't. Joel paid for her to go to a salon for a few hours to get her out of the way. Isabella is lecturing Joel about something. Danny and I talk on the other side of the room until she's done. Joel is ignoring her anyway, watching us. Then she directs Chris to begin loading things into her SUV. Apparently, someone wants a private show. Danny offers to help take things down to the vehicle.

Even with the extra help, Isabella is still barking orders at Joel to get moving. "I want Churchill impressed enough to tell his friends."

Joel continues to ignore her and lights a cigarette.

"That's who it is, Churchill? He's following through with his invitation?" I keep my voice casual.

Joel meets my eyes briefly. Then shrugs. "You were invited, too. Remember?"

"Yeah, but I'm going to help your mom." Ken called Gloria over the weekend and said he wanted to talk things out with her. She's only going to spend a couple hours with him, but I'm going to be in the area in case of trouble. We insisted she meet him in a public place.

Joel gets up and starts searching through his racks and cabinets. "Yeah, I know. Bad timing. She just had to go see him today. And damn it, I *know* she's going through my stuff. I *know* it. She used to do that when I was a kid."

Isabella says, "Joel, we don't have time..."

"Just *wait* Iz. I don't want her nosing in these." He takes his notebooks down and puts them in the Macy's bag I had brought over. "Take them to the apartment. And this too, Gabriel." He tosses me a switchblade. It's stiletto style, with a telescoping blade.

"I thought you had a hunting knife."

"I have other knives. This is one of those other knives."

He's being a bit of a smartass, and trying to aggravate Isabella, who is waiting for him.

I say, "You afraid your mom will steal it? Go mug some people on the 6 train?"

"I carry it sometimes. If she sees it, she'll ask questions I don't need."

"Maybe you better carry it today. You can impress Churchill."

He comes over and takes the knife. "I could. Watch this."

He clicks open the knife with a *snick*, and holds it by the blade. "Left or right? Right. Third shelf." Then he throws it across the room at one of his wooden storage shelves. It lands in the right side of the third shelf, next to a set of delicate tools.

"Uh huh. That's impressive. Don't ever do that again with me in the room."

"You're a good shot, and I can use knives. We have complementary skills. I can do that thing in *Aliens,* with Bishop and Hudson. Want to try?"

"Let's not and say we did." I go over to pull the knife out of the shelving. "Damned show off."

They all finally take off, and I drive Gloria to Wayne. While she talks with Ken at a restaurant, I watch them through the window. She tells me afterward, as might be expected, that nothing came from the conversation other than Ken getting angry with her when she refuses to come back to him.

Later on that evening, Isabella comes by my apartment with Joel. "I'm dropping him off for you," she tells me, her hand around his waist possessively. Or maybe I just imagine that. She gives me a genuine hug. "I so want you to be at a showing with the paintings of you. It would be very surreal and fourth wall. Take it all off."

"Come on, Iz..." Joel's voice has a warning note.

"I'd like to see the two of you naked together."

I decide to ignore that. "How did this showing go with Churchill?"

"He saw two pieces he liked and bought, and he's thinking of sponsoring a private party for more. He got a little touchy-feely with Joel, but no worries."

Joel briefly glares at Isabella. "She's exaggerating. It's just how he...I mean, I got the impression it's how he is. You know rich people; think they own everything."

I notice Isabella isn't bothered by what he says. She puts her arms around him and rocks her body against him.

I watch this, saying, "Uh huh. He doesn't own *you.*"

"I know that, Gabriel. I can handle myself. I have experience doing so. Iz likes drama, so you have to discount half of what she says. Churchill said he'd like your advice about something; he asked you to email him to set up a talk." He gently separates himself from Isabella and hands me Churchill's card.

"Did he invite you along to that?"

"Joel has to see someone else this week; he has a recording to do in London." Isabella explains that she has set-up some meetings with wealthy patrons in London. Joel is going to be filmed talking about the paintings they buy, and those recordings will be installed under the respective paintings or sculptures, like a museum experience at home.

"And it's this week?"

Isabella shrugs. "Thursday. Sorry it's last minute." She slips her hand in the waistband of his jeans.

"Iz, *time to go.*"

For a second they lock eyes, then she shrugs again and heads for the door. "I'm very proud of you, baby."

I go to lock the door behind her. Isabella kisses me. I like her, but I'm thinking all of us have been sprayed with some kind of jealousy compound. Maybe another MK-ULTRA experiment.

And so, after I lock the door and listen for her getting on the elevator, I turn around and say, "I like your new girlfriend. How long you been together?"

He regards me with a slight smile. "You're such a hypocrite."

"*Excuse* me?"

"You and Danny. In my loft. I see it with you two. You and he had something at one time, didn't you?"

I laugh at that. "We'd kill each other. Besides, I was kind of a player when I was younger."

"I don't believe that for a Goddamned minute. You forget I know you."

I go to my kitchen to get a bottle of water. "You read too much into things."

"No, I don't. When you two are off guard, there's something close between you. Nothing that bothers me, okay? If anything, it makes me understand you and him. I didn't do that with Chris. Maybe we could have, but it was better for us *not* to. And then maybe it was better for you and him to have done that. It has something to do with much he cares about you."

"You see that in everybody I know? How about Michaela? Jim? Or Bob?"

"I notice you didn't say Veronica. You don't hide things that well."

"That isn't something I'll go into, but I'll acknowledge."

"Really?"

I shrug. "Hmmn. Things happen. Did *you* try anything with Veronica?"

Joel sits on the arm of the sofa and takes out his phone to plays with it. "I thought about it briefly last year, when I considered that maybe you and I wouldn't happen and I needed someone to care about me. But although we love each other, it wouldn't have been fair. Anyway, you haven't answered about you and Danny."

"Yeah, I haven't. Because there's nothing to answer."

Joel nods sarcastically. "Okay. I'll just imagine worse than what you tell me, until you do."

"Like you and Isabella?"

"We were fuckbuddies on occasion. It isn't a secret."

"She still wants you."

"She'll get over it. See, *I* can tell you things."

I sit on the bench in front of my keyboards, watching him. "You going to tell me about what Jan left you?"

That gets him. He puts the phone down carefully. "I did. You saw the boxes."

"So you say. And in the same way, I told you about me and Danny. So we're good."

We've checkmated each other. He tries to think of something to say, lighting a cigarette.

I change the subject. "I want you to know I am knocked out by how this is moving forward for you with your work and I'm proud of you too, for what it's worth. I'd just like to be kept in the loop on where you'll be during the week...like *three thousand miles away.*"

"I'm not staying. I'm flying back Monday. I can't really say no to these gigs at this point. Iz has an issue, and I'll talk to her about it."

I can't help but say, "Don't let her get you in the bathroom alone on the plane."

"*Really?*" He stares at me, and I see a sudden fury in his eyes that makes me wish for my own cigarette. "I was outside this apartment watching out for you when that guy was trying to break in here last summer, and you were inside fucking Alex. I saw him walk out the door swinging his dick, and you were protecting him--*before* he decided you were too low-class. I guess at first it was real meeting of the minds, huh? And after all that you're going to act injured because of *my* friend?"

My face turns red; I invest my attention in my water bottle for a few seconds. I guess we still have some issues.

He turns red as well, glancing at me as he plays with his pack of Djarum.

I say finally, "I thought you told me not long ago "*It was how it was.*" Now you're going to bring up shit?"

He exhales. "I guess I'm still angry. Doesn't mean I don't love you. I must feel more secure about us because I was afraid to tell you that, and I tried to pretend it didn't matter. But I guess somewhere it did matter and I'm still angry, yeah, especially when he's still trying to break us up."

"It's not going to happen. What are you still angry about?"

"That you wouldn't give me a chance when I came back. That you treated me like I was *dangerous* but you let me in here, gave me keys, confided in me stuff you wouldn't tell anyone else. I wasn't good enough to fuck, though."

I get up and move closer to him, to the ottoman. "Joel, that is not a fair way to put it. Remember, you came back at the end of July. By December we were together again. That was a pretty short time in the scheme of things. Keep in mind that you did not say *one word* to me for two years before that. Two. Fucking. Years. I called you, I emailed you, I asked Chris to give you messages. Not one damned word in return. You hold people at arm's length and expect them to read your mind...Jesus, *I don't want to do this.* I don't want us to be like this."

We look at each other; he gets up to blow smoke out the window. "I know. I'm not saying it's logical. I just didn't understand what you saw in him."

"It's over. People make mistakes. I don't think this will help us move on and build something if you're going to hold that against me for the foreseeable future."

"I'm not. I swear I'm not. But I can't help my feelings, that I wasn't not good enough. That's me, not you. You see where that comes from now? It's hard for me, but I try. I just don't understand *your* jealousy. Iz isn't trying to get between us. You think she is, but you don't know her. *I* do. We fucked around some. But she wouldn't do anything to jeopardize her business, and she likes you."

I feel more that we've both allowed emotions to take over us. Maybe for a reason. To clear the air and move on.

I'm not ready to admit that, though. "You just said she has issues."

"You know, you *wanted* to meet people in my life. You'll have to deal with how they are like I deal with Danny and Jim." Jim Pollan is another lawyer friend of mine.

"*Touché*. And Bob?"

"Bob doesn't judge me. Veronica and Michaela don't judge me. I give Danny a lot of slack because I have to. Jim not so much--he isn't as bad--but they both think I'm going to get you in trouble. Nonetheless, I give you the benefit of the doubt that you can spend a day with them and not be fucking them."

"Is that so?"

"You do have an ego at times. And you think you can gather everyone in a box and arrange them as you please. As mad as you might be about Alex, you don't see how he's a threat to you. If he apologizes and asks for another favor, you'll do it. Don't look at me like that. You think I don't know from my past work what people do to play someone? You aren't casual about sex, so you have emotions. That's why I'm angry. Not for the sex, but because you were intimate with him. He'll use that against you because he wants you for a pet. If he can't have you, he'll just try to screw us up. I guarantee you he's said something about me to you already. Probably that I'm ruining your life."

I really want a cigarette. Gum just doesn't work for this although I unwrap a stick from a pack on the coffee table.

Joel stares out the window. But I see in the reflection he's watching me watching him.

I think about what he said. I don't want the rest of the evening to just be us railing at each other.

"You haven't ruined my life. You made it worth the effort to keep living."

He blushes once more, but doesn't respond.

"I'm not talking to Alex again, period. Nothing. Not a text, not a call. If he's drowning in the East River as I'm walking by, he'll have to call 911."

Another couple of minutes of silence go by. I think about all he's told me, and how the past plays into how both of us handle life. About the lies and what those did to him.

I watch him pick up Archie and hold the cat in his arms. We're not sure how to proceed with each other. Then I make a decision.

"Okay, so. There's no reason not to tell you. Danny and I very briefly hooked up when we were 16. We didn't have anyone but each other to be close to; there was no Gay-Straight Alliance at John Philip Souza High. We were really close to each other almost as soon as we met. Not just because we were the gay ones. We had each other's back. Anyone fucked with one of us, the other would come running to help. If one of us got caught alone for a beat-down, the other would be searching for the fuckers who did it. Having someone's back like that is rare and that's why it's important for me to be that kind of friend."

I pause for a moment, thinking about it. Joel is facing me now, listening intently.

"My uncle knew about me, but he was very protective like a mother. He didn't want me on the streets getting laid. No one was good enough for me. I'm not kidding. He knew everybody in the Village East and West, and I had people I didn't even know spying on me if I was in the neighborhood. He was very community-oriented; far more than I've been. He had a lot of friends and respect. He was tough; Golden Gloves in college. He'd been in street fight after street fight, just like me. He was tough enough that no one wanted to cross him in his community either from respect or because he'd kick their ass. So he was a real cockblocker in a sense."

I have to smile at that. "And Danny had his entire family to handle in his situation. You know that story. And so back then because we were close and had no one to turn to, it seemed natural-- teenage emotions and sex drive. It didn't last, obviously. A matter of weeks...and we almost lost our friendship over how we couldn't handle our jealousies, especially when we were hiding the whole thing from our moms and classmates. That jealousy seems real familiar right now."

Joel lights another cigarette, plays with Archie while I talk.

I continue. "Danny's thing about not being able commit to anyone longer than overnight was true back then, too. But we both had fragile egos. And afterward no one I was ever involved with gave me the sense that it would last, like indefinitely. You are the only person I ever truly desired to make it last...the only person I would go to the end of the world for to make it work. The only one I can see infinity with. Is there anything I can tell you that will make you feel less angry with me?"

"You have. It's anger at myself, how I have trouble dealing with things. I have to find my role in your life."

"You don't have a 'role.' We're together, that's what counts."

"I guess. Thank you for sharing about Danny. It makes a lot of sense, how you tell it."

I wait as he nervously scratches Archie's ears and inhales deeply.

"So, uh...Jan, he left me eleven million dollars."

He looks at the floor then at me.

Jesus fucking Christ. I figured it was a few hundred thousand. No wonder he was reluctant to mention it, after many occasions of listening to my rants on class and money issues.

It hits me what kind of man Joel is. Jan left him that money rather than whatever family he had or even charity. Jan wanted Joel taken care of and knew he'd be responsible enough to handle it.

"Guess I got me a *rich* boyfriend, then. Dinner's on you."

He smiles.

∞

Thursday I exchange emails with Churchill and he calls me that evening. He wants me to check on an employee who may be selling inside information to a competitor. I get the retainer and talk to Veronica and Geneva about surveillance.

Joel texts me all day about what he is doing in London. --*Do you want to come here for a weekend?*

I'd like to; I've never been. But I have work to do. Nonetheless, I'm prepared to pick them up from JFK when they come back on Monday. But then Ken calls me that morning.

"I want to talk to you."

"Fine, what's on your mind?"

"Not on the *phone*. Just come here to the house."

"Why? What do you want to talk about?"

I can practically hear him gritting his teeth. "About what you said. Look, I have the day off today. I can't talk about this with Gloria, she wouldn't understand."

"Okay, I wouldn't bring her. But I'm picking Joel up from the airport now. Can this wait?"

"No! You said you wanted to help, didn't you? I don't want Joel involved in this. He...he doesn't need to know. I mean, I don't want him to know. Him or Gloria. You're such a hotshot, can you deal with that?"

I'd like to hang up, or maybe throw the phone in his face if he were here. But that isn't going to help. "You want to talk right this minute?"

"Yeah, 'cause I have to do something *fast*. It's not just me, you see. That's where I need...I need your advice."

Huh. It's quite a turnaround. While I don't trust him, the prospect of getting information is too good to turn down. I do some of my own teeth-gritting and say, "Okay. Where do you want me to meet you?"

"At the house. Don't tell anyone."

"I got you. I'll be there in an hour-hour and a half."

I hang up and text Joel about what I'm doing. He won't get the text until he turns on the phone after the plane lands.

I set up my work phone. It has an app that records what's going on even if the phone appears to be turned off. Just to be sure that the recording is preserved, it's sent to a cloud-based function Joel set up. So should the phone be taken out and stomped on, the recording is still extant.

∞

"He's on his way," Ken tells the other two men.

Meese nods. He looks at Cody. As per Cody's mental quirk, he is staring with fascination at the knife he holds. A Bark River Bravo III. It's an 11-inch blade and suitable for setting up a campsite--to hack small limbs of a tree or debone an animal. He also has a khukuri, a Nepalese knife with an inward-curving blade. Cody's like a kid at Christmas; he doesn't know which to play with first.

Meese rolls his eyes, but not so Cody could actually see. The man is dangerous and Meese knows better than to get on his bad side. Cody is already annoyed at Ken for having to do this. He's not really upset with Meese. Adding Ross onto the tab just gives him more fun to have, before they have to clean it up. Meese knows with Cody to just indulge the monster.

Cody has been to Ken's house once before. He remembers that Ken has no weapons except one. A shotgun hidden on top of a wood and glass cabinet in the living room. When Ken has his back turned, Cody pulls on a pair of thin black gloves and casually reaches up--he doesn't have to reach very high at 6'5, and inside the depression behind the cabinet's decorative scroll. The shotgun is still there, a little dusty. Just good to know.

"I don't like it done here," Ken finally says. Knowing he can't change what's set in motion, but still. Meese thinks Ross needs to be taken out so he'll be taken out. It's rough; it'll be rough for Joel. But hopefully this shuts up both Joel and Gloria and life goes back to normal.

Meese doesn't even look at him. "We'll clean the place, dump him in the Passaic. Nothing traces back here."

"If you use those," Ken tells Cody, "He'll bleed out all over my rug."

Cody raises his eyes from his knives. As Ken is going to go next right after Ross is killed, bleeding out isn't a problem. However, Ken has no idea of the real plan in action.

"I told you, take him to the kitchen. It's tile. Tile cleans. This is my expertise, right?"

Ken nods and looks to the front window. Cody and Meese exchange glances.

Ken's actually biting his nails.

"Cut it out. Don't look so nervous."

"What if he can tell?"

"Tell what? All right, if he thinks you're too nervous tell him it's because you're going to admit to something. Be angry with him. He'll believe it. He's not a rocket scientist, and he's probably eager to get dirt on you."

Meese is perfectly calm. Cody has his knives and can use them. They have to use something other than a gun because of the noise. Ross wouldn't likely meet them somewhere out of the way. He's not that stupid. So they have to be careful of noise. Cody won't do something sensible like strangling because he wants blood. Again, Meese isn't going to argue. It's the endgame that counts.

At least it will be quick for Ken. Cody is probably a sadist but Meese isn't. Ross can bleed out slower, so long as he can't yell. It's what fits the plan.

But it will bring Gloria back here. And Joel will have to come along, to be with her. The sheer emotional storm that will take over-- Joel is a sensitive boy--means Meese steps in at just the right time to help them out.

Joel will likely be sad about Gabriel Ross. No doubt the son of a bitch has some kind of psychological hold on Joel. With how Meese's plan is set up it will be clear that Ross and Ken got into a fight. The police will think Ross probably threatened Ken. Ken's calling the cops when Joel and Ross came over was good. That sets the narrative. Ross stabs Ken, and Ken defends himself. Unfortunately, both die before help arrives.

Cody's ridiculous knives may draw some attention, but deal with what you have. Meese found out Ross writes about Eastern religions, so a Nepalese knife...you could buy that he would have one. Something like that.

Joel will realize then how close he was to danger. That this worked for the best. And now he's free. Free from the father who kept him from Meese for so long, and free from the fucker trying to corrupt him.

It may take a bit but Meese anticipates Joel turning to him for comfort. What he needs to do to pick up his life now. And what they can do together.

Don't get lost in that, Larry. It's show time. He puts on rubber surgical-type gloves and stretches his fingers.

Ken McFadden wanders into his kitchen and now stares at the floor. *He's going to be killed here. A man is going to be killed here.* Ken was so angry the day Gloria left. And then again when he talked to her and she refused to come back. His anger made him call Meese.

He thinks of Carson Smith. He was only threatened. Would they kill him too? Cody might. He likes that. Meese said they'd have to think about it. But this thing with Ross, Larry says, *this* is necessary.

He'll find out everything. We can't let that happen. You've gone too far, we've all gone too far. Just let Cody take care of it. That fucker would probably try to blackmail you. He's scum. You're too smart to let that happen, Ken.

And yes, it's this or prison or something else terrible. It's just been a whirlwind since Gloria left. But now the anger is ebbing, leaving him with a strange feeling. Even knowing what Larry says is true...Ken keeps thinking, *a man's going to be killed in my house.*

∞

I park outside Ken and Gloria's house. My phone rings. It's Joel.

"What's going on?"

"You landed okay and everything?"

"Yeah, baby, we did. We're getting a taxi; it's okay. I just don't understand what my dad wants."

"Neither do I, but I want to find out."

I notice that in the house directly across the street, a curtain twitches. I'm pretty sure I see Dell for a brief instant. Must be wondering what's up.

"I don't like it," Joel says. "Wait for me."

"I'm already here. I won't talk to him long. I'm thinking he has some kind of secondary scheme he wants me to buy. But whatever bullshit he tells me may lead us to what's really going on. I have the recording device on."

"Oh, good. I was going to tell you."

I laugh. "I'll check in with you. Don't worry."

"Don't hang up...we're in the cab now. Keep me on."

"While I'm talking to him?"

"You can do that." He explains what I need to set up. I take care of it.

"I got it, but don't say anything so he can hear. He might get mad if he finds out."

Joel mutters something. I see John Dell's curtains twitch again. "Well, just come out and say hi." I tell Joel that Dell is spying on me.

"Fucking cops."

"I know. Time for me to go in." I set up the phone to look like it's shut off, and get out the car.

Ken has the door open before I even get to the porch. *Anxious, aren't you?*

I see some kind of hesitation in his eyes. He jerks his head to indicate I should come in.

"We can talk in the kitchen," he says.

Even though it is not a warm day, he's sweating. He turns suddenly. "How do I know you're not recording this?"

I shouldn't say it but I can't help being a smartass. "You want me to strip so you can see?"

"No!" He draws back. But frowns at me. I'm wearing a plain white rough weave button-down shirt over my jeans. I lift the shirt so he can see--no wires.

He looks at my pocket. "What's there?"

I reach into my front pockets. "Wallet, keys, phone. It's turned off, as you can see."

He swallows hard. "So...so...we should go into the kitchen to talk."

He starts to lead me there. I look into the living room on the left. Nothing. I can even see up the stairs. Nothing.

And yet. The feeling something isn't right. Whether it's him sweating and looking back at me or my own experience and instincts. I stop. "How do I know *you* aren't recording this?"

That throws him. He stares back at me. We're almost to the dining room. "Are you kidding? What...what...what do you think this is?"

I stare hard at him. "Why don't you tell me what this is, Ken?"

At the same time, I bring my senses to try to feel if someone else is here. Something is wrong and the more I stare at Ken, the more he shows it.

"Why are you nervous?"

He has difficulty speaking. "I...I have to tell you things I don't want to. I'm embarrassed. Goddamn it, it's not fair."

He looks away and a trickle of sweat runs down the side of his face.

"Okay, I understand that." And it could be true. But it's not. I have 25 years of being jumped in various circumstances to give me heightened senses. When I don't move his eyes widen.

"So come on then."

"Yeah, sure." I lean closer to him and say very softly, "What is it? Who's back there?"

His eyes lock with mine. He opens his mouth. "Let's..."

I shake my head. "What, Ken? What did you set up?"

His mouth quivers. He finally says in the same low tone, "*Go!* Just go."

I draw up and look around quickly. I don't see anything, but he seems close to freaking out.

"Call it off."

"Go! *Now.*"

From his face I realize whatever it is can't be called off.

I put my hand on him. "You come with me."

He shakes his head.

I feel something behind me and jump to the side. I turn to see a very tall man in black. He's come through the living room and circled to stand between me and the front door.

He's so tall he blocks the sunlight from the front door window. He's dressed in black, including a black hood over his head and some kind of glasses over the eyeholes.

In his hand he has a long, curved knife. He slashes at me and I jump back again, just missing the blade.

Something my dad says comes back to me in this moment. He's the same height I am. "*Tall men use height to intimidate. They expect you to run, to freeze in fear, or hit them in the gut. You have to use their body against them.*"

The best thing to do in a knife fight is leave. But he's already slashing again. By instinct I use a variation of a Krav Maga defense: ducking away from the knife, grabbing his arm and twisting while moving to his side and behind him. At the same time, I kick his kneecap. Not straight across--down. With a big man, my father said, use gravity. Up or down.

The big man actually loses his grip on the knife and I take it and throw it as hard as I can away from us, in the dining room. It's too large to try to use it to fight him.

I can only hold him for seconds then I back away from him to the dining room. He follows trying to grab me.

The fighting I'm trained in isn't good for everything. Baguazhang is an art that's good for multiple opponents. Boxing is good against a person similar in size. Otherwise, the best defense is not to be there. But still, I remember--leverage. Make them put their body in unnatural positions. Use angles. He's trying to grab my head and my arms and I'm moving to the side to throw him off balance. I swing a chair at him; not his head, his legs.

He pauses momentarily from that and I use the opportunity to get in the living room. Ken is suddenly right behind me. "Stop! Just call it off!"

He's yelling at the big man but the big man isn't listening. If I was Jason Bourne, I'd crash out the front window. But I'm me; I want to get to the hallway and the front door.

Ken seems to be going with me. Until he stops and holds his hands up. "Call it off!"

I look back. The giant suddenly reaches up to the top of a cabinet and brings down a shotgun. In a swift move he shoots Ken in the chest.

His blood splatters my face. The noise deafens me.

Pounding on the front door. "Open up! This is the police!"

It's Dell.

Then something hits the back of my head.

∞

Meese pauses after hitting Ross with the butt of his service weapon. "We have to leave. Go out the back kitchen window, through the woods, down to the creek. I'll pick you up."

"And him?" Cody points to Ross.

"Back-up plan. Go!"

Dell yells, "Open the door. Put down your weapons now!" He's trying to see through the front door window.

Being careful not to be in view of the hallway, Meese puts the shotgun by Gabriel's prone body. And puts Gabriel's hand in the trigger guard.

∞

Eight

George Santayana said, "Those who do not remember the past are condemned to repeat it."

∞

Monday, April 11, Continued
Whitestone Bridge, 11:07 am

IN THE TAXI the terrified driver stares in the rear-view mirror at Isabella trying to talk to the police on her phone while Joel is yelling into his.

Isabella says, "They're going over. Can you call somebody?"

"I don't want to hang up." He stares wildly out the window. "Get your car. I need to go there."

Isabella gives her address to the driver.

Joel then uses Isabella's phone to call Michaela. She can't understand exactly what's going on, but once getting the address she says, "I'm on my way."

Joel hears something from his phone. Someone muttering, and a pounding sound.

"Gabriel? Are you there?"

He hears Gabriel say faintly, "Someone hit me..."

The pounding sound ends with a boom, like a door being slammed open. Another voice in the background. Joel recognizes it as Dell's. "Put that down! Stay on the ground and put your hands behind your head!"

The call ends.

∞

Forty minutes later Isabella is driving to New Jersey, trying to stay calm, smoking, watching Joel.

He's on the phone with Michaela. She arrived at his parents' house ten minutes ago.

"Where is he?"

"In a police car. I'm outside the car. He can hear me. No one else is here."

"Why is he in the car? What happened?"

A pause. "He's in custody right now. Your father was shot."

"I heard a gun. Is he dead?"

"Yes. I'm sorry."

"Okay. Who did it? Wait, they think this was Gabriel?"

"He saw what happened and told me, and I told them. Another man was there. But when the cops walked in the shotgun was in Gabriel's hands."

"No. No, there was someone there. He was knocked out."

"I know, he told me. Hold on the best you can. This is something that needs to be straightened out. Clearly whoever did this dropped the gun on Gabriel to make it look otherwise."

"He was on the phone with me the whole time."

"I know he didn't do it. I need to take care of some things and take some pictures."

"Of what?"

"Evidence. Gabriel's face. The blood on it. The mark on his head from the gun."

"Jesus. Can I talk to him?"

"Not at the moment. They have some kind of forensics unit coming from the state police and I want to make sure they do this right. They aren't going to let him out the car, anyway."

"I'm on my way."

"Tell me where you're going."

Joel thinks about it. "The parking lot of the police station."

"Check to see how your mom is. Someone might be calling her now."

Joel ends the call and stares out the window. Isabella takes his hand, and he starts crying.

∞

Michaela arrives at the east side of Wayne, in the little plaza that holds the police station. She's a minute ahead of the police who are bringing Gabriel in.

And she sees a SUV pull up. Joel jumps out of the passenger side and runs to her.

At the same time, the police cruiser pulls around.

"That's him," Michaela says. "They'll go around the side."

Without a word he runs around the side of the building.

Michaela hurries to catch him before he gets in trouble.

The car stops and Dell gets out the front seat.

"Joel, you can't be here." Dell's voice is kind. "You're going to have to leave; you can go in the station."

Joel stares in the back seat. Gabriel looks at him. *It's okay,* he says silently.

"Let him go. He didn't do anything." It's so crazy, Joel can't believe he's saying it.

Dell sighs. "Do you know about your father?"

"Yes."

"Have you told Gloria?"

"Yeah. I told her to wait for me at my place. But there was someone else in the house."

"Who?"

"I don't know." Joel looks at Dell imploringly. "Please."

Michaela takes his arm. Dell glances at her. "We're undergoing an investigation. I need you to step away, Joel. You don't want any trouble for him."

"But this is wrong!"

A couple of officers get out of another car. They silently move closer in case something happens.

"He'll be okay," Michaela says. "We're not interfering, Detective."

Dell nods at the other officers. "Joel, we'd like you to come in and make a statement, okay?"

And that freezes him. The idea of going in the station. Where Meese is or was.

In that frozen moment, Dell opens the back door and takes Gabriel out. His hands are cuffed.

Joel's eyes go over him. The blood dried on his face and shirt.

"Don't worry." Gabriel says. It's meaningless. They are worried. But it's the most he can say. Joel holds back from saying anything else. Gabriel looks over his shoulder at Joel before he goes in the back door of the station.

"Oh Jesus."

The tears come back. Michaela puts her arms around him. "Come on. Come with me."

Joel sits in her car and talks to her. Isabella waits outside her own car, smoking.

Michaela then goes inside to speak with the officers. At the moment, Gabriel is under arrest. The county prosecutor in Paterson is being called in.

From her conversation with Dell, Michaela gets the police perspective. Gabriel was known to have had a conflict with Ken McFadden. The police were called to that conflict. The shotgun was in Gabriel's hands. People are more likely to be killed by someone they know. Easy to imagine that Gabriel, a man with a record for assault, might kill his boyfriend's father in anger. No one else was seen in the house, other than by Gabriel.

Michaela made sure to point out that the blood splatter on Gabriel's face was a fine mist type--clearly indicating that it was front spatter from Ken's exit wound. And therefore, it would have been a little impossible to achieve shooting Ken from the front and get that kind blood splatter. They'll be testing Gabriel's hands for nitrates, which may or may not help. But Dell agreed to allow a blood splatter expert to come by and take pictures.

She returns to Joel, who's still waiting in the car with Isabella. "They want to talk to you."

"Can you go with me to talk to them?"

"All right, so long as you understand that a conflict of interest could exist—I'd be remiss if I didn't tell you that."

"That's fine." He falls silent, lighting a cigarette.

"You want to go in and talk to them now?"

The look on his face when he glances at the station tells her 'no.'

"We can discuss what to tell them. But for now, he's okay. He wants you to know that."

Joel looks toward the building. Is he somewhere that he can look out the window? "What's going to happen?"

"He'll have an initial arraignment in municipal court where he receives a Complaint notifying him of the charges and he enters his Not Guilty plea. Then it goes to a grand jury for indictment. That could take months."

"Bail?"

"Municipal Court will deny it. I can apply again at County Court."

"I can take care of the bail."

"You won't need to. He won't get bail for murder."

"He has to get out. Can you challenge a denial?"

"Of course. But don't get your hopes up."

"Do that, please. Whatever you need to do, please do it. I'll take care of you. I'll write you a check right now."

"You don't have to. I wouldn't let Gabriel have anything but the best. I'm going to call the blood expert to come over today."

"Good. Is he going to be held here?"

"He'll go to Paterson. He'd be held for a little while with some other new arrivals. He won't go to general pop right away."

"Jesus, Paterson. That hellhole."

"I know. If I can find another solution..."

Joel regards the police station. "Who's the detective on this? Dell?"

"Yes. What's wrong, Joel? You look scared to death."

She can see it on me.

He tries to speak. It's simple. *I know someone. A detective who was friends with my father. He abused me. I'm afraid I'll see him again. Now I'm afraid of what he'll do.* But the words won't come.

She puts both her hands on his head. "Something's bothering you. You can tell me later. You can't do anything here. Let me go tell him you're taking care of things for him, right? See about your mom, then you need to tell people what happened—especially Veronica, to handle the business, and Danny and Jim and Bob."

"I told Gabriel they thought I'd get him in trouble," he says dully.

"Bullshit. This isn't anyone's fault but who killed your dad."

"And Gabriel *did* see this person."

"Yeah. He said the man was big. Gabriel's kind of fuzzy on it, but he was dressed in black with a mask. So he didn't see the man's face, but he's at least 6'5. You'd think he'd be noticed."

The faintest idea comes into Joel's head that just maybe, he's seen that person too. A long time ago.

∞

Wednesday, April 13
Paterson, New Jersey, 2 pm

I'm waiting to see what's next at the Passaic County Jail. I was processed at Wayne on Monday; I was processed again here in Paterson yesterday. I've gone through the strip search, which is routine. Not the first time I've done it. I already had a medical eval with the personnel here to determine if I have TB or STDs, or if I'm insane/suicidal. I've been interviewed about gang affiliation. Everything was routine. They left me in a cell by myself until I was to be put into the general population.

The only way to handle it is not to freak out. Let the process go along until the error is rectified.

Today, three correctional officers have just told me I'm going back to the medical facility. They walk me in a pattern then stop at a holding room. I sense something's wrong when only one of them takes me in the empty room.

This guy says flatly, "We asked you about who you know and who you're working with."

"No one."

"Why are you so upset about being asked that?"

I look around the room for a camera. All of these rooms and all transfers are supposed to be on camera.

"I want my attorney here. Right now."

"You seem to be getting upset over this issue," he intones. He goes up to me and rips the jumpsuit, from my shoulder on down my chest. He's dispassionate about it. I just stay still. If this is on camera eventually someone will see it.

He continues until he basically rips the suit off me. It takes some doing, difficult with me being cuffed.

When the suit is around my feet and I'm just naked and standing there he says, "You're getting too upset over what you might be holding and who for, and threatening me. Threatening yourself." His voice is flat yet strained.

"Is that what the story is supposed to be? Who told you to do this? I haven't done anything against you people."

He looks away for a second. I get the idea this is a job. No more, no less. He may not even want to be here.

Which doesn't make it easier when the baton goes against my ribs. I hear the other officers come in.

Five minutes later I'm strapped down to some kind of restraining device, coughing and trying not to choke to death from what they sprayed in my face, and being taken to the medical facility.

The blood is pounding so bad in my head...a migraine coming on from the blows or the mace. I can barely hear whatever they're lying to the medical people about...

∞

Thursday, April 14
Canal Street, 6:00 pm

"Joel, I don't understand..."

Joel and his mother are in his loft. He knows she's still in shock from Ken being killed. Joel, by comparison, is nearly out of his mind with worry. Especially as Gabriel has not called him, and when Joel went to the Passaic County Jail yesterday, he was told Gabriel wasn't allowed visitors. Michaela's looking into why.

He's also had to handle the Wayne police and Passaic County prosecutor's office having the NYPD executing a search warrant on Gabriel's apartment. He was barely able to get Archie out in time before they showed up. He took the cat to his loft, and then went back to try to straighten up the mess the police made. That search infuriates him.

Right now, Joel is trying to counter his worry with action. But even as he takes care of things that Gabriel can't, like Archie, he stays with his mother, trying to 'be there' for her grief and other mixed feelings.

Her guilt is palpable. "I asked you to investigate him, and this happened."

Joel doesn't have time for what he feels is unnecessary guilt. "Not your fault. What he did, he did."

She frowns at him. "He's your father."

"So what? He didn't want to be." Joel does feel a little bad. Because he's human. The human capacity for regret. *Things didn't have to be this way.*

Gloria switches subjects. "You really feel Gabriel did not do this."

"I *know* Gabriel didn't do it. He doesn't kill people. Ever. You don't know him like I do. He doesn't have a knife like the one they found. He doesn't like knives. Michaela, our attorney, says the blood splatter--sorry--shows he was nowhere near Dad with the gun. He should be out now."

"Why isn't he, then?"

"Your friend Dell says when he broke the door in, Gabriel had hold of the shotgun. That doesn't mean shit, but since his fingers were on it that was enough to put him in custody."

Gloria tries to take his hand. "Don't be mad. John doesn't know Gabriel. I'm sure if you talk to him, he'll help."

Joel draws away from her and gets up. "I don't talk to cops."

"But John is a friend...he's called..."

"He's not *my* friend."

"Larry called too..."

Joel whirls around, scaring her. "What the fuck does he want?"

"He was checking in on me. He wants to talk about what happened."

"Don't say a Goddamned word to either one of them."

"Joel, what...what's the matter? What is it with Larry?"

He lights up one of his cloves. "You don't see, do you?"

And even though she hates the smoking, she puts her arm around him. "Joel, I don't understand. But with your father dead, we have to be here for each other. Did Larry do something to you? Please tell me. I need to know...for what's between us."

Joel looks her in the eyes for a long minute. He doesn't want to tell her. He wants to tell her.

From how he stares at her, Gloria becomes uncomfortable as if she realizes what's coming. But still she meets his eyes. "I have to know. I can't let you just suffer from this alone."

Joel turns away. She keeps her hands on him.

"I've had this...lived with this alone since I was 15. He raped me on his boat. Like, a couple weeks before Dad threw me out. And he did it again, and he brought in his friends the second time, to sell me to them. He made me have sex with them, too."

When he looks back at her, he sees the blood draining from her face.

"Why didn't you..."

"Why didn't I tell you? Well, you hero-worshipped him and thought I was making your life miserable, so who would you have believed? Dad sure has hell wouldn't have believed me. Instead, Meese tells you I'm a prostitute, and that you believe. Also, I *did* tell you. Right before Dad kicked me out, I told you and asked you for help. Do you remember now?"

Gloria starts crying. She falls prone on his small couch from the weight of what she heard.

Joel gets up and stares out his window at the buildings across Canal Street. For a moment, her tears have no effect on him other than satisfaction. To finally have this shit out in the open. She's crying; *he's* the one who went through this.

The sensation of coldness fills him to where he feels nothing. But he's not a person who feels nothing. Even the old Numbness doesn't come back as often anymore. The coldness in him begins to evaporate almost as soon as he feels it. He can't believe he actually feels sorry for her for having to hear this and realize what a fucking bad job she did as a mother.

What happened with Meese did not take away his humanity; did not define him as a person, did not mark him as a lifetime victim. He could have become too hard to feel, but he isn't. He finds some empathy for her. He's gotten past what happened to him, mostly. Saying it out loud to Gabriel and now her helps with that. But it'll take her time to be able to deal with it, once the guilt hits. He draws hard from his cigarette and walks back to her. She tries to say she's sorry through her tears.

Joel sits next to her and puts his arms around her. "It's okay now. It's over."

Gloria digs in her purse for tissues and gasps. Joel sees that the picture of Meese is still in her purse. Meese and Joel standing nearby with Tim, and a couple other boys.

"Give it to me," he says.

Her face turning sorrowful, she hands it to him. Joel looks at it for a long moment, then starts ripping it. Crossways, crossways again, and again and again and again, until it's in tiny pieces. Then he drops those in a stone ashtray on a table, and takes out his lighter.

Both of them watch the pieces turn black and become ash.

∞

Friday, April 15
Newark, NJ 8:45 am

Michaela opens her office door. She rents a large private office in a suite controlled by a divorce and family law firm. "Come on in."

When Joel and Veronica are inside, she hugs them briefly, seeing the expression on his face. "Can I get you something?"

Joel shakes his head. Veronica says, "I'll get him tea. He should have some."

Veronica starts using the Keurig machine.

Joel asks Michaela, "What's happening with him? Did you find out why I can't see him?"

"Yes. Okay. First off, I gave them the recording from the phone. The prosecutor said it didn't prove that another person was there. You hear Gabriel and your father talking--I can spin it as Gabriel trying to help, but the prosecutor says it could just as easily be a fight just between the two of them."

She rolls her eyes. "Anyway. More serious. You know that reputation he now has? Here in Jersey, it's that he's some kind of gun for hire. This rumor got around the jail, and the admin feels that makes him a security risk. They put him in 23-hour ad-seg."

"He didn't start the rumor. He just takes advantage of it."

"Which has kind of backfired. All right. I know this isn't really his fault. Remember I told you that the prosecutor would weigh the evidence? I thought the forensics would spring him, but the prosecutor heard of this reputation that he has and thinks Gabriel set this up about your father. The first bail hearing went nowhere; I have another hearing on the 27th. We'll see what happens."

"Ad-seg, what is that? Administrative Segregation. I got it. They think he's gang affiliated."

"Possibly. But more likely just a hardcore criminal. Now for the second part of the story. You can't see him because he's under psychiatric evaluation and observation."

"For *what?*"

Michaela snorts. "Supposedly, they're concerned he's suicidal. He isn't. They've given me trouble, but I've seen. But he's not allowed regular visitors, as you found out."

"What the hell does that mean, suicidal?"

Michaela watches him closely. "Okay. As a new inmate, he's held separate from the general population for a bit. That's normal. But on Wednesday, he's suddenly pulled into the medical unit. They say he flipped out; afraid he was going to be searched, like he was hiding something. He tried to get away from the officers. The officers claim he ripped his jumpsuit off and started acting violent, and saying he was going to hang himself. So he's locked down 24/7 in an isolation cell."

Joel takes this in, biting his nails. "I went there Wednesday morning. They didn't tell me anything about what happened. He didn't do that. I know he didn't."

"Of course not. I went there after you called me. I saw him...I'm going to try to have this investigated."

"Is he okay?"

She sighs. "It's been rough. I can tell they beat on him; self-defense, they said. You think I'm not mad? This is fucking Passaic County, one of the most corrupt counties in New Jersey. I'm going to try to get him transferred. I might have luck there. The emergent judge for this week happens to know my dad, who used to be a prosecutor in Bergen County. With what's going on in the news, the federal investigation and the ACLU lawsuit..."

The Passaic County Jail is routinely over capacity by about 150 inmates. Single-inmate cells house three people. The dorm areas have no space; inmates sleep on the floor, some within feet of a toilet. The jail is so vermin-infested inmates have to cover their faces when they sleep so as not to have a rat or roach get in their mouth. The ventilation system is horribly inadequate, putting inmates at medical risk. The jail has been cited for fire code violations numerous times, and the ACLU has reported that the inmates are forced to deal with incredibly unsanitary conditions. Like many other county jails, Passaic County houses inmates from outside the county in order to generate revenue. In 2008, a federal judge was so disgusted by the situation, she reduced the sentences of some federal inmates as the conditions were too punitive. Soon after, all federal inmates were removed.

Veronica says, "We need some press on this. I'll call Mankiewitz."

"We should call Clark, too. Where would he be transferred?"

"Back to Wayne, most likely. See what happens at the bail hearing after that. Joel, you haven't spoken to the Wayne police as yet for that statement. Can we arrange that?"

She notes Joel's face now frozen in fear.

Veronica says, "Honey, what's wrong?"

Joel picks up the mug and stares in it. "Uh...I can't go there. I can't. There's....there's...I can't."

Michaela knows this is unusual for him. She reaches across the desk and touches his arm. "Someone in the jail? In the police department. A cop?"

He nods. "Uh, he's...his name is Meese. He...he..." Even though he was able to matter-of-factly tell his mother, now it's become the stumbling block again.

Michaela says gently, "This man is a cop at the Wayne PD?"

"A detective. Larry Meese." He brings his eyes to hers, almost crying. "He knew my father. He..."

"Did something to you."

"Yeah. He...I can't talk about it. But he lied to my parents after. It's why I was thrown out."

"Larry Meese. He was there at the scene."

Joel's eyes widen. "What do you mean?"

Michaela gets up now, and does her own pacing in the room. "He says he wanted to check on your father. He said he's Ken's friend and he was worried."

Joel makes a noise somewhere between a cough and choking.

"Detective Dell was across the street. He went over to see what was going on and when he heard the gun, started knocking at the door. He says Larry Meese came up to the house to see what was going on."

Joel shakes his head. "Dell may live in that neighborhood but Meese doesn't. That's too much a coincidence."

"Meese isn't a detective anymore, I remember that. He's..." She checks on her computer. "Undersheriff in charge of corrections for Passaic County. Lawrence Meese."

Across from her, Joel's intake of breath is so sharp she's afraid he's having a panic attack.

The look between them says the same thing. Meese being in the Department of Corrections has to be connected to what happened to Gabriel.

"This was set up," Joel says. "The whole thing is *set up*. We have to get him out of there."

"What do you think happened?"

"We were looking into what my father may have been doing. Mom was worried he was in trouble. He's connected to Meese through some dummy company, and I just remember the two of them planning something when I was young. Some kind of scheme. It might have gone on for years. Dad's job was good for that to happen."

"And Meese in law enforcement. I know the game." Michaela picks up her own mug.

Veronica says, "So if Meese was conspiring with your dad, and Gabriel was looking into what your dad may have been doing..."

"He might have called Meese. And then Meese would know we were investigating him. God only knows what my mother told him on top of that." Joel feels a tremor in his body from the realization. "He knows I'm here. He *knows* who Gabriel is. He probably knows I went to see him in the jail."

Veronica gets up and puts her hands on Joel's shoulders, to comfort him.

"Could Meese have been the killer?"

"Gabriel said the man he saw was really tall."

Joel says, "Meese is maybe 6 feet, but not over that. I feel like someone else could be involved. Meese wouldn't expose himself like that to kill someone. He'd have help. I keep thinking I might have seen this person way back when. The height. But no names. It would have been brief."

"It scares me now." Michaela stares at her computer screen. "I was angry, I was going to get a lawsuit going, but knowing this...people who aren't crazy can be made crazy in the Special Housing Units."

"I think it's worse than that. He's in real danger. What can we do?"

"Call the press, like you said. Let's see if we can get some light on this just to make sure nothing further happens. I'll put in a motion today with the emergent judge. I think I can talk him into a transfer until the bail hearing. He really liked my father. I'll go see Gabriel too, so that he doesn't lose touch."

"What about bail?"

"Unlikely, Joel. It's a murder charge."

Joel falls silent, thinking. "I need to make a call. I might have to look into something. Michaela, let me know when the bail hearing is."

"Even if it happens, it'll be high."

"That, thank God, is not something I need to worry about."

∞

Friday, April 15, Continued
Englewood, NJ 11:22 am

An hour later, Joel is in a private office in a geometric modern building on the edge of the city.

Travis Churchill smiles at him. Billy Strayhorn is playing in the background. Joel knows this is for effect.

"Did you want to follow up to see how the paintings are being framed?"

"No, I trust you on that. I wanted to see you about a different situation. I need some help."

"I'm very glad to see you again," Churchill says. "A little strange calling you Joel, but it fits you better than 'Dylan,' when I think about it. Did Jan know?"

Joel remembers that Churchill and Jan were in some same social circles. Jan was discreet about his sex life, and Joel doubts he would have recommended Joel specifically, but he once indicated to Joel that he had recommended the escort agency Joel worked for. Churchill and Jan were very different men, and Joel had a very different relationship with Jan than Churchill. But Churchill always treated him well, and with respect.

"Yes. Not at first."

"You were close to him."

"Yes."

"I admired him greatly. He helped me when I was starting out...I mentioned you once or twice. I guess...well, he was protective of you."

"I appreciate that."

"What can I do for you?"

"You've read about what happened to Gabriel? Let me explain..." Joel gives him a short version of events, enough to get across that Gabriel is not in trouble from his own doing.

"I didn't think he was that kind of person. I hope this gets rectified soon for your sake. And his. I know my investigation is delayed at the moment."

"No, Gabriel's partner will take care of it. I'll make sure."

"You're very conscientious, as always. I valued that about you. And don't worry, I have no problems with keeping Gabriel under my hire. I know how the media and government can screw people over. They've tried with me enough times. I'm sorry to hear about your father, by the way. How can I help?"

Joel nods, accepting the sympathy. "You're a man of considerable influence in this state. I need someone who can get Gabriel out on bail. I can handle the bail amount, whatever it is. I just need him out. He's being abused in custody. Right now, no one can do anything about that."

Churchill leans back at his desk. "Who's presiding over the case?"

Joel gives him as much information as he knows, including the name of the judge who's handling the bail hearing.

"Mmmm. Not *that* big a problem." Churchill makes some notes to himself on his tablet. "I'll call someone today who can help out."

Then Churchill wants to talk over old times. "My God. I have to say this. It's been a few years. You look the same and different. Such a different look than when I knew you, but this suits you. Your demeanor suits you as well. I almost felt lucky you were willing to speak to me in the club..."

"That's kind of you to say."

"Well, it just brought up the effect you had on me. I haven't stopped thinking about it. You know what else I valued about you...?"

He lights a cigarette, as does Joel. Churchill then replays the music and in conjunction with that, graphically describes the sexual activities he used to pay for. Considering the circumstances, it's inappropriate, but Churchill lives in his own world to a large extent. Joel remembers that about him and knows it comes with the territory. So he listens to Churchill's reminiscing, keeping composed. He wonders how far he will need to go. Right now, as happens with people who have power, it's the power itself that is intoxicating.

"I can't believe we ran into each other again..." Churchill says. "Seeing you the way you are...I'm very impressed with how you take care of things. Uh...I want you to see me again. Doesn't have to be right away. That would be a return favor, we might say."

Joel leans forward in his chair. "Can you make that call now?"

Churchill stares at him. "Yes..."

He watches Joel while he murmurs into the phone. Joel gets up and moves away; through the floor-to-ceiling windows he can see other buildings in the area being coated in rain.

Churchill calls him over. "It's taken care of. I know I can trust you, Joel..."

"Of course you can. It's a matter of honor with me. I hope Gabriel will be cleared soon, and I have to work on that, but I'll see you within the next couple months. Is that okay?"

"Yes, you are always professional. I look forward to it."

Joel pauses, and changes his voice slightly. The way he used to with Churchill. "Whatever you want."

The way he says it, and how he looks at Churchill, is enough to make the other man draw in his breath. He gets up and takes Joel's arms; runs his hands down Joel's body. Joel watches him with a subtle expression Churchill is also familiar with.

Then he leaves.

Outside, in his leased SUV, Joel lets the Numbness take over to help him cope.

Jan, with a cigarette, is in the passenger seat. "I can't believe he's asking that of you. I thought he was better than that."

Joel speaks softly. "What's important is getting Gabriel out. I'll do what I have to. I can handle it."

"Money, even the good deal of money I wanted you to have, doesn't seem to make anything better."

"Sure it has," Joel says. "More than you know. But this isn't money. If I knew how to pay a bribe in this situation I would. He knows how, so I had to ask him. It's power, not money."

"Gabriel will understand."

"I have to take care of him. He took care of me; I'll take care of him. It's what you do. Always. I learned that from..."

Joel glances down to see Jan has another notebook open. "Jennah."

∞

JENNAH

Marcus Aurelius said, "Never let the future disturb you. You will meet it, if you have to, with the same weapons of reason which today arm you against the present."

∞

No matter what else, I took care of her.

It is May 1, 1994.

EVENTUALLY JOEL FINDS HIMSELF in front of the Stephen
Schwarzman library. He was going to go in and try to read, but ends
up just sitting on the steps, sometimes with his face buried in his
knees. Sometimes crying.

People walk past and ignore him; punk kid, sullen teenager.
They don't see the bruises on him, nor the blood on his shirt under
the jacket. He's too tired to do anything about it. He doesn't feel the
time pass. He tries not to think but the images rise up. His father, the
gang of kids. Pastor Sal and Meese. Art. Grace...

Footsteps stop next to him. Someone standing there. He gets
wary. What if it's a cop, someone to harass him?

It's a girl, not that much older than he. Curly hair, olive skin
indicating multiracial heritage, no make-up, U2 t-shirt and jeans. She
looks concerned but friendly. "Hey, are you okay?"

He doesn't answer, just eyes her cautiously over his folded
arms.

She smiles, showing pleasant, slightly large and crooked teeth.

Her smile causes him to raise his head slightly. He sees her
eyes go wide at his bruises, and sinks his head down in his arms again.

She crouches next to him. "Somebody hit you? You hurting
bad? I think you are. My name's Jennah. Can I get you something?"

Again, he doesn't answer. He wants her to both go away and
to comfort him. He misses Grace, and he's scared.

His not speaking doesn't dissuade her from staying with him.
She sits next to him on the step, watching him watching her over his
arms.

"You're really cute. Too young for me. But cute. What are
you, thirteen?"

"Sixteen." He says it without thinking.

She smiles again at the success of the ruse. "Oh, sorry. Are
you going to get in trouble if you go home now?"

"I don't have a home.'"

"No parents?"

He shrugs. "Long story."

She puts her hand on his back. "You've had a rough time. I know about that. I had some bad stuff happen too. I thought maybe I could figure it out here. I like libraries, you know?"

He lifts his head a little. He had thought of that. He's been back in libraries since Grace disappeared, as if maybe he could find the reason why it happened.

Jennah smiles at him again. "You want to come home with me? I'm alone right now too. I'd really like someone to talk to. I have a place in Brooklyn. It's a squatter building. I know the way in. No electricity, but it has water at least. I think the city doesn't know about it."

Now he looks at her head on. Trying to figure her out. She winces a little seeing the blood on his shirt. "Oh, someone did hurt you."

"A couple people beat on me. They were looking for a friend of mine. Why are you asking me home? You don't know me."

"I would if you told me your name."

"Joel."

"Well, Joel, you can come with me. If you want a book, I got a card, but we have to go to the Grand Central branch. This one doesn't really let you check out books. I got candles to read by. I was going to get chicken on the way home. You like chicken?"

He stares at her, unable to formulate an answer. *I don't know what's up with her, but she's either too trusting or not to be trusted.*

"Come on. Better than sitting here, right?"

Her greenish eyes are guileless. As he stares at her, his instincts tell him she's okay. Maybe she hasn't really learned what it means to be on the street. In any case he takes the hand she offers. She walks with him to 46th Street and they spend time together, looking for books. She ignores the people who stare at Joel's face and shirt, making him feel a little less like a freak.

On the train to Brooklyn she holds his hand and hums to herself. She works hard to be upbeat, but at times her face falls into a shadow, a lost world. Joel watches her in between flipping through the books.

He finally asks, "How did you get here? Did you run away?"

"Yes...my mom and dad fought all the time, and it was like I didn't exist except to be yelled at. I couldn't take it anymore."

"What bad thing happened to you?"

She stares down at her book, *Imajica* by Clive Barker. "I had a guy when I first got here; he found someone he liked better. Bigger boobs, blonder, whiter, whatever. She threatened to kill me if I came around him again. He was okay with that."

"Why?"

"I guess he just isn't a good person." Jennah smiles at him thinly. "And I told him I was pregnant. I was in the library trying to figure out what to do. He's not going to help, that much is clear."

Out of the train, she takes him to the empty building slated for demolition. The entrance can be accessed through a lot. She lives in one of the old studio apartments on the third floor. Inside, Jennah lights candles; the religious kind in long glass jars. Joel bought them from a corner *botanica* on the way to the building. The people who beat him were not looking for money and so he still has a little tucked away.

The apartment has some furniture scrounged off the street. Jennah's done a pretty good job fixing the pieces up. There's also a queen mattress and some battery-operated cooking devices.

"Other people live in the building. We're part of a group that split off from a larger place in Williamsburg. The city found them out and served eviction papers. Our group felt that a smaller building might fly under the radar. Like I said, we have water, but no one can figure out the electricity. They took out and replaced the fuses, but..."

"Maybe I can look at it. My shop teacher was pretty good; I learned a lot from him about this stuff."

"I'll introduce you to the others tomorrow. There are six apartments in use here. We're trying to be quiet so that the city and any drug people don't find out."

Jennah pulls him down on the mattress with her, and they dig into the take-out chicken, listening to news on the radio.

"What happened to your friend? The one those people wanted to find?"

"I don't know. We were together since I got here, up until a week ago. She was...we were like...she was my girlfriend. I think she was the only person *anywhere* who really cared about me."

Joel tries not to cry, but the tears come from fear and frustration. "We usually met at this place in Times Square, the McDonalds or the arcade. She didn't show up when she was supposed to. A guy I know said she came through looking for me earlier and that she was near the Meatpacking district. I went there to find her. We just met up, then we saw a couple men doing something to another man. They saw us, and we ran. We could run pretty fast, you know? And we got around a corner, and she saw an open doorway and told me to hide there. She was going to call the cops. I waited, and then I heard the men coming and they had guns. They cocked them, just like in the movies."

Jennah is staring at him wide-eyed. "Oh my God."

"They were going to go in. And I heard her say, "You looking for me?" She made them go after her. To save me. I ran out and they were all gone. *She* was gone. I looked all over for her."

She touches his face. "What happened here?"

He winces from the touch, and then smiles to try to cover it up. "Today. Some guys were looking for her. I don't know if they were like the other ones we saw, but they started hitting me, saying they wanted to know where she was. Then the cops came around and I had to run too, because what was I going to tell them? But I hope that means she's alive."

Jennah caresses his hand while he talks. Then they both read. Jennah curls against him while reading, and falls asleep. The dried blood on his clothes doesn't bother her. Being inside and almost alone makes this a luxury.

The next day, Jennah says she's taking him out since they are now roommates. First, she introduces him to the other residents. One of them takes Joel down to the basement. He's able to figure out why the electricity hasn't been able to start and to repair the connection. That seems to be his price of admission to the building.

He's surprised at how he and Jennah bond quickly. Much like he did with Grace, and yet this is different. They weren't thrown together, and there's a little distance and boundary between them.

Joel spends time with her walking or reading in the library. Or drawing in the apartment during the daytime. A stray cat that's sort of collectively owned by the tenants often comes over to spend time with them, and sits with Joel while he draws.

He also looks for Grace when he can—traveling over their shared routes, searching for mutual acquaintances, particularly Mario. No trace, no word. Mario looks too, but eventually they both give up.

Jennah socializes with the other tenants, but Joel picks up they aren't thrilled with him. Maybe because he's too young and could draw attention. Even his electrical skills just seem to garner jealousy. He just remains cautious that he might have to leave in a hurry.

Joel knows nothing about pregnancy but he's grown concerned for her. In wanting to care for her, he starts coming back to the apartment with things he's 'acquired.' Jennah insists he not steal—that other ways exist to survive.

Joel hasn't done his way of surviving for several weeks now. He doesn't need much to live on, although food is always an issue. And for Jennah, it's a much more serious issue. Two of the other tenants are women, and one of them has suggested several times she take over Jennah's care, and after the birth, the baby itself.

Jennah is no way giving the woman her baby. But figuring out how to survive—it taxes the capabilities of a 16-year-old and 17-year-old.

"Can you get food stamps," he asks her.

"They'd take me back to my parents. I ran away. They'd probably take my baby, too."

Jennah is reluctant to risk being with her parents again. And Joel understands that.

One of the nicer tenants thinks he can get Joel some odd jobs doing illegal electrical work. It's a fuzzy prospect as Joel has no way to enforce payment. Still, he helps on a few jobs. It's either illegal wiring that would be outlawed by the city, or a landlord who doesn't want to pay a licensed contractor. It's not enough to be a real income.

Jennah had freaked out when he told her what he used to do for money when he was with Grace. But what other options does he have? Panhandling isn't his thing. She tries to talk him out of it with logic, but the logic doesn't make sense to him.

"I'll just look for a better class of tricks."

Jennah hates this talk, and how it makes him seem much harder than he is. But he's determined. He begins moving in a dangerous boundary from quick street tricks to find those willing to spend more time and money.

It means hanging around in places, waiting for someone to notice him and approach him. And developing illusions for the tricks. The married man who takes him to a hotel can feel like he's really helping Joel with college tuition, that kind of thing.

Jennah cries over Joel when he makes the mistake of being rather proud of his success with this.

"I think you should go to art school," she says.

Joel gets upset. "How the fuck am I supposed to do that? Just like you can't get welfare I can't try to go to school. We'd both be put in foster homes. You want that?"

He knows she loves him, even though they haven't done anything together. In some sense she's living a romantic fantasy that gets more difficult to deal with every day.

"You can't sell your body; you're going to get AIDS."

"I know how to use a condom."

"I don't want you to get hurt! You could lie about your age and work on a magazine or graphic arts company."

"Yeah, in an office just like my father. That's going to happen."

He's irritated with her, because he's angry he can't do anything. He can go out and have sex for money, but he can't get a real job.

But she has a way of making him not mad at her, because of her faith that he can do better. Even though he has no idea how. She says he has something special. He doesn't like that word, but recognizes she means something much different than Meese did.

The tension grows between them during the next couple months. The next stage of her fantasy is talking about some imaginary new guy she's going to find and marry. She says she'll take care of Joel when that happens. Joel suspects this is revenge for him hustling. He ignores the bait.

In spite of this tall, dark and handsome fantasy proxy boyfriend, her hands start to wander ever closer to his thighs and between them, each night. He feels helpless here. She loves him but says it's more like a friend, when it isn't. He loves her but feels she's driving him away with her fantasy, that he's not good enough. And then she feels it's okay to touch him. What is he going to do--refuse? That wouldn't be nice; she's gets comfort out of it. But it's bothersome because it gets him hard and he can't do anything with her there.

The nighttime Jennah is the fantasy Jennah. The daytime Jennah is the practical, protective dreamer. She gives up trying to change his mind about hustling. So now she wants him to tell her where he goes. That at least has a solution; he's able to get a couple of pagers. He wants her to let him know in turn if she gets ill, and she feels better that he has an emergency number to call her.

It's August. She's six months along. One night Joel doesn't respond to her beeping, and Jennah is worried sick.

She beeps him over and over. When he doesn't respond she hits the streets to try to find him. He doesn't talk a lot about where he goes, but she tries every place she can remember he's mentioned including Times Square, marching up to other young men and asking if they know him and where he might be.

Mario is kind enough to help her. He remembers that some older man was looking for Joel as well, supposedly a client. He tries not to let on that the man gave him bad vibes. Another teenager tells them that Joel was over at Columbus Circle, and the man had said he could be contacted at the Paramount Hotel.

First, they go to Columbus Circle. No luck.

Then the Paramount. It's on Bowery; and it's not the Plaza for sure. The clerk pays no attention to them or anything else other than OTB results. Jennah approaches him and demands to know if the older man is here. The clerk still ignores her. She threatens to call in a police raid, saying Joel is underage. The clerk relents and mutters a room number on the fifth floor. Jennah's already on the way to the elevator.

At the room she's bangs on the door with Mario behind her. The door swings open and a white man in his forties stares at her, a belt in his hand and a wild look in his eye.

"What are you doing," she screams at him. But bravely, she pushes past him into the room. The man grabs his jacket and wallet, and runs out.

Jennah finds Joel curled up on the bed. He's covered in bloody welts on his back, and more smears of blood around him and on the sheets. A pillow case has been ripped up and wound around his neck.

But he's not dead. In spite of being nearly unconscious from what the man had done to him he's shocked for her to see him naked in this bed, looking worse when she first met him. She ignores that embarrassment, and gets Mario to help her clean him up.

They use all the towels in the place to blot the blood from his face and body, where he's been hit hard. The man had rings on his hand and these cut his face open. Despite Joel thinking he could handle all kinds of tricks, this man was practiced in overpowering people. He started hitting Joel with the belt while choking him. He was going slow and probably working up to a marathon torture session.

The sense of having just missed Joel being murdered brings a graveness to their interaction. Jennah does not show anything but concern to see him like this, and gets him back to Brooklyn and in their home.

It takes two weeks for the bruises to go away. But he can't sleep well. He feels shadows coming in to attack him. He can't sleep with his back to her. She stays up late watching over him.

After he recovers, she caresses him again. He shrinks from this, but she keeps on. This time she kisses him. Takes his hand and puts it between her legs. Recognizing his hesitance in what to do with her, she tells him.

Jennah's next scheme is to do something with Joel's drawings that he leaves around. He never bothers to do anything with them. She copies and colors them, pastes them to backing and sells them on the street like other souvenir peddlers. She's sometimes run off for not having a peddler's license, but she manages to sells a good deal of his work. Her pregnancy keeps her out of trouble with the police. To her, that helps since she is not going to chance the baby being taken away.

They still argue over whether he should keep up the sex work. He has no feeling over her selling his art. He doesn't think it's going to lead to big-time money and has no interest in pursuing it even when she points out his potential. She reads about the success of Jean-Michel Basquiat, who was also thrown out as a teenager and struggled to support himself with street art. Joel listens to the story and they even go see Basquiat's grave in the Green-Wood Cemetery. But Joel does not apply the analogy of Basquiat to himself.

Jennah is angry that he doesn't have the faith in himself that she has in him, and he'd rather let her be mad at him than attempt to live up to that faith.

But he has another interest to keep him from prostituting full time. Hacking. He's found out about a casual meet-up of hackthusiasts in Chelsea. When he shows up at the meeting place in the basement of a music club, he's shy at first. A tall and lanky young man his age smiles and waves him over. "Don't be a stranger, sweetheart."

This is Chris Szala. He vaguely resembles a young Tim Curry and sometimes likes to wear make-up, or Madonna-style fingerless gloves, or lace stockings under jeans, or long multicolored scarves. He's impervious to criticism and has a sharp enough wit to keep haters at bay.

He seems to like Joel a lot, although others think Joel is too quiet and probably stuck-up. But not Chris. He sees beyond this and fills in silence with his own theories on gaming, comics, aliens, sea monsters, government conspiracies, and rather good knowledge of gender fluidity in different world religions.

The hackers call each other by code names. Chris bestows the name Mephisto on Joel, and rarely calls him anything else. Upon finding out that Chris likes poetry, Joel gives Chris the name Satyricon.

Joel and Chris begin hanging out outside of the hackers' meetings. Joel doesn't tell anyone where he lives; he crafts many stories to keep people away from him. But Chris wins his trust with his guilelessness. He even takes Chris to meet Jennah.

He's worried about her now, in her eighth month. She refuses to see a doctor, *any* doctor. She won't talk to the female tenants, fearing they will force her to give the baby up. He presses her: "Go to Planned Parenthood."

But Jennah's like him; refuses to trust others. So Joel takes it upon himself to research about pregnant women and babies and birthing at home.

Jennah bestows her faith in his caregiving, which is preternatural, and Joel accepts that as his duty to her.

She starts labor at a bad time, not surprisingly. No one is around in the building. She pages Joel and he runs back to her along with Chris. Joel has memorized and prepared for what to do and amazingly the actual birth goes okay. Joel finds out he can be calm and effective in an emergency, and like Jennah, he can handle parts of life that aren't pretty. Chris, supposed to be helping, nearly passes out and Joel has him wait in the hallway until it's over. Jennah's child is a girl. The baby is fine. But Jennah's not. She stays sick after the birth and the next day.

That throws Joel. He's able to care patiently for the baby girl, having read and prepared for that. But Jennah being sick overwhelms him. She complains of pain in her legs. She doesn't eat much, and can't sleep or stay awake. She wants Joel and the baby girl she named Jaycia to sleep with her.

Joel is terrified. Seventy-two hours after the birth, Jennah is not better. She's not bleeding but she's in pain constantly, and swollen. Joel tells her she has to go to the hospital against her protests. He promises that Chris and he will watch the baby so she won't be taken away.

She gives in from fear. He calls Chris over to help. Jennah forces herself to sit up. Joel is ready to help her dress.

Then she doubles over in pain. Joel panics and gets down beside her.

"Don't leave me," she says.

"I won't. It'll be okay." He wraps his arms around her. He'll have to call an ambulance.

And then she stiffens. Her head snaps back. He's not sure what happens, but suddenly he feels the life slip out of her.

He can't believe it. Chris gets on the other side of the mattress staring at them both. Across the room, the baby girl begins to wail, as if she knows.

Chris is still in shock. "What do we do?"

Joel picks up Jaycia. He thinks carefully. "She wouldn't want the other people here to be thrown out. If we call the police, they probably will be. Her baby will go to foster care."

He's not sure if he can handle the fact of her death but he recognizes an internal force that steps up to be rational and pragmatic, leaving the emotional for later. Like what he had to do to leave Wayne. Call it the practical side of the Numbness.

"We have to take her outside, Chris. Then I need to figure out about the baby."

Chris doesn't question this. Joel has far more life experience already, between the two of them. As with the birth, Chris sees the side of Joel that is self-possessed. They wrap up Jennah in a raincoat with some of her personal effects, and carry her outside carefully. They keep her upright as if just helping her walk. It's early morning in Brooklyn. Not many people on the street. A park bench is not too far away. They place her there, and Joel calls the police from a pay phone. The two of them hide where they can watch. The police come, then an ambulance. A couple officers walk around the neighborhood trying to ask questions, then eventually leave.

Joel goes back to the apartment and comforts the baby. "It was taking care of her. Whatever I had to do. Now I have to take care of her girl."

"You can't stay here."

Joel agrees. Without Jennah, he's likely to be kicked out anyway. And they'd take the baby, maybe. He won't let that happen.

"There's a place in the basement of my building." Chris's dad is a super in an apartment building in Brooklyn. He's Hungarian and doesn't speak much English. Chris usually translates for him. He also spends a good deal of his time inebriated, leaving Chris to go about his business. "Dad's not going to care if you sleep on a cot there."

Joel collects his stuff; mostly just the baby things, his few clothes and books and his notebooks.

In the temporary quarters he does what he can with the baby girl. She is fine for a week, two weeks. He can't think what to do other than keep her. Chris is equally bewildered but willing to support his friend. He even babysits when Joel has to start his 'work' again for money.

But Jaycia develops a cold, some kind of cough. Joel knows he can't take chances with her health. He cannot pretend she is his, and he realizes he has to give her up. But the idea of her in the city's foster care system...

He researches again, desperately. He finds a story about a Connecticut fire department where newborns can be left anonymously, a 'safe haven' place. Due to recent scandals in surrounding counties regarding adoption and foster care, this particular county has a nonprofit agency with a stricter-than-typical screening process for prospective parents.

Please God. Let this be true.

He and Chris take a train to Connecticut on Metro-North. They wait until nightfall and then set Jenna on the fire department steps in a carrier they bought in a thrift store that morning.

"I don't want to do this," Joel tells the baby. "But I won't let you be lost."

He immediately goes to a pay phone and calls that particular fire company. Several firefighters pour out the door to find the baby girl. They take her inside.

One the way back, in spite of his relief, he stares straight ahead with an empty sensation. "If I was older, I could have kept her and taken care of her."

"You had to do it. Jennah needed a hospital and she wouldn't go." Chris talks pointblank with him. "You stuck by her and did the best for the kid. You took care of business and you *did* take care of her. This'll hurt *you* more."

"I didn't want to do it," Joel says. "She would have loved me."

He and Chris are close enough now that Joel can cry on him, and Chris can hold him while he does so.

∞

NINE

Edgar Allan Poe said, "It is by no means an irrational fancy that, in a future existence, we shall look upon what we think our present existence, as a dream."

∞

Friday, April 15
Alphabet City, Avenue A, 2:00 pm

TRYING TO DO PRACTICAL THINGS to keep calm, Joel checks
Gabriel's work voicemail and work email. Walter Cleveland has left a
couple messages asking if he can help.

"Oh, yes," Joel says, and calls the number Walter left.

"Joel!" Walter says his name like they already know each
other. "I'm so glad you called. Is there anything I can do?"

"I hope so. I'm afraid Gabriel is in real danger." Joel explains
what happened. "And needless to say, he's innocent. I'm afraid they'll
kill him in there. They've set him up for some reason."

"I'll go over and hold a press conference. I can get Ariana to
publish something immediately. Do you have any idea why this is
happening?"

Joel hesitates. "Maybe. But I can't tell you right now. I mean,
you'll still help Gabriel, right?"

"Of course; if it's something you want or don't want to talk
about, that's fine."

Joel closes his eyes. "I really, really, thank you for helping out.
I'm pretty scared about this. I know Gabriel is going to work with you
on a book. I'll help you too. Just, you know, it's hard to get public
interest on what happens in a jail. No one cares. And a jail or prison is
like its own little planet."

"Have no fear," Walter intones dramatically. "I'll make it a
sensation."

Later that evening, Joel is back in Paterson. Walter has lived
up to his promise and has a story breaking in the Huffington Post.
He's speaking with some media persons on the street outside the jail.
And Mankiewitz is there too, agitating live on his blog about what
happened to Gabriel.

Having spoken with them both, Joel takes a cigarette break
while watching the jail. He hopes Gabriel has gotten word that people
are trying to help. Michaela is trying to get in to see him again, and
submit her motion in to the emergent judge.

Joel's phone rings. He recognizes the number. "How did you
get this?"

Alex says, "Does it matter? Is he okay?"

"No. I was waiting for Clark to call back."

"I saw something that Mankiewitz published. I should tell Clark to go there?"

"Yes. That's why I called him."

"What happened?"

"I don't know. He didn't do this."

"Of course he didn't. What do you know about it?"

Joel can feel his teeth grinding. "I *don't* know. If I did, he'd be out." He hangs up.

∞

Monday, April 18
Paterson, NJ, 4:08 pm

"What do you want to do about that situation?"

"Just hold off. Don't do anything else." Meese ends the call.

He goes about his work, or tries to. Things are not happening the way he wanted. He felt he had a very good alternative plan when Ken fucked things up at the last minute. Cody was able to get out of the house (if he didn't, Meese would have taken care of that too). Meese found him later waiting quietly, out of sight. Of course, no one questioned Meese being around the neighborhood.

Except John Dell. But Dell knows nothing, really.

With Dell outside, risking another shot to kill Ross was not going to happen. Meese improvised, knowing Ross was likely going to end up in his custody. Which is exactly what happened.

Since Meese already had extensive background information on Ross, he allowed that information to make its way quickly to the Passaic County prosecutor's office. That meant Ross wasn't leaving jail any time soon.

And Meese wouldn't need long. He's in charge of the jail, effectively. Being in charge has its benefits. He has a thing going that Ken and Cody didn't know about, arranging with some long-term inmates to let them get government benefits of which he takes a cut.

He's had other incidents arranged as well. Out of any given set of correctional officers, a couple are always willing to go over the line, just like cops. The rest will not say anything. Even if they despise the other officer, they won't rat on him. Just like cops.

Meese set up his new improvised plan carefully. It was working out. It's delayed him having to help Gloria and getting to see Joel. But Gloria isn't answering his calls. He knows she's staying with Joel at his apartment. She should call him--he's Ken's Goddamn best friend. But nothing. That is seriously aggravating.

Roll with the punches, Larry. Think of the endgame.

He has access to security feed, showing visitors to the jail. He told the staff at the jail to be alert if Joel showed up. Joel wasn't allowed to see Ross, of course. Only the lawyer can do that. But he has the video of Joel. Still trying to do good deeds. Not realizing he needs to cut that PI loose. When Meese saw Joel show up, he figured it was time to set up the beatdown with Ross, which was going to quickly lead to a 'suicide.'

But then that fucking New York writer showed up. And the reporters. Showed up and got the media to put out stories about how Ross was being abused. The whole thing about the jail being 'inhuman' was hashed over again.

Now Ross's lawyer got a judge to approve a motion to transfer him. The judge ordered that Ross be under hospital observation over the weekend, and moved to Wayne on Monday.

Meese has to be careful with this new spotlight on the jail. The press talked with him briefly, and he promised an immediate investigation and assured Ross would be given all possible protection. Well, Ross is not going to *stay* in Wayne. He won't get out at his bail hearing, and then he'll be transferred back to Paterson. People will forget about him and move on to the next story. And then accidents can still happen. It has to, before any trial occurs.

Meese doesn't realize he spends an hour just replaying the video of Joel arriving at the jail. For the brief moment Joel glances at the camera. He knows. He must know Meese is watching out for him.

∞

Tuesday, April 19

On Tuesday Joel picks up his mother and takes her back to the house in Wayne. He's in a much better mood. Michaela had followed Gabriel's transfer to a hospital, where his injuries were documented. A psych eval found he was not suicidal and other than being in pain from the beating, was in fair physical shape. She also made sure he was taken to Wayne and set up in the jail with no problems.

Today, Gloria wants to get some clothes. John Dell and a uniformed officer meets them there; the house is still taped off as a crime scene, which means a law enforcement officer must go with them. Dell acts protective of Gloria, discretely standing in front of the living room entranceway to block the sight of the blood on the floor and walls.

Gloria goes to her bedroom by way of the kitchen stairway, accompanied by the uniformed officer. Joel waits by the front door, folding his arms. He knows Dell is watching him but ignores the detective.

"How's it going," Dell says finally.

"Seriously?"

"Yes."

"I'm surviving."

Dell continues to study him. "Gabriel is okay. I want you to know that. We had him transferred over this morning. He's in a holding cell. Really, he's in a good place. This isn't Paterson."

That makes Joel uncomfortable. Dell doesn't have to give him that information. So why does he? Joel just nods shortly.

Dell's expression is not unkind. "You haven't given much of a statement."

"I told you he was on the phone with me. He's innocent. You should already know that. Michaela Connor told you about the forensics. I know you found nothing in that search of his apartment."

"The prosecutor feels otherwise about Gabriel, not just because of the forensics. However, I'm investigating this. A good cop, and I try to be, keeps an open mind. Hunches are good but you have to be open to all possibilities."

"Just like on *Law & Order.* You must be Wayne's Bobby Goren."

"Could do worse. I'm willing to listen to you if you have anything--*anything*, that can point me in a better direction."

Joel smiles humorlessly. "Why? Because you know my mom?"

"I have a little insight because I know her. She's mentioned problems with your father. I don't know you, and she doesn't really know you either. Hiding things will not help your case."

"Neither will telling you anything that you'll use against him."

"You don't trust police, do you?"

That gets Joel to glare at him, and Dell is taken aback a little at the ferocity in Joel's eyes.

"I don't have *any reason to.*"

Gloria comes downstairs now with a large suitcase. Joel takes it from her and walks out. A couple minutes later Gloria comes out as well.

He asks her, "Is this everything?"

Dell is waiting by the front door. She holds up her hand to him and then turns to her son. "Joel, they're going to release his body."

"Okay. Whatever."

"Honey...you've been through a lot. I don't know what happened. And with your boyfriend in jail..." She bites her lip.

"I don't know why he's even in jail except they probably think I'm lying."

"I can talk to John..."

"Don't. You can't trust cops no matter how nice they are. Everything you say is something to use against you. Tell him nothing-- *got it*, Mom?"

She flinches from his tone. "Is this because of..."

He sighs; the flare of anger goes down. "Not now. I don't want to talk about it."

"But Joel, we need to do something with Ken. I mean, I don't know about his estate, I think he had a will but I'm not sure. Everything's a mess."

"He's a trained accountant and his personal affairs are a mess? That's what being a drunk does for you. I did better than that being..." he stops. "Being on the street."

"I know. You have something he never had. I need your help. I don't know what to do."

"Do you have an attorney?"

"Just the one who helped me in the DUI. I can ask around…"

"*I'll* ask around. We'll get it settled. I'll take care of you while this is going on. Take a leave of absence from your job. Or quit it."

She puts her hands on his shoulders and start combing his hair. The same look in her eyes as when he was young, after he would clean up behind her. He's getting used to her doing that again. Not a comfortable feeling and yet something about having her not only accept him but treat him as her hero, is so gratifying…

What if she's faking? Being nice just to have me as her whipping boy again?

Gloria puts her head on his shoulder. He puts an arm around her, uncomfortable as Dell is watching them.

"He needs a wake and a funeral," she says.

"Why?"

"Joel…" She lifts her head. "We *have* to."

Joel so doesn't have to. He wouldn't even have the body picked up if this was his decision.

"Please." She starts crying.

Fuck, he says to himself. And Dell spying on all this. He holds her closer so Dell doesn't think he's causing her to cry. She clings to him even tighter, and that makes his guilt rise. He remembers what Gabriel did helping Giselle's brother arrange her funeral. The TCOB part of him gets in gear. As it always must. No time to break down. "Okay, Mom. We'll set it up. Tomorrow."

"What…the wake?"

"All of it. Tomorrow."

"Joel, that's not enough time…"

"For what? You need to announce it somewhere? I'll help you, Mom, but I'm not drawing it out. Tell me the funeral home in town and the cemetery. Let's do it now."

"Joel, it should be the weekend…"

He gets angry again and tries to calm himself. To spend money on this man who never loved him, didn't want him, and threw him out of the house. But he tells himself it'll look better for Gabriel's situation.

"Make it Friday then. Give me the name of the funeral home and cemetery."

She thinks about it. "The one that's nice is Michelson Brothers. The cemetery is North Woods, just past the highway. I called them this morning to see what we could get, and they have a plot..."

"Yeah, all right."

"Oh, I need clothes for him..." She turns around and goes back to the house. Joel takes out a notebook and calls the funeral home first. Funeral homes are used to handling services fast under unpleasant circumstances. He arranges to stop by with his credit card and to get a viewing room for Friday. Then the cemetery. Joel makes that the first stop for the next day.

The process comforts Gloria in helping with the responsibility of making decisions. They start at the cemetery. He doesn't bother to go with the manager when she takes Gloria out. He stays in the office, paying the bill and checking his messages. Then to the funeral home. She goes through the service, the casket, the remembrance cards, guest book and other accoutrements. Joel cannot remember his father ever being in the slightest way religious, but the director arranges for a minister to say a prayer. Whatever. More for him to tune out.

The next day, Joel checks with Michaela about Gabriel. He isn't allowed visitors except Michaela. The bail hearing is next Wednesday. But Michaela is working on Joel being allowed to visit on the weekend as her 'assistant.' Nonetheless, Gabriel is allowed to make phone calls as of this morning. Soon Gabriel is indeed calling him.

"Yes," Joel says when the mechanical voice asks him if he'll accept the charges.

"Oh my God, there you are."

He sounds okay. Joel almost can't say anything at first. He starts to choke up. "And you. Are you safe?"

"No, it's "*Is it safe?*"" Quoting *Marathon Man*.

"Goddamn it, I guess you're all right if you can do that."

Gabriel laughs. "I miss you so much, baby. Just hearing your voice, even angry at me, is good."

"I'm not angry..."

Gabriel wants to ensure he's good, Archie is good, and his friends are well. Joel doesn't tell him about Churchill's help because he wants to be sure it happens, and these calls are probably recorded.

Even knowing what Gabriel's been subjected to, Joel finds himself breaking down on the phone about having to handle this funeral.

Gabriel's calmness comforting to him. "You're doing great, baby. I know how this makes a difference for her."

"I can't believe I'm doing this. For *him*. He should just be buried in a landfill."

"I know. Things in life are weird. The reason why it happens this way is because you're a good person. Look, I'm pretty sure whoever was there wanted to kill me. But at the last moment, Ken told me to leave. He tried to stop it. I don't know what that means, but you should know it. If Michaela talks a good talk, you can come in and tell me about the funeral on Saturday."

Saturday. He has a hard time believing this is all happening. That he has to visit Gabriel in jail. *Do something*, he says. Not to any higher power. He doesn't believe in that. But to any forces in the universe willing to listen.

Joel stays in Gabriel's apartment to take care of Archie, who he's moved back home. But he stops by his loft to check on Gloria. She's calling people who might come to the funeral. It's an odd situation, since they'd be coming to a funeral arranged by the son who hasn't been here in 17 years, and whose boyfriend is accused of killing the deceased.

"Is any family coming," Joel asks her when she hangs up.

She looks at him. "His people didn't stay in contact much. His brother is going to try to make it. He lives across the country."

"What about you? Your sisters?"

"Oh, well..."

"Well, what? What the fuck goes on with this family?"

"Joel, please. Your language..."

"Don't police me. Just answer the question."

She shakes her head.

"Did you tell them?"

"Yes. They aren't really speaking to me."

He pauses. "Did you tell them I'm here? I mean, I'm back. Or whatever the fuck."

"No. I didn't have a chance."

"Do you want them here?"

"God, I don't know, Joel. I don't know if I can handle them on top of this."

That, Joel can agree with. But in spite of her attitude, he gets some contact information from her and leaves her two sisters a message by phone and email. He's not sure why he does this, but perhaps hearing that at the last moments of his life Ken was attempting to do what was right meant something. He feels that real change means he has to do things too.

∞

Friday, April 22
Wayne, NJ, 11am

The day of the funeral he helps her get ready in spite of the tension that remains between them. The strange pattern they're in. Dealing through passive-aggressive behavior. So this is what having a family is like again. Annoyance balanced with the strange familiar role of taking care of her.

Gloria's older sister called him back the previous evening. She isn't coming, but she had a short formal conversation with Joel asking him about how he was doing. He felt she meant well. Margaret emails him. She lives in Spain. She can't get back in time but wants to know all about him, almost gushing in her email. He has that put off for now, not wanting to explain his life.

A fair number of people attend the wake. Ken's colleagues and neighbors. Most speak to Gloria. Joel doesn't get involved in conversation. If they read the news, they know the alleged circumstances of Ken's death. The stories don't explicitly state Gabriel and Joel's relationship, but it can be inferred. Joel feels like everyone who comes in the funeral home is judging him.

He has his own support. Geneva, Veronica, Michaela, Bob and Chris are there. Joel stays to the side of the room with them, only leaving when Gloria insists he come over to accept some person's respects. Some of the visitors stare at him as though he might be the murderer. He stares back, making them all nervous.

Things go well during most of the viewing; only one is held so that the burial can proceed more quickly. Gloria is handling the situation okay. Dell is here, of course. For her support, she says. The man is every-fucking-where. Gloria moves anxiously back and forth in front of the closed casket, to Joel's group, and to the people visiting.

Then he sees a man he knows and is glad to see. The swim coach from high school. Jon Lane. Lane greets his mother, who then turns to gesture toward Joel.

Lane walks over. "Joel. I can't believe it." He holds his hand out.

Joel takes it. The man shows genuine warmth.

"I'm so glad to see you, although I'm sorry about the circumstances."

"It's okay. Nice to see you as well."

"I heard you were going to be here. Are you holding up?"

"Yeah. This isn't..." he doesn't know what to say. The coach scrutinizes him.

"I hoped you were all right. This isn't the time to talk about it, but I was sorry when you left."

"Thank you." Joel blushes. "I appreciate that."

"Come see me at the school if you get a chance."

That makes Joel feel some measure of brightness, that this man who knew him for a year and a half would remember and care about him.

And then a group of men come in the room...and he hears the voice of the Monster.

"Gloria! Finally. I've been trying to reach you."

Joel freezes in attempting to respond. Across the room, the Monster has hold of his mother. He puts his arms around her. She looks over at Joel, helpless.

Lane turns to see what Joel is staring at. He says softly, "Joel, are you okay?"

"Yeah, yeah. I mean..."

For a second Joel and Lane look at each other. From the expression on Lane's face it's clear to Joel. *He knows. He knows about Meese.*

"Do you want me to stay around and help?" Lane's words imply something deeper.

Joel turns red, as if the whole world knows about him. He feels exposed and vulnerable, like when Jennah found him in that hotel room. Shamed. Marked.

His eyes drop to the floor. "No, but thank you. I'm grateful for what you said."

Lane reaches to hold Joel's hand briefly before leaving. "I'm going to leave, then. But I'd like you to stop by and see me at the school."

Joel nods. He feels his friends' hands on his back. He hears the Monster trying to sweet-talk Gloria. He'll come by and help her clean the house. Help her arrange Ken's effects. And he's sorry to say hello like this *but he really wants to talk to Joel, who can use a friend right now.*

If I get up and run, people will think... Dell is watching him closely right now. Then Dell gets up and discretely moves between Meese and Gloria, on some pretense. Which Joel should be doing, but he can't move. He can't move at all.

Joel can hear the footsteps coming toward him and looks desperately at Michaela. Seeing his face, she's up and standing in front of Joel. Bob stands up with her, on instinct.

Around him Joel's friends feel his horror even if not all are sure why. The man coming towards them is six foot, white, around sixty. Slightly ruddy, graying thin hair, eyes narrowing. He's focused only on Joel.

The room drops away for Joel; he's back inside the boat. In Joel's mind, he changes the outcome of what happened. He has Meese down on the floor, choking the life out of him. Beating him. Over and over, until he dies.

But that isn't happening. Instead, he's forced to sit here while Meese briefly frowns at Michaela and says, in a voice tinged with...what, *happiness?* "Joel. How are you holding up?"

Joel doesn't answer. He's trying not to hyperventilate but to keep his eyes on Veronica's hand holding his. She squeezes tight to anchor him.

Michaela says, "Officer Meese, may I help you?"

"You know who I am, do you, Ms. Connor? I know you of course. I know you're working on the case of the man who was arrested for this. If you need anything at all, please call me."

Then the minister comes in. Gloria walks quickly over to them. "Larry, come sit here with me for the service."

"Well, of course, Gloria."

Joel's eyes start to water. His mother took the Monster away so he wouldn't have to talk to him. He knows she trying to help.

When the Monster is away from him, Joel feels his entire body coated in sweat.

The minister begins the service. Joel can't hear a word the minister says. He only hears the blood pounding in his ears. He feels the Monster staring at him. He doesn't look at Meese, but he sees Michaela and Veronica both glaring at Meese.

Meese, however, only sees Joel.

Meese stays through the service. He gets up to look at the casket, and then goes back to where Joel is. He is not the slightest bit uncomfortable.

"I'm a friend of Ken's," he tells Joel's group. "I was a detective sergeant here for many years. I knew Ken for a long time. Known Joel since before he was born. Nice to see you back, Joel."

The last sentence is said with such a strange tone they all frown at Meese. Except Joel, who can't look at him.

Sometimes nightmares have levels that even demons can't comprehend.

Bob has already gotten up and is standing in front of Joel. Meese frowns at him, but doesn't take the hint to walk away.

The silence becomes awkward. "The funeral is over," Joel says finally. His eyes are still downcast. "Time for you to leave."

"It's a sad day, terrible what happened to Ken." Meese acts like Joel didn't say anything. "Ms. Connor, I saw that the man accused of this crime was transferred to Wayne. I can put in some influence for you, if you need it. But now, Ken was a good friend of mine. I certainly hope for justice in his case. That the person who did it pays for it."

When he looks around Bob to see Joel again, his whole posture and breathing changes.

"But what I'm really concerned about is how Joel is doing. Joel, we should catch up anyway, now that you're back. You're welcome to come by and talk to me. I can help you get through this."

He steps closer, and Bob steps in front of him again. Meese barely contains his anger at Bob, but this isn't the place to start something.

Joel glances at John Dell, now sitting in the front row. Dell isn't looking at him; he's looking at Meese's actions with a *what-the-hell* expression.

Gloria pushes gently past Meese again. "We have to go now. We need to go to the cemetery."

"Would you like me to drive you, Gloria?" Meese puts his hand on her arm.

Joel finally stands and brings himself to look at Meese. "She's with me." He pulls his mother away from the Monster.

They stare at each other face to face. Joel is shaking slightly. Meese is giving him a once over as if he's trying to absorb Joel with his eyes.

He turns to Joel's mother. "Gloria, you need anything you just call me."

"She doesn't need anything from you."

That gets Meese's once-over again. "Joel...I know you must be grieving over your loss. I'm glad you're taking care of her." Then his voice gets lower and strangely guttural. "I'm glad you're back here after all this time. Can you tell me what brought you back?"

The question hangs heavy. Joel finally turns away, steering Gloria towards the doors to the room. "If you have any questions, you can direct them to my attorney. As I said this funeral is over, and it's time to leave."

He indicates his friends should follow, as he leads his mother out. Meese stays inside, now staring at the casket.

∞

Monday, April 25
Wayne, NJ, 10am

In the morning, Joel is at the Wayne Police Department to see Gabriel. He's taken to a room with a counter-like structure. Joel is in a white linen shirt, black linen trousers, long black leather jacket, and boots. He is uneasy being in the jail. He's never really been here, but feels Meese's ghost in the building. This is exacerbated by seeing Meese's picture in a photo array of current and former officers. *Don't show any emotion; you need to stay here.*

This smaller town jail isn't really set up for visitors. Michaela said Joel was helping her on the case and would need to talk to Gabriel. They know it isn't really true, but let it pass. Looking around, he doesn't recognize anyone else in the station, other than Dell. Dell actually greets him and asks how Gloria is. He says he'll get Gabriel himself.

Joel is coursing with adrenaline, waiting. Finally, Dell brings Gabriel in the room. He's in an orange jumpsuit and thong sandals. His beard is significantly thicker.

Joel looks carefully at Gabriel's face. Michaela had told him that Gabriel was hit with something. It's been over a week, but the faint bruises are still visible. Michaela has pictures for whatever action she's planning later.

Joel stares at his eyes, to get a sense of how he's holding up. He sees is his own feelings reflected back.

They hold hands across the tabletop. He notes Gabriel looks pale, tired, but not lost. Gabriel's hands hold his tightly.

"You look good," Gabriel says. "Real fucking good. I appreciate that." He smiles.

Joel smiles too. Reminding himself he needs to do that. Looking worried isn't going to help. "I can't say the same about you."

Gabriel shrugs. He closes his eyes briefly. "What are you going to do? No fashion consultants here."

They stare at each other.

"What did they do to you in Paterson?"

"Joel, don't worry about me. I'm fine."

Joel frowns at him. "Don't start that 'fine' shit again. Michaela told me."

Gabriel looks down at the counter. "I didn't want you to know."

"I *have* to know. You can't protect me from that. I'm going to worry anyway. What did they do?"

"Someone ordered these guys to hit me a few times. They maced me too. That was a bitch. It triggered a headache. I couldn't talk for a while, so they said they thought I had a psychotic break. And then there was the *cavity* search."

He stops talking and stares into space a moment, then smiles as if he said too much. "Not even getting kissed first, you know?"

"Jesus. You don't belong in here."

"I agree with you. I don't know why I checked myself in. If I don't like it, I'll get the fuck out. Call the bellhop for my things."

Joel ignores that levity. "Is it happening here?"

"No. They leave me alone, so far. No one's friendly, but they're cordial so long as you don't make trouble. I actually was allowed to read. I'm able to shower, but I'm not allowed a razor due to my delicate sensibilities." The sarcasm shows his hidden anger.

"What else happened there? In Paterson?"

Gabriel smiles grimly. "I woke up from whatever drug I was given, and I started demanding Michaela be called."

"They wouldn't let me see you, so I called her. She went right over. I guess that was good timing."

"Sometimes that works out. But then I was eventually given some kind of paper jumpsuit, the kind that you can't turn into a noose. They put me in something like a padded cell and someone would look in on me every fifteen minutes. Suicide watch. I felt like a Goddamn lab rat."

Joel squeezes his hands. Gabriel smiles again. "This was only what...two days. But it's like...you're on another planet, a desert island. You have a limited amount of information in jail anyway, but segregated in a Special Housing Unit...nothing. I kept thinking...someone could kill me and no one would know. I had to fight with myself not to break down, because that would make it worse."

His voice gets lower and tenser. "I couldn't read, you know how I hate that. And I missed Archie. Being in the hospital, even cuffed to a bed, was paradise by comparison." Now he seems like he's going to cry. "Needless to say, I know what you were going through. I missed you every minute. I worried about you."

"I was out of my mind."

"You're strong, baby. I see that more than ever."

Joel looks down at the counter.

"You are. Mikki told me. She came by after the funeral."

"Then you know?"

"I wish I could have been there. He wouldn't have come near you. That's what kills me about being in here."

Joel struggles not to get upset. Gabriel somehow manages to comfort him just in holding his hands and looking at him.

"We got this far."

Joel nods. "Your hearing Wednesday. I'll be there."

"Okay. It won't add up to anything. Once the forensic evidence is in, maybe..."

"We'll see."

Gabriel considers him. "What did you do?"

"Who says I did anything?"

"Me. It's written on your face."

Now Joel smiles. "I called in a favor. I hope it works."

"Okay. I'm not going to complain about that. Can you check on things for me? With the business? See how many clients have scattered like rats abandoning a burning Bronx building?"

"No one has left. You have a lot of media support this time. And Veronica is an excellent manager and so good in dealing with clients. She installs confidence or comfort, whichever."

"I'm so grateful for her too, to have my back through this shit. I heard about the media. Saw some of it. You got to meet my new BFF Walter. I'm grateful to him, though. Joel, I'm sorry. About your father and this whole thing."

"Don't be." Joel leans forward. "The funeral...it was weird."

"Honestly, that man sounds fucking batshit crazy from how Michaela described him."

"Gabriel, the way he looked at me I swear to God he thought I was glad to see him. What the fuck?"

"I don't want to talk about it too much here, but I thought about how Mikki said he was acting. These people...they imprint. He doesn't see you; he sees the 15 year-old you. And if he thinks that you're glad to see him, then he was dealing in fantasy in the first place."

Joel shudders. "Back then too, he thought I wanted him to do what he did. And him being in charge of the jails--he wanted to hurt you."

"Hum. Maybe."

"I'm afraid about what he thinks about you. What that *means.*"

Gabriel starts to speak and stops. Dell is walking by looking at them. Not unfriendly and not friendly.

"What's with that guy," Joel mutters.

Gabriel nods. "I can't figure him out. Seems like he wants to help, but I can't trust anyone now. Because yeah, I think you're right."

They spend some time talking about other things. Joel eventually has to leave but then it's hard.

"Go," Gabriel tells him. "It's hard for me too. I can't argue with you now. You'll win everything."

"Jesus, I can't believe we argued before I left. If I had known. Never again. It's all over, that stuff, right?"

"Sure, baby. It was always over."

"I mean it. I'd do anything to have you out."

"I know. Life is precious and all that."

"Don't be flip to show off. Call me later if you can. Do you need anything?"

"You. My cat. A pack of Camels. Some decent food. My own shower and soap. What else..."

"I'll ask them what I can bring you. I know other people want to visit you. I'm lucky Michaela even got me in."

"I'll be all right."

But when Joel stands, a look comes over Gabriel's face that makes Joel feel guilty.

"Call me tonight. Do you need money here?"

"Michaela brought me change and a couple books. Jails have very little. They get all meals from a local diner. Better than Paterson, though. The change is for vending machines if I want to pig out on Three Musketeers and Doritos. The library is on the same plaza as the jail--I can see it out the window--but I can't get any books there. They might let you bring a few."

"I'll bring you some. But I think you're not going to need too many."

∞

Wednesday, April 28

The motion judge, Judge Brettone, is a nice enough man and reasonably fair. Michaela has been in his court numerous times. Although he is overwhelmed with cases as are most criminal court judges, he's willing to listen to a defense attorney for the sake of fairness. Michaela feels lucky to have him for this motion. She's surprised when he stops her in the court hallway and asked her to step in his chambers.

"Michaela," he says, looking at a notebook he keeps. "Suppose you ask for home detention as a condition of bail. In the Paterson area, of course."

"You mean wearing an ankle monitor?"

"Yes. If he can find someone to stay with here."

"Well, yes...but judge, the evidence is so weak he should really be out."

"This is a murder case, Michaela. Gandhi wouldn't be out on bail without conditions. I'm going to say again--suppose you ask for home detention?"

Michaela doesn't hesitate anymore. It's not a suggestion, it's a statement. "Yes sir. But Danton won't go for it."

"I'll hear your arguments on the merits." His look tells her what's going on. Not unheard of in New Jersey for a judge to make deals. She has a feeling Joel was successful in his machinations.

Since the hearing is in a matter of minutes, Michaela needs to find a place for Gabriel to stay. Something could be rented, but Bob's place is easier if he's up for it. She finds his number and gets ahold of him.

"No problem. What do you need me to do?"

"Get anything out that would make a probation officer nervous. They'll be by to check it out before he's released."

"No problem, I've helped my clients clean out their places enough times. I don't have alcohol. Maybe porn."

"You don't mind stashing it temporarily, *n'est-ce pas?*"

Then she's in court. Gabriel is sitting along the side of the courtroom on a bench with other defendants, all in chains. He has not shaved but looks better than when Joel visited him--more alive. He spends the time before court begins keeping watch on Joel and Veronica, who are in the bench row behind the defense counsel's table.

The hearing goes perfunctorily at first. One of the bailiffs unlocks Gabriel from the row of men and leads him to the defense table. He smiles at Joel and Veronica before taking a seat beside Michaela.

The assistant prosecutor, Charles Danton, argues valiantly that Gabriel shot and killed a fine upstanding citizen who was also a respected state employee. He recommends against bail and does not appear to worry over his likelihood of losing.

Michaela in turn argues that Gabriel has an outstanding reputation as a private investigator and community advocate. Plenty of persons will attest to his character and integrity. The prosecutor doesn't even really have a motive for Gabriel other than a vague revenge theory. No evidence other than his presence in the house. No fingerprints, no witnesses.

Danton then goes into a rebuttal to Michaela's argument that Gabriel has had a history of violence in New Jersey. Hitting a preacher and being arrested for that. Getting into a violent fight with another man in which Gabriel had broken the man's leg and arm and some ribs. Plus, he has a reputation as a gun for hire, even comparing Gabriel to Omar on *The Wire*, which impresses no one other than the line of defendants on other cases waiting to be heard.

Michaela matches Danton's scornful tone. "Those rumors are completely unfounded and irrelevant. Mr. Ross has in fact been subjected to severe physical abuse in the Passaic County correctional system by virtue of officials acting improperly on these unfounded rumors. A complaint has been filed on this matter. And regarding the fight Mr. Danton is referring to, Mr. Ross was in a situation of self-defense. The other party involved, Donald Mathers, is an accused serial killer and human trafficker, and who had broken into a building to follow up on a threat to another person's life."

That person happened to be Michaela, but she doesn't want to overdo her argument. She continues, "He also discovered several bodies of women who had been missing for years, along with the son of the victim, who is here today to support him. And he helped organize an international mission to identify these women. The Governor even sent him a thank-you letter."

Danton pretends he can barely keep from laughing out loud. "The Governor isn't here today, is he? I don't think he'll want to testify on Mr. Ross's behalf. Ross is just too much of a risk to be released, your honor. Not for *murder*."

Judge Brettone turns to Michaela. "Ms. Connor? You have some merit to your argument, but the charges are quite grave."

"Your honor, I have a proposal..."

Five minutes later, the prosecutor is squealing with rage at the judge's ruling, which makes Joel smile. Brettone looks coolly at the prosecutor and cuts off his protests. "Mr. Danton, my decision is made. Perhaps you need to collect better evidence before an arrest. Bail is set at two million. The defendant is required to wear a monitoring device and confined to a residence within the Passaic County area until further notice. Ms. Connor, do you have such a residence?"

The other defendants waiting for their hearing stare at Michaela, wondering how she got that little miracle performed. While Danton was pitching a fit, Joel had quickly spoken to Michaela and now when Judge Brettone asks her the question, she looks up. "I have a residence and the bail ready, your honor."

The judge nods. "Get a hold of the Department of Probation for the monitor and to arrange for the officers to check out the residence."

The prosecutor, frustrated, glares at Gabriel. Gabriel smiles at him politely.

A court officer leads Gabriel out. Michaela, Veronica, and Joel leave as well.

Joel asks, "What now?"

"He goes back to Wayne. You need to pay the bail, certified check. I'll go with you. On the way I'll call the Department of Probation. Hopefully we can get this set up in 24 hours. You'll need to pay for the monitor as well."

"I have it. Let's get this started."

A few hours later, a probation officer is sent to Bob's apartment to review it and ensure no guns and drugs are present. By late Friday afternoon, Gabriel is released from the Wayne jail and police officers escort Gabriel to the apartment in a squad car.

∞

Friday, April 29th
Paterson, NJ, 5:30 pm

Veronica has a gym bag for me that Joel gave her. He's not here at Bob's place right now. Veronica tells me that Joel's mother called him, and some sort of problem is going on at her house and he has to check it out.

The officer at the Department of Probation, a white woman in her late 30s, stays to program the ankle monitor. She explains to Michaela and me that I'm not allowed to leave the apartment perimeter, which is calculated for the building and about 25 feet outside the building. If I trespass that boundary the ankle device will go off and I'll be tracked down and re-incarcerated. I'm allowed to make arrangements for legal and medical visits as long as the Department approves.

Once she leaves, Michaela and Veronica help me settle in. Bob gives me a long hug, and the women join in.

"This is surreal," I tell them. "Suddenly out of that place, that isolating environment, and now I don't know what to do."

"Let's see what Joel brought; maybe some disposable Schicks." Veronica teases.

"Maybe a Norelco," Bob says helpfully.

"I got the message. Actually, not being *allowed* to shave has changed my perspective. It goes tonight." I open the gym bag and find new clothes, a new small laptop, and a new cell phone. As always, Joel knows how to take care of business.

But I'm worried about him. The cell phone's already been charged and has all the previous apps he installed on my regular phones. He's that good. I text him on the new phone.

– What's going on baby?
--I'll tell you later. Are you better? Is everything okay?

--Fabulous.

--I'll be over soon, if Bob doesn't mind.

I use that moment to discuss the prospect of being roommates with Bob for a while. "I don't know how long this process will take. But we can rent a place and get transferred."

"Don't worry about it. It's why I have a two-bedroom apartment. You don't care if I have a woman over, right? The dangerous criminal in the place might be a turn-on. In exchange, Joel can come and go as he pleases so to speak. I know he doesn't abuse that. Just don't be loud; There's a bawdy-house clause in my condo agreement. Just kidding! Anyway, tell him to come over and I'll give him a key. What Gabriel really needs is food. That's what makes you feel like a human being again--to choose your own food. Pizza? Chinese? Cheeseburgers? *Coq au vin?*"

"Pizza sounds human enough right now." I let Joel know by text that he's welcome.

After dinner I start calling people, feeling like I'm exploding with the need to be normal. I call Danny, Jason, Bertrand Herrmann, and my Baguazhang mentor Chiang. My father had called Michaela earlier in the week to ask what's going on and asked for me to contact him. I didn't while I was in jail, but I do now. Surprisingly, Jeffrey doesn't give me a hard time. In fact, he asks if I'm all right. The conversation doesn't last long, but I'm speechless when my father says, "I know you aren't guilty, that you're being railroaded. Let me know if I can help."

After an hour of calling while the others talk among themselves I finally feel exhausted.

Veronica tells me, "Give it up. The rest can wait, right?"

We're in Bob's kitchen. Bob doesn't drink much, and I'm not allowed to as a condition of bail. However, Bob does have a fancy coffee machine for lattes and cappuccinos that he's working for everyone like a barista. "I guess. I just need to start repairing things."

"We're good. The cases haven't fallen behind, with Geneva's help. No one's canceled any jobs. We've picked up more inquiries, if anything. Perhaps you should get arrested more often?"

"I'll only allow *you* to say that, and only today."

∞

In the evening, Joel arrives at Bob's apartment in his rental car. Bob greets him at the door. "Hey man. He's sleeping in the bedroom. Veronica and Michaela have left. They wouldn't tell me what they were going to do to each other or provide pictures, damn it."

Joel smiles. "Sorry about that. Did everything go okay?"

"Absolutely. I've been in jail. Nothing like *not* having someone watch you get up, watch you go to sleep, watch you take a shower or piss. Or saying *sir* every other word. He's re-acclimating."

Joel walks around the living room. He likes the fact Bob's place has a lot of plants and posters from 1960s era rock groups. Bob hands him a set of keys. "For you, as long as you need."

"You're a good man."

"He's been there for me more than once. I'll back him up. How is your mom?"

"Things are weird."

"Roll with it. You look tired. Go on in if you want. I've got some sexting to do."

Joel shakes Bob's hand formally, which just gets him a hug in return. Then Joel opens the bedroom door softly.

Gabriel is lying on a double bed in the blue and white room, clad in a t-shirt and shorts. The monitor on his left ankle is small and thin, really a two-inch strap with a black box the size of a flip phone on the outside.

Joel sits next to him on the bed for a while, watching.

Gabriel moves in his sleep then and wakes suddenly, looking over his shoulder as if for an attacker. Joel knows that feeling.

Gabriel sees Joel, and takes a moment to focus. Joel smiles, since Gabriel is now clean-shaven. "This is what it took, huh?"

They embrace each other. Gabriel brings Joel's face to his, taking him in.

Eventually he asks, "How is Gloria? What happened?"

Joel looks away for a moment. "Mom wanted to get some papers out of the house and asked Dell to go with her. While they were there, Dell saw Meese outside the house, in his car."

"What did he do?"

"Stayed in the car. Dell thought it was strange. When he looked out the window, Meese drove away. Dell asked some questions but Mom didn't say anything—listening to me for once."

"For Meese to leave when he saw Dell looking out..." "Right. I didn't like it. When I came over, Dell kept trying to get me to talk to him, like he's my substitute father or something. Bullshit. I took her back to the loft. I asked Chris to stay with her tonight and keep her distracted with stories about Area 51."

The darkness in his face makes Gabriel concerned. Aside from what is going about Meese, Gabriel senses Joel is holding himself back in his feelings. He must be in a rage of emotions under the surface.

Eventually, in the quiet of room and the night, and being able to feel the safety of Gabriel's arms, he breaks down and cries some.

They lie entwined on the bed until the tears have stopped. Gabriel asks, "Do you want to talk about anything?"

"I don't know. Right now, I'm glad to be alone with you."

Gabriel says, "I missed you so much. Life can be so unfair."

Joel sits up and takes off his shoes. "Sometimes. But we're here now, right? Isn't that Buddhist?"

"Yes, but Buddhism is not on my mind. You know that play, *Bent?* It was made into a movie with Clive Owen. Dominic took me and Mom to see it. Two gay men in a concentration camp. They love each other but can't look at each other or touch each other. They express themselves verbally to be sexual--really, to be intimate. And they do that right in the middle of the camp, with the guards watching. That couldn't be taken away; it was a victory, a triumph for them. This whole time locked up, I thought of that. And I talked to you, as if you were there. I felt like that could be us. Even if we weren't in the same place, we could be together. Thinking of that kept me sane. *You* got me here, not religion."

Joel lies down again to be face to face with him. "What did you talk to me about?"

"Umm. What we did, what we would do. Not just sex, but sex makes me feel alive. With *you*. I can't believe it makes such a difference, but it does."

"I feel that too...You want to do something?"

"Jesus, yes. But it's been a very trying day for us."

"Maybe I need to."

Gabriel keeps his hands on Joel's face. Joel moves his hands down Gabriel's body, feeling him responding.

"Tell me what you said in jail, like in the movie..." Joel says.

Gabriel tells him as Joel takes off his clothes and Gabriel's, and then sits on Gabriel's legs. He brings his hands down, stroking them together. A very intimate, low-key act. But intense. Then Gabriel eventually gently pulls Joel down beside him, and moves his mouth down Joel's body. And stays there for some time. Joel closes his eyes and just feels.

Gabriel pauses to say to him, "You asked me not long ago if I remembered our first weekend together. What do you remember?"

∞

It is August 25, 2006, Continued

What he remembers...

He follows Gabriel back to the sofa in the living room, and curls up with him, running his hand down Gabriel's leg.

And Gabriel spends a long time just kissing him. At first it's strange, then he finds the experience more powerful in its slowness.

And Joel tells him. "I knew you were different."

"Is that right?"

"Yeah. I never fucked an angel before." He presses against Gabriel for emphasis, half under his body. Sees Gabriel's eyes flash at feeling Joel's desire.

"I never fucked a prophet. I guess we're both in for something." Gabriel takes Joel's hand and puts it on his crotch. Joel moves his hand gently, hearing Gabriel's breathing become heavier. Joel unzips the jeans and slides his hand in, enjoying how Gabriel reacts.

Then Gabriel touches him in turn. Staring up at Gabriel's eyes while Gabriel is stroking him, he finds himself lost in it. Why? Something in his hands, in his body, in his being. The difference between a person and the *right* person doing it.

It makes Joel start to tremble from feeling that power. *Give in to it.* He tells himself. *Give in. He's different.*

"What," Gabriel whispers, clearly enjoying this.

"You're making me feel..."

"I'm making you feel. Feel both of us, Joel. Tell me what you want."

Joel shows him, and then Gabriel does the same.

During the next day, Saturday, Gabriel is content to just have Joel lie on the sofa with him, watching James Bond movies on BBC America. Joel lies in front, and Gabriel has his arm around Joel, and a leg wrapped around him as well. Sometimes. He shifts back every so often.

Joel finally turns his head to look up at Gabriel, who's paying attention to *Goldfinger*.

"You don't have to hide it."

"Hmmn?" Gabriel looks down at him. "Hide what?"

Joel moves his hand behind him, to feel between Gabriel's legs. "This."

Gabriel smiles. "I didn't want you to think that was all I want. Because I like what we're doing now, too."

"Oh, I was worried you were just really into Pussy Galore, there."

Gabriel bites his lip and then moves his fingers on Joel's ribs until he hits a ticklish spot.
"Oh, that gets to you, does it? Be careful with the smartass remarks."

Joel giggles helplessly. And suddenly Gabriel pulls him in closer, grinding against him. With his mouth he finds an area at the back of Joel's neck that Joel didn't even realize was so sensitive to touch.

"Yes," Joel says. For a couple minutes, everything is forgotten in that experience. The combination of hardness and softness. The point of Gabriel's tongue tracing nerves he didn't know he had.

"Wait here," Gabriel says, his voice low with urgency. He sits up. "No. Take your clothes off. Then wait here."

Five minutes or so later they're back in the same position, but now Gabriel's fucking him. Slowly. Barely moving in this relaxed position, like at a Roman banquet. The magic works here too, for some time. Joel can't even speak coherently, seeing Gabriel's hand move up and down his body while he rocks his hips against Joel. Watching Gabriel's hand go down to stroke him in rhythm. "God, your body is so warm," Gabriel says as he moves his hand. "I love feeling that."

The safety and power of being in his arms. Then Gabriel puts his mouth on the back of Joel's neck again, making him tremble.

"I'm going to come..."

"Yes...I want to see you come." Gabriel moves harder, faster. Driving him. Making him explode in release, and in tears at the same time. Then coming himself, saying Joel's name over and over. He has tears as well, and they're both in astonishment over this intensity. Joel's head is turned up to Gabriel's; Gabriel cradles his face, keeping them close together. They kiss, and again, and again, mixing saliva and tears and sweat.

What is he doing to me?

∞

"Is that what you wondered..." Gabriel asks him. "What I was doing to you?"

Gabriel had kept his mouth on Joel while Joel remembered the story out loud. And now he's lying behind him again. Joel feels the activation energy between them so strongly, the exothermic reaction of them both getting hotter from touch. And by now Gabriel has started re-enacting the memories. He has his mouth on the back of Joel's neck, and massaging him like he did then. That has Joel helpless.

He whispers, "You scared the fuck out of me..."

"That was intimacy, real intimacy. Not only fucking. Just like now, intimacy. Being scared is worth it, baby."

"It still scares me. I've never had this kind of...whatever I have with you."

That makes Gabriel smile; spurs him on. "I know. You're so fucking special to me. Isn't that why we went through what we did, to be together? Just feel it now. It scares you, and you're not going to trade that for anything. Anything."

Joel starts trembling, and Gabriel holds him tight, their bodies together. "Look at me."

Joel turns his head up. Now they're both sweating and breathing hard. Joel has tiny tears in his eyes.

Gabriel says, "Tell me you love me."

He breathes, "I love you."

"Tell me while you're coming. Don't stop looking at me."

"I love you..." tears spring in his eyes as he comes in Gabriel's hand, as Gabriel climaxes in him. And Gabriel is saying it back, his hand cradling Joel's head close to his. They stay in their mutual gaze long after bodies have calmed, sweat has cooled. *A victory...*

∞

Ten

Frederick Douglass said, "We have to do with the past only as we can make it useful to the present and the future."

∞

Tuesday, May 3rd
Alphabet City, Avenue A, 10: 27 am

JOEL IS SO ANGRY about *another* search that he can't read the warrant. He just trusts Michaela that it's properly written and executed. Dell had let Michaela know that he was going to search Gabriel's apartment again. Joel took Archie out of the place and over to Veronica and Geneva's apartment. They have a new orange kitten, Farrah, and Archie enjoys other cats.

Gabriel had insisted upon giving Joel a temporary power of attorney so he could handle certain things that Gabriel cannot get to, like paying bills. One of the disadvantages of being a criminal defendant is that while you are considered innocent until proven guilty, your life goes to hell if you cannot be outside to maintain the status quo. Joel is willing without question to handle that which would go to hell—checking Gabriel's mail, fielding messages, keeping utilities going. Joel's stress level is balanced by the appreciation of trust Gabriel gives him to fully handle Gabriel's life, to step in for him where he can't.

He has help. Michaela, of course is handling legal aspects. Veronica, with Geneva's assistance, is working the open caseload and dealing with new clients. This shows that their decision to pair up was a good one. And in fact, as Veronica had said, no one has asked to cancel their contract due to Gabriel's being arrested. Quite a change from last year. Now positive notoriety makes him more appealing to a public who is looking for an antihero.

But at the moment, Joel and Michaela are at the apartment to accompany Dell and a couple investigators from the Passaic County prosecutor's office, as well as the requisite NYPD officers necessary for jurisdictional purposes.

The violation of being searched is hateful to Joel. Michaela keeps an eye on him as well as the officers. Geneva texts him while he waits for this to be over. She promises to help clean the place up and burn sage to clear the vibes of police officers.

In the first search, the police had taken computers—to look for evidence like documents, emails showing collaboration, or Google searches on how to kill someone. The hard drives have been backed up but the invasion of privacy is sickening. Joel knows they have reviewed Gabriel's bank account, credit cards...searching for relevant purchases (like the knife), payments, statements, phone calls. They found nothing, but the prosecutor's office is trying again.

The revenge killing theory is the prosecutor's baby. The fact it's not the truth is irrelevant--just like the Warren Commission, Gabriel would say. Joel smiles for a moment. And as the son of the victim, and a possible suspect, they might investigate him. Investigate his past. Well, take that as it comes. He's survived worse.

One of the more unpleasant Passaic County investigators looks around the living room, with a notebook in his hand. He seems disappointed that the apartment isn't a murder repository. He says to Joel with impatience, "Are you *sure* this is everything originally in the apartment?"

"I took out the videos of me banging your mom," Joel replies. "Didn't want to embarrass you."

Dell steps in between them before further interplay occurs.

A few minutes later, Gloria shows up at the apartment.

"I want to be here for you," she says to Joel.

But she's also friendly to Dell, like she's okay with this. She doesn't seem to understand the situation here, at least to Joel's reckoning. *She wants me to be friends with her pet detective.*

Dell is cordial during the search and careful in how he talks to Joel, as Michaela is watching. However, after she and the officers leave, he stays around. Chit chat Joel wants no part of. But there's Mom, acting like it's no big thing. She tries to interest Joel in Dell's work history.

"John started out in the department—when?"

"I started patrol in 1992. In the Youth Bureau. I made detective there."

"You two never had a chance to talk much."

Joel tries not to glare at his mother. "I didn't know a lot of cops. I wasn't a delinquent. Just neglected."

"Joel, really..."

"No, John. That's true. I was not good to him at that time. It's not his fault he was gone. Ken threw him out, and I let him."

Joel collapses in a chair as she starts sniffling. Dell murmurs something to her. Joel's irritation rises. *He's* the one who was abandoned, but somehow, she gets the attention.

Joel says to Dell, "You're done. It's time to go."

"Joel, don't be rude. He's trying to help."

"Get my boyfriend out of custody then. You know he's innocent. You fucking know it. *He was trying to help Mom.* If you do any investigation on Ken, you'll see. Why do you let this go on, if you're such great friends with her?"

Dell meets his eyes. "Joel, I'm neutral. The prosecutor made the decision to hold Gabriel. I'm looking for all relevant evidence. If you have any ideas, you're welcome to share them."

Joel lights a cigarette and stares back at him. In his experience, police don't listen. They have their view of the world. Everyone's guilty of something. They'll say anything, do anything, to trip you up.

But his emotions get the better of him. That a Wayne police officer is in his world, his sanctuary.

"The corruption started from your own department," he says.

Gloria gasps, no doubt from his infernal rudeness. But Dell takes it neutrally, because he's so damned neutral. "What does that mean?"

"It means you'll find more looking there, than here. Now get the fuck out."

He's not abiding by Gabriel's courtesy theory.

Dell is not insulted. Just as Joel has his perspective, so too do police officers who are well aware that they cannot be separated from their job in people's minds.

"Let me talk to you alone."

Joel indicates to Gloria she should go to the bedroom. She does so, reluctantly.

"So, what?"

Dell, sitting on Gabriel's sofa, observes him carefully. "You said corruption goes to my department. Would you like to elaborate on that?"

"No, I would not." Joel exhales, rolling his eyes.

"Is Larry Meese a good friend of yours?"

That gets a reaction despite Joel's inner and outer barricades. "*Fuck* no."

"A friend of your father's though."

"So I heard."

"For a long time?"

"Yeah. I guess."

"You know I was planning to go through Ken's papers. I thought maybe, just maybe, Ken was involved in...something. And got killed for that. However, his storage unit was broken into and nothing is left."

Joel wants to ask if the Dewars bottles are still there but doesn't. "We turned over what we have. Like Michaela said, Gabriel was trying to find out what Ken was doing."

"And Ken called him over to the house, Gabriel says, and a big man killed him. Don't look at me like that. I'm not saying it isn't true, I'm saying I'm looking to see what *is* true. From the little we've been able to make out, the papers you found seem to indicate that Ken had some offshore accounts. We're trying to get more info but these banking places don't like to cooperate. You think he was in a conspiracy?"

Joel shrugs.

Dell continues. "If so, he covered it up pretty well with his various companies. You know what's funny? One of the companies has the same name as Larry Meese's boat."

"Yeah, that's hilarious."

"What is it with you and him? What happened?"

Joel lights another cigarette and looks away from Dell. The idea of telling a stranger, another cop...

"Joel, I suppose you're working with Gabriel's lawyer. If you find anything, I could help. That reporter seems to be investigating too."

Joel snaps his head around. "Who?"

"What's his name--Barclay? He asked me some things."

Joel frowns. "Whatever."

"Hmm. Not friends, huh? He asked about you. And Ken. He seems to know a lot about you."

That just makes Joel burn inside and shut down. Dell tries a little more than finally gives up. Gloria walks Dell outside, sputtering some sort of platitudes about how *we're all in this together.*

Yeah, right. Joel locks the door behind them and goes back to scowling at nothing.

But he's also irritated that Gabriel hasn't really talked about where to begin with his own case. As if depending upon forensic evidence is such a grand-slam. Tell that to the innocent people on death row still waiting to get out. Meanwhile, Alex is being not-helpful by investigating Joel. Of course he would, the asshole.

Since Joel's stepping in for Gabriel in one way, he's going to step in for him in another. Before the first police search of the apartment he did his own search. Aside from a few leftover packs of Camels he's confiscated, he found Gabriel's notes on a legal pad on top of the folder of papers regarding Tartarus. Gabriel noted that his next plan was talking to people who worked with his father.

∞

Friday, May 6th
Hackensack, NJ, 10:02 am

Joel knocks at the apartment door. It's the residence of a man named Carson Smith. Joel has spent the last couple days at the Division of Development. He developed an idea to play up sympathy over Ken's murder to get people to talk. And then since the staff would not likely talk about state business, to then ask them a more offbeat question. *Has anything really out of the ordinary happened that was in any way connected with Ken?*

A sympathetic colleague who was Ken's underling told him about an auditor who was trying to get Ken to look into an old contracting deal, and then suddenly quit. The colleague needed the auditor's signature and had to deal with getting the man's supervisor to write it off. Not only did the auditor not give notice, he took all his leave so he wouldn't have to be in the office at all.

A white man around 50 looks out cautiously.

Joel says, "Are you Carson Smith? Could I talk to you a minute? About your work at the Division of Development?"

"Who are you?"

"I'm investigating the case of Ken McFadden. I believe you worked with him?"

"That fucker. Don't talk to me about him."

"Did you have a conflict?"

The man breathes hard. "He fucking ruined my life. How's that for a conflict?" He slams the door shut.

"I guess that would work," Joel says out loud. He waits outside the door, sensing the man inside is watching him.

The door opens. The man stares out at Joel.

"Are you kidding me?"

"No, I want to talk to you."

"I told you, I have nothing to say about McFadden."

"Nothing good, anyway. I understand that. I don't either."

"Oh yeah? You worked with him too?"

"He was my father."

This surprises Carson so much he just gapes at Joel. Then he steps back. "Well, I know this is bad, but I can't say I'm sorry he's dead."

"Neither can I. However, I have reasons to find out who really did it. The man arrested for it didn't kill him. So, maybe you can tell me why you're not sorry he's dead."

Carson bites his nails. "Seriously? You think I did it?"

"I don't know. You can tell me if you didn't. If you did, I'll find out. But in any case, you probably would like to vent about him, and whatever you tell me can't shock me."

Carson lets go of the door and moves aside. "Fuck it. All right. Come in. Sorry if it makes you think less of him."

Joel walks inside. "I doubt anything can make me think less than I already do."

In spite of his anger, Carson gives him a strange look. People aren't supposed to say that about their fathers. Even bad fathers.

Carson waves him to a chair.

"I've just applied for disability benefits. I think I have PTSD. I know that's going to be a rough road."

Carson seems to think Joel should understand why that happened.

"You quit your job all of a sudden."

Carson begins pacing the living room, getting visibly upset. "Fuck. This has been a nightmare. I was too scared to say anything. I had to quit. I had no choice."

"I'm sorry to hear that," Joel says. "Did Ken have something to do with this?"

Carson stops pacing and stares at Joel. "He caused it. I think. It had to be him, because it happened after I talked to him. I was told not to talk about it...but now I'm angry. Just, I'm not going to talk to the cops. Don't ask me to talk to the cops. I'm not going to court, either. You don't know what I went through."

"Tell me about what happened."

"I found something odd in a review of some contracting assignments. A job given to a guy who I know to be connected to one of the Jersey families. Not so unusual, right? Well still, not supposed to happen. This guy isn't even a contractor. It's a shell company. Yet Ken's office approved a bid *after* the man was sentenced to probation. A rudimentary background check would have found that out. I didn't think at first Ken had anything to do with it--maybe a field officer was bribed or something. I told him we should look into it further. He acted like he didn't believe me. When I came back with more info, then he turned all serious and concerned, and said he'd help out."

Carson takes a pill out of a bottle, among several bottles of prescription drugs on the coffee table. He swallows it dry. "And a few nights later I go home and find this man in my apartment. In that chair." He points. "He was a big guy, all in black. Hood and all. Even dark glasses."

Joel leans forward intently. "What happened?"

Carson shudders. "He said I should stop asking questions and just be a good little bureaucrat. If I didn't, he'd come back and I'd see my blood and brains exploding from my head. And even though he wore a Goddamn hood, I could tell he thought it was an interesting idea. He wanted to see my blood. He was emphatic about that."

Carson now looks like he's getting mad. "What else could I do?" He suddenly sweeps everything off his coffee table with his arm.

Then he stares at the bottles and papers on the floor. "What else could I *do?*"

Joel waits for Carson to get himself under control, then thanks him and leaves.

It's enough for Joel to work on. He still has contact information for some former clients, as well as acquaintances, who might be useful. Some of them have gotten in touch with him over the years. Joel still has one email he's never changed, from that life. Even though the life is over, he keeps the email as an identifier for those whose phone number he can't obtain.

Joel begins an assessment of who out of these people he knows might help him in this case. He sends some emails, makes some calls. He nets a few sexual offers he turns down politely.

The right person calls back. "My husband might be able to give you something. Is this a New York thing?"

"New Jersey."

"You want a contact there?"

"I don't know that I can trust anyone here. I'm looking for information on a suspected hired killer. I don't have a name, but I have a description of sorts."

"Let me have it, and I'll convince my husband to talk to you."

Two days later, Joel's flying to DC to meet with his former client's husband, a man who works for the Department of Justice, Organized Crime and Gang section.

They meet at the Martin Luther King Jr. memorial.

The man says, "I got the information from the New Jersey office; I told them it was a routine inquiry. I'm going to follow up and say that my non-existent suspect isn't theirs, so they don't ask questions. But for you, it probably is the right guy."

He opens the file to show Joel.

"Stephen Cody, 55. Six-five, probably 250 lbs. Suspected contract killer for some of the New Jersey families. Some of what's said about him is probably bullshit. He was supposed to have put one victim in a tank of piranhas, like a James Bond villain."

The man hands Joel a surveillance photo. "They haven't been able to hang anything on him. His taxes have been pulled, but whoever's handling that for him is clever. He's a consultant on business operations. That can mean whatever the fuck he wants it to. Gives him cover to travel." The investigator sighs. "I just gave up smoking. It's hard, when reading about this stuff. Cody is a suspect in at least a dozen mob hits."

"Any current operations on him?"

"No. It's an open file but not active. They'd reactivate if some new info comes in. I can tell you who to call, who'd most likely listen."

Similar to what Gabriel told Ken. The DOJ man surveys the spring landscape. Some cherry blossoms are coming in. "This part *isn't* bullshit. He likes blood. He tries to do his kills so they are as nasty as possible. The more blood the better. I looked it up. Hematolagnia. Bloodlust. It's his thing. He wears the hood at the killings. Makes him stand out more, I'd think."

"Anything else outstanding about him?"

"This was a rumor; an associate of his supposedly said he might film his hits. I looked that up too. Scopophilia."

"Really?"

"I like to research things. Whenever my coworkers come across anything weird they check with me." He laughs.

"I know someone a lot like that."

Joel studies the file on the way back to New York. As soon as he can, he drives to Paterson.

∞

Tuesday, May 10
Paterson, NJ, 3:08 pm

I'm getting a text from Joel that he'll be coming over soon at the same time I hear knocking at Bob's door.

He opens it and says, "Oh. Hello." Someone he recognizes, but isn't sure how to handle. I look out the bedroom door to check.

Then I hear: "Hello, Bob. I guess my son is here. May I talk to him?"

Bob looks over his shoulder at me. I nod.

My father walks in. Jeffrey Ross has shorter, darker hair than me, graying now. He's in his early sixties. We have the same dark eyes, body type, same defensive posture. He's remarkably fit, and has an air of being on guard for threats.

"Gabriel."

I swallow hard. "Hello." Outside of his phone call when I was released, I haven't spoken to him since after the incident with Don Mathers hit the news, and that conversation was brief and perfunctory. He sent me a birthday card with the photo of me at 16, the one Joel had found before. I haven't *seen* him in...God knows. In my mind, I see the father I had when I was young, and his anger and scorn, alternating with a strange camaraderie when he would take me to practice shooting or other military survival exercises in the woods. Teaching me to do what he did.

Bob edges around the sofa. "I'll leave you two alone."

"Thank you," Jeffrey says.

Behind him, Bob looks at me, and I nod at him. I prefer to have him around close by, as this is making me extremely uncomfortable. He pretends to go upstairs but then slips into the kitchen.

Jeffrey puts his sunglasses in his blazer pocket and takes out a pair of glasses. Like me, he prefers wire rims.

I find myself mentally flailing. The unexpected visit gives me pause. I don't know what to say.

He asks, "How are you holding up?"

"Uh, I'm okay." I see he's scrutinizing me. "You can sit down if you want."

"Thank you. I'm glad your friend is helping you out."

"He's a real good man."

Jeffrey nods. He sits in the side chair; I sit on the sofa. He looks down at the monitor I wear. "Ridiculous," he says.

"Excuse me?"

"It's ridiculous, Gabriel. You being in this situation. I know you. I know you'd never kill someone. That they would even consider this tells me that they aren't doing their job right. You don't waste time with people who aren't viable suspects. Is this because of you finding those dead women?"

His eyes tell me he's sincere. "Well, I don't think so. The prosecutor in that case didn't like me, but this is a different county. They don't really know each other. It's the conflicting physical evidence."

He nods again. "Your friend is your attorney still?"

"Yeah. She's pretty sure that it will be dismissed."

"It should be. You don't handle life that way. You seem surprised to see me, Gabriel."

"I...yeah. You're here to...what?"

"To see how you are. I hate to pull a cliché, but you're my son. I know you're in trouble, and you don't deserve to be. What you did with that serial killer was a hell of a thing. I'm glad you got some acknowledgement about that. I don't like seeing you in this mess."

He laughs, startling me. "Jesus, you should see your face. You're like God hearing the Devil admit he has a point."

"I can't say I have any history of this happening."

"Is it that bad, Gabriel?"

"I appreciate your support. I really do, but yeah, it's that bad. You've told me everything I've done is wrong from as far back as I can remember. My wanting to play baseball. My liking to read. My not wanting to be in the Army. My not wanting to hunt. And let us not forget your gentle critique once you found out I was gay. I always thought you hated me. That I was a disappointment to you. You told me I was an idiot for what happened in Buckston."

"Life is tough, Gabriel. I wanted you to survive. I didn't want you to be a target. I didn't say everything you did was wrong. And about Buckston with that preacher, I said pick your battles. I did neglect to tell you what was right; I admit that. I let your mom do that. I never hated you, and you weren't a disappointment. I didn't agree with much of what you liked and who you were, but you did it, right? You always stood up for yourself. You learned that."

"From Mom."

"Of course. She may have been artistic, but she was tough."

It's hard to accept the words, even if the feeling is genuine. "If it wasn't for her, I'd have turned out to be a psychopath. All I heard from you was how terrible it was that I wanted to be some kind of fag."

Jeffrey looks away, out the front window. Then he calls out, "Bob? If you don't mind, do you have any coffee?"

No sound from the kitchen.

"I know you're there backing Gabriel up. Nothing is going to happen."

I say, "It's okay, Bob."

Jeffrey looks back to me.

I tell him, "The only time I had your approval was playing your war games. Any other time I was nothing to you."

"That isn't true. But I understand why you saw that. That is my fault. Except for one thing--I was good with you wanting to be an investigator. Dominic gave you a lot of trouble about that; it wasn't "good enough" for him. But it was clear to me you would have no problems doing that work. I told your mom to get off your back about it."

That's a jolt; I have to think back for any evidence it's true. And then I remember it was. I carried so much anger towards him, that his surprising support for my career choice meant nothing at the time.

Bob brings him a mug of coffee. Jeffery thanks him, and when Bob goes back into the kitchen, he asks me, "How'd you get out on bail?"

I start to answer and stop. "I'm not a flight risk."

"That's not the issue. This is a serious charge. Please tell me. I'd like to know what's going on."

I lean back on the sofa. My relationship with him is such that it wouldn't occur to me that he'd want to know. I have to think if I can trust him. His background is in intelligence, so he understands confidentiality.

Staring at him, I say, "Joel called in a favor with a man who pulled strings with the judge."

"Joel? The man's son. The one who was killed."

"Yes. I don't know what you know about this."

"What I read in the stories. I read them all. They only say so much. He worked with you, Joel did. Is that right?"

"He's my boyfriend. When he was 15, his parents threw him out of his house because of who he was."

Jeffrey keeps my gaze. He nods once more, slowly. "That explains it. They think it's a domestic thing because of you and Joel."

"Yeah, it's a theory."

"What they did was wrong, to throw him out. You're looking at me like I'd think otherwise."

"You didn't help when you threw us out."

He sighs. "You don't entirely understand that, Gabriel. Another thing that's my fault for not trying to talk to you before this. We're alike that way. Stubborn. Not hearing what we don't want to hear. I figured someday we'd talk, and then time just keeps going with nothing happening. I never threw *you* out. Kate and I had issues. She didn't like my line of work, what I did in the military."

He nods at my surprise. "She didn't tell you that, because she was not a person to badmouth. She knew that the work was my life. Remember when you called me at Christmas, and told me you ended a relationship because that man didn't appreciate your job? That's what went on between her and me. I told her she could leave if she couldn't handle it. I was younger, had a lot of passion for her *and* for my career. So it didn't always go well between us. But I would have had you stay with me if I could. I would never throw my son on the street.

"At the same time, it would have broken her heart to *not* have you. And if I was on a mission, well...I wouldn't know what to do with you. When we split up, you went with her. I know we had a tempestuous relationship at times. When we got back together, it was for real. We both changed."

Hearing that is so strange to me, as a description of him and Mom, as a description of me and Joel; he can see my reaction.

"What?"

"Nothing...nothing. Look, tempestuous doesn't aptly describe living in a car because you have no money."

He frowns. "She never told me about that, you know. She wanted child support, which was what I could afford. She didn't say she was homeless. She went to her brother for help but not me."

"Dom had a heart."

"I'll never be what he was to you, I know that. But I loved her nonetheless."

"So much love, you had to share it with other women. And your drinking."

"That's none of your business. What was between her and I was *our* business. I never cheated on her when we got back together. And this was at a time you were making her miserable by refusing to talk to her, and fucking around getting in trouble with your friend Danny."

That hurts, because it's true in part. I gave my mom a bad time for a couple years after she reconciled with him.

"I'm glad Dominic watched over you. I'm glad you made things right with her. She loved you like crazy. She'd be very proud of you now. And I am, for what it's worth. And as for the drinking, I don't do it now. It was hard to deal with some of what I saw and went through back then. That's not an excuse. It hurt you. It damaged what was between you and me. I said things I shouldn't have. I saw you hate me. It's hard to see your own kid hate you, but...I accept my responsibility for that."

I can hardly move, from the waves of feeling going over me. Him here, talking about my mother. I feel a jealousy; she's mine, not his. I never thought about her in terms of her relationship with him.

And I can't just let it go that he claims to have these feelings. I understand Joel's turmoil with his mother better now. "You've thought of me as less than you because I'm gay."

He looks away for a long minute. "You know, the military has changed. Don't Ask, Don't Tell ended, and I rolled my eyes because I had no idea if this would hurt military effectiveness or not. And then I started finding out that people I knew were gay. One of them, a colleague who saved my life once, said, "Jeff, doesn't it get tiring carrying around that attitude? It only hurts you, and your son." I was mad for weeks, but he was right. He was a good man who had to hide himself, and who he was had no impact on his skills. I broke it down and thought about it. An intelligent man can't carry that prejudice."

"So your friend could teach you something I couldn't? Nice."

"Yes. I'm sorry. You don't give in easily. Me either. It's strange to see you the same way. I created you in part and you learned the good things of survival, and the fucked-up things of never giving in, never relenting even when someone's trying to reconcile with you. Because I need to take the accountability for this, I'm going to share something with you."

He breathes deeply, and I find myself in anticipation of this. I know so little about him...as little as he knows about me.

"The work I did...that I still do on occasion...it nearly killed me several times over. Not just being in danger. There's that, but physical danger never bothered me. It's where I had to go in my mind to do what was necessary to take care of my people, to take care of a mission. I couldn't tell Kate. Some of it was classified, but also I didn't want to be diminished in her eyes. She had such a strong sense of ethics that I couldn't hold to. I knew she would not see me the same way. I had to accept the bargain that I would just not tell her the dark places I went to. The drinking was the proverbial pain killer. Dealing with memories, dealing with waking up and thinking for a moment: *who's there? Who do I have to look out for? Who's trying to kill us?* But also afraid that she'd see through me and leave me again."

I can't say anything. I'm struck mute. He meets my eyes.

"I know something very similar is in you. You have to watch out for it. When you fought that man in Newark--the serial killer--I heard how badly he ended up. I'm not the kind of asshole who says, all right, my kid can beat the shit out of someone. I know where you went to in order to do that. Bob knows it too, right, Bob?"

"Yes," Bob says from the kitchen. "It was pretty bad. I know those places as well."

"And at the same time, maybe I was jealous of you in way. You didn't put up a façade. I took my anger out on you when you were younger; anger meant for myself. But you didn't break. You didn't turn into a drunk like I did, and that meant you were stronger than I was."

He smiles. "You may not realize or want to, but we're pretty similar. You have the same skills. You're as good a shot--probably a better shot than me. You know how to find things, how to go places. You don't let people intimidate you. You can take a lot and don't complain. Look at you here. An ordinary person would be freaking because of what happened. But you--you're tough. I know they beat you; I saw it on the news. I was trying to call people to help, but you got out. And you can be tough on other people's behalves. You did that for your mom plenty of times. You know how to get in the street and take care of business. You did what I would do and you did it well."

I want to check my ears. Maybe my brain. Perhaps I'm hallucinating.

"If you were working on my team in the field," Jeffrey says, "I know I could drop you in an operation and not worry about you losing your shit. That's valuable."

"Thanks."

"We have the tough bloodline. Did you know your great-great-great grandfather was an Irish immigrant who lived in Five Points?"

I have to smile. "The toughest lowlife place in the city. You didn't tell me."

"I'll go over the history sometime. But it shows in you. The toughness, not the lowlife part. I know you'll get through this but I want to help. Is there anything I do for you? Do you need money?"

I can't help it. I grab the pack of cigarettes that somebody left here on a visit and light one. Drawing it in, I answer. "No. It's covered. Thank you for offering."

"Your friend is pro bono?"

"I'm taking care of it."

"A good defense is expensive. I have investments."

"Really, it's taken care of."

"I can see if anyone I know has pull in the prosecutor's office. Or if you need some feet on the ground looking for evidence."

"Um, I have people doing that. But...I guess I could ask you to check something that has nothing to do with this."

"All right. Something in another case?"

"Not officially. And it's sensitive. I know you know how to handle that. It's something maybe in your area."

"I got you."

"There's a man in an intelligence agency here. Aaron Comstock. He might be connected with some kind of MK-ULTRA type operation. I wanted to see if there's anything...I don't know, that says who he really is. But I don't want you to put yourself in danger or get noticed, in finding it out."

"I can do that. I appreciate that you trust me."

I think about changing. It means having to consider changing everything, even my relationship with him especially as he seems to want to change it with me. This may be the hardest thing for me, as he doesn't realize how bad it was for me as a kid. It still hurts.

"Gabriel, about military culture. It really makes you feel separate from civilians. Only another military person understands. It made me feel you didn't appreciate me, that you didn't appreciate how good you had it. And I didn't go for help for myself because the culture discouraged that."

He gets up. "If you need anything else, the offer still stands. I'll check on you later."

I just nod and get up too. "Okay, thank you. Why...what made you come here?"

"You're my son. We have differences. Like I had with my father. I guess Kate rubbed off on me finally. Maybe her ghost is haunting me. I didn't want it to be the same way. You just turned 37. I can't believe my son is almost 40 and a tough man. A man who deserves respect. I have to support you. Just don't go to those places I did."

He puts his hand on my shoulder briefly and doesn't wait for me to reciprocate. Unlike Gloria, he isn't asking for anything.

Turning towards the door, Jeffrey peers out the front window in a manner that seems familiar to me. Like he's ready to go psycho on whoever is outside. Did I look that way to Joel with the UPS man some weeks ago?

"Someone's coming," he says.

I look over his shoulder. "That's Joel."

He turns to me. "Your boyfriend. I guess you'll introduce him to me?"

"If you say anything unpleasant to him, I'll knock you the fuck out."

He actually smiles. "Just as I would, had anyone said anything to Kate. I wanted to kick *your* ass more than once for that. She wouldn't let me."

Joel knocks, not wanting to use the key Bob gave him. I open it and step back.

"Hey, he says, coming in. I'm pleased to see he has a cat carrier with Archie inside. Then Joel sees my father. He recognizes him from the photo. His eyes widen.

"Joel, this is my father, Jeffrey Ross. Dad, as you said, I'm introducing you to my boyfriend. Joel McFadden."

"Joel." Jeffrey holds his hand out, and Joel takes it. Jeffrey shakes his hand formally. "I'm sorry about your father."

"Um. Thank you. You were here...talking to Gabriel?"

"I wanted to see how he was. To see if he needed help with his legal bills, or investigation or whatnot."

"Oh. Well, that's appreciated. I'm making sure he's taken care of."

I see Jeffrey appraising him. "Good. He needs his back covered. He's damn good at what he does, but still everyone needs some cover at some point."

"He has it. That's kind of my responsibility."

Jeffrey nods. "I have to leave now. I'm glad to know Gabriel has backup." Jeffrey looks from Joel to myself and back. He nods again, to himself. God knows what he's thinking.

"*What*," I say, a little roughly.

"He's as tough as you, Gabriel. I can tell. Better be, with the trouble you cause."

Joel tries not to smile, seeing my glare.

Jeffrey takes out his wallet and a card. "Gabriel has my number, of course. Buried under something so he can't see it, or maybe in a voodoo doll. Nonetheless, if you need my help for anything with him, whatever that may be, get ahold of me." He hands the card to Joel.

"Thank you," Joel says again.

Then Jeffrey leaves, shutting the door behind him.

"Holy shit," Bob says, having left the kitchen. "We must be in Bizarro World."

"Ain't that the truth." I exhale smoke.

Joel is letting Archie out the carrier, then notices the cigarette. "That's gotta stop right now."

"I'm entitled. My father said he was proud of me. A Hallmark moment." My cat jumps in my arms and I stroke him.

"Maybe he meant it." Joel takes the cigarette away from me. "What else did he say?"

I give him the details of the conversation. Then, because I see he's edgy to get to some other agenda, I say, "So what's going on with you?"

"I want to show you what I found. I followed up on what you were going to do with the agencies."

Now I have a second chance to be utterly surprised. We haven't been talking much about the case. In this role of defendant, I've had a hard time adjusting to the idea of proving my innocence. I've been working too hard on just trying to feel normal.

I should have known Joel would be relentless about it. He lays out his handwritten notes and file on Stephen Cody. I read the notes about Carson Smith and Cody's home invasion, on what Joel's father was doing, and then the file. Carefully, slowly, holding Archie on my lap. Joel nearly goes crazy waiting for me to finish. I still have to shake my father out of my mind in order to concentrate. But then the case file becomes clear.

Joel starts talking. "It has to be Cody, don't you think?"

"Makes sense. That stupid knife. He was probably planning to cut us both open to bleed out."

"He killed Dad deliberately, you said. This was a setup."

"I don't doubt. Ken was the lure. They probably thought with both of us dead, it would look like Ken and I had a fight. I'm just not sure of why. Ken wasn't going to go flip on them. And I knew nothing. So why kill us?"

"Maybe they thought Ken and you were trouble."

"Cody could believe that. He's a hit man. Meese..."

Joel twitches at his name.

"Has he tried to call you?"

"No, thank God. He calls my mom. She doesn't answer."

"Can you ask her to answer once? See what he wants?"

"Ugh. Okay. He must have freaked when they moved you. If she pretends they're friends maybe he'll leave you alone."

I say, "Actually, I think the opposite." He's lit one of his own cigarettes and I take it from him to draw.

"What do you mean?"

"See what he says when she talks to him. Then we'll go over it. In the meantime, this was good information. Cody's an interesting person, not that I'd want him as a neighbor. For a hit man, he's pretty sophisticated and kind of psychotic. Hit men are all basically serial killers. But he's very pathological."

Joel shrugs. "That's not what jumped out at me."

"There's a reason it's important. How he kills, what he does."

"Sexual."

"Even sexual is playing to something *else* in the brain. The brain is the key organ. Physical arousal is nothing compared to mental arousal. Cody's playing to that mental arousal. It's important."

Joel's paying attention to me. "Okay, why is it important?"

"To understand what evidence may be available. To understand his vulnerabilities. In any case, I'm thinking of different approaches. Were you able to get anything from Ken's laptop information?"

Joel's eyes flash impatience at me but he answers. "Some of the banks he visited online, and I think some account numbers or passwords."

"Good. I want to look at the copies of Ken's papers we have. I want to get a paper trail started with him and these offshore accounts. We can build a case of corruption with Meese. That will bring them down, and that will end this."

"Or, and I like this *better*, I start following Cody and find out what he's doing."

"Or, and I like *this* better, you do no such thing."

"Excuse me?"

"Hell and no. No. Don't scowl at me, I'm beyond that. You do nothing with him. This is not up for discussion. I need you for your ability to get into these bank records."

"I thought you weren't supposed to break the law while out on bail."

"I'm not planning on using Bob's computer or the one you brought me, for Christ's sake. If you can get me the equivalent of a burner laptop I'll pay you."

Joel falls quiet. Burning me with his eyes. Bob, intelligently, refuses to offer comment.

I see Joel turning over things in his head like a steampunk machine. Gears and cogs and wheels in their own difficult rhythm.

"I have to take care of things on your behalf, with Veronica, and my mom, and my own stuff. Chris will work with you with the information I found. You know you can trust Chris like you do me."

I don't like his tone. I stare at him for a long time. "Joel, please don't make this a thing between us."

"You know I have to keep our lives holding together, right? Why are you looking at me like that?"

"*I know who I'm dealing with.* Don't do anything that I would have to kick your ass for. Jesus, I just threatened my father and my boyfriend. No wonder I'm a Goddamned criminal. Can you have Chris get here soon as possible, when you're doing things on my behalf?"

∞

Joel gets into the SUV he leased and lights up one his cloves.

"Just like our dear Angela," Jan says, smoking one of his expensive cigarettes.

"Angela smoked Marlboros. She made me quit the cloves because the clients would smell them on me. She didn't know everything."

Jan laughs gently. "You don't feel Gabriel knows everything."

"How can you love someone so much, and be so angry at him at the same time?"

"You're trying to protect each other. One of you has to give."

"He's not in a position to tell me what to do. Even Angela realized that eventually."

"But first you had to learn from her."

Joel looks over at Jan sitting next to him. "This is a different situation, I would think. No one's life or death depended upon me learning how to fuck."

"More than you think. What did she take you from, when she took you in? You *bristle* from people telling you what to do, but at the same time you're so good at learning from others."

Joel can see it in the notebook Jan holds.

∞

A N G E L A

Samuel Taylor Coleridge said, "And in today already walks tomorrow."

∞

Learn what you can.

May 27, 1996
Times Square, 12:07 pm

JOEL REALIZES SOMEONE'S watching him. He looks around to see if it's a pickup, or a rival. He almost doesn't realize the watcher is a woman.

Much older, late thirties maybe. Or forties with some work. A brunette well-dressed in a black and white checked skirt/jacket combo.

She walks up to him. "How old are you?"

The question is disconcerting enough that he answers. "Twenty-one."

"I doubt that. Please tell me you're not 17..."

He backs up from her. "Who the fuck are you?"

For some reason she smiles at his anger. "My name is Angela. I want to talk to you, okay?"

"I'm not interested." He walks away. She stays beside him.

"Hey, seriously. I'm not hassling you."

"Yes, you are."

The woman pulls out a fifty-dollar bill. "For twenty minutes of your time?"

Joel glances at the money then at her, and assumes an impervious expression. "I don't do that."

"What, with women? Never had a woman?" Her tone is so amusingly skeptical, he actually turns a little red.

She continues. "I'm not asking you to fuck me. I asking you to listen."

Joel recovers his bearing. "I get more than that."

"Maybe. That's why I want to talk to you. And this fifty dollars you don't have to spit out right after. Whatever you think you're making now, I can get you three or four times--probably more."

Joel remembers Mario's advice that he has to be careful about people offering things. Mario disappeared a year ago, while Joel was off the streets for a bit. Over the last two years, he's been back and forth between couch surfing and trying to do regular work like Chris does, trying to be a street artist as Isabella encourages, and going back to hustling.

God knows what happened to Mario. People in street life disappear like an alien abduction, or a reverse rapture.

"*They'll offer you all kinds of shit...the more they offer, the more likely they're planning to carve your face off.*"

Joel tells the woman, "Whatever you're selling, I'm not buying."

"*You'll* be selling. You'll be making money for both of us, honey. What's your name?"

"I don't have a name. I was born without one."

The woman laughs. "You're a smartass. Some people are born without names; I've met them. Some even work with me. It happens when you're abandoned. That's not you, though. You have a name."

"You don't need to know it."

"I will if you work for me."

"Why the fuck should I?"

She takes his arm and steers him down the street, away from the other boys. Her voice lowers. "Because you're smarter. I see that. I could be nice and say all the boys here are smart and beautiful, but I'm not nice. You're *miles* away from them. A couple years from now even more so."

He takes the fifty from her hand. "You've already taken enough of my time."

This doesn't bother her. "I like you. I think we can understand each other. Here's the deal. I need to see a birth certificate; no jailbait in my clan. Then you need to be tested. Then again after 30 days, then again after six months. In that time, you stay with me and stay clean. If you take drugs, I kick you out. I take in a lot of men, and I kick a lot out."

"You make it sound so great."

"You want to earn a thousand in one night? For just a few clients? You'll do it my way. I take very few people in to start new, usually they want to transfer to me because I run a good operation, top quality. I screen clients. I'm careful about who hires my boys. I'll protect you all the way, as long as you don't fuck with me. I'll get you out of jail in a sting, and I'll hire someone to beat the shit out of anyone who hurts you. But you have to play by my rules."

Joel stares at her. "And why couldn't I just do that on my own? Why should I have you pimp me out?"

"Because you don't know how to do it, jackass. I'm only crossing my fingers you're still clean."

He's still suspicious, but a part of his mind is considering it. "I've been doing this longer than you think. I can take care of myself. You want me to just live with you? Like a foster child?"

"At first. It doesn't cost that much. I keep track of expenses, and that's paid out of what you take in."

"Oh, like a Ponzi scheme."

"Not quite. A Ponzi scheme is fraud. What you're thinking is something else, like vigorish on a loan. But I'm not doing that. You'll make money. You'll get your own place. If you're smart, you'll save or invest it 'cause you'll have about five good years--ten if you keep your looks. If you're stupid, you spend it all and that's that. If you fuck up, you're out. Get hooked on drugs, you're out. Get a non-curable STD you're out. Hold out on me, you're out. Poach clients, you're out."

Joel stares at her.

"Let me take you to lunch."

She turns and walks away, and he follows. Why? Because his instinct says she's telling the truth and he can learn something. They go into a French bistro nearby, to a quieter table in back. She has some fancy cocktail and he has a Coke.

She's business-like. "How long *have* you been hustling on the street?"

"A couple years. Not all the time. I do other things. I can do electrical work, computer stuff, some things with carpentry. People around the city will pay for it...but not all the time, you know? I'm not licensed. Sometimes I get burned. Sometimes some guy will have me work with him and try to take the money."

"Like a pimp."

"Yeah. I don't have one, and I don't want one."

"I'm not one. If you're so good why do you hustle?"

He smiles. "I'm good at that too."

"Is that right? Is your attitude impressive to the tricks off the pier?"

"I've walked away when I wanted to. I don't want this to control me. But it's easier than trying to do the other stuff without a full-time job or a license."

"It's easier than working nine to five *with* a license. If you do it my way."

He toys with his straw. "I don't take well to being told what to do."

"Bull*shit*. You're picked up off the street by some fat fuck from Jersey or Staten Island. He tells you to suck his cock. Do you do it? Yeah. So you take to being told what to do."

Joel turns red. She waves that away. "I'm not sensitive, I can't be. I wish I could hold your hand but I've been burned too many times myself. We'll see where it goes. You need to be told what to do because you don't *know*. Get it through your head. You're 18, we presume. I want that birth certificate. You need to know how to be an adult. I have an older worker, Jake. Jake is aging out, he's 32. But he's the best. He never judges, he's cool, he handles emergencies well, he doesn't screw people over. Never did drugs, never tried any bullshit young workers think they can get away with like I'm old and stupid. I'm not. And I always know, I'll always find out. Jake will tell you what you need to know over the next few months while you're getting cleaned up. You'll have to fuck him but he has to know how good you are, what you can do and not do. He's clean, he'll show you."

"Show me what?"

"Sucking cock, getting sucked, fucking, getting fucked. Yeah, I know you think you know how to do it. There's a difference between street work and escorting; that's why you'll get paid more. BDSM, we have that if you can do it. Threesomes. Not often with mixed men and women, but that happens too. Other, more specialized services can be offered, but I'm not making you do what you don't want to. That doesn't benefit either of us. If you won't, one of my other boys will."

She starts eating. Joel is not as hungry; he's trying to absorb all she said.

"How did you know what I do, anyway?"

"That's a smart question. I knew you had something. I don't recruit from the street. You're an exception. Sometimes I have to be down this way. My place is on the West 90s. Anyway, I'm here, I look. I know the game. I see these boys on the street all the time. You don't dress obvious or effeminate. You have the Brando look. T-shirt and jeans. Both tight. *Really* tight. We can all see you dress to the left, and you're going commando. You could get away with the redneck or preppie look, but you like this. Your shoes and jacket are pricy for a street kid. I'd like to know how you ripped them off, and why someone else hasn't stolen them from you, but you can save that story for another time. You like clothes, and that's going to work out. You can *wear* clothes, like a model.

"Also, you have charisma. I've seen hundreds of them out there, and I usually don't *see* them, if you know what I mean. But I *saw* you. So did everybody else. I saw the other boys. They like you or they're jealous. I saw men with their wives check you out. That charisma is the biggest difference, the biggest money maker. I'm not blowing smoke up your ass. You can be smart and pull in 200 an hour, or stupid and piss it away for fifty.'"

"I make more than fifty."

"Not all the time. Not on the street, you don't. Don't try to fool me. Have you tried in bars?"

"No..."

"You'd make more. Never mind. You're going to now. How do you approach? How do they approach you?"

He thinks it over. "I don't mind spending time talking to them first, in conversation. Is that bad?"

"No, that shows you have a good attitude. People will appreciate that. What else?"

"Most of them ask if I want company. If I want to hang out, or go for a drive. Some will be more crude--do I like to fuck, and how. Some ask if I need money, and can they help."

"Sounds about right. I'm not saying the subtler ones are always the safer ones, but there's a correlation if you study it long enough."

Joel says, "If I see a guy who's checking me out, I might ask if they're looking for some place that I could help them find. I say I'm looking to build up a college tuition fund or pay a bill. Or sometimes they lie about where they're from and I say I'd like to hear more. Or I tell them I noticed them 'cause they're really hot, and ask if they want a date."

Angela pauses in her eating to laugh. "And they buy that. The hot part. I know they do; you don't have to say. They want to believe it, coming from you."

She indicates he should eat, while she watches him. "You work out somewhere."

"The Y on 18th. They have a pool. I like that. I don't pick up there because I don't want trouble. I want to be able to go back when I want."

"Good. Some boys have their heads up their asses. I knew I liked you. We have some rich clients. *Really* high dollar. Men who can't be gay openly, but can pay for it the way they want. And their wives don't care. Money makes up for everything."

She eyes him like he's a new car she's thinking of buying. "The more I look at you, the more I think you can handle it. Keep working out. No steroids for you, it would ruin your look. Some clients think they want 6'1, 200-pound muscle boys. Some want twinks. Don't try to change to either. You have a sell; you just need to work on it. Cut out the Brando bit. Go upscale. The ones who *will* want you will go nuts for you. I know some of my clients would eat you alive. Do you read?"

"Of course I do."

"We'll see. You want a GED, you can get that. Go to school and get the damned license if you want. On your own time. I'm interested in what you can do with my top roster clients. Don't mouth off to them. They have money, so they think they own the world. Let 'em. Who gives a fuck? They pay, that's what you remember."

She signals the waiter for the check. As if on cue, the waiter spends a brief moment looking Joel over, just a pause too long. And smiles. Out of habit, Joel smiles back.

Angela says, "If this wasn't business, I'd be insulted. One more thing. You top or bottom?"

"I don't do that. I mean, I don't want to. I don't like having my back to people."

"It goes for oral as well as anal. Yeah, on the street I understand. But this will be different. Also, that particular act can be done face to face."

He frowns at her. "Okay. Either, I guess. I mean, I've *done* it to people, but..."

"I don't need the details. You top, but can be versatile. Your rate just went up. You have no idea how much tops are in demand."

She gives him a business card. A consultant. Of course, what else? As he turns it over in his hands, he thinks about the prospects.

Five years, maybe. Doing what he's doing, but more money. Joel has no interest in drugs, no interest in partying, no interest in cars, houses, whatever people spend money on. He's also aware he's limited in what he does know. How to save money, how to invest. He'd have to do it slow, and observe. Angela probably knows; he wonders if she'd tell him.

"If I did, can you help me save money? Not hold it for me, but show me where to keep it."

"For retirement? Yeah, I can, but it's up to you to be disciplined; to be in control. As I said, some blow it as fast as they earn it."

"I don't have those habits. I know how to be in control."

"I don't doubt that. I see your control. You just need the knowledge, and to learn. You can set up some tax forms as a consultant. Don't fuck with the IRS. I'll have you down as an independent contractor if you want."

"I know computers pretty well; you could make it a computer consultant."

"Do you? I've thought about going online, but I don't know if it's worth the security risk if the DA decides he wants to hassle the sex businesses."

"I know computer security. I can show you."

"Well, we can help each other then."

And Joel does it. He does what he can to check her out. A couple people tell him she has a highly unusual operation. She's very hands-on and micromanaging. Most escort agencies would just look the escort over, maybe ask him or her to strip. Not Angela. But apparently, she's very exclusive as well. And as a practical matter, that appeals to Joel as opposed to spending hours trying to collect the moist, crumpled up twenties from street tricks.

He moves in her townhouse. It's almost like a prep school, except less fooling around. Angela doesn't allow secrets, and she doesn't want the new escorts who stay there fucking each other. Ones who try too hard are thrown out. The first day he's there, Angela throws out a man Joel's age, with the help of Harry, a large bald guy of indeterminate age who seems to be a general enforcer.

If this was a movie, or TV show, here would be the montage of the next six months.

Angela gets Joel a bank account and some basic health insurance. He knows his Social Security number, so she registers him to vote and gets him registered in Selective Service. It's past his 18th birthday, but the agency is okay about late registrations. All of this is to keep him off government radar and to get him ID. Once he has a bank statement and a voters reg card, he uses those and the health insurance card to obtain his birth certificate from Passaic County. And with that, he gets a learner permit from the DMV. Angela wants him to have a driver's license. Harry likes Joel and actually gives him driving lessons, telling him about various baseball players and classic Yankees games while they drive in Westchester County.

Her older worker, Jake, is tasked with training Joel in everything else. Jake gets him in shape: haircuts, clothes, skin treatments, exercise, rudimentary manners, and sex talk. The boring kind, about clients and how to handle them. Jake even has a notebook--more like a play book, in which he drills Joel about every possible happenstance. This is both for what escorts should not do and what clients should not do. It seems amusing at first but Joel sees Jake is serious. It's to protect the escorts, let them be in control. That Joel appreciates and he gives Jake less trouble than most new escorts do.

Jake does not touch him sexually until after the three-month mark, and then only with condoms. It's much like the playbook, designed to get Joel over any self-consciousness, embarrassment, hesitation, or vulnerability a client can take advantage of. Jake repeats Angela's mantra: "It's business, only business."

The sex part is the easiest and also the most difficult, as giving someone a blowjob is uncomfortable when the person is rating him, writing down notes, and sharing them with Angela. And, every person in the townhouse knows what's going on. Angela even watches. Not with any apparent lust but to assess him.

Joel wonders if she'll make him have sex with her too, but that doesn't happen. What Angela does in her off time is unknown but she is strictly hands-off with the escorts. No doubt to avoid any emotional contact that could be used against her. She does however bring in a female escort borrowed from another agency to see how he handles women. This is for the occasional bi threesome that comes along. Some bi/straight men want to have sex with a man, but feel more comfortable having a woman along. Some gay men want to have sex with a woman, but want a man along.

And the last couple months involve the final polish. Jake and Angela both get him practiced in the subtleties that make a difference in escorts. The way to talk to different clients, to pick up on their needs and wants—most importantly, to put them at ease and make them feel desired. Joel's charisma and manner of dealing with people blossoms here, and even Jake is impressed.

Now Joel knows the financial drill. He's told Angela what he's willing to do and not do. He's good with the boyfriend thing, with role-play (exception—no cops), with bondage. He has no interest in other fetish acts. She respects that. He has enough for her to market his appeal.

Angela takes him to meet a couple long-term clients who are comfortable dealing with her openly. That is where he finally sees her unabashed approval. Whatever charisma and natural charm he has suddenly butterflies almost by instinct. It's something he's born with, part of the self-possession that so often impressed others since his youth. He has the clients enraptured by the time this cocktail party or whatever it is over. Both clients book him. Dollar signs practically light up in Angela's eyes, like in a cartoon.

After the first few bookings, she ups his rate.

Classically good-looking masculine blond, sophisticated and well-spoken. Very discreet, excellent companion for gentlemen desiring dinner, overnights, travel, meetings. Top in bookings, top in action. Talents include role-playing, romance, domination. Call for rates.

∞

ELEVEN

Agathon said, *This only is denied to God: the power to undo the past.*

∞

If I learned anything from Angela, it's that business is business. This isn't proving something to Gabriel about what I can do, it's business.

FOR A FEW DAYS Joel and Geneva watch Cody's house in Ridgewood, which is north of Paterson. Joel uses the SUV for this venture as Gabriel's Camry is being held for evidence.

Cody lives in an anonymous upper-middle class home. He's married, with three kids nearly grown. For the first few days they watch him he does little interesting. He engages in serious yard work, maybe another fetish. He drives his three daughters around. He talks to neighbors. He works on a project in his garage--a birdhouse. Jesus.

On the third day Cody leaves the house with a large satchel. Something about his expression seems different. They follow him to Paramus. He stops at an electronics store. Geneva goes inside to check it out, as Joel can't be sure he wouldn't be recognized by Cody. Ultimately Cody spends over an hour inside.

"He was looking at camera equipment," Geneva says, getting back in the Rover. "Serious specs, even infrared. I have to wonder if he had some specially made. From what I was able to hear, he's getting some refurbished."

"Just like the report. He uses special stuff to record his hits."

Cody finally leaves the store. He's wearing clunky glasses and would seem to be a mild-mannered professor, were it not for his massive height and build.

Now he's back on the road, driving north. A forty-minute drive gets him to a remote area, outside a town called West Milford.

He eventually turns right on a small side road. According to the Google map Geneva consults, the road is less than a mile long. It appears to be wooded on both sides as they drive by. Joel continues down the highway a few hundred feet to a convenience store. He parks by the phone. "Let's walk back."

The two of them start back to the road. Charter Road. As soon as they can they get within the first line of trees in order to avoid being observed.

They walk down the entire end of the road, which has five houses. One appears to be in use. One other is for sale. Cody's car is parked at a third house. The house is set well back from the road. Anyone coming down the driveway would be obvious. The house is a wood-faced one-story structure with a porch. An alarm system is indicated by a sign off the driveway. His family house doesn't have that particular alarm company.

Back in the car, Joel checks the address of the house in the public records. The owner is a corporation. The corporation name looks like one of the ones his father sent bank drafts to.

"Let's see what we can do with this," Joel says.

∞

Danny is visiting me today, and Chris has come over to see what I need done. As they both watch, I lay out the papers to see the connection clearer, and to point it out to Chris. "Ken's original shell company, Eastern Division, was transferred to Tartarus. Then another company, Nazgul Industries, bought Ken's other company, Northern Division. Ken's very clever with names. And looks like Cody is a Lord of the Rings fan."

Archie, who is staying here now, decides to lay down on the papers and give himself a bath.

Chris asks, "Why all the selling, Danger Man? Why not hand over the cash?"

"The more transfers of assets and the more shell companies used, the harder it is to trace the original source. We're able to get into Ken's account with the information Joel found. The shell companies here in turn sold to three others, and those deposited the assets into the various accounts. You see we've managed to track some of the transactions. All three of them are doing this the same way. Ken probably handled it all."

"We've reached the River of Jordan."

"Where you're baptized in no taxes and no questions asked."

"So you want to hack into these accounts?"

"They're accessible online. Ken must have wanted it that way. We have Ken's online access, so it's not that difficult. I really want to see Cody and Meese's accounts if possible. That's where some hacking may occur..."

The door opens; Joel and Geneva comes in. Geneva waves at us and shakes Danny's hand.

Chris jumps up. "Hey Mephisto. Danger Man is making me his personal Boy/Girl Wonder. I'm taking your place, 'cause you got glamour shots to do with Izzy and shit like that."

Joel is affectionately amused. "If you don't *mind*, we need to talk to your boss."

"Just don't give him a hard time. I'm going to be his bodyguard. Gotta protect the Danger Man."

"Good luck with that."

Now I get up to embrace him. "Everything okay?"

"Why wouldn't it be?"

He glances at Danny, who's speaking to Geneva, and asks me in a whisper, "Does Danny think I got you in trouble with this?"

"No, he doesn't. Because you didn't. Danny's not looking for blame. Listen, Blackbird. No one gets between us."

Chris is watching us with amusement. "What a soap opera. Mephisto is such a drama queen."

Joel says, "I hope you're helping and not wasting his time, Satyricon."

Danny and Geneva then come over. Danny to say goodbye, and Geneva to say hello. After that, I take Joel aside to speak to him privately in the kitchen for a moment. "Did your mom talk to Meese?"

"Yeah. I told her to be friendly."

"What did he say?"

"According to my mom, he said he needed to step up and help me through this "difficult time" and that he wanted to meet with me. God. I can't even think about it."

"Okay. We'll talk about it later." I bring him back into the living room.

"We have some stuff to go over with you," Geneva says, sitting on the couch.

I had been feeling less tense, but that changes. "I wish I had a cigarette right now, because I know something's coming."

"I'll explain it," Geneva says. She goes through what they've discovered about Cody's secret cabin and propensity for electronics.

Instead of smoking, I just unwrap some gum really slow. It keeps me from freaking out.

Geneva concludes, "It looks like a classic double life. The house could be a base camp."

I nod at her. "It's a terrific lead. And it's a connection to Ken. Nazgul owns the house, and seems to be Cody's company."

Joel is sitting next to me takes my hand. "It could be more than that. I need to get in that house. It's a Turner alarm system. What do you know about getting around that?"

I put his hand to my lips for a second. "Okay. What our friends here may or may not know is that I did not want you to follow Cody. I'm just concerned for your safety after what we've been through. However, the two of you backed each other up and stayed far away from him. That's great. Geneva, I know you have serious abilities. As my father would say, you're tough. However, I don't want either of you going in that cabin."

Joel frowns, his face getting red. "What the hell?"

"*I* wouldn't go in there, Joel. There are limits. You're not going in there."

"Don't give me that bullshit now."

"Did you forget that report on him? This is a man who shot people on the street to test out new weapons. He fed a guy to rats in an abandoned train car. He tied a person to a street lamp and a delivery truck to be pulled in half. This isn't someone to treat lightly."

"Where did you get the idea I'm treating him lightly? You said this was good evidence with him. What was *your* plan?"

"I told you, we're going to continue to collect evidence and approach the right people."

"You would call the police? *You?*"

Both Geneva and Chris seem a little out of sorts from the conflict rising, and that makes me uncomfortable.

"Chris is helping me on this," I tell him. "Listen. Michaela and I have talked about it. She feels she can get this case dismissed. And just like with Sophie's case, if we have evidence of someone else this works in our favor. A paper trail of connections can be given to the right authorities, or the news, or both, in order to make this happen. But Cody is too dangerous to put yourself in his path."

Joel jumps up now, furious. "Stop overprotecting me!"

His anger gets to me. I'm feeling pretty tense as well. "Against a fucking hit man? I will. I don't care how angry you get. I'm not going to help you with that."

"I'll do it on my own. You'll just hold me up by being a control freak."

I'm shocked enough to be speechless, and suddenly feel very tired. The amount of stress the both of us are going through...and then to be carrying around the collective weight of our past on top of it.

"You know better. I'm not going to go there especially with others having to listen to us. We'll talk again."

"You'll give me orders again, you mean."

"I don't give you orders, Joel. If Cody's into tech, he has cameras around the place. You won't know where. The security system may just be one set-up he has."

"You know how to get around it."

"I can hypothesize, that's all."

"That's enough. Look, I know how you feel being here. I hate it. I wanted to bring Archie here for you, whatever I can do to make it better. And you're trying to handle this the best you can, because you feel you have to handle everything. Doing your *War Games* thing with Chris is taking control in your way, I guess, but I don't want to risk your freedom waiting a year for a Goddamn trial..."

Joel stops. At least I think he stops. All of the sudden I can't hear him. My head has gotten warm, and the warmth seems to have a sound. Then the pain comes up like it was injected.

∞

"What's wrong?" Chris, who was closest, actually caught Gabriel before he fell. "His eyes just rolled up."

Geneva comes around and puts an arm under Gabriel's side. "Just ease him to the sofa, okay?"

Gabriel mutters something. She says, "I got you."

Bob is up too. "Oh God, it's starting again. I'll get the heating pad."

Joel has been frozen. "He has the headache." He gets on his knees by the sofa. Gabriel's eyes are open but he's not seeing anything.

Bob returns with a heating pad. "Yeah. He can't hear you at this point." Bob puts the pad under Gabriel's head. "I've been kind of nursing him when this happens--don't look like that, I used to take care of my junkie friends. The heating pad helps but he's not available for a few minutes."

"When did this start," Geneva asks.

"Day after he got here. He says these headaches have been coming for a few weeks. I think stress is triggering them."

"Oh my God. And he had one in jail. He didn't tell me he was still having them."

"He's afraid if he tells you then you'll argue about it and that triggers more headaches."

"That's my fault. He needs to see someone. We need to get him to a hospital, a CT scan or something."

Geneva puts her hands on his shoulders. "Okay, don't panic. Things are going to be okay."

Joel takes one of Gabriel's hands, but Gabriel doesn't respond. He mutters something unintelligible.

"It'll pass in a few minutes," Bob says. "He says the pain is so loud he can't tell otherwise what's going on."

Geneva gets up to put her hands on Gabriel's head. "Positive energy." She gently rubs his temples. This gets a little grunt from him. Archie climbs up to lie beside him.

"He'll be all right. Veronica taught me this. She has real healing powers."

They watch her massage his head. Joel is distressed because he needs to take Geneva back to New York, but doesn't want to leave Gabriel. Bob offers to drive her.

Joel sits on the arm of the sofa, watching Gabriel talk to himself.

"Don't you worry." He makes sure Gabriel's head isn't being burned by the heating pad. "You haven't seen tough yet. I'll take care of this."

∞

Monday, May 16
The 2 Line, 1:17 pm

Monday afternoon Joel takes the train uptown to a specialty store for some supplies. On the subway car he tries to read. Gabriel is having a CT scan on his head. Michaela was able to get that scheduled and approved. She accompanies him as the probation office doesn't allow anyone else to. Rather than worry, Joel tries to stay busy until he can go over and find out what's going on.

"You need help," Jan says, sitting next to him on the bench. "Sometimes it helps to have professionals."

"Who the hell would I get to help? I can handle this."

"You can but professionals ease the way. Just think about it." And when Jan turns the pages of the notebook, Joel can distinctly recall what Jan is referring to.

Although that distracts him, he also gets the feeling someone else is staring at him.

He looks up. Standing next to him on the nearly empty car is a white man, early fifties. Around 5'11, dark grey hair, trim in a dark elegant three-piece suit. Sharp eyebrows, deep brown eyes that are almost black. A manner around him that could only be called imposing.

Joel recognizes him, although he only saw him once, and under very strained conditions: drugged and in the middle of a showdown.

The man smiles very faintly, almost not a smile at all. Yet it's genuine. "Mr. McFadden."

"How did you know..." Joel doesn't finish the question. This isn't a man about whom one would wonder how he does things.

Zest leans against the pole in the middle of the bench. "I hope Mr. Ross is well."

∞

Ty and Dean

The Daodejing says, "Being and Nothing come from each other; Difficult and easy depend on each other; Long and short demonstrate each other; High and low incline to each other; Sound and voice harmonize each other; Front and back follow each other."

∞

I admit sometimes help is needed.

It is June 5, 1998.
Chelsea, 10:27 pm

THE MAN STAYS next to the bar, staring hard at him. "My name is Ty. I know who you are. I've heard about you," he says. "I want you. I have the money."

Joel briefly considers giving him the agency number, but the man's eyes stop that thought. They're a window to Crazytown, Population One.

"I'm sorry, you have me mistaken for someone else." He glances at Chris, indicating they should leave. Chris is already standing, taking out money for their tab.

Joel moves away from the bar but the man is having none of it. He reaches to grab Joel's jacket. "I said, I want *you*. I have the money."

Joel keeps his expression neutral. "And I said, you're mistaken." He has to yank his lapel away from the man, who stares at them as they leave.

"Jesus," Chris says when they're on the street.

"Whatever."

They go back to Chris's one-room apartment on West 29th Street. They spend a few minutes discussing a coding issue in a game and how to bypass it.

Chris is just suggesting they try to find Iz and go somewhere, when the front door to Chris's apartment slams open, making them both jump.

It's the man calling himself Ty. Joel feels the danger from him--his breaking the door open only confirming that theory.

And which is even more confirmed by the gun the man holds, pointed toward them.

Ty is focused on Joel. He shuts the door behind them, and moves closer. "Who the fuck you think you are, walking away from me?"

Joel tries to think of possibilities to calm Ty down and disarm him. He moves away from Chris slowly, to keep Ty's focus on him.

"You think I'm not good enough for you?" Ty points the gun directly at Joel's head. Chris is frozen in absolute fear and silence.

"No, I don't." Joel wants the man's attention away from Chris. "I was mistaken. I'm sorry."

Ty twitches at the words, which he wants to hear. But he's not finished. "You're a fucking whore. You have no right to act better than me."

"You're right. I'm sorry about that. I'll take care of you. We can go."

Ty wavers, the gun moving jerkily in his hand. "I don't have anywhere to go."

"We can go to a hotel."

The man takes strange offense to that. "I don't want to go to a hotel! You think I'm stupid?"

"No, I don't." Joel makes his voice soft, placating, subjugated. "What about here?"

Ty doesn't say anything, as if considering.

"Here. I'll take care of you, make it good."

Ty's eyes wander over him, then his posture eases somewhat. "Okay. It better be good."

"For you, it will be. The best."

Ty unzips his pants, still holding the gun.

"My friend should leave."

"Why?" Ty swings the gun toward Chris. Chris tries not to choke on his own nervousness.

"So we can be alone."

"Why shouldn't he see? You think you're so good sucking my cock, no one can watch you?"

"No, I thought you'd like it better to be alone. My friend will stay. Whatever heightens your pleasure."

"Now we're getting somewhere." Ty relaxes a little more. He pulls his trousers down halfway, and helpfully indicates his genitalia. Joel gets down in front of him.

Joel can feel Chris' horror that Joel is doing this. But Chris is smart enough not to protest. Especially as Ty keeps the gun against Joel's head during the act.

Joel lets the other part of him take over while thinking about how to get them away from this crazy fuck. He's sorry he stopped carrying a knife. He thought at this point in his life, he didn't need to. But then, could he use the knife with the gun at his head? No matter, hopefully, Ty is the type who gets tired after. If not, he'll make Joel do more, maybe Chris too. And then kill them.

Joel gets in his survival mode and uses what he knows that will make the man more into it, more intense, more physically strained.

Ty can't keep his mouth shut. He grunts, comments, asks Chris for comments. Chris doesn't say a word.

Finally, it's over. And when Ty staggers back Joel discreetly spits on the floor.

"Uh...that was all right..." Ty seems disoriented now as his brain chemistry changes.

"I'm glad. Do you want a drink?" Joel slowly gets up off the floor.

Ty's looking wobbly. "Uh, yeah. Then..."

"Whatever you want." Joel steps past him to the old dresser against the wall. It has a table lamp with an iron base.

In one swift motion, he picks up the lamp and swings the base at Ty's head, as hard as he can.

Ty goes down to the floor.

Chris finally moves, jumping up, shaken and near tears. "What the fuck!"

Joel is far more collected. He shoves Ty's body with his foot. "Take it easy. He's out."

He picks up the gun. Chris is in no shape to hold it, so Joel shoves it in the back of his jeans. "We're going to drag him out to the street."

"And do what?"

"Call the police. Your friend Drew's in the area, right? Tell him you need a bag, now."

"What? What are you..."

"*Just do it,* Chris."

Chris is stunned by Joel's composure after being forced to have sex with a gun against his head. In awe of this calm, deferring to Joel's authority, makes the call. "He'll be downstairs in ten. You're just going to leave him?"

"I can't drag him all the way to the Hudson River, right? As much as I'd like to. We're going to leave him outside, put the bag on him, call the cops. Let them deal with it."

"Didn't you say Angela has someone who handles this?"

"I take care of my own problems."

"What if he comes back?"

Joel looks away, angry. He allows the anger to envelope him, then goes back to his inner calm. Chris is right, it's getting help when needed. He takes Chris's phone and dials a number. Chris hears him give a very short version of what happened. Some back and forth. Joel talking to a man and a woman.

Then Joel sits on one of Chris's chairs, staring into space. Drew buzzes the building and Chris goes down for the bag.

Shortly after that, Harry arrives with Angela. They don't introduce themselves to Chris, who is still too nerve-wrecked to attempt conversation.

Harry nods. "I'll take him out..."

Just then, Ty starts to stir.

Joel jumps up.

"Don't worry," Harry says, but Joel isn't worried.

He kicks Ty in the chest. Chris gasps, but Ty doesn't move. And in a fury, Joel kicks him over and over. It's hard to tell if Ty is conscious or not. Neither Harry nor Angela say anything while this happens.

Joel finally stops, breathing heavy. He gives Harry the gun, and the bag of coke. Harry picks up Ty as if he was a bag of laundry and takes him out the apartment.

Angela has a strange look on her face. She does something Chris doesn't know is decidedly unusual. She embraces Joel and holds him for a couple minutes. He cries briefly into her coat and she strokes his back.

Then they break apart. Joel sits in the chair and lights a cigarette. Angela walks to the door. She looks back at Chris. "You need to have this door fixed. I'll send someone over." Then she's gone.

∞

It is September 4, 1998.
Columbus Circle, 9:07 pm

Dean, the client, had asked for a variation of the 'boyfriend' experience. This turns out to mean meeting him at a high-end cocktail bar in a world-renowned hotel. Dean has already rented a room at the hotel. He has Joel follow his lead that they are on some kind of date. Dean treats him like a long-missing lover, flirting with Joel almost bashfully while they're at the bar.

Finally, he has Joel come with him to the room. Dean sets up a portable stereo to play various romantic songs. He seems to really be into Berlin's *Take My Breath Away,* as he has the song repeat over and over. In bed, Dean spends a long time kissing and caressing Joel, as if they were in love. The song becomes the soundtrack to this and continues while they're fucking.

Dean's smile and passionate demeanor, and the emotion in his eyes, seems so genuine. He is an attractive man around 30, dark hair and bright smile, dark eyes with a hint of upturn at the corners, even a smattering of freckles. Anyone in this position would be overwhelmed. Because he seems like he's sincere in the emotions. He asks Joel to talk to him like they're in love. *Tell me you want me. Tell me you miss me. Tell me what I do to you, Dylan.*

Then, as soon as Dean comes, he jumps up and runs into the bathroom. Joel is exhausted by then. It's not just the sex but the intense, enforced dialogue that accompanied the act. He sits up in the bed, waiting to see what's next.

Dean comes out a few minutes later. His face is completely blank. He has a robe on. He doesn't look at Joel. "You can leave now." He tosses a folded hundred-dollar bill on the bed. A tip.

The agreed-upon fee is on the dresser until after the session is over. A tip is unusual, and good escorts don't ask for a tip. Dean's manner is so cold and indifferent--even hostile--that Joel slips out of the bed without a word and gets dressed as quickly as possible. In the incredibly uncomfortable silence, Dean does not look at him but stares at the curtain on the window until Joel leaves.

Outside the hotel, Joel stops to light a cigarette and wonder if he did something wrong. That truly almost never happens.

But everyone makes mistakes and he might not even know what. It could be a misplaced word or glance that disrupted the fantasy.

He finds out two days later he did nothing wrong. Angela tells him Dean has high praise for him. In fact, he's booked another appointment with Joel in two weeks.

Joel is confused. He doesn't raise his feelings to Angela. Maybe, he thinks to himself, Dean was embarrassed by having to pay for sex. That happens. Some clients have gone to great lengths to justify it to Joel, as if he cared.

He doesn't think about it again until the next appointment. It starts off the same way. Meeting Dean in the bar. Dean greeting him like a lover he's longed for desperately. Taking him up to the room, with a conspiratorial, flirtatious air. What seems like hours of foreplay, set to that same Berlin song. Energetic, passionate sex where he demands Joel says even more intimate, affectionate words to him.

And then Dean comes, withdraws, and jumps up, striding towards the bathroom. This time before he goes in he tells Joel, "You need to go now."

His face burning, Joel again, gathers his clothes and dresses as fast as he can. Dean opens the bathroom door and Joel is just then grabbing his bag and starting for the door.

"Hey," Dean says flatly.

Joel looks over his shoulder.

Dean tosses more folded money on the dresser next to Joel.

Joel is tempted to leave the money. The act of reaching over and picking it up is somehow degrading. Not as if Dean threw it at his feet, but still. Nonetheless, it would insult the client. Be professional, Angela says. What *they* think doesn't matter. Still, in just the act of how he gives the tip, Joel knows Dean is sending a message about how he feels regarding Joel's worth. He picks up the bills--two hundred dollar bills this time--and walks out.

He stays on the street pacing around the block, needing a long time to shake off the bad vibes. Then he heads downtown. Somewhere around the Village he sees some people from a local LGBTQ youth center, looking for donations. He stuffs Dean's tip in one of the workers' cans.

Why does Dean bother him so much? Rudimentary psychology. He'd like for Dean's feelings to be sincere. He'd like a relationship. Joel's relationships in past years have been studies in power imbalances one way or the other. Eventually, people lie. Eventually, people trick you. In some cases, they get off on it--making you think that love you, and humiliating you. Joel's fallen for that before. Not with Grace, who disappeared. Not with Jennah, who died. But those who have come since seem to be targeting arrows at him.

You still want your mother to love you. The relationships are a poor substitute.

Joel doesn't want to think too much about that. He tries never to think about *them*. Instead he goes for practicalities. He asks Harry, who knows so much about underground life, how to follow someone. Harry wants to know why but Joel charms him. The only one of Angela's coterie who can. Without telling Angela, Harry instructs Joel on how to follow and not be seen. How to observe and change your look, your posture, even your vibes. He does this because he knows Joel is not going to get any of them in trouble.

After the next session with Dean, Joel follows him. Gets his address, his last name, his work. Financial, not surprisingly. No emotion, little human contact that requires emotion. Also not surprisingly, Dean is very superficial with everyone he's in contact with, male or female. A touch of contempt. He goes into gay bars and enjoys attracting attention and rejecting that same attention.

Control freak. No one's going to get one over on Dean. He'll reject before he's rejected. He almost gets off on listening to the men compliment him, and then scornfully dismissing them. Not just turning them down, but being nasty about it. To see them get confused and hurt. You'd think that eventually that would get around, and people would ignore him for being an absolute asshole. But no, there's always someone who tries. A victim for Dean to play psychic vampire with.

It explains to Joel, why Dean hires escorts. Not just the classic "I don't pay them to have sex, I pay them to leave." He pays them to not reject him. He pays them to be the rejected ones.

Joel can actually understand that. He finds himself empathetic to an extent. He doesn't change anything in his manner or words the next time he sees Dean; he knows better. But somehow Dean picks up on something. The tiniest changes in vibrations. Maybe Joel shows a little bit more confidence in the sex than Dean wants. And afterwards, before even getting out of bed, Dean says, "Don't look at me. I don't want someone like *you* looking at me."

This time, he actually does throw money on the floor. Rather than pick it up, Joel kicks it under the bed. Let housekeeping find it.

That's it, he figures. No more with Dean.

But Dean has told Angela he wants to set a regular thing with Joel every month.

The fact that the extra contempt and humiliation must have excited Dean disgusts Joel. "Not interested," Joel tells Angela.

"Joel, that's not like you. He's paying premium. That's more for both of us. I know he freaked you out; you don't hide it as well as you think. I hinted you may not have time for him, and he offered to pay more. So why do you have this problem?"

"I don't like how he treats me."

"Tell me what he does." She's serious. Angela has continued to live up to her word about taking care of her workers. Angela also has a no second-chances policy with clients who hold out on money, verbally abuse the escorts, no-show appointments, or try to force acts the escort didn't agree to. And of course, she helped in him in how she handled Ty. Without her being explicit, Joel has figured out they have shared some of the same experiences.

With some reluctance Joel describes the interaction with Dean. Angela is not unduly concerned, but she does feel some understanding of *his* feelings. "It's not you. He'd do that to anyone he hired. The self-hating client. Projects it on the guy he pays for. I don't analyze them--why bother? He doesn't want to have an emotional connection."

"It fucks with my head."

"Joel, it's business. You know that."

"I know sex is business. This is different. Only a psycho does this shit."

"The romance part? His fantasy. You're the fantasy. Think of it like a movie. Actors pretend to be deeply in love for a living, then go home and snort a kilo of blow or fuck a sheep or whatever. You're an actor."

"Yeah. Speaking of actors, you know I never refuse a regular except the actor with coke-dick who wanted me to get it up *for* him. And the Viagra-abuser who was going into extra innings. I hope you take me seriously."

"I do, and that's why I'm telling you don't get emotionally involved with the clients' bullshit. It will do you better in the long run. You never know what other people are thinking, but it's less about you and more about saving the tattered remnants of their own self. You take care of yourself, first and foremost."

Joel tries to be professional about it. Angela is right in a way, and he knows he's right in a way. He sees Dean three more times. By the third time, his indifference almost makes the experience matter-of-fact.

But for some reason, that doesn't make it better. It's almost that Joel feels like he's losing himself, becoming hardened. He can see himself eventually *becoming* Dean. That is repulsive to him. And so, during the next appointment, he actually ignores Dean's command to not look at him. Risking his standing with Angela, he tells Dean, "You have no right to talk to me like that."

Dean calls Angela to complain. If it had been any other escort, he'd have been kicked out of the stable, or at least on probation. Angela knows Joel enough to know he doesn't break his role unless he has to.

Dean tells Angela he wants Joel to see him for free, and to apologize. He describes graphically what he wants Joel to do.

"No," Angela says. "You don't treat my people badly. I don't want your business."

Dean does not take that well and threatens Angela. The only people who know this is happening are Joel and Harry and Angela's attorney. Joel is scared Angela is going to be in serious trouble because of him but Angela tells him not to worry.

"I protected myself better than that. You know I have contacts in the police. Not only can't he prove anything, I can cause more problems for him if he wants to push it. He's not in a position to risk a lawsuit and be exposed. Protect yourself, have a good attorney, and don't be afraid to come down hard when you have to."

Apparently, that's the end of the Dean matter. Angela then tells Joel, "You need a break. I'm going to set you up with some people with more class than that fuckwad."

Joel expected to be torn up one way and down the other. Even to be told he'd have to leave her employ. "Why?"

"You said you don't want to lose yourself. I'm going to help you with that. I do have a heart, you know. Bad for business to let clients be sadists, so we're better off. I have someone better for you, a recommendation from another client. This guy is a Euro moneybag, if you know what I mean. He's Dutch, and very continental. You, honey, will be perfect for him. His name is Jan and he's interested in having a sophisticated young man going with him to Berlin. I need someone I can trust to go overseas and not be an idiot. He's low key and *nice*, I checked him out. And you, I know I can trust."

"As long as it's Berlin the city, and not that damned song again," Joel says.

∞

Twelve

Maxim Gorky said, "In the carriages of the past you can't go anywhere."

∞

Monday, May 16, Continued

JOEL GETS PAST his initial shock at seeing Zest. "How is Gabriel? Under the circumstances, what do you think?"

Zest smiles. "I think he's very strong. I've kept up with what's going on."

"So what do you want?"

"I want to help."

Staring at him, Joel tries to read his intentions. "Why? He doesn't want it."

"I can understand that. But I would wager you *do*."

Joel doesn't answer that. He's very disconcerted by seeing Zest. He remembers Zest in the warehouse, kneeling down to cut the binds around Joel's wrists. Before making Joel and Gabriel leave so he could kill the man who kidnapped Joel.

"You have a different perspective. Which is why I'm talking to you. You aren't depending on the legal system to extricate him."

"I wouldn't depend on it--you got that right."

"I would not either. Mr. McFadden, what you want is proof of who really did it."

"Right. We're both doing that, just..."

"You perhaps have different approaches?"

Joel feels a rush of adrenaline. "I shouldn't talk about that. There's this man...a killer. Stephen Cody. He's a contract killer with the Jersey mob. He did this."

"How do you know?"

"He knew my father...and another of my father's friends. I think my father got himself killed."

"We could talk more about that. I imagine you have good reason. I can help you with this. I hope to convince Mr. Ross of my sincerity."

"Call him Gabriel. I can't stand that 'Mister' shit."

Zest raises an eyebrow. "You don't like pretension. You've seen too much of it. I respect him and you, or I wouldn't use it. If you want familiarity, I can do that too."

"Whatever. Why are you so hot to help?"

"I'm sympathetic to how much you care about him. You need to stay calm to reason with him because he's going to know you've spoken to me. He won't be happy about it. That's why I approached you; you are helpless to my speaking with you. *Why* I want to help is a complicated question. Do you really need to know, is it important? Because if I am in fact sincere the motive shouldn't matter."

"It matters."

Zest contemplates him. "Might we step outside to smoke?"

They get out at the next stop. Columbus Circle, which Zest finds amusing. Joel remembers that Zest had contacted Gabriel here, making him go to the Met Museum to speak with him, to threaten him. Really, to threaten everyone Gabriel cared about if he didn't stop investigating the Tertullian Society. Remembering that is why Joel needs to know Zest's motives.

Outside, smoking Dunhills, Zest looks up at the golden statue in the plaza at the tip of the park. "Gabriel quoted something to me when we spoke the first time. I was amused, but rather taken with his courage. I've had people get angry, try to bluff me, certainly be scared. He accepted the situation, but he was not broken by it. Instead he turned to me and questioned me about my life. He told me there must have been a time when I could have chosen differently. That was the chink in my armor. It stayed in my mind."

Zest sighs, keeping his eyes on the statue as Joel keeps his eyes on Zest, listening intently. He barely touches his own cigarette. Around them, several unlicensed vendors hawk bicycle rentals to tourists. Zest and Joel are an oasis of seriousness in midst of this commerce.

Zest continues. "I wasn't sure why. Why would this young man in a bad way manage to get through to me? He wasn't powerful or influential, certainly no one within the Society would think so. But I realized they underestimate him badly. He is a true believer of principle and an intelligent one. He also knows when he needs to protect others; when that is right, without ego getting in the way. Nelson tried to use that against him, and underestimated him as well.

"By the time we got that far, I respected Gabriel for what he was doing. I didn't want to hurt him. I didn't want you to be hurt. I was glad he made the decision he did. It was the best way, as I was telling the truth. He did me a favor as well, made the situation much more...malleable, shall we say. I wasn't lying when I brought up professional courtesy. And he understood."

Zest now meets Joel's eyes. "You may not believe this, but I think it's unfortunate he distrusts me. I felt from the beginning I'd enjoy talking to him. You see, Mr...you see, Joel, I'm not redeemable. I've done too much to ever change my karma. I've read what Gabriel wrote about karma, everything he said in his articles before and since the summer. I don't believe in God, but I do understand powers of the universe. I'm too much in the red to serve any good purpose. Somehow, helping Gabriel would be like being able to live a different way by proxy. Does that make sense?"

Joel draws from the cigarette, his mind reeling. "Yes. I know what kind of man he is."

Zest smiles, with a hint of the regret he speaks of. "And I know what kind of man you are as well. You've been going to great lengths to help him. I've been watching."

"*Following* me?"

"I have no work at present. I wanted to see what was going on. So, yes, at times."

That doesn't bother Joel. Rather, he uses his internal intuition on Zest. "You want to leave them, don't you? You're done with the Society."

Zest's smile gets deeper. "One doesn't leave the Society. There's no retirement plan."

"Like the Mafia? I suppose not. But you would if you could."

"I'm in a strange place, Joel. A very strange place. I have nowhere to run, no one to help. There is no other destiny for me. But I can perhaps help someone else. I think Gabriel is a good choice. I can't exactly run a marathon or volunteer for a soup kitchen. But helping him will help others."

"This is redemption."

"I told you I'm not redeemable. I don't ask for mercy from the universe. But I can say that I did right once."

Joel wishes Gabriel could see this, see the look in Zest's eyes. As if he knows, Zest takes out a pair of Bollé sunglasses and slips them on. "I appreciate the time, Joel. We'll need to convince him, I'm sure. Remember this number to contact me, text or call." Zest recites the ten digits and then turns and walks away.

Now Joel finds concentrating on anything else more difficult than ever. He recovers his SUV and drives back to Paterson.

"There's our superstar," Bob says when he opens the door. "Why don't you use the key?"

"I just don't want you to get sick of me."

"As if. The new intern at work says that a lot, *as if.* I told her it's not 1995 anymore, but she thinks it's funny. I'm hoping she'll get me up to date with any current sexual argot."

"I'll keep you in my prayers for this to happen."

"If you're going to pray for something to happen, Joel, the first ten items are..."

"Don't tell me, I still want to like you. Let's just say I hope you get happy."

"You too. So feel free to just come in when you need to for him. I'm going to a conference this weekend and plan to get happy with a colleague I've been talking to on Facebook. I want to like her page. Like it many times."

"Facebook is passé, Bob."

"Nothing is passé for pussy, my friend. She could be on CB radio for all I care. Eastbound and *Down.*" He claps Joel on the shoulder as Gabriel comes out of his room.

"I was just giving an update to Walter on things. He wants to visit, and I guess I'll let him. Is Bob going on about that woman again? I've been hearing about her for 72 hours straight. If nothing happens, I'm afraid *I'll* have to blow him when he gets back."

Joel frowns. "He's having a bad influence on you. We need to get this case over with fast before you start talking like him full-time."

Bob laughs. "Don't worry, I love him like a brother. I'm not saying I *never* did that back in the days I was trying to score junk, but I also don't remember if I liked it or not. Other things on my mind."

Bob then leaves them alone in the living room. Joel finds himself settling into Gabriel's arms on the sofa. "How are you?"

"Learning more about porn actresses than I ever wanted to; I hope that comes in handy later."

"I mean about the CT. What did they say?"

"Post-concussion syndrome. Sometimes it happens months after the injury. It's sort of like post-traumatic stress."

"What's the treatment?"

"Migraine medicine. Same stuff I already use, higher dosage. Also, I should avoid stress. The doctor seemed to be serious about that, and didn't understand why I was laughing when she told me."

"That's all they can say to do? My God."

"It'll go away in time. I should check back in three months, unless I'm in prison, of course."

Joel falls quiet. Archie jumps and sits near them both, purring.

"What's bothering you, sweetheart? You know I can tell that something's going on, right? We know each other too well. I feel it burning in you. Just say it."

Joel shifts around nervously. "Later."

Gabriel moves his fingers through Joel's hair. "Are you afraid?"

"You'll be angry."

Now Gabriel puts his hand against Joel's face. "No. It's not like that. We have to stop with this anger as a blockade between us. Don't ever be afraid to talk to me. More than ever I need that. I'm helpless here."

"You're never helpless."

"If I go 25 feet beyond the door, the perimeter of this building, I'll go to jail. I feel pretty helpless. You can just drive off anytime. I know this will work out and at the same time I'm scared."

"I'm sorry, Gabriel. It's why I want to help you."

"I know. You know I need you. I trust you. I love you. Tell me about what is on your mind."

A few moments go by. "I was on the 2 train. Zest had been following me; he started talking to me on the train."

He waits.

Gabriel keeps his hands the same. "You think I'll be mad about that? That you talked to him? We must be super-stressed. You know better."

"You were very... *vehement* about things. That's a word of yours. And then the headaches. I don't want to set you off."

"Don't worry about that. You didn't set me off, and I can't stop living because of headaches. We've lost perspective at this point. I'm not angry at all. Okay? Tell me what he said."

Joel recounts the conversation. His voice is hesitant at first. He tries to see if Gabriel's hands feel different on him, being attuned to the subtlety in emotions. But nothing changes.

When Joel's finished, Gabriel says, "I'm not upset with you, so forget that. We have different analyses. Zest is not a benign person. He's not a Shakespearean tragic king. He's a man who's made a living killing people and destroying lives for an organization that shouldn't exist. He could say anything for any reason."

"You think I don't know that?"

"No. I think you're scared. He's offering something and you want to believe it's legitimate."

"I think sometimes help is needed, and he's offering to help. What would he get out of this otherwise?"

"I don't know. But I just can't let a man like that help me. It's like taking help from the devil."

"At this point, that doesn't matter. And especially if he's not with them."

"Even assuming he's not completely full of shit, he can't give them up. He can't leave them. If he tried to do anything and his superiors told him to stop it and kill us, he would."

"You think I did something wrong."

"I already told you, you did nothing wrong. Maybe it's even better to know his alleged agenda."

"Maybe you should talk to him."

"I'm not going to go that far." Gabriel sits up. "I just can't. Not knowing what he would have done to you and everyone else in my life."

But now Joel burns. "You don't want to talk to Zest. You don't want me to get into Cody's house. What the hell am I supposed to do?"

"Okay, now *you're* getting angry. That isn't helping."

Joel sits up suddenly, looking away. Frustrated. The blood pounds in his head. He takes out his cigarettes and lights up. Gabriel watches him, hugging his knees.

Joel tilts his head to look back at Gabriel. "You can't control everything. You have to step back and let me take care of it."

"I know I'm not in control."

"You're trying to, though. Whatever you can do. Maybe I understand that, what you must feel being here. But you're talking to me like I don't know what I'm doing."

"Not true. You know what you're doing."

"Then it's...it's like when you were in Michaela's basement. Locking yourself in because you couldn't let anyone help. You don't think I'm capable enough."

"That isn't it. I swear. I know you are a capable man. But I have a responsibility to you. Not to let you risk your life."

"Goddamn it, Gabriel." Joel gets up, agitated, stalking the living room. "I fucking told you, I'm with you no matter what. That means I take a risk. You can't keep me in a bell jar. What if the situation was reversed? You wouldn't think twice about not listening and doing what you want. You'd say it was the right thing and you had to do it."

He stands on the other side of the coffee table staring at Gabriel, who still has his head down on his knees, looking back at him. "What is the difference between us, for fuck's sake?"

Gabriel speaks quietly. "The difference is I'm okay with risking my life, not yours."

"Fuck it, I'm going to risk it. You aren't making me do it. I can decide what I want to do, and live with the consequences. If it kills me, whatever. I did it for a good reason. You can't make that decision for me; you have no right."

Gabriel turns his face down. Joel is shaking inside. He doesn't want it like this. He wants it to be okay. Feeling overwhelmed, he turns around and leaves the apartment.

On the way back to New York. Joel feels horrible. He shouldn't have left. But this isn't a relationship issue. It's so much more.

And he's going to do it. Gabriel may not tell him how to get in Cody's house, but he can figure it out.

∞

Later on during the night, Gabriel texts him. --*Are you okay?*
He doesn't know how to answer. -- *Yes.*

--How you go on and on. Keep to short responses.

Joel smiles. Strange that when he wanted to get Gabriel back, he'd say everything on his mind. But even to get over their conflicts he's reluctant to give in.

As if Gabriel knows what he's thinking, the next text says, *--Separate 'us' from what we disagree about. We can disagree without it getting out of hand.*

The next day he's watching his mother start to pack things, such as what she wants to give away. The police have released the house as a crime scene. Joel arranged for a crime scene cleaning service to come by this week and take care of the living room and the blood stains.

The process has been started to put Ken's estate in probate. He had a very simple will, not updated for years. Joel knows some snags are going to happen. Like about those accounts offshore. One of new his concerns is if Ken's machinations are exposed, the government might try to impound the house and any other assets.

However, as far as Joel's concerned the more household items that get trashed, the better. He's ready to get a junk truck to haul it off and sell the Goddamned house. Gloria is grieving for Ken. He understands that. But she alternates between trying to make plans to move on, and breaking down and having Joel decide. Right now doesn't know where she wants to do--stay in the house, or get a condo in Wayne, or something closer to Joel.

Joel is getting annoyed at her stopping to clean and sort things. "Just throw it away. I'll hire a regular cleaning service for this place."

"Joel, you can't just pay for things all the time. I can clean."

Not that I remember. Why not just walk away? What's to hold on here? She said she wanted another life. And she wasn't against his paying for everything up to now.

Gloria stares into the living room at the dark red blood splatters on the rug. While she's dealing with that, and he's feeling guilty over not feeling anything about it, a shadow crosses the front door and the bell rings.

Joel goes over to the door and looks out the window. Meese is standing there. He looks expectant.

Joel feels both anger and dread. He says through the door, "What do you want?"

"I know your mom's here, but I really want to see you."

Joel has no idea how to respond to that--the conspiratorial, intimate tone.

"You need to leave."

"No, we can handle it. It's time."

"If you have anything to say, you can call my attorney."

Meese's face changes; his eyes go cold. "Joel, you might remember your friend over in Paterson. You think I can't make trouble for him just because you bribed a judge to get him out?"

Joel doesn't want to give in to this, but better to see what his game is. He turns to look back at his mother.

"Do you have to," she whispers.

"Don't worry," he tells her.

Then he opens the door. Meese's expression goes back to...pleasure. He reaches out briefly to grab Joel's arm. Not expecting the touch, Joel is speechless.

Meese smiles at Gloria. She doesn't smile back.

"You don't look good, Gloria. This must be taking a toll on you."

"I'm fine," she replies, her voice shaky.

He walks to the living room entrance and glance around. "Looks like you're getting ready to move. Maybe that's for the best."

Joel interrupts the small talk. "What did you need to say?"

Meese focuses on him. "It's time for us to talk about the plan. You've been through a lot, but I think getting our life going now would be good for you."

Joel stares at him in disbelief. "What the fuck are you talking about?"

"Joel...you don't have to be afraid anymore." He reaches out again to put his fingers on Joel's face.

Joel jerks away from Meese's hand. Meese looks furious for a second, then lowers his eyelids and nods. "Your mom's here. We can send her away."

"You're out of your fucking mind."

Gloria has moved to get between them. "Larry! Keep your hands off my son."

Joel catches something in Meese's eyes that's dangerous. He says to Meese, "Leave her out of it. This is between you and me."

"I know. But she's getting in the way. I suppose she doesn't mean to, but..."

Joel takes Gloria's hand and pulls her away from Meese. "Mom, just go in the other room."

Gloria reluctantly leaves for the dining room. Joel is alone with Meese, and that makes him extremely uncomfortable. *He can't do anything to you. Not now.* Joel feels surreal that this man is even here. By reflex, the Numbness seems to be returning, freezing his muscles, his reactions. Joel can barely bring his eyes up to look at Meese. "What is it?"

And he sees again that Meese is watching him with a strange expression. Not anger. Not really desire. Something else dark and strong.

Meese's voice goes gentler, and seems all the more malevolent for that. "It's so great to see you. I know you wanted to come home again. Was this for her? Maybe, but I know you're looking for *me*. You had to come back for *me*."

Joel now stares at him in shock. Meese actually starts to reach for him again, and he backs away.

"Leave me alone," he says, and thinks his voice sounds juvenile, like he's gone back in time.

Meese isn't listening; his eyes have gone dreamlike. "You couldn't stay away; I knew you'd be back. You owe me but I'm not mad about that. It was Ken's fault but that's over. You were always meant to be mine. Now we're going to work together on the plan."

An internal shower of adrenaline, cold as ice, makes Joel feel sick. "Whatever you're thinking, you're insane."

Meese's face slowly changes and goes pale. "It's that fucking PI, isn't it? He's done something to you. *Poisoned you.* I should have...it's not too late. You don't have to be under his control. I'll take care of him. He won't keep us..."

Meese goes back to his dreamy look and takes Joel's arms. The Numbness makes Joel almost helpless. He becomes 15 again. *Feeling Meese digging his fingers in Joel's shoulders and face, to make him do what Meese wants.*

Meese then leans to whisper in his ear. "Joel, you don't know about him. I found his record. He's a criminal. He robbed and beat a man when he wasn't much older than you. You need to stay away from him. You know, deep inside, you're *still mine*."

Joel hisses, "Fucking perverted bastard." He struggles to get out of Meese's hold.

Meese holds on to him. "I wish I found you after they threw you out. I looked all over. It was *them*. And she's still trying to control things, isn't she? I thought she knew better. I'll take care of that too-- I'm sorry about this, I know you don't want to hurt her, but it's for the best." Meese speaks in a louder voice. "Gloria, I just want to say something."

Gloria comes back in the room. She sees Joel's face and puts her arms around him. "Just leave," She tells Meese. "I don't want to hear it."

Meese smiles. "Suddenly you think you're a family now? Well, you know what he did, Gloria."

"He didn't do anything. You lied to me about that! You made Ken throw him out with your lies! I want you out of my house, Larry."

Meese's expression doesn't change. "Really? Well, let me tell you. You don't know everything about him. I do. I found his record. Yeah, just like that fucking PI, Joel has a record. I see that's news to you. Joel, you didn't tell Gloria? *You* did it to him, Gloria, you and Ken. You could have let me take care of him, but no. You threw him out, and what do you think he did? Your son's a whore. He has an arrest record from way back of street hustling. Who knows if he ever stopped?"

Joel feels her stiffening in his arms. He lets go of her and goes to the front door and yanks it open. "Get out of here."

Meese shakes his head, coming up next to him. "No, you see-- she won't bother you now. You're not good enough for her anymore. I think you'd better see how you could make me happy, instead of pissing me off. You still look like you, but you're...*older*. I don't want you that way."

The Numbness gives way to anger in the face of Meese's fantasy/perversity. "I'm not listening to your bullshit. Get the fuck out."

Meese moves past him, but keeps locked to Joel's eyes. Joel feels helpless again to that stare. "I know you and what you're meant for. That's why you were mine in the first place. I'm coming back for you and our plan. You're going to work with me the way I intended."

Joel slams the door shut practically before the last word leaves Meese's mouth. He's breathing hard. He watches to make sure Meese actually drives away. Behind him, he can hear his mother starting to cry. He can't turn to look at her. He leans against the door, wishing the world would go away. That the world would fall on them all. Just like that day on the boat.

Eventually, he turns around. His mother is leaning against the sideboard, her hand over her mouth, tears rolling down. Clearly, he is no longer her hero.

She says, "Is that *true*, what he said? Did you even tell me the truth *before*?"

The fragile bond between them is breaking into pieces. Her tone is horrified. Just like when he was young.

For a moment he feels 15 again with her. When he did something that displeased her and would suffer from her turning on him. "No, Mom, don't you see, I wasn't doing that when I was still living at home, but when I was on the street..."

His voice trails off. He realizes Meese has him defending himself to his mother. His mother, who was too drunk to stop his father from kicking him out to the street. Who wouldn't believe him about Meese's abuse. And now she's judging him. *She's* judging *him*.

She says, "Did you really *do* that?"

"*Fuck* you." Joel grabs his jacket, and leaves.

∞

I'm worrying about where Joel is. He hasn't responded to my text from some hours back.

Bob is answering his front door. I hear him say, "...No, he isn't available...I can't do anything about that..."

I recognize the voice on the other side and get up, angry. Bob looks over at me and shrugs.

"I'll take care of it."

I go to the door as Bob leaves. Alex is standing on the small cement stoop.

"What? Why are you bothering my friends again?"

"Because you won't talk to me. For God's sake, Gabriel, I've been worried."

"All right, thanks for that. Nonetheless, I don't have anything left to say to you."

"I apologized for what I said. You agreed to help me out with my source's problem, then abandoned the whole thing without telling me why."

"I had good reason. The problem is now you and your insistence on stalking me."

"I'm just trying to look out for you."

"I don't need you to do so. The only thing I have to say is what I said before. To drop your story."

"Can you at least give me a reason why?"

I roll my eyes. But I have what I feel is an obligation. My father had called me back to say he had found something on Comstock. Comstock's real name is actually Damon Clement, and he was known for having been involved in some sort of intelligence-based drug/hypnosis experiments with intelligence agencies. That's as much as I even want to know.

"Your source isn't telling you everything. I found him talking to a man who I also saw Comstock talking to. That's all I'm saying. I have reasons, which I'm not going into, to say sincerely Mesereau is *not* who he says he is. And you getting any further into this story could be extremely dangerous. Don't do it."

Alex frowns. "All right. All right, then. I appreciate that. I understand you enough to believe you. I think..."

"What?"

"You care. I'm glad you care."

"I don't want you killed."

"We still have something, Gabriel. You and I."

"Don't start this again. No, we don't."

"I'm serious about what this is doing to you. I'm trying to investigate and find out what he's done, to try and help you."

"What he's done...you mean Joel? Are you out of your mind? Leave it alone, Alex. Seriously. You do not understand."

"I understand what kind of person he is--"

"What kind of person he is, is someone who helps me warn you when he doesn't have to. Stay out of this case with your 'investigations.'"

Alex shrugs that off. "I just see so much more in you. You still care about me. When I think about it, the last time we slept together, I felt we were so close. Something happened to you right after...I think that's when he got to you."

This makes me so infuriated I speak without checking myself. "The last time we slept together, I didn't want to do it."

He's taken aback by that. I'm angry at myself for saying it. It's true but wasn't necessary, and I don't like to be hurtful.

"That isn't true," he says. "I was there."

I can say nothing that will make this better or worse. I can only get entangled with him, which is what he wants. I shut the door.

∞

Joel sits in his SUV for an endless time. In the parking lot of Willowbrook Mall. Hiding, like he used to do when he lived in Wayne. He had nowhere else to go back then. He feels the same helplessness. But it's not the same. He can do something to take control. He takes out his phone.

Then he drives back to Paterson, to Bob's apartment. It's one in the morning. He sees Gabriel through the slats in the blinds on the windows. He's moving around the living room, pacing. He's still restless. Their disagreement doesn't sit well with him, either.

Joel moves up under the light shining from the eave over the door. Gabriel sees the shadow or movement through the window and is instantly at the window to check it out. They stare at each other through the glass.

Joel, wavering between past and present, expects Gabriel to reject him. To turn away.

Gabriel does move away from the window--to open the door. Seeing Joel's face close-up, he pulls Joel inside his arms. "It's okay, whatever it is."

Joel holds on to him. He wants to cry and can't. Gabriel murmurs, "It's okay. It's okay. You're with me. You're safe."

Joel talks into Gabriel's shoulder. Telling him about Meese showing up at the house.

Gabriel is still holding him but his mind has started to go elsewhere. Joel feels that too. He looks up and sees Gabriel's gone distant. But his eyes are raging.

"Gabriel."

When Gabriel looks at him, his expression changes. He embraces Joel tighter. "He's not going to hurt you again."

Joel speaks into his shoulder. "Please."

"I swear to God, I'm going to do something to this fucker..."

"I'm scared. He threatened you, and he's crazy. What is this damned plan he's talking about?"

Gabriel holds him hard, putting his hand on the back of Joel's head, cradling it. "I'm not worried about him. He some kind of fucked-up fantasy. It's not important. You don't want to know what it is. But I have you now. I want you to listen to me, baby. No matter what he told you, that part of your life is over. It's over. He's got nothing to do with you. You're with *me*."

He repeats this over softly, taking Joel to the sofa. "You're with me..." Until Joel stops shaking.

"No one is going to hurt you," Gabriel says with finality.

"Do you mean it? Do you still love me?"

Gabriel frowns over Joel asking this, but just holds Joel tighter. "Yes. I mean it. I love you, baby. Don't ever worry about that."

Joel thinks about what Meese said--something about Gabriel robbing someone? He didn't tell Gabriel that part. It can't be true. *He's making you question everyone like he did your mother. Just forget it.*

Then Joel gets a text alert. He reads it, and falls silent.

"What is it?"

Joel texts back quickly then gets up. "Something we need to talk about now." He looks out the window next to the front door.

"Joel, what's going on?" Gabriel is up now as well, apprehensive.

Before he can do anything else, Joel has unlocked and opened the front door.

Zest is standing there. In another three-piece suit, with a faint smile. "May I come in?"

"No," Gabriel says, but Joel and steps back and lets Zest come through, then shuts and locks the door behind him.

Gabriel exhales, angry. "Goddamn it, Joel." He says it quietly, so he doesn't wake Bob.

They glare at each other.

Zest says, "Gabriel, don't be angry at him. He's helping you."

"*You* don't tell me what to feel."

Joel gets agitated again. "Just fucking calm down for a minute."

Gabriel's fists are clenched, frustrated.

Zest keeps an open posture; his hands are facing Gabriel. "I'm alone. I'm not armed."

"Your friends with you?"

"They were not my friends. I'm sure Joel explained my conversation with him. No one knows I'm here. I think it's time to talk."

"Talk about what?"

"You know what, Gabriel."

Gabriel sits on the arm of the sofa. "So you're going to convince me now? Is that it?"

"I want to, yes. May I sit down? I am rather tired this time of night. Age hits once in a while."

Gabriel doesn't look impressed.

"Go ahead," Joel says.

"Search me if you wish." Zest holds his arms out some from his side.

Gabriel walks over to him, still in his fury. Zest takes off his jacket, then his vest. Gabriel goes through the pockets of the jacket, then pats him down. Staring in Zest's eyes, Gabriel yanks Zest's shirt out of his pants and feels his chest, checking him for a wire. Zest's return expression is neutral, even complacent when Gabriel runs his fingers through Zest's carefully combed hair and tells him to take off his shoes.

Zest has no identification or phone with him, only keys, cigarettes, and lighter. Gabriel examines all of these. Then he moves back to the sofa.

Zest resets his clothes, smooths his hair. He folds his jacket over his arms. He nods at Joel, who has taken a side chair. "I realize I'm making a presumption that Joel has told you of our conversation."

"You had no right to approach him about this."

"We're not talking about rights now, Gabriel. I understand your philosophy, I understand your protectiveness. But this is beyond that now. I'm not here on behalf of the Society. I'm here on my own accord."

"You think I can separate that? You told me my friends would be horribly killed, even raped beforehand. That I'd want to kill myself before it was through. And now I'm supposed to just overlook that because you somehow have a crisis of conscience."

"I did tell you that and I would have done it. This is why I was glad you listened to me, even though I know you did not want to do that. I'm not insulting you by pretending it was a lie or that I'm secretly good man. But is it beyond you now to hear me out?"

"How am I supposed to believe you?" Gabriel's voice is quieter.

"My actions. The Society has nothing to gain or lose from your situation. Only you and Joel do."

"And what do you expect in return?"

"Nothing. I told Joel I have no way to create a new self, a new life."

"You would go against them." Gabriel takes Joel's jacket and finds his cigarettes, and lights one. Joel chooses not to call him out on it.

"I did not say that. They have nothing to do with this."

"If you're sincere, then tell me who the three men were who beat me."

Zest leans back crossing his legs. "May I borrow your lighter? Thank you. Gabriel, that's petty revenge. Those men do not remember you at this point. I don't know them; Nelson hired them."

"You have access to Nelson's life and what he was doing. I'm sure you know the identity of the man who called himself Smoke. I don't care about him, he was doing his job, so to speak."

"As were the three men."

"It's different. I would like to know. And the New York contact, Jacobs. What's his real name?"

Zest leans forward, meeting his eyes. "That is extremely dangerous, Gabriel. What do you think you're going to do?"

"Learn the name of the man who wanted me dead. Who killed my client."

"That was Nelson. Jacobs is merely another pawn in a larger scheme."

"Does he give you orders?"

"I'm a consultant. He's neutral to me."

"Then it shouldn't bother you to give me the name."

"Gabriel, if you choose to provoke them, to expose them, whatever may be in your mind, I cannot protect you. I won't participate. But I can't stop it."

"I'm not asking you to. I wouldn't trust you to."

The tendrils of smoke rise between them. "One matter at a time. Once this is taken care of, once we establish your innocence, then we can discuss this issue."

"Use that for leverage, huh? Is he a politician or business person?"

"Business. That's all I'll say. I will also emphasize that you should not look into Jacobs. You're too smart for that. I know what you've done."

That gives them both pause. Is he suggesting he knows about the YouTube videos?

Gabriel says, "Is that so? What have I done?"

"How you handled the matter in New Jersey and upstate New York. I know what was in the papers was half the story of how you accomplished those tasks. A man who uncovers crimes and traps a serial killer as you did is not the type of man who deliberately provokes someone far more dangerous for no reason, for no benefit."

"Duly noted."

"These people exist, Gabriel. You can't control that. Now may we discuss how to help you? Joel is already on the right track."

Joel paces the room much like Gabriel was doing before. "We need to figure out what to do with Cody. How to get in his cabin."

Gabriel rolls his eyes. "And we want to do that *why?*"

Zest says, "I was able to use some of my contacts to find out more information on Mr. Cody. Cody's associate, the one Joel's source mentioned, actually later turned up dead--a one-car accident where he was cut in half by a highway sign. I guess the families wouldn't like to know Cody films *everything*, and so Cody must have regretted telling his associate about that.

"However, the now-dead associate had told my informant that Cody saves a copy of each kill. The associate *saw* the videos. That's stupid, because it leaves evidence. But he's compelled to do it. He films his hits, including when the police eventually arrive. The associate described several of these videos."

Joel says, "He has to have all these videos somewhere. Somewhere his family won't find them, but where he can watch them--like the cabin. That's why we need to get in the cabin."

Gabriel nods with some reluctance. "Fair enough, I see the connection. You saw that the cabin had a Turner system. Turner Systems are good; they base their demos on people who like high tech. What would help is if he's using their mobile service. Crack the phone, you have all the apps, passwords, info."

Zest asks, "Difficult to handle?"

"Depends," Joel says. "Apple has tight security on its phone apps. Android goes through Google Play. That's why phones in the US are so much harder to hack than other countries that have standard service. If I can get the phone for a minute, maybe less, I can copy the phone. I need to pick his pocket. Don't look at me like that, Gabriel."

"Pick his pocket. No danger in that."

"Picking pockets is a matter of diversion. If he's diverted sufficiently, he'll have no damn idea what's going on. This is it, damn it. The proof. He films everything. He probably filmed killing my father."

Zest lights a cigarette, leaning back and crossing his legs. He asks Gabriel, "Do you remember any indicia of that?"

"He wore glasses...they were odd glasses. I guess he could have been wearing a small camera."

"Such cameras exist. He had the knife there to kill two of you. He wouldn't have wanted to miss an opportunity to film that." Zest gestures with the cigarette.

"He keeps them." Gabriel takes one of Zest's cigarettes and Joel decides not to complain. "Trophies. He'd want his trophies where he can be among them to engage with his passion. This kind of passion he can't share with his family."

Joel takes the cigarette from Gabriel's hand and draws from it. Zest watches them. Gabriel continues. "He hunts for people in the same mindset as hunting animals. The filming is the proxy for stuffing and mounting. His way of killing people is his mark, his signature."

"How soon can we do this," Joel asks.

"Joel..."

"It's not up for debate. He threatened you. I don't have time for you to investigate the intricacies of high finance. No more *Paper Chase*. We have to get this film, now."

Zest says, "I need to go out of town for a few days. I'll be back. Please don't try this until I get back. I need to go to handle a matter. If I put it off, I'd draw attention to myself. When I return, we will set this up."

∞

Thursday, May 19
Paterson, NJ, 11:09 pm

I've been mostly alone all day, working. Now it's after 11pm, and I'm trying to concentrate on some notes. Walter is here; he brought some books for me and wanted to talk about my exploits with Don Mathers, and my current predicament. I can tell he wants to be in on this investigation and play it out in the upcoming book. Walter asked me write about everything I was feeling about Don Mathers. I've been trying, but all I feel about him is rage.

Bob is home tonight, and right now he's on his cell talking to a client. The client is having a crisis; he's out of prison after 20 years, and not sure he can make it in an undisciplined, unregulated world. Prison nerves.

While Bob is counseling, my attention wanders. I'm starting to like Walter in spite of myself; he has a dry humor I can appreciate. But I miss Joel. Joel doesn't want to come here every night, afraid Bob will get tired of all the visiting. I know Bob better than that. He has the second bedroom because he likes company. I'm frustrated I can't get up and go out and find Joel. He's like an element in space, tumbling around in a chaotic mass. I'm afraid for him and even more so since Zest is now part of the equation.

"You look lost in thought."

"I miss my boyfriend."

"I understand that. My wife had a terrible illness and was in the hospital for nearly a month. I missed her every night."

I take off my glasses. I have mild farsightedness, and I'm being careful to use reading glasses so I don't trigger the headaches. When Joel isn't here, I've been sneaking cigarettes. Walter has become one of my suppliers. He takes a couple out now.

I can see distance fine. And getting up to look out the window as I light up, I see something in the black shadows that seems blacker than the night and the trees. The blacker shape suddenly moves.

∞

THIRTEEN

William Shakespeare said, "Things without all remedy should be without regard. What's done is done."

∞

Thursday, May 19 *Continued.*

CALL ME PARANOID. I don't like people lurking outside when I can't tell what they're doing. I move to my bedroom. The windows there face the same way as the living room. The light is off in there, so I can look outside without being seen.

Picking up on my feelings, Walter has followed me. "What's going on out there?"

"I'm not sure. Maybe nothing. But I just want to see."

Now Bob is here. "Someone's outside? Should I turn the living room light off?"

"Not yet."

The shadow splits. Now I'm sure two people are there, about ten yards from the front door. Moving in opposite directions. The way they leave seems too deliberate.

"Turn it off now..."

Bob goes for the lights, and I move toward the kitchen. Walter is right behind me. The apartment is now pitch black. Archie, sensing something is up and smarter than any of us, hides in one of Bob's bookcases.

"How are the locks, Bob?"

"You put them in, buddy."

"The deadbolts are set on all of them?"

"Let's check. Walter, keep an eye on the window?"

Now we split up. I go for the front door, and Bob to the back door in the kitchen. We meet back in the living room and nod at each other.

"The patio door?"

"I have the bar in the groove."

We're talking low by design. The curtains are drawn across the glass doors. Bob doesn't have weapons. I consider calling the police, which granted, I rarely do. But nothing's happened.

That changes when we hear something at the glass door. Scratching. The lock tumblers fall. But the door can't open, because of the bar. We hear someone struggle with the door briefly.

"Oh my God," Walter says quietly.

"What *is* this," Bob whispers. "Let's get them."

"No." I put my hand on his arm. "Not a good idea."

Now the person is at the back door. And we hear the front door as well.

Bob exhales. "Fuck. I hope those bars work." On both doors, I installed sliding bars that would require a police battering ram.

Whoever's outside tests that theory. We can hear something in the bolt turn.

"That's some fancy tricks," I say softly. But I'm nervous, with nowhere to go. Bob reaches under the sofa for a softball bat.

Walter, eyes wide, asks, "Do we call the police?"

Bob says, "Or is this the damn police? You said that man from the Sheriff's office threatened you..."

"I'm pretty sure he intended more fun for me in the lock-up."

"This could be set up to look like a home invasion."

"Drugs planted."

"Suicide-by-cop setup."

It's bad we're both so paranoid. It's bad we're justified in being that way. Walter is looking from Bob to me like he's watching a tennis match.

Some force is pressed against the door. We can hear the thump.

"What do we do?"

"I'm not waiting for them to figure out something worse." I pick up the phone and call Veronica to have her enact an emergency measure.

"Hold on, just a couple minutes..."

Whoever's outside works the doors the entire time I'm on the phone and afterwards. All we can do is watch them and be prepared in case the barrier is breached. I'm afraid they may use something like a Halligan bar to break the door open.

The front door seems like it's bending. Bob gets a fire extinguisher and hands me his softball bat. Not much, but we'll be ready to make the most of it.

"Walter, if they get in run upstairs and start screaming out the window like your life depends upon it."

Walter scurries to the staircase.

And then we hear fire engines.

"Thank God." I exhale.

Bob suddenly laughs. "Did you have her call in a *fire?*"

"She has burner phones for such a purpose. We don't know these fuckers *weren't* going to set the place on fire."

Bob sighs. "I'm not complaining. I'm just going to get you a copy of *How to Win Friends and Influence People.*"

I smile. "In some places in Jersey, I'm less popular than *Batman and Robin* and *The Phantom Menace* combined."

Walter has come back. "Is it over?"

We watch outside for a while as firefighters go from house to house; lights go on, people go outside.

"Welcome to my world, Walter," I say, lighting another cigarette.

He leaves shortly thereafter, promising to check on me in the morning. Nothing else happens during the night, although I can't sleep. Neither can Bob. We stay up until it gets light, playing cards.

∞

Veronica is helping me put in the cameras when Joel arrives.

I've been calling and texting him. He finally said he was coming over. I'm just glad to see he's okay.

He rushes over to me. "I'm sorry. I was taking care of something. If I'd known..."

"The scary part's over. We're just trying to prevent it again."

"What the hell happened?"

I check the signal on Bob's tablet. I can see the high angle, wide angle. And Joel staring at me.

"Some people were trying to get in the apartment. First, we're going to set up security. Then I might look into another apartment if I can get permission to move."

"We can fight them off ourselves, man."

I give Bob a *you're-not-helping* look.

He's not impressed. "And you aren't moving. As if I'm scared of this? I'm thinking of getting another Harley. Eddie's keeping an eye out for a bargain ride for me."

"I'll help you too," Walter says, having returned as promised. Since the man's life had been in danger, I can't complain about him being here taking notes. And I feel better with a lot of people around.

Veronica gets down the ladder. "How's the camera working?"

"Fantastic. We could wire up a damn building together."

"We had a few inquiries about that, actually. Maybe it'll be our new specialty."

Joel comes over to look at the video feed. "Do you have any idea who they were?"

I put my arm around him, and he puts his head on my shoulder. "Not specifically. But I have this set up for night vision."

"You're worried and trying to pretend you aren't. You were smoking too. It's in your hair."

"No comment. If I could put cameras on other parts of the building, I would."

"We could late at night. Use a compound glue for the brick. Or, we could put them in trees."

"Trees. I like that. Some of the trees are beyond my range, but trees are all around the building. Some at the parking lot."

Joel starts toward one of the trees. I follow enough to the limit of my range. I have the range measured exactly in my mind.

I watch him examine the tree. He looks over his shoulder at me. I feel my frustration rise. He walks to me, standing just on the other side of the imaginary line. "This is hard for you."

"I won't call it fun. It's not fun for you either."

"You remind me of a caged animal."

"No one's ever used that analogy before--clever."

He smiles. "A dog with the invisible fence."

"Did I *do* something to you?"

"You said to have a sense of humor. I'm trying. I'm really trying not to freak out. I know this is Meese. I'm going to watch the place from my car tonight."

"No, don't do that, stay out all night. You can be inside."

"Bob..."

"Bob is fine with it; this isn't like you to not listen to me. You can't relax here for some reason I don't understand. Bob used to shoot up with criminals and homeless people in abandoned houses. He's a mellow guy. He wouldn't have offered if he wasn't okay with this, and it may be a year or more. He can handle you staying the night."

Joel looks away when I mention the prospect of the future. "I can see what's going on better from the car. I'll have Veronica with me." He slips his arms around me. "I'm scared."

I run my hands through his hair. "We just need to be proactive."

"I want to end this."

I think about that. "The danger quotient has gone up. We know that they are aware of what we're trying to do."

"If they know, then we need to do this fast."

"I don't feel good about his house, Joel, no matter what Zest says. There has to be another way."

"For Cody, I don't think so. For Meese...maybe."

"Meaning?"

He shrugs. "I've considered what's going on from a strategic sense."

"Let's talk about it. Stop teasing me with your freedom of movement and come in the DMZ." I bring him inside.

A few minutes later we have a little lunch party. Walter is kind enough to spring for it despite my protests, and in turn meets my other friends: Jim, Geneva, Chris, Danny and Mikki. After the fear of the previous night, having people around is comforting.

Joel and I keep exchanging glances. He isn't speaking much, and seem to be mostly in some internal world.

"What's on your mind, baby?"

"I've come to an epiphany from what's happened over the last few days when I heard the danger you and Bob were in." He turns to look at the others. You know we're trying to find evidence to get Gabriel out of this situation, to find out who really killed Ken."

They all acknowledge that.

"I had a plan, a strategy--I'm not going to say what it is, so stop getting hyper, Gabriel. I wouldn't tell the lawyers. Let's just say it could very well work, but has...risks."

Mikki and Jim look at each other. Jim is my age, a defense attorney in New York City. He's a nice-looking Jewish guy with a perpetually worried demeanor. I tend to make that worry worse.

Jim says, "So that's every idea Gabriel's *ever* had. He taught you well."

"This one's mine. He doesn't want to do it. He's gone soft in old age. It may still be done because it's a good idea. But I'm also considering other angles. You all have an idea who we think is behind this, and why. Walter doesn't, but the fact he was out there making sure Gabriel didn't get killed in jail...I'm including you in. Just don't print anything right now."

"Of course; I appreciate being included."

Joel is making me nervous. "You know, Chris has helped me a lot; I'm not going into that in detail, but I think the records trail is going to be the primary evidence."

Joel smiles at me. "See? He went from Jason Bourne to Mr. Rogers. I'm thinking of another angle that won't make him crazy."

"Too late," all my alleged friends say.

Joel, sitting on the floor next to me, tents his fingers under his chin. "This other idea is a different kind of risk and I guess I want to know what you think because if I do it, it's public. However, I'm very serious about this."

His demeanor is grave enough that he has everyone's attention, waiting to find out what it means.

He looks at Jim and Mikki. "It doesn't take long to file a lawsuit, right?"

Jim nods. "Only as long as it takes to write a complaint. That can be mere hours with a template. Well, if *Gabriel* was writing it for me, then we'd be talking about three or four months..."

Jim's amused by his own insult, but quickly gets back in professional mode when I glare at him. He says, "What are you thinking of doing?"

Joel looks at everyone then focuses on the attorneys. "Listen. This is going to come out. When I was 15...my mom and dad had pretty severe problems. They weren't watching out for me and maybe I was more vulnerable because of that. My dad's friend, Larry Meese...he got me into a situation."

Everyone knows what's coming, and the room is heavy with expectation. I put my head on his shoulder so I can't look at anyone else. I hear his heart rate rise considerably and feel him break out into a sweat. But he goes on.

"He got me alone on a pretext. On his precious *boat.* And...sexually assaulted me. He threatened to have me put in juvenile detention. I had messed around with a teacher and he knew and used it against me. I felt like I had no choice. He made me come back and did it again, and then had three of his friends...he sold me to them. I don't know how else to put it. But I escaped."

At this point, I have tears. He keeps his voice calm but he's trembling, and he takes my hand. Chris gets up and starts massaging Joel's shoulders.

"Meese made up some shit about me to get Ken to turn me over to him full time, like I was a delinquent. But Ken just threw me out instead. That's when I went to New York. It may be strange to say that as awful as it was, better to be thrown out then being under Meese's control."

Without looking, I can feel the reactions in the room.

Bob says simply, "That's fucked up, Joel. I'm sorry."

There's a general consensus of empathy for him. I can finally look at him myself and see how he holds himself together. Allowing himself to acknowledge what happened without judgment.

"It's okay," he tells me in a low voice. And then to the others, "It's time. Meese is dangerous. I see now, with what happened to Gabriel in jail and with these guys trying to break in, I need to put heat on Meese. Get it out publicly. Whatever Cody is, he may think twice about being involved with a pedophile rapist. Even killers have standards. Pedophiles are too much heat. Even the accusation is too much."

And then he says after pausing a moment, "I want to sue Meese."

The quiet gets even quieter.

The attention focused on Joel makes him nervous, but he continues. "Like the people who sue a Catholic Diocese. They can do that years after the abuse occurred, even when the victim is an adult, right?"

"Yeah," Jim says. "The statute of limitations is tolled in those cases, but only six years in New York."

Mikki exhales slowly. "You're thinking to sue him for what he did to you. To take it to trial."

"Yeah."

Now my own heart has tripled hearing this. I can't say a word.

Mikki says, "It's a powerful solution. I only want to acknowledge, because you need to know, the excruciating process of what's involved, Joel. You are already looking at testifying in at least two within the next year or so. It's the discovery process and waiting for the trial that's so hard. The deposition will be brutal on you, as well as everything surrounding this particular case. Media coverage, motions, interlocutory appeals, and so on. The litigation becomes a part of your life."

"Yeah, I thought about it. I can deal with it. I need to repeat the story of what he did to me, to be questioned on the story, to have my credibility attacked. To have my past brought up and used against me. I know. I know what people think of sex workers--that they deserve what happened to them, that they can't be raped. That suing 17 years after the fact means I'm trying to shake him down, maybe making a false claim for revenge. I can handle it. I've had worse said to me. It's going to come out in public anyway, since I chose to be public. Someone we know is determined to make sure of that."

He means Alex, and I feel my face go red. Feeling it's my fault.

"Stop," he says to me. "That isn't on you. If anything, it's because of you that I can handle this. I don't have anything to be ashamed of. You taught me that."

Veronica says, "You're still very brave. Saying this now is hard."

"Thanks, V. I know. I know what people say in comments to stories about rape and sex abuse. People are vile sometimes. Nonetheless, those who've been abused, they'll understand. That's what's important."

"What's involved with getting this suit happening?"

Jim and Mikki glance at each other. "In New Jersey, Mick?"

She opens her tablet to consult online. "Allege the tort, and the damages. This involves the case of a minor at the time of the incident. It'll be automatically confidential. You couldn't talk about it, what's in the complaint itself. However, the statute of limitations is only two years. Some legislators are trying to get a new bill in, because of Church issues. But the Church also has powerful lobbies working against that."

That makes me angry. "They're following JP II, who was too "pure in thought" to conceive that pedophile priests even existed."

Joel looks irritated at the legal aspect. "No way around that?"

"You could try, but unlikely. However, the committee with the bill is hearing witnesses. If you're looking to get this public, that's one way--aside from just going to a newspaper."

"I've considered that."

"Wait," Jim says. "Let's not take lawsuits off the table. Any loopholes in the state law?"

"Well...wait a minute. Discovery. There is a tolling provision, I think." Mikki does research on her phone.

"N.J.S.A. 2A:61B-1(c) allows a plenary hearing. Statute of limitations can be tolled in a case because of the plaintiff's mental state, duress by the defendant, or any other equitable grounds. The case I'm looking at involved a 30-year gap. If we get past that, we can do a regular torts claim."

"Plenary hearing," Jim says. "That'll be rough. I still like 1983; maybe the plenary hearing could be tied in...more research--Gabriel could do it."

"Explain so I can appreciate this, please." Joel lights a cigarette.

The lawyers look at him. His decision has given him a gravitas we can all hear, all feel.

"Well, you'll need to argue before a judge as to why the reporting was after the two-year SOL. It's what, 17 years later? Duress isn't exactly involved here. I'd bet case law backs that up. You'd have to argue mental state or other "equitable" grounds."

Joel raises his eyebrows. "And those are?"

"Fuzzy terms courts don't like. We could think about it. Mental state...you aren't crazy. You don't have recovered memories. I'd have to argue PTSD. You'd need a diagnosis that said only the current trauma *vis a vis* Gabriel's situation and your dad's death somehow enabled you to pursue this. That is stretching it...but..."

"Go ahead nonetheless. I can handle it."

Mikki and Jim look at each other again.

"You'd do this, right? I'd need *you*. A stranger would be too difficult."

"They'll do it," I say out loud. I make sure by my tone what I say isn't a question.

Michaela says wryly, "Don't get cross, Gabriel. You know I will. I don't do much civil, but I'm here for you, Joel. I wouldn't leave you alone. I'm already planning to sue the state of New Jersey and Passaic County on Gabriel's behalf."

I turn back to look at Michaela. "Thank you. For helping him."

"He's a friend. You all were here for *me*. I'm not letting him be handled by someone else."

"It goes for me too. Of course," Jim says. "I do civil. I still have my Jersey law license." He leans forward. "You'll have to tell us what happened. I know you just did, but...you know, in detail. You'll have to read the complaint. You'll need to testify about it."

"Yeah. I know. I don't care. I want it done as soon as possible before Meese thinks of some other way to try to kill Gabriel."

Jim looks at me now. "The complaint..."

"No, I'm not writing it. I can't."

Joel says, "I understand it will be difficult, but..."

"I'm not. I support you doing this. But I cannot write that."

"I'll write it on my own, if you show me how."

"Write a narrative," Mikki says. "I'll give you some parameters. Jim and I can do the complaint within a few days."

I say to Joel, "You don't have to do this for my situation."

"It helps both of us." He lights up. "Does it hurt Gabriel's case?"

"Meese shouldn't have anything to do with Gabriel's case. However, a possibility may exist that if the suit goes public, the facts of your abuse could be seen as motive for revenge."

"To kill *Meese*, yeah. But he's alive."

"I mean if you thought Meese was colluding with your father. If Gabriel was enacting revenge on your behalf for that."

He shrugs. "That doesn't seem feasible."

"If it's not public, it doesn't go in as evidence in trial. If it does go public, then it could, if the prosecutor thinks it's motive."

Joel doesn't respond, but turns to me.

"This case should have been thrown out long ago. I'm not afraid. We'll tie it into Cody somehow. Ultimately, this is your decision."

Joel tells Michaela and Jim, "Start it now, and I'll make a decision when it's written. But I'm already pretty sure. I want him to answer for it. To drag him out in the light."

"It's still confidential."

"Not for long. He'll know. Something will be set in motion, to bring this down. Maybe I can find other people he did this to, and have them join in. Wouldn't seem so crazy then." Joel smiles wryly. "Sorry to make this day a downer of sorts. But this has to be done. Meese is more dangerous than just hurting kids. He sent somebody here. I know this has to be true."

Everyone tries to assure Joel that he hasn't done any harm. They get up and start preparing to leave. Joel speaks with Michaela, Jim and Veronica about the complaint. Bob takes me outside to have a cigarette. Then Joel talks to Walter. Probably catching him up on Cody and Meese.

"It'll be okay," Bob says.

"Holy shit. I'm so fucking frustrated, being here. If I could get around on my own, he *wouldn't have to do this.*"

"He *wants* to. Let him. The past is a bitch. This can restrain the bitch. Hitting back helps. He wasn't able to as a kid, but he can now. Let him hit back."

Through the glass door, I see Danny say something to Joel. They talk for a moment, very intensely. Danny eventually grabs Joel's shoulder briefly, what seems to be a positive manner.

Veronica comes out to join us.

"What was that," I asked her.

"He told Joel he was sorry. I think about how they didn't get along before. Joel told him that he didn't have to apologize, that everything was good between them."

"Joel doesn't want pity."

"Danny wasn't doing that. But true, most people don't know how to handle someone going through that. I know."

Now Joel comes out. I see exhaustion in his eyes, but also a new sense of purpose. He says to me, "You think you have the excuse to smoke?"

"Don't harass me; I'll still kick your ass."

He smiles. "I've been waiting for that to happen for years now. But I'm not doing anything with this tonight. Let's forget about it for a while."

He hugs me, and then Veronica hugs both of us.

"I have to get in on this," Bob says. And so we're wrapped up tight.

Later on, I ask Joel, "What's next?"

"God, you're asking *me*. That's a switch. This was the worst. I'm not giving up on Cody's cabin. We'll see what we can do when Zest returns. For now...the next thing won't be easy, but easier than this. Finding other boys Meese molested."

∞

Joel is taken by the fact that Gabriel told him his plan to find other victims was a good one. He knows he doesn't *need* to have Gabriel's approval, but getting it means the world.

"This is hard for me not to be there to protect you," Gabriel says. "But you have handled this admirably. You were right."

Joel blushes some and smiles, looking down.

"You've lived a lifetime in the past few weeks." Jan, next to him again.

Gabriel has gone to talk about something with Bob.

Joel finds turning the pages of the notebook Jan gives him to be much easier than other eras he's reviewed. "Time has seemed to speed up."

"You're getting to your present. You have a chance to see the difference in your life. It's a turning point."

"Too many times I said this has to change...but now it is. Now it is."

∞

SAM & LAURA, RIZA, ANTONY

Søren Kierkegaard said, *Life can only be understood backwards; but it must be lived forwards.*

∞

This has to change.

It is January 20, 2004.

Battery Park City, 5:23 pm

Dylan, Sophisticated Blond. Bi, straight-acting, well-read. Top or versatile. 23, 5'8, 165 lb., blue/gray eyes. Muscular swimmer's build, moderate hair, no tattoos/piercings. Smoking ok. Big and cut. 100% safe, drug free. Out calls, travel, overnights. Very discreet. Easy-going, fun, no attitude, affectionate. Client, LTR friendly. Over 90% repeats. Role-play, CIM, COB, couples, deep throat, domination, bondage, erotic massage. Romantic, boyfriend, kisser. No barebacking. Email for more info.

It's just after his 26th birthday. He's called Angela to thank her for her gift, a cashmere sweater. It's very expensive, and shows how much she values him, even though he's been on his own for four years now. But sensibly, he stays in touch with her. He only wants to do this part-time, hoping to gradually just not do it at all.

Angela understood. He is smart enough and professional enough to be absolutely reliable to her, but that also means he grows out of needing her. He's taken fewer and fewer calls anyway, and Angela is about maximizing business. She keeps his contact as a referral, for clients she knows would appreciate him (and that he is always good for a referral fee) and he in turn sends business her way he doesn't want.

The only thing he doesn't send are men who occasionally ask him how to be an escort. Sure, they *want* to be. Some even feel--hey, they want to go out and have fun anyway. Why not get paid?

Joel is not ashamed of his work. He feels he found some sort of strength through his abilities, his skills. He doesn't feel worthless or low-class. He takes pride in his ability to be professional and good at what he does. No one can take that from him. The world runs on eroticism and money, and he's tapped into that and earned his accolades. He treats other sex workers with respect as well, regardless of their status.

Yet he does not encourage or recruit. Maybe some would handle it better than he. Nonetheless, had he gone back in time with better circumstances, he wouldn't have chosen this. He had it for survival, and mastered it. But he will not be part of someone's decision to get into it.

However, if he finds out good or bad info on a client or escort, and Angela needs to know, he tells her. They've spent years going over these things, and Angela trusts him, probably respects him as much as she can respect anyone.

For business, it's important to know who's a serial caller, who are bogus appointment makers, who are clients with narrow, picky tastes. To know the high-dollar clients who are difficult, or heavy drug users. The clients who tend to turn escorts away at the door too often. Clients who no-show or withhold pay. The escorts who only want body worship and high prices, who emphasize cock size and say they're 'spoiled.' Escorts who don't return pages, go on drug binges, disappear or collect customer complaints. Dishonest ones, no shows, those who can't be confidential, and escorts with personal issues that interfere with good work.

Joel is still known to most clients and other escorts as Dylan. It's his brand name, and Angela lets him know if others in NYC try to use it as a stage name, or try to pass themselves off as him. Unusual for an escort moving into the 21st century, Joel does not do photographs, web cams, stripping (except privately), or porn. He doesn't enter Hustlaball pageants. That cuts down a premium-premium rate because he's not famous. But he is selective, expensive, and known to a range of clients as highly desirable. No wonder a few hustlers out there try to pretend they're him. Except that brings him a bad name, so he has to act on it and borrows Harry to visit them and give them friendly advice.

Because his client list is mostly repeats, he has fewer problems. Long gone from hustling on the street and getting beat-up, or burned for money (which in essence is a form of rape). Gone is having to be in family cars complete with a baby seat in back, guessing whether someone is a junkie, psycho, or has other serious health issues...evaluating risks about being alone on the street or in a hotel room. Joel no longer has bruises but he remembers them.

Gone also are the past relationships where he's let others use him, stalk him, or consider him an audience for their particular brand of personality disorder. He's promised himself it's going to be different.

Angela says she has potential clients for him, a couple. Couples can be opposite sex or same-sex. This one is opposite sex and looking to be repeat clients.

The couple want to meet him and at a bar in Battery Park, so he goes to check them out. Quite often, clients who meet in neutral places are bullshit. An escort doesn't need to be felt out or seduced. He doesn't need to be told this is the client's first time with a man. But Angela says for these two the meeting is actually part of their fantasy and they'll pay $500 straight up just to talk for a couple hours. For the trouble.

They meet him in the bar at a private table. They're both white. The man in his late forties is Sam. He's tall, thin, black hair with some gray. He has the decadent professor thing going. The woman, Laura, has dark brown hair and is about 10 years younger than Sam. She has classic features, resembling Lena Olin.

Sam introduces them both and does most of the talking. He makes a point to Joel that he and Laura are married, not that Joel cares.

They're both immediately into him. Angela has good instincts about that. Sam is very taken with him in particular. He reaches over and touches Joel's arm and leg every few minutes. Laura just eye-fucks him in the background as she nurses her red cocktail.

Joel turns on his charm like Zen, automatic. Yet inside Joel is not thrilled with it. He's going through the motions though Sam and Laura cannot tell. And the money they are offering is serious for a recurring appointment.

Sam continues prattling on, explaining the two of them live in Westchester and neighbors might notice any erotic visitors and so they like to have 'date-nights' in Manhattan. Apparently, they've tried this a few times and it was okay, but they're still seeking the right partner, so to speak.

Joel listens to him, nodding, smiling provocatively at times. That has Sam almost blowing his load at the table.

It's business, Angela would say.

This is what I do for a living. Fuck a pretentious yuppie couple.

So don't do it. You have a choice.

And yet as he considers getting up and walking out, he knows that chasm is not crossable as yet. He has to figure out how to do this right. To be able to walk away and burn the bridge.

He agrees to a 'test' evening. A test as much for him as them as he makes clear with a touch of put-on arrogance. Sam, besotted with him, is acquiescent. Laura goes along with what Sam says.

They meet at a hotel a week later. And then continue to meet every month for three months. Then Sam ups it to every three weeks.

Surprisingly the sex is good, perhaps the most actually physically enjoyable for Joel out of any of his clients. The chemistry with both of them works well in that strange way where you can seriously get off with someone even though zero emotional attachment exists. At least for Joel.

Sam more or designs the show; he's the one with the fantasies. He likes a little cuckold/control thing: to watch Joel fuck Laura, to suck off Joel while Joel goes down on Laura, to have Joel fuck him while he fucks Laura, both of them fuck Laura at the same time. He seems to be able to come up with exponential permutations on this. He likes for Joel to give him orders, deny him, to suddenly take over and direct the action. He watches Joel throughout the sessions, and holds on to him afterward in a way that raises a few red flags.

Joel picks up on serious psychodrama between Sam and Laura, which is the subcontext of the sex. But Sam wants to draw Joel more into the psychodrama. It becomes Sam's *life* to have those sessions. Joel hates to think what their regular home life is like, how they treat each other. He doesn't want to know. But Sam has a worsening habit of confiding details about their life to Joel that Joel doesn't want to hear. More red flags. But Joel's fallen into the habit of keeping on with them, since nothing has gotten definitively bad.

At seven months in, Sam wants Joel to come to the Westchester house. Now even more time (all paid for) is spent listening to Sam talk. Like Sam feels Joel is his friend. Joel sees that Sam is developing an attachment to him that isn't healthy.

In late September, Sam calls him to come over just to talk. As soon as Joel gets in the house Sam sits him on the couch and finally proposes that Joel live with them. He'll make up a story as to why Joel's in the house, saying he's a boarder or a personal trainer.

Joel saw this coming weeks back. Maybe since the first night they were all together, when Sam practically threw himself at Joel's feet.

Joel turns this offer down gently. Laura isn't around that day, and Joel has no idea if she's part of this offer or not. It doesn't matter. Still, Sam spends an hour, then two, trying to convince him to change his mind. Out of kindness Joel stays with him--watching Sam crying, listening to Sam saying his life will have no meaning without Joel. To keep Sam from losing it, Joel spends some time holding him.

"You're not going to leave me, are you?" Sam cries into Joel's chest.

"Take it easy. Everything will work out."

Eventually Sam takes a couple of Valium and falls asleep. Joel makes sure he's breathing okay, then leaves.

The next day, Joel changes all his contact information except his working email, which Sam and Laura don't have.

This has to change.

He books a flight to London at midnight that night. A musician friend he ran into a week ago in the city invited him to hang out if he had the chance.

The musician, Reynaldo, who often works session for major bands, introduces Joel to some minor and major celebrities. One of these, Antony Savage, is the singer in a Britpop band, Ellipses. Savage fronts Ellipses with his brother Duncan. The British press has fun with the Savages' last name, as they are known for fighting with each other, the other band members, and paparazzi.

Antony Savage is part of a little get-together with some alternative artists, musicians, and hangers-on. Reynaldo is invited to this party and brings Joel along. Joel stays in the background despite varying levels of interest in him. Reynaldo doesn't use drugs, but music and drugs are inevitable in these parties and Joel wants nothing to do with that.

Savage follows Joel when he steps out on a balcony to smoke.

"Can I have one," he asks. But instead of taking it, he moves closer to Joel and starts kissing him. In his frame of mind, Joel goes with it. It seems daring and outrageous, for a celebrated rock star to be kissing him where they could be seen by anyone. Joel's used to being discreet.

In the heat of the atmosphere of music and reefer in the background, probably harder stuff as well, Savage gets down and unzips Joel's pants. Joel feels a little dizzy, with the people in the room watching this little encounter through the glass doors. People on the street can probably see as well. Joel keeps his face turned away from the street in case someone takes a picture of Antony Savage blowing a random man.

Joel leaves right after but Savage manages to convince Reynaldo to give Joel a message and a number. Joel talks to him a couple times, and Savage is crazy strong to meet up with him again. But Joel isn't sure. Reynaldo is a professional, but a lot of rock 'stars' are fucking crazy, like actors. Totally out of touch with reality. After the Sam and Laura Variety Hour, he can do without the psychodrama.

His semi-regular clients somehow find out where he is. They have a sense about him. His email fills up. There's a few he'll call back, Jan for one. Since he's in Europe and Jan is home in Amsterdam, Joel goes to see him for a week.

Then another semi-regular invites him to India. Joel feels better about doing this if he feels he doesn't *have* to. Since he rarely spends money except for clothes or computers, he has enough bank to not take jobs for money. Whereas seeing Jan is for the friendship, going to India is for the experience.

The contact is not Indian, but he has a friend who is. That friend, Riza, is Indian *and* Muslim. He has money and lives like a decadent expatriate prince. After Joel's client sees Joel for the weekend, Riza impulsively invites Joel to visit him.

Savage has managed to find one of Joel's emails and is writing constantly. But Joel ignores him and stays with Riza. For the next several months.

Riza decides he wants to go to out of the way places in India, live more ascetically and meaningfully. Joel obligingly goes with him. He watches Riza talk with locals, spends a lot of time with him isolated in mountains or forestry.

As often happens with Joel, the person who falls for him thinks he or she is running the show and then at some point becomes an appeaser, afraid Joel will leave.

Riza starts showing those signs. It conflicts with his religion which is still strong with him; he stops to pray often. He finds quiet places for them to stay and likes to drink tea and go over points of his study of theology with Joel. He has books of Sufi poetry, and reads them to Joel. Joel has picked up some Arabic and Hindi words, as he often does with international clients. But Riza is not a client. He's a companion.

Riza is a very peaceful person. For the first two weeks, Riza does not even attempt anything sexual. From the frequent phone calls Joel overhears between Riza and his family, Riza is torn between his proclivities which burn in him when he's with Joel, and the ascetic ideal of his Islamic studies.

But eventually the conflict gives way to the physical. That leaves *Joel* conflicted, as Riza is a remarkably beautiful person. The more they continue on the journey through Southeast Asia, the more Riza leaves his money and the trappings that go with it behind. But he keeps saying how he has to go back. That a wife has been chosen for him and he's supposed to step up and get that taken care of.

He has a tendency to explain this after sex, as if feeling the guilt. Well, he is feeling the guilt. When Joel tells him he'll leave rather than cause more conflict, Riza gets extremely upset and begs him not to go.

Joel gives in, but that doesn't change Riza's mind about doing what his family wants.

Joel asks him, "And what power can make you go ahead and do that, really?"

"It's an obligation. You have to understand."

"You're aren't physically held down to them. Would they assassinate you?"

"No, but I'd be shaming them."

"That's their problem. You can live on your own, right?"

And Riza could. But even though he listens and considers the philosophy of autonomy and freedom, he insists he has none. A higher power draws him. It's not only enculturated, it's in his genes. Or so he says.

All the amusing things they do together become more bittersweet, some version of *Brokeback Mountain* set in India, because Riza is moving around a clockwork, edging back to midnight.

Joel even prays with Riza, although Joel has no real belief in any particular higher power. Not a specific one, with a name. But he likes the beauty of the words, and the haunting, compelling music of the muezzin's call to prayer. Riza is in harmony with him then, sharing the same appreciation of beauty.

But family will often trump everything. The family is the past that decries the future. The family that underscores the past. Joel can see the clock winding down by the number of family phone calls that increase, by the prayers Riza now insists on having by himself. He does, however, suggest that Joel live nearby where Riza and his future wife will be making a home.

It's January again, right around his 27th birthday. Joel's surprised by how he personally feels. Hollow, because he can't change anything. Frustrated, because he has feelings, and knows Riza has feelings. These feelings could be called love. But they are absolutely teardrops in an ocean for how much effect they have on the situation.

He's not going to stay and be a hidden lover, risking serious danger if he's ever found out to have a sexual relationship with Riza.

The only way to save yourself is to leave first. Just as with (almost) every past relationship he's had.

When midnight strikes, Joel already has bought a ticket to go back to London. No sense trying to talk Riza out of his life choices, and fuck goodbyes.

This has to change.

He's barely settled in a hotel in London, looking for contacts who might have a flat to sublet, when Savage somehow finds him. Shows what money can do.

Savage shows up at his hotel room at 3 in the morning.

Joel opens the door and raises his eyebrows. "And?"

Savage smiles. "Want to shack up with me?"

∞

It is December 1, 2005.
London, noon

The year seemed to go by so quickly...except that when Joel got fed up, time crawled until he moved out of Savage's flat.

But since Antony wants to still be civil, Joel comes over after Antony calls him.

Antony is cool but welcoming. "So you're doing what now?"

"Nothing. I'm taking a vacation."

"Well. I might be going to Tibet or Nepal. There's some spiritual retreats there that might be good to reawaken my creativity."

"That would be good for you," Joel says kindly.

Antony is restless. "I want you to listen to our new release, then."

Joel settles into one of Antony's strange expensive designer Sixties throwback beanbag chairs. "Sure. I appreciate that."

With some formality, Antony plays a few selections. A highlight is the first single from Ellipse's next album, a hard-driving song called "Play for Pay." In the music industry, 'pay to play' is a term like payola, paying off radio stations to put a song in heavy rotation. But Antony's song is about a person who does things for money, and has little concern over the feelings of the song's protagonist, who declares he is taken advantage of, and not surprised that the person is leaving the relationship for better and richer opportunities.

Joel supposes that the motivation behind this bitter song is his not catering to Antony's every whim. And not forgiving Antony for screaming at Joel whenever he was dissatisfied with life: dissatisfied with his batshit-crazy brother, with an interview, with a review, with his tea not being made the right way. Also Antony does coke and that Goddamn sniffing is annoying. Aside from personality changes on a moment's notice. Although Antony has his caring, loving side, Joel sees he's never going to change indulging in his demons. Without those demons, he wouldn't be Antony Savage, rock star.

Which is why Joel packed his bags with the few things he had in Antony's flat and took off while Antony was in rehearsal. After he discovered Joel's treachery, Antony cursed Joel out in voicemails, in emails, through mutual acquaintances, and finally in song.

Antony stares at him after the song is over.

Joel gets that he's supposed to feel upbraided by becoming a topic of Antony's song. He doesn't want to laugh at this, but it's so ridiculous. Antony was overdramatic when he went down on Joel in public, he's overdramatic fighting with his brother on stage, and he's overdramatic about a breakup that's his own fault for being a grade-A jackass.

"Not bad," Joel says. I'd swear it's a lot like that old Asia song. The one with the gymnast in the video. You've seen it, right?"

Antony is highly insulted by the corporate rock comparison, as Joel intended. He still talks civilly to Joel for a couple hours, while maintaining a hurt-martyr posture. He doesn't want Joel to leave and at the same time he wants Joel to break down and admit he's wrong. They talk over and around each other, until Joel finally wearies of the game and leaves.

A few months later Antony emails him to say he's is in Tibet. The song *Play for Pay* is released to critical acclaim. The accompanying video portrays the play for pay antagonist as female, although a mysterious blond male turns up repeatedly. Rumors abound about what that means, since Antony is not openly gay. Joel keeps his interpretations to himself.

This has to change.

∞

Fourteen

Dylan Thomas said, *The function of posterity is to look after itself.*

Monday, May 23
Wayne, NJ, 12:09 pm

AT JOEL'S FORMER high school, a security guard asks him his business. Joel tells him he wants to see Jon Lane. Actually, Lane is now head of the athletic department for the school. The guard leads him to Lane's office. Lane is on the phone, and looks up at them.

"Is it okay, Jon?"

"Yeah, Bill, fine." Lane waves the guard away. He gets up from his desk and comes around. Joel holds his hand out, and Lane takes it, and hugs him. "I can't believe you're here. I'm glad you came by."

Joel feels overwhelmed by again being around the one man who tried to make something of him before he left. Lane looks overwhelmed as well.

"What happened, Joel? Back then. Maybe I shouldn't ask, but..."

"What did they tell you, Coach?"

Lane moves back, his hands on Joel's arms. "Your mother told me that you ran away, maybe that you were staying with her sister."

"I wasn't. I went to New York."

"I had a feeling. I thought about looking for you. I know something was wrong with *them*, your parents. I don't want to upset you saying that, after seeing you with your mom."

Joel feels tears in his eyes. "You're not. There was a lot wrong. I guess I should have talked to you. I didn't trust anyone then."

"How bad was it?"

"It was killing me. But it wasn't just them. My mom...she says she's sorry. Back then, I told Mr. Jeffries..."

Lane snorts. "He's long gone. Worthless SOB. What's going on now, Joel?"

"My father's murder...I'm working on it. My boyfriend was the man was arrested but he's innocent. I was on the phone with him when it happened, for God's sake. But the cops don't buy it. Our friend representing him thinks the charges will be dropped but I don't trust the system. So I'm looking into it. And now that means having to deal with what happened back then. I guess you're the only person in town I can really talk to about it and even now, I'm not sure."

Lane squeezes Joel's shoulder. "I know when a kid is going through a bad time. Now, the administration is all over that, from liability if we don't ask. Back when you were in school, the liability was if we *did* ask. Whatever you need to talk about, we can. I was going to check on a swim class. Come with me."

Joel follows Lane to the swimming area. A bunch of young men and women are huddled around the pool listening to the assistant coach give them some prep talk. They stare at Joel, who's introduced as an alumni and top swimmer. Joel stares back at them, as if looking for himself.

"He could dive, too." Lane tells them. "Better than anyone, including me. Maybe you could show them sometime."

"I'll come back." He and Lane leave, and walk outside to the track, passing several students who greet Lane and openly gawk at Joel.

"You wear pretty expensive clothes," Lane says. "That catches their eye."

Joel shrugs and smiles.

"Do you need my help, Joel?"

This is the hard part. Joel isn't even sure how to start. They both survey the empty track and the bright sun making the green field beyond sparkle.

"One of the reasons I left is because a man in town, someone with influence, abused me. I don't know how else to say it. I never really told anyone so I don't know what the right words are. But it happened, more than once. He was going to..." the words stop in Joel's throat.

Lane looks at him. "Larry Meese."

"You know?"

"I saw how you reacted when he arrived at the funeral."

"He was going to sell me to other men he knew. He made me do things, and lied to Ken. That's why Ken threw me out."

Lane sighs. "Fuck, I wish I knew at the time. "Damn it. Damn it. Something about that man always bothered me."

"What?"

"Nothing to prove. But he picked out boys to mentor, and almost every time, at least one of them would flip out--drugs, jail, or running away." Lane folds his arms. "A cop in a small town, you can't just make accusations. He got married again after you left, and then divorced. I wonder if his wives knew."

"No one ever said anything, then. I'm not surprised."

"No. He's not someone who lends himself to accusations."

"I saw in a Pennsylvania paper that some accusation has been made against a guy who worked at Penn State. You can imagine how working against the system of a major university can be. This is similar."

"Are you planning to do something, Joel?"

Joel sits on the last bench at the edge of the track. "Yeah. I want to see if I can get anyone to talk about him. I don't know who he may have abused. I remember some kids older than me, but I don't know their names. If you can give me any names, I want to find these boys, these men, and see if they'll talk."

Lane sits beside him. "For what purpose?"

"A lawsuit. Doesn't matter if it works or not, the important thing is turning over the rock, exposing him. Some people talk, others might come out."

"How does that help your boyfriend?"

Joel considers how much he can tell. "I think Meese was involved in something with my father. I can't prove it completely, but exposing him might lead to other information coming to light."

"It's a hard choice to make."

Joel looks down at the ground. He finds himself speaking in a way he had not before. "You say you wished you knew what was going on. I do too, because I was 15 and had no way out and no one to turn to. What does a 15-year-old know, after being sexually assaulted by a cop? My father threw me out and my mother was drinking too much to care. I spent a few months on the street in New York City until my girlfriend disappeared because someone was trying to kill her; then I lived in squatters building for another few months until my next girlfriend died. I had no one to help me there, either, without going into the foster care system. I just hustled on the street. I guess I felt that since Meese had already done what he did, this was what I was good for. Really, it was all I had. Because of him, because of them, I had no choice about what to do with my life."

He hears Lane breathing heavy. *I know I probably shouldn't do this. I shouldn't exploit what happened to me.*

"I did that for a long time. I was an escort. I was good at it, because I felt, you know, it was what I was good for. That took a part of my life from me. He took a part of my life from me."

He looks up. Lane is frowning at him. "Joel, you think I meant it was a hard choice for me? It's a hard choice for you to face him. Not to give you the names. Meese left here in...2002. The last kid I remember him taking an interest in was Andrew Reading. He was 15 at the time. Andrew dropped out and left town just after Meese retired. I'm not thinking sequentially right now, just who comes to mind."

Joel makes a note on his phone.

Lane stares into the distance. "Robert Casey. 2000. Around 16. Tony Blake. 14-15. 1998. Yeah, 1998. Chris Ellman. Also 1998. Randal Jeffries, 1996. Jimmy Skolos, 1996. Dennis McNally, '96 or '97."

"Thank you. I didn't want to do that. Manipulate you. You're a decent man. I'm sorry. I imagine you don't want to see me again." Joel gets up.

Lane takes his arm. "You'd be wrong. I want you to come back. Maybe this sounds stupid, but I want you to show these kids how to swim. You had a love for it, even if you didn't want to admit it. You're an artist now, right? I think you put your love for swimming into your art. I saw you in that pool for hours, practicing."

Joel did not remember that before, but he does now. Yes, as much as he thought he spent time in the woods and in Willowbrook, he also spent hours alone diving and swimming. No one ever questioned him on that.

He takes out a business card. "Give me a few weeks. I'll come back and show them."

∞

Wednesday, May 25
Stroudsberg, PA, 11: 23 am

Joel locates three former students whom Lane identified. Robert Casey is in Maine. Casey lives outside of Glenburn. He's far away from anyone, nearly living in a cabin, sporadically employed. Chris Ellman is in Baltimore, Maryland. Ellman is a grad student, who's dropped out and gone back to school several times.

Joel first speaks to Casey and Ellman, and then goes to see the third, Anthony Blake.

Anthony Blake is in Stroudsberg, Pennsylvania. He's a counselor in a drug rehab facility. He spent 19 months on a meth charge in 2000. Got clean and a certificate a few years ago. Former drug addicts tend to be open about what happened to them. Disclosure is important after the years of secrecy that is inherent in addiction.

Blake's job isn't high on the hierarchy, so when Joel goes to the facility, he takes a chance on just asking for Blake, saying he wants to speak about a former client.

Blake is white, a small, thin, dark-haired guy; his head is nearly shaven. His eyes are bright, but reserved.

"What can I do for you?"

Joel introduces himself. "I need to speak with you privately. I really need your help."

"I have a cubicle; that isn't really private. You say this is about one of my clients?"

Joel nods.

Blake manages to get a meeting room that's empty, and leads Joel to it. "Are you an attorney?"

"No, I'm working on a criminal case."

Blake frowns. "Police?"

"Private."

Blake sits at the corner of a long table in a simple room with some books on the walls and posters advertising the various programs in the facility. "And my client was involved? Which one?"

Joel sighs. "I'm sorry about that. It's not a client. It's you. You went to high school in Wayne, right? I did too. Five years before you did. I dropped out because of Larry Meese."

Blake freezes in place and stares at Joel.

"What do you want?" His voice goes low, severe.

"I want to expose what he did. I'm setting it up, with a complaint that has anonymous plaintiffs. The court is pretty friendly to filing under a pseudonym or a "Doe" thing, when it's a sex abuse case."

"You're going to do that? You're going to sue him?"

"Yes. I have to. He can't do this anymore. Do you feel like I do? Like you escaped, but always feel guilty, thinking about other kids that are out there? I was fifteen. I didn't know what to do. But I feel guilty that this happened to you."

Blake jerks away from the table. "How do you know? How could you know what happened? Did he tell you?"

"No, no. No one told me. I did research on dropouts from Wayne. Ones who fit a pattern of victims of sexual abuse. I fit that pattern. You did too."

Blake stares at him. "He made you..."

"Yeah. Probably the same thing that he made you did. Him and his friends. I've spoken to two other men who went through what we did. One is willing to go along. I think the other man might if more than a couple people file this. Safety in numbers."

Blake looks away, disturbed. "How do I know who you are?"

Joel takes out his driver's license. He hesitates. Gabriel could do this so well. He feels awkward. "Did you hear about the serial killer in New Jersey?"

Blake frowns. "The women who were killed? Like, mass graves? Some Bundy-type guy, right?"

"Yeah. He was a lot like Bundy. My boyfriend tracked him down. He found those women. I was with him. I'm not telling you this because I'm trying to impress you. I'm telling you because I don't want you to think I'm trying to hurt you, or that I'm some kind of nutjob."

Blake examines the driver's license, then puts his head in his hands. "I heard of that guy, your boyfriend. Got into a fight with the killer."

"Yeah, he did."

"I don't remember his name. He's the same guy who hit the preacher."

"He'd rather forget that, but yes."

"I'm not gay, you know."

"I don't care one way or the other. That doesn't have anything to do with Meese. He's not gay, either. He's a pedophile. Or at least, someone who is imprinted on raping teenagers."

Blake swallows hard, nodding. "Yeah, that's true. Why are you doing this now?"

"He may have done other crimes. I can't say worse crimes. You know like I do, it's hard to say worse crimes happen."

"I got over it." But that isn't quite true.

"You had problems after."

"Yeah. Why I'm here. They know, the agency."

"I had problems too. Not drugs. Other things. I spent years thinking I wasn't a good person. Then you get close to thirty, and things start to change. That way of thinking gets old, but you don't know how to change. Either you do something different or get worse. We did something different. But it's not complete without doing something about him. I don't know about others like him, but I know him. What he's doing now. He's still a cop."

"In Wayne?"

"Paterson. Sheriff's office."

"Do you live there?"

"No, I live in New York."

"Wait a minute," Blake says. "He was arrested, your boyfriend. That was in the Huff Post."

"Yes, he was. He was accused of murdering my father, which isn't true."

"Do you...do you think Meese did that? Is that why you're doing this?"

"I don't know for sure who murdered my father. I can't say what Meese did, without proof. What I know is that he can't be arrested for what he did to me. Maybe for what he did with you, because the statute of limitations doesn't apply to what happened to you, if it was in 1998. But more can come out in a civil trial, anyway."

"Are you trying to get money from him?"

"I don't need his money. I want him exposed."

"But if it's private, no names, that doesn't happen."

"I'm willing to talk to the press. I'm not going to give any other names, but the case would clearly be from two, three people. Eventually, it will come out."

Blake stares at Joel. Joel can clearly see Blake is remembering things he doesn't want to, and Joel is sorry to make him do that.

Blake says, "You were before me..."

"Yeah, 1993. He lied to my parents afterwards. They threw me out at 15, so I didn't have anyone to tell."

"He lied to my parents, too. He said he caught me stealing. You mentioned his friends. Did he..."

"Sell me to them? Yeah. I'd like to know who they are."

"You don't *know*? They were his fishing buddies. I mean, I'm not sure of their names but I know they have boats at one of the marinas Meese would take his boat to."

"Not Acquackanonk?"

"He went other places. He made me go with him sometimes." Blake shudders. "Franklin Lake, the Pompton River sometimes. He knows the marinas."

Joel had not thought about the other men involved. But now his interest is raised. He understands why Gabriel wants the names of the men who beat him up. Just to know, for one. And leaving the possibility of something else.

Blake leans back in his seat. "God. I don't know about a suit. I don't know. Can I get back to you?"

"Of course. I'm filing soon. Even if I do, you can join as a plaintiff. My lawyer would get your information. I just want to act on this. It's time he was stopped. And if you remember any more about those men, can you let me know?"

∞

Friday, May 27
Chinatown, 1:00 pm

Michaela calls him. "I had him served."

Joel takes a deep breath. "Any reaction?"

"Not yet. My process server didn't stick around, given that this was the Sheriff's Office. No one has called or emailed me."

"Okay. I appreciate the heads up."

Joel's phone rings again an hour later. An unknown New Jersey number.

"What do you think you're doing?"

Meese.

"You can talk to my attorney."

"Fuck that. I thought you understood, Joel. Don't do stupid things. You and I, we're bound together more than you'll ever understand. You think you're going to get somewhere with this? You really think you're going to get money out of me? Are you that much of a whore?"

Joel tells himself, *Don't say too much. Don't give him an upper hand.*

"This isn't about money. It's about justice."

"Bullshit. Everything you did, you did because you wanted me. You were always drawn to me. We had that special thing between us. Feeling guilty about it now doesn't change it. You wanted my help; you wanted what happened. If your criminal thinks you're damaged goods, that's because you didn't stay with me like you should have."

Joel starts to say that other boys can back him up, but no. Don't let him know that. The complaint is going to be amended. He'll know then.

"It's all going to come out about you," he says.

"No, it's not. Because you're going to withdraw this. And you're going to do this right now, before you get yourself in bigger trouble. Do you understand me, Joel? We're sticking with the plan. *You and I are connected.* We always will be."

"You are fucking demented."

Meese breathes heavy over the line. Joel feels stronger, without Meese in front of him in person. His voice turns, as it does. Always moving from the malevolent to the seductive and back again. "You're acting stupid, but that's others' influence. You're still special to me. I told you, you're always mine. You should be trying to make the best of that, instead of risking your criminal's life on provoking me."

Joel feels like throwing up, like he did the first time on Meese's boat. The idea of them being connected.

Meese continues, "You're not who you were, when you were here with me at first. That's too bad. You've probably fucked thousands of men. I hope you don't have AIDS. But I can see you at 15. I think I can still see that. What you did for me because you love me. I think about that all the time. It almost makes up for what you are now. But you still owe me, because you left before we put the plan in action. And that's why you came back. I'll always mean something more to you than the criminal does. You know that."

Joel pictures Meese in front of him, and his being able to kick the shit out of the older man, until Meese is broken, crumpled, bleeding. Someday.

"When you're dead, and you'll die long before me, I'm going to make a special trip to piss on your grave." Joel hangs up.

To try to counter the feelings rising in him, he searches for Zest's number on his phone. Zest returned a couple days ago and called him. Joel enacted a little mission with Zest he did not tell Gabriel about. It was successful.

After summarizing the situation, Joel says, "I'm not sure what to do."

"You're on the right track. It's a very delicate business to set them against each other, but I can't say I'm not experienced in that."

∞

Looking at Joel, after he tells me about the phone call he got from Meese an hour ago, I really want a cigarette. Well, I want one all the time, but this just exacerbates it. He watches me looking at his cloves. I take his hand.

"I'm not afraid of him. Let me see the number he used. It's not his office phone, I take it."

"What are you going to do?"

"See if he'll flip."

"He won't, for sure unless I withdraw the case."

"And you're not going to do that. I don't care about lying to him."

After three rings, I hear a male voice say, "Who's this?"

"Are you Larry Meese? I want to talk to you."

A pause. "Oh, the *criminal's* calling. All knight and shining armor, aren't you? Going to threaten me?"

"Threats are your domain. Mine is probabilities. The probability is you're going down for whatever you were doing with Ken and your hit man buddy. No doubt he handled your dirty work for you that day. Were you in the kitchen waiting for us? If you get smart and turn him in now, you come out better for it without unnecessary unpleasantness being exposed--you dig?"

"Game player, you are. All on Joel's behalf. He sure does have stellar help, a drunk mother and a criminal boss. I guess you got some kind of hold on *him*, to control what he does. But he was mine first. Want me to tell you about it?"

I ignore that, trying not to let my anger show on my face as Joel is watching. "Maybe you should think harder about how Cody's going to reconsider your partnership if he finds out about your predilection for underage boys."

Another pause. Then Meese laughs shortly. But it sounds a little forced. "You seem to think you have some kind of leverage. You can't go outside your door without County permission. Am I supposed to be scared of what you can do?"

"Things are already in motion. You can get ahead of the game or fuck it up. And maybe I'll look for your friends, the ones with the same sickness you have. The ones you sold your victims to. I bet not all of them are willing to keep secrets."

Meese's voice turns angry. "You listen to *me*, criminal. You're trapped there with your junkie friend. Anything can happen. Cops can raid the place. Maybe it blows up from a gas leak, or catches fire from bad wiring. Maybe it's the crossfire of a drug shooting. Just another Tuesday in Paterson. You know I can make that happen. If you're as smart as you think you are, you'll get out of my way. He isn't yours."

He ends the call.

Joel is staring at me.

"Unlikely," I tell him. "But he's worried. And that will throw him off."

"Did he threaten you?"

"Standard operational procedure. Don't make him out to be more than what he is."

"Don't pretend he's less than what he is. He's psycho."

I smile. "You know who you're dealing with?"

"*Because* I know who I'm dealing with. Zest is here."

"Is he, now?" I get up and look out the front window. "Is this the irony of the Tertullian Society protecting me?" I give Joel a stern look.

He says, "Do you know who *you're* dealing with?"

∞

Zest has an idea I don't like but I realize I can't do much about it. They want me to get part of the plan working, with Chris's help. Chris is already on his way to Bob's place. In the meantime, Zest and Joel are going to find Cody.

Before they can I go I ask Zest, "Are you going to give me those names? At least Jacobs' name?"

He appraises me. "Gabriel, let's get this taken care of. Then...I don't know. I think it's dangerous. Once this is done, I'll leave you a contact number, in case you need to get in touch with me. This can be a matter for future discussion."

I start to argue with him about it, but a movement outside the window catches my eye. It's Dell, approaching the door.

"You better leave the other way," I tell Zest.

"I'll meet you around the other side," he says to Joel.

I wait for Zest to go out the front door, then open the back, which faces the parking lot. As Dell approaches, I say, "These are not the droids you're looking for."

He raises an eyebrow at me and actually smiles. "Gabriel. How's it going?"

"Another day locked up wrongfully, what can I say?"

He nods. No disturbing his placidity. "Joel is here too; I saw his car."

Joel hadn't told the police that he leased a car, so Dell is checking up on us.

Joel is now right behind me. I know he's anxious, and I'm kind of on guard. How do we know Dell isn't working with Meese?

"I'm here," Joel says. "What do you want?"

"I'd like to come in."

I can't really tell him no, since technically I'm in custody. He takes the sofa and I take a chair. Joel just stands, staring at him.

Dell says to Joel, "Gloria is looking for you. I kind of take it you and she had a fight. That's not my business, but I know she's looking for you."

"You're right, it's not your business."

Nothing ruffles Dell. He turns back to me. "In any case, Gabriel, I've been talking with my captain. Ms. Connor called the prosecutor's office to say again you should be released. They called my captain and asked what evidence we've found support the case against you."

"And you found none. So I can go home."

"Not quite. He really is holding to those fingerprints on the shotgun and your relationship with Joel. But listen. I attended a few conferences to be a better cop. I saw Barry Scheck talk about how even fingerprints aren't always reliable. I thought it would be good to know what bad forensic science is, so I can make better cases about the right people. I also heard a talk by one of those profilers. He was interesting, because he was called in as a private consultant about a closed case. He profiled the guy who was convicted and concluded he wasn't the killer type. That helped get an appellate court to overturn the conviction."

"Good for you, getting your continuing ed credits in."

"Both of you have real smart mouths and a lot of hostility. I'm not one of those cops who rises to bait. I consider victimology; every cop should. But also what I'd call suspect-ology. Evidence is not the sole thing with me. It has to be balanced with what makes sense. I'm looking for a killer who makes sense."

"Why? It was clearly two crazy, violent homos planning a murder, because that's what we do."

Dell snorts. "Please. First off, I'm gay. Oh well damn, you're surprised. Guess *that* doesn't happen often. Second, this isn't the Seventies. I saw that shit on shows like *Streets of San Francisco* and *Police Woman,* but that's not a viable theory today."

I tell him, "I commend the Wayne Police Department on their diversity in hiring."

"You don't let up, do you? I researched you both, because I wanted to know more about who you were. I wanted to know if anything about either of you made sense with this case. Granted, a good deal of my concern was over Gloria. In light of that, I did some pretty extensive checking."

Dell looks at Joel. "Joel Kristofer McFadden. DOB January 21, 1978. In New York City in 1996 you obtained a driver's license, selective service reg and a passport all within a couple months."

"I was thrown out of my home in 1993. I believe Mom confirmed that. It took some time to work up to being a citizen."

"You should have come to the police when they threw you out. We wouldn't have let that happen."

For a moment I think Joel will explore in fury. He turns red and his eyes get wide. But he stays quiet.

I know Zest is waiting for him, but Joel doesn't want to leave me. He lights up to try to cover his anger. "I had reasons. I told you I had reasons. Why don't you look in your history--the department's history?"

Dell studies him. "Okay. You told me that before. Maybe I will. You weren't on the radar much in your life much after 1996. No rentals, no leases, no marriages. Just a *lot* of international travel. You were known to be associated with a woman named Angela Gold, real name Annabelle Lucovitch."

"So?"

"She has a record of prostitution charges in the Eighties. And she attempted to set up an escort agency in Houston in 1988, but was encouraged to leave town. She is thought to be currently running an agency in Manhattan."

"So?"

Dell shrugs. "You have a record too. A charge for solicitation that was reduced to a Desk Appearance Ticket, which in turn was dismissed. This was 1998. Angela must have paid it or paid someone on the force using her services. You also have three arrests under the name Dylan Yeats when you would have been 16-17. The fingerprints match those taken for the Desk Appearance Ticket. You like Irish poets, Joel?"

Joel freezes beside me. I speak up. "Dylan Thomas was Welsh. You didn't research that well. Why don't you leave him alone? I think he's been through enough."

"I understand your feelings, Gabriel, but life doesn't work that way, unfortunately. For Joel it must be quite a change from the days working with Angela to working with you. Gabriel Ryan Ross. DOB February 15, 1974. Now you have some interesting records. Three arrests going back to the first when you were 16, for suspected drug activity."

"That old one should have been sealed. No conviction, no booking. Just a bunch of cops screaming at us and running their hands up our asses. Much like the Passaic County Jail. Me and a bunch of friends were pulled in because this guy we happened to be hanging around with had forgotten to pay off the precinct captain. "

"Take it up with the NYPD. Then we have suspicion of grand theft auto and breaking and entering in 1994 with one Martin Traynor. This is Union County. You weren't arrested there but he was, and someone said you were his cohort. It's in Traynor's file."

My turn to shrug.

"Then there's assault in Buckston last year, and the material witness warrant for the Mathers case most recently."

"Thanks, I was wondering what my rap sheet said. This saves me trouble."

"What's not on it is another case with Traynor. You and he beat up a known drug dealer and robbed him. Can you explain that?"

"Yeah. It didn't happen."

"Is that right?"

"Believe what you want." I see Joel staring at me. I realize he's heard this before. How? Jesus, Meese and Dell have been looking at the same records. Meese must have said something to him. I feel some of the horror Joel must be feeling.

Dell continues, "Your mother and father were questioned about it. You couldn't be found at the time. They alibied you. And so that was dropped. Traynor was held for a few days and tried to put it off on you, but again, you were alibied. And no evidence tied you to it."

I feel cold from hearing this. I had no idea anyone talked to my mom and dad.

Dell continues, "I would like to know what happened."

I speak carefully. Not for him, but for Joel. I don't want him to wonder. "Martin had some problems. I didn't know he was planning to do that, and I left when I saw what was going on--when he started getting violent. I wasn't going to help him. I didn't *call* for help, but he was my boyfriend. Well, until that night. That was a side I didn't want to get involved with. Whatever he said about me...I don't know why he did that. I do not rob people and never have. Jesus, I didn't even know my parents talked to the police. I was 19, for Christ's sake. I was still in school, on the edge from one life to another."

"Your parents were protecting you, I guess. But if it was true, it would fit in with your alleged violent streak. That's what cops focus on, but I also saw you have a very strong reputation as a good investigator. Your uncle was a respected community activist. You've never had ethics problems in your work, other than with Reverend Bunton and that wasn't about your work. You're cleaner than a lot of investigators. And you work for Ms. Connor. Her reputation is pristine."

"She'll be glad to know."

"And interestingly, Captain Daniels' father was in the Army. Turns out he knows someone who knows one Lt. Colonel Jeffrey Ross. You're surprised again. Your father was Army Intelligence. Maybe still is."

"He does a lot of things. I'm not involved in them."

"Well, Daniels' father's friend has been advocating for your release. That's not proof of innocence, but it does get the Captain to at least notice the case could be stronger."

I have to smile. That is kind of funny, my dad trying to get me out of trouble.

"You're not Army, but I get the sense you have intelligence skills. And an authority problem."

"We have reasons. Were you going somewhere with all this?"

"Yeah. I did what I had to do to make up my mind about you both. And you're looking into this case. I don't know how and where and who, but my intuition tells me you are. If you have a lead, you should let me in on it. You can only go so far on your own."

"I will ask Ms. Connor's advice on that."

"Fair enough. I'm willing to take a look."

Joel says, "I have to go."

Dell turns to him. "And I'll look into what you said. I have to be very, very discreet. So do you want to point me somewhere?"

Joel meets his eyes. "I don't know who you know. I don't know what side you're on. I know cops protect each other. All I can say is I knew a cop, and he..."

Then Joel locks up and his face gets pale.

"Was it Larry Meese? He seems to be all over the place here. Some of the records I wanted to look at--he's already requested them. Tell me, Joel. He can't hurt you now."

Joel explodes in fury. "Are you fucking kidding? He already has. You're here raking over *our* history, getting off on it. What about *his*?"

"You think I haven't looked into him? I already saw something was up. I'm not stupid. Yeah, because he's in the Sheriff's Office, not much I can get people to say. I've been trying to track you, though, and you've been talking to people who used to live here in town. I can see the connection. But if Larry's bent, we want him for murder. To get Gabriel off the hook."

"What have you found out, then?"

Dell turns back to me. "I can't go into much. But I'm finding some strange financial things. The US Attorney's Office here ran an inquiry on Ken before he died, and that makes me suspicious about what they both were doing. Once the subpoenas from the offshore accounts are answered, I suspect we may uncover some connections. If you have anything else that can help..."

We do. But we can't tell him. Or...I look at Joel. About to leave with Zest. Little does Dell know.

Joel meets my eyes. This isn't the time, but we're both a little shaken. Things we weren't ready to tell each other. Maybe things we would never talk about otherwise. And God, what if my mom thought I actually did that...

Joel gets up. He says again, "I have to go." His parting glance tells me he's going through with the excursion with Zest. Which means we're moving on, and without Dell.

Dell looks at the closed door. "I know you two are up to something. I have my own sixth sense I developed in combat about trouble brewing. Too bad you can't feel that I can help."

"You see what's on my ankle right now? You're starting to get the idea something's *wrong* here. Well, if I'm in this situation because *I* was trying to help, then you get why we're cautious about who we think can trust."

"Give me something, Gabriel. I'm trying to trace what Ken was doing with those accounts. I'm not an expert on it, and so far I can't convince the department to let me use a forensic accountant."

I think about it and make a rash decision. Probably because I'm worried about Joel being out there with Zest.

"Well, I'll speculate off the record about what might be going down..."

I give him some information, enough that if he followed on it he could make the same connections I did.

He takes notes, but he's frowning. "The feds are going to get in on this. They'll take over jurisdiction."

True, but it pisses me off. "Why am I talking to you, then? Little ole' murder doesn't mean anything."

He looks up at me and holds my gaze for a minute. We stare at each other man to man.

"I'm not that kind of cop. I wasn't that kind of soldier. In Iraq we didn't have to help the locals, but when a problem was there I could do something about, I did it because *not* to do it was wrong. Didn't matter if it wasn't my job. At the very least for Gloria I would not just let this go because the US Attorney is going to yank the case from us."

I think he's sincere. "Then you better get to work before the other parties involved decide to skip town."

∞

Ridgewood, NJ 3:35 pm

"It's always better to take the dangerous ones out," Zest tells Joel. "However, for evidence, we should try alive."

"I know. But Meese bothers me more; he'll want revenge."

Zest softly opens the door of the black SUV. "Cody is deadly. I'm handling this as carefully as I can."

Zest saying someone else is deadly. Joel watches Zest walk up to where Cody is watering his hedges, like any suburbanite. Zest has a phone with a listening device that Joel has used before with Gabriel.

"Mr. Cody?"

Cody turns his large head. "Who might you be?"

Zest stands about 15-20 feet away. "My name isn't important. This isn't official."

Cody stops spraying. He doesn't look unduly alarmed, but his being changes. He's looking at Zest, probably considering how to take him out if necessary. Zest appears to be looking at Cody the same way. If this was the Old West, the citizenry would be scattering inside by now.

"Then what is it?" Cody's voice is very flat.

"You and I are in the same business. Contracting for similar organizations. Cutting to the chase, I'm dealing with you as a professional."

What he said to Gabriel last summer.

Zest continues, "I'm not wired but you should treat this as if I am. I would."

Cody looks around without moving his head, for Zest's back-up. He stares into the windshield of the SUV, but it's tinted.

"You have something particular to tell me, Mister?"

"Yes. A man named Meese. He's involved with some corruption in this state with a man who was recently killed, Ken McFadden. What McFadden did, that's coming out. Including his bank account in the Caymans."

"Really."

"What's also coming out--which Meese hasn't told anyone--is that he's a pedophile, and he's being sued for that."

Cody's eyes crawl over Zest. He doesn't show much reaction, but Joel strongly feels Cody wasn't aware of this.

"Since Meese is aware that evidence has turned up regarding the corruption scheme, he's planning to leave. With his own evidence implicating others."

Cody shifts his stance, drops the hose, and frowns at Zest. "You seem to know a lot."

"Let's say he went to the wrong person for advice."

"And why are you telling me?"

"You never know what information may be relevant. You never know who might need a favor. We're professionals. I thought I might extend a favor. There are some people you can't afford to be in business with. If it was me, and I had accounts related to this, I'd check them."

Zest walks backward slowly, not turning around fully. Cody just watches him, not moving.

∞

When Joel returns with Zest, I'm working with Chris. Chris doesn't know who Zest is, and is smart enough not to ask.

I say, "Now what do you think is going to happen?"

"The players have to move. They both know they cannot sit on this information, what is happening. Meese has to decide what to do before the lawsuit is public. Cody has to check on his accounts."

I think about it. "I'm worried about Cody's cabin. If he has any evidence there, he might move it or destroy it."

"Joel has a camera on the cabin."

I don't look at Joel. I already know his defiant expression by heart. "Okay, that was one of your projects you didn't tell me about."

"Yeah. So, the cabin. It's time. We need to get in. Anything we find is admissible, right?"

"So long as we are not police. Is there anything on God's green Earth I can say to convince you not to do this?"

"No. You aren't going to change my mind. We have to get in there. If you're not part of the solution, you're part--"

"Don't give me that. I know what I'm up against. The first thing is getting to the alarm system to control it. Like we were talking about, he might have it on his phone."

"He does, and I'm already in his system and have it on my phone. That was the other thing Zest did with me. We pulled a temporary pickpocket thing while Cody was shopping." He holds his phone up, proud of himself. "Don't look at me like that. I knew you'd agree with me eventually."

"You know me well."

"I do now," Joel says.

"That wasn't always true." Joel knows Jan is with him when he goes outside to smoke. "If I knew him then, I wouldn't have fucked up the first time."

"If you *didn't* know him," Jan replies, "You wouldn't have come back."

∞

Coming Back/Breaking Up

Eleanor Roosevelt said, "The future belongs to those who believe in the beauty of their dreams."

∞

March 3, 2006
Chelsea, 3:00 pm

CHRIS OPENS HIS DOOR. "Mephisto. You're back from the Holy Empire. They finally get sick of you?"

"I left. Antony was bugging me about joining him in Tibet for his spiritual crisis. I figured it was time to get off the continent. Are you going to let me in? What the fuck are you doing in cycle shorts?"

"It's my day off." Chris pulls him inside and hugs him.

After some time, feeling comfortable around each other again, crashed on the couch, Chris says, "So when are you leaving again?"

"I'm not. A guy I know has a sublet for a year. I think it's time to stay awhile."

"Finally." Chris gives Joel an eyeroll. "Are you having a spiritual crisis too?"

"You could say that. I'm too old to fuck for a living."

"Oh, you're giving it up again. Roxanne, you don't have to put on the red light."

"Thanks for the support."

"Mephisto, you need to know who you are before giving up the game as American Gigolo."

"What does that mean?"

Chris drops the persona for a moment. Joel sees real affection in his friend's eyes. "You need to actually believe in yourself."

"Maybe I do. Isabella says she's interested in promoting my work some more."

"Not *all* she's interested in. You're catnip to her. *Rrrrow.* Bow-chicka-wow-wow. But turn that to your advantage. Do something with your stuff this time--that's what I mean about believing in yourself. You're not afraid of anything, but you're afraid of that."

"I will. I want to think about what to do in life. What I want. Who I want."

"Someone in particular?"

"No. I don't do well with *that* either. I keep finding out who isn't good for me. I'd like to think somewhere there is a so-called 'right' person. If who I am--who I was--doesn't scare him or her off."

"That's also part of believing in yourself. Don't run away..."

Joel lets Iz know he's back, and she starts with plans for him. She takes him around her new gallery, showing him some of the other artists' work. "And I have plenty of room for you. Even a showing."

"I don't want to do that. Having a couple things here is okay."

"I know you have enough for a show."

He doesn't respond.

"God, you frustrate me sometimes. Stubborn. But I'm not giving up. You can do a mural, right?"

"Of what?"

"People fucking. This guy I know wants a modern-day take on those bathhouse images in Pompeii..."

"So you figured, I have so much experience..."

"No, asshole, because you're a great painter."

He glances at her. She's smiling. "C'mon let me introduce you to the guy. He's a trust-fund kid, so we can charge him up the ass."

"Okay. It might be a thing."

After meeting the guy at his over-large apartment and sealing the deal, Isabella takes Joel back to her place.

She gets a little drunk and he doesn't, but he has a glass or two from the bottle in her meritage collection.

She curls up with him on the floor, on her thick rug, while *True Blood* is on TV.

Her hand wanders under his shirt. She feels him tense up. "What?"

He takes time to answer. "I'm trying to live different."

"So what does that mean, no sex or something?"

"No, just that..."

"You want to get involved."

He shrugs.

"Well, you know *we* can't, 'cause I'd shoot you dead the first week. I don't run a babysitting service. God help whoever has to be your nursemaid."

"You and Chris. Really backing me up here."

She sighs. "Okay, you're right. We need to believe in you. I'm sorry."

Isabella takes her hand away and pats his shoulder so sarcastically, he has to laugh. He leans over and kisses her. It's affectionate, but Isabella holds on to him, stroking his hair, keeping him in an embrace. Despite his earlier statement, he's still drawn to the affection. And Isabella's persistent sensuality pulls him in. Soon, the TV show is forgotten as their clothes come off.

Sometime later, her legs are shaking and she's screaming. "Oh, God, Joel...ohmyohmyomyGod!"

He raises his head from between her legs. "So, it was good for you, then?"

He crawls up beside her and closes his eyes, tucking his head into her shoulder.

"I love it when a man eats me out after he comes in me."

"I'll put that on my resume, under 'skills.'"

While Joel is pleased in this way to make his friend pleased, he recognizes he can't still do this and seriously change his life. The emotions get him mixed up. In the weeks to follow, he stands firm on that despite Isabella's heavy hints. Finally, she gives up and just goes back to pestering him on his artwork, as he designs, preps and begins the trust-fund kid's mural.

He does that during the day, and hangs out at this bar near NYU at night, where a friend bartends, and where he can draw without running into anyone he knows from years back. *It's not much of a plan for moving forward,* Chris says. *Who are you going to meet at a grungy Goth bar?*

∞

March 27, 2008
Maiden Lane, 5:13 pm

Joel had only been in the apartment for a few minutes when the doorman calls Joel's client. The client frowns and hands the phone to Joel.

It's the doorman. "A man named Gabriel Ross said to tell you he's waiting outside, sir."

Jesus Christ. "I'm coming down."

Joel puts his jacket back on, and tells the client he has to leave. The client says he'll wait, but Joel has a feeling he's not going to return.

In the lobby he ignores the doorman, who pretends he doesn't see Joel, and stares out the door.

Gabriel is across the street talking to Danny. He's in a fury, Joel can see. Danny grips Gabriel's shoulder briefly and leaves.

Joel has no idea what to say or how to act. He realizes he's still slightly in working mode, although once he crosses the street, in the impossible spotlight of Gabriel's vision, he feels that mode crumbling.

Joel takes a deep breath. "You brought Danny with you? Why?"

"That's what you have to say?"

Joel fishes out a cigarette. He sees Gabriel looking him over. The clothes he wears, which are a different style with clients. Seeing that he shaved. Joel feels briefly defiant. "You know what I do."

Gabriel shakes my head. "I know what you *did*; I thought this was over."

Joel shrugs. "It's complicated in a way, simple in a way. I wasn't doing it to hurt you. It was a favor to someone."

"That sure as hell does not make me feel better. Honest to God, you don't see what this does to me, do you?"

Gabriel's voice cracks. Joel frowns, reaching out to touch his arm. "Baby, it's not that big a deal. I can explain, if you let me. I know Danny won't want you to listen, but—"

"This isn't about Danny. This is a betrayal of what I thought we were trying to build."

"It's just sex."

"Sex isn't the problem. *Sex* isn't why I'm angry." Gabriel turns away and leans his head against the building in back of him. "I worked so hard trying to get you to trust me, so you wouldn't have to do this. As long as you can't see that, we can't have a relationship. You don't know me, or don't want to know me enough to believe me. To believe in yourself."

"No, no, no...that's not true." Joel can't be certain he's actually talking. It doesn't seem to have an effect.

Gabriel's staring out in the distance, and Joel cannot believe the expression of pain he sees on Gabriel's face.

"I can't repeat this experience over and over. Every time you do this, it's part of you shutting me out. Refusing to be with me in any *real* way."

Joel hears something in Gabriel's voice he never has. *Finality.* He tries to touch Gabriel again and but Gabriel backs away.

"Gabriel, you're taking this too seriously." Joel hears the fear in his own words.

"*Trust* is serious. You gave this work up before you met me, and then went back to *because* you met me. To keep distance between us. Do you see that? You don't want to let me in. Ever. But I care about you too much. I can't let you hurt me because of that...I can't be with you anymore."

For a moment what Gabriel says hangs in the air. In Joel's mind, as he's desperately trying to process the words, he's saying to himself *no, no, you can fix this. He's not going to...*

And then Gabriel turns and walks away quickly, not looking back.

He has to look at me. He can't leave me. I know he loves...
But he's gone.

Never, ever, has anyone walked away from Joel. Grace disappeared. Jennah died. But the others...Antony, Riza, Sam...Joel did the leaving. But then, other than Grace and Jennah, no one believed in him like Gabriel did.

But he's gone.

∞

FIFTEEN

Walt Whitman said, "For what is the present after all, but a growth out of the past?"

∞

Saturday, May 28
Paterson, NJ, 7:22 pm

WE HAVE SET MORE in action. Chris has managed to hack into Cody's account. We arrange a transfer of money from Nazgul to Tartarus. If Cody isn't concerned with Meese's perversion, perhaps he'll be concerned his money is being stolen. Joel and Chris finish testing what they want to test on Joel's phone. They're doing another version of the phone recording app.

Walter is here again. I'm not crazy about this, as I feel things are about to happen. Things chaotically dangerous.

Walter asks, "What does all this do, now?"

Joel smiles, pleased with their work. "Cody's calls are duplicated to me. We can hear what he hears, and it's recorded. Even if he uses a different phone, if he has this phone nearby, we can hear it."

Joel and Chris then discuss some technical aspects for a few minutes. Then Joel's phone buzzes. "It's working. He's talking. Or calling. It's set to detect by call or voice activation."

He turns on the phone and watches the trace on the laptop monitor.

We hear Meese say, "Who is this?"

"I need to talk to you." Cody. He sounds flat.

"What about?"

"We have a problem. I have an idea to take care of it, but I want to run it by you."

"Go ahead."

"Not on the phone. Let's be discreet."

A pause. Then Meese says, "Come to my house."

"Sure. How soon?"

"I'm leaving now." The call ends.

Joel says, "Meese wants Cody on his territory. Like that matters. This is the chance to catch them together."

"Joel, Cody is going there to kill him. He's clearing out. First Meese, then he'll probably go destroy any evidence in the cabin."

"One thing at a time," Joel says. "I get some feed of them together, then I'll go to the cabin."

I take him aside, out of Walter's hearing. "Uh, no. If you're going to the cabin, go now with Zest. I'll call him. Use the window of time while he's with Meese."

"I want proof they know each other." Joel grabs the camera and goes over to where his jacket is hanging.

"Wait for Zest."

"No time." He meets my eyes before he goes out the door. "I'm doing what you would do. I learned from the best."

I watch him run for his SUV.

Walter asks, "Is he actually going there?"

"Yeah. I can't stop him." I tell Chris, "Please start tracking him."

"We got him, boss. He'll do good."

∞

Meese's house is situated between two small copses of trees. Joel has chosen the one with the better cover to stake out the area. Meese arrives home, goes inside the house, and then twenty minutes later heads out the back door down to the dock. Joel records him doing this.

Meese has a gym bag and a laptop under his arm. He takes the objects to his boat tied up at the backyard dock. He's only in the boat a minute or so before returning to the house. Then Joel sees Meese sit on his stone front steps, smoking.

Joel considers the boat. What did he take to it? Why? Could he *really* be considering bugging out? At the north end of the lake is a larger dry dock. People haul their boats out there to be repaired or moved. Or maybe he's just hiding things there because Cody's coming.

It could be evidence. That nags at Joel. Then he gets the signal Cody is calling someone again. He puts in an earpiece and listens.

"I'm almost there."

"Just come on in the house. I'm here already."

Joel decides to take the risk and moves quietly to the dock and then goes up the short ladder and over the railing. He makes his way down the stairs to the kitchen/living area.

And he stops for a moment. It's dark, just tiny side lights giving any illumination. The room seems the same. The sofa where Meese forced him. The bed where the other men forced him. Two of him are here. A boy and a man. The boy wants to fall away in horror.

Then Joel realizes he hears agitated voices through the phone. He got distracted by the being on the boat...

Cody and Meese are approaching. *Go.* Joel sees the bag and the laptop on the dining table. He opens it. The bag has a few guns, bundles of cash, and papers.

He feels the shift of the boat as Meese and Cody get aboard.

Joel moves back in the bed area behind the curtain. He gets on the bed so he can see through the window to the deck. He sees Meese has his arms folded and is staring at Cody, who seems relaxed.

"All right, we're here outside," Meese says in an irritated voice. "What is it?"

"Let's go downstairs. Be discreet."

"No one is here, for God's sake. What's wrong with you?"

"I'm being careful. Let's go downstairs."

"Look, if you don't want to talk, then don't."

Cody shrugs and turns as if he was going to leave. But then he whirls around, fast for such a big man, and hits Meese in the face. Meese acts quick to block it, but the blow still knocks him down the stairs. Joel hears Meese land on the floor.

Cody shuts the hatch leading to the downstairs, and locks it.

Joel risks looking around the curtain. Meese is crumpled at the bottom of the stairs, struggling to get up. Joel carefully moves to the kitchen and takes everything out the bag except the papers. He shoves the laptop in the bag.

Meese groans and mutters something. Joel heads back for the bed.

"Who's down here," Meese asks. And then repeats it. "Who's here? Who's down here?"

Joel gets on the bed and looks out the window. Cody has come back, and now climbs aboard. He has a small box with him that he sets on the deck of the boat, and leaves again. Joel sees him taking his phone out his pocket as he walks down the dock.

Joel opens the window, and shoves the bag out.

"Who's here?" Meese's voice is closer. Panicked, Joel hauls himself up through the window.

He hears Meese behind him: "Joel?" He thinks he feels a hand on his foot, and kicks away desperately. Then he's on the deck. Joel grabs the bag and jumps overboard into the water, hearing or imagining hearing an angry muffled voice behind him.

He begins swimming away as fast as he can. As he approaches the property next to Meese's, another repeat of 17 years ago, he looks to see if Cody has seen him.

Cody has his back to Joel. He puts on his hood, and then his glasses. Joel realizes he's wrapped up in his fetish, filming this. Cody takes out some device and starts messing with it.

Joel continues swimming for the pier of the house next to Meese's. He's almost there, when the boat explodes.

Joel goes underwater to cover himself. The water vibrates from the explosion. Debris falls around him under water. He counts ten and then climbs out carefully. Down on Meese's backyard, Cody is watching the debris in the water.

He'll probably be there a few minutes filming the aftermath, if he holds true to form. Joel makes his way through the thread of woods to the road.

Meese probably wanted Cody in his house, maybe to take him out. Cody clearly wanted Meese in the boat for the same reason.

Cody seems to have won this one, and if he's going to wait for the cops to show up, Joel still has time to get to the cabin.

Joel manages to make it to his SUV unseen. Behind him, he can hear the sounds of neighbors freaking out. Sirens are in the distance, not too far away. He unlocks the door and tosses the soaked bag in the back seat.

As he starts the car, the passenger door suddenly opens. Meese gets in the car quickly, breathing hard. Joel stares at him in disbelief. Like Joel, Meese is soaked through. He carries the scent of the explosion with him, burnt wood. He's bruised and bleeding in places, not that Joel's struck by concern over his health.

"I saw you," Meese says. "I saw you jump out the boat." He looks in the back seat. "You saved my stuff. Were you trying to help me, after all?"

Joel briefly considers if he can kick Meese out of the car, physically. Then Meese takes a gun out of his waistband. It's wet, but that doesn't mean it can't shoot.

"You should go talk to the police about what happened," Joel says, wondering if Meese is now completely insane.

Meese gestures with the gun. "Where are you going?"

"I have to check on something."

Meese frowns. "You were going to do something to me. That lawsuit..." He holds the gun up.

"Forget it. It's already withdrawn."

Meese clearly isn't normal. Probably a head injury, but he's not about to pass out. He says again, "Where are you going?"

Joel's mind turns. He has to get out before the road is cut off. "Cody's cabin. He probably has evidence there."

Meese leans toward him with the gun. "What do you want with that?"

"You take his evidence, he can't do anything to you. You'll have that to hold against him."

Meese smiles. "God, I forgot how smart you are. Looking out for me. I knew it."

Joel decides to go ahead and drive. Meese doesn't protest but he doesn't lower the gun either.

Joel makes it back to the turnoff for the highway seconds before police cars turn down the same street. He hits the gas.

Meese mutters, "You know about that cabin...I followed him there once."

"Yeah. You can put that away, so it doesn't go off accidently."

Meese wavers, frowning. "I don't know. I know you're trying to help me, and that will make up for what happened before. This fucking son of a bitch trying to kill me. But you--you and that criminal." He stares at Joel while he drives.

Joel pulls on his seatbelt. In doing so, he takes out his phone without Meese seeing. The phone is waterproof and should still work.

"He made you do that, didn't he?"

"I didn't understand what was going on," Joel responds.

"Of course not. I knew he was up to something. I tried to get rid of him, but we'll think of something."

"Do you mind if I smoke?"

"Your mom wouldn't like that."

"But she interferes. You told me that."

"All right. But I don't want to see you do that too often."

Joel reaches for the glove compartment and takes out his cigarettes and lighter. Meese touches his hand. Joel remains calm, knowing he cannot lose it now.

As he fusses with the cigarettes and lighter, Meese lets the gun sag a little in his hand. He's staring at Joel's face, not his hands. Joel can slip the phone in the driver's side door storage. He presses hard on the power button. And can't help but sigh when it lights up. He turns off the volume and presses other buttons he knows by touch and can see with his peripheral vision.

∞

"Where *is he,* Chris?"

"I don't know. He hung up on us. Hopefully, the phone is still working."

"Fuck!" I pace around the apartment, trying to think.

I see a shadow at the door. I open the door and let Zest in. He and Walter stare at each other.

"I can't introduce you," I say. "Joel suddenly went quiet at the lake and we're trying to find out what happened. Chris, call him again."

"He's back! I see his phone!"

"Where?" I lean over Chris's shoulder.

"He's heading north."

I pick up my cell and call him. It rings and goes to voicemail. "Joel, call me back."

I meet Zest's eyes. "He must be going to that cabin. No other reason to go north."

"I'll meet him there. Just in case."

"Why wouldn't he answer? Not just to be stubborn. He knows I'm worried."

"Gabriel," Walter interrupts. "I just heard there was some kind of incident in Wayne. An explosion."

"Bob has a police scanner." I run over and turn it on. We can hear a report of a boat blowing up at Acquackanonk.

"Goddamn it, he'd know I want to know he's okay." I call him again.

"It might not work if it was damaged somehow," Zest says.

"Are you contacting the police," Walter asks.

"Not until I know where Joel is and if he's safe."

"Danger Man," Chris says, "Joel is signaling me."

I look at Chris. "How?"

"We have ways to do that. He can't talk."

"Why...Chris, does he have one of those recording apps you made for my phone?"

"Of course," Chris says with a touch of scorn. "I'm already there to get in his phone."

Chris works frantically for about 30 seconds as we listen to more reports of emergency responders heading to the lake.

"Got it," Chris says. "We can't talk, but we can hear. I sent him a signal we're listening."

I hold my breath.

A little roughly, we can hear Joel's voice. "You said you followed him there once. Then you know the layout."

His voice sounds calm and flat.

And then another voice. "I didn't trust that fucker. And then he tries to kill me. After all I've set up for him..."

My entire body is cold with adrenaline. "That's Meese."

Joel says, "You don't have to keep that pointed at me. If something happens, it could cause an accident. I don't want anything to happen to you."

"I know. But...it's hard to trust you, Joel. This is it. The endgame. I've gone too far now. I'm not being taken. By anyone. Cody or Dell, anyone. If we get pulled over, you and me go together. ..."

I turn to Zest. "Let's go *now*. Do you have any weapons with you?"

He just raises his eyebrows. I should know who I'm dealing with.

"Danger Man, aren't you supposed to stay here?"

"That's why you're leaving too, Chris. Now. Cops will be here as soon as I take this monitor off. Get somewhere safe."

Chris jumps up and shuts the laptop. "Can I do anything?"

"Take the monitor and drop it somewhere--into a moving vehicle preferably."

Walter says, "I'll drive him. We'll take care of it."

Chris doesn't waste time getting his shit together. I call Bob to let him know chaos will ensue soon. Then I put on my zippered sweatshirt and grab my own stuff and one of Bob's boxcutters. I leave my work phone and take the new personal phone that the police shouldn't know about, and the laptop. We go out and lock the door, wait at the boundary line.

Zest starts his car. I take out the knife and slice through the monitor. It has one long continuous beep, then falls silent and just blinks. I give it to Chris and Walter, and run for Zest's car.

As Zest pulls away, I use the app on my phone to check where Joel is. He's about 20 miles ahead of us.

∞

Meese snaps out of his reverie. Joel sees he's bleeding from his head. If only he'd pass out.

"Cody may be on his way here too. He'd want to hide whatever he has here."

"I know what he's doing." Joel notes they are close to the turnoff for Cody's cabin.

"How do you know?"

"I hacked his phone. I know where he is by his GPS." The gun is now just lying in Meese's lap, but Joel is careful in how he moves so he doesn't make Meese nervous. He holds up his phone and checks it with one hand. "He hasn't left the area yet. Probably hard to get out now."

Meese looks impressed. "You went to that kind of trouble?"

"Uh, yeah."

"You're good with computers, then."

Joel nods, glancing at him.

"That will work out for our plan. It'll help in meeting new people."

Joel checks the phone. Chris's light is still on. He knows Chris, and no doubt Gabriel, can hear the conversation. *You're not alone,* Joel tells himself.

He asks carefully, "What do you mean, about the plan?"

"We're almost there, right? Our plan. You're going to be my partner. You'll meet other young boys, like yourself. I always noticed how people are drawn to you. We can break them in, together. We were going to do that. *But Ken got in the way.*" Meese slams his hand on the dashboard.

Joel tries to watch Meese's gun hand. "It's over now."

"But he took you from me. You and I, we wouldn't be very long together *that* way. Boys grow up. But you were special enough to stay with me anyway. We would have built upon our special relationship to find others like us. Boys who would look up to you, and..."

Joel has a hard time not jamming on the brakes and jumping from the car as he finally *hears* what Meese is saying. That Joel was supposed to stay with him back when he was 15, and then when he aged out of Meese's imprinted age range, he would recruit young boys for Meese. To keep the cycle going. *That's* the plan that he thinks Joel came back to Wayne to fulfill.

"The criminal corrupted you, didn't he? You're not gay."

Joel keeps his voice steady as the car approaches the gravel road. "He didn't corrupt me. It wasn't what you think."

"Oh. Of course not. But he tried."

∞

"I'm going to kill this fucking man," I say, barely able to control myself. "How far away are we?"

Zest glances at me as he presses the gas pedal down. "We'll be there soon. Gabriel, don't let your anger check you."

I look over at him. "I can be cold. You'd be surprised."

I get a text from Veronica.

--Detective Dell called me to say he knows you left and wants to talk to you. He wants to help.

Dell. He could easily trace the phone. It could all be a trap.

--Send me the number.

I consider whether it's safe to explain to Dell what's going on. He could get the state police to pull over Joel's car. But Meese with a gun, and utterly fucking insane...Meese will kill them both. I don't want to risk his life with cops who don't understand the situation.

∞

Joel parks his SUV down the road from Cody's cabin, and then gets out. Meese follows him to Cody's back porch. Joel examines the door.

"It has an alarm system," Meese says. "We'd need to see..."

"I have control over it." Now Joel opens the alarm system app on his phone, logs in, and checks the security parameters. He turns off all the cameras, and the alarms.

A pop-up window asks, *ARE YOU SURE?*

He clicks 'yes.'

The red light in the door goes out. He can see a keypad by the back door go from red to green.

Meese is saying more about how great Joel is, and how he wished Joel had been around to do things with him before. Joel ignores that. Taking out one of Gabriel's pickguns, he works it in the door. Nervous, more than he thought he'd be, it takes him a couple tries.

Then the door is open. No time to waste. He's in the kitchen, with Meese behind him, still carrying the gun. The living room ahead of the open kitchen is plainly furnished. To the left of the kitchen is a room with a shut door, then a bedroom, a bathroom, and another shut door.

He swiftly uses the picklock on the left room that's been shut and locked. It probably was a dining room. It's been turned into a workroom, one you might find in a garage. Boxes and bins and a worktable. A smell of sawdust and chemicals.

Where he makes his weapons, maybe. Saws, drills, a regular TrueValue set up.

Meese looks around with a cop's eyes. "God only knows what sick things he dreamed up in here, right?"

Joel banks on his ability to remain cool. "No doubt."

The bedroom and bathroom don't look promising. Joel tries the second closed room. It's set up like a den. A huge black loveseat is the main piece of furniture. A small table is to the right, with an ashtray and a small reading lamp with an iron base and green glass shade. Cody clearly smokes cigars in here. A small humidor and bottle of whisky are on an ebony wood table against one wall.

Joel quickly looks around. It's the only one with a carpet. Heavy red curtains are on the windows. Against one wall, facing the loveseat, is a 50-inch TV. A computer is on a small stand next to the TV, wired to it.

Meese wanders in. The drive has given them time to almost be dry, but Meese is still messed up in his head. "Where could his stuff be? What would he have?"

"Videos. He tapes everything, right?"

"Oh, you know about that...yeah."

In Joel's mind he can see Cody on the loveseat, watching the TV. The videos. None are around that he can see. He turns on the computer and opens the closet, which has folding doors. He sees camera equipment on gray metal shelves. It ranges from large movie-style camera to cameras that could be attached to eyeglasses. The smaller monitors are also connected to computers and video editing equipment. Damned if there aren't a few black hoods on the top shelf.

Breathing harder, Joel goes back to the computer, and opens the small desk drawer under it. Bits of junk. No, it's stuff that belonged to people. Drivers' licenses. Rings. Articles of clothing. More trophies.

Meese is suddenly looking over Joel's shoulder, nearly making him jump. "He's an idiot. Like a fucking serial killer. Saving evidence..."

When the computer screen lights up Joel checks the files. Nothing, other than video playback software.

Where could the videos be? If not on a computer, then they had to be in hard copy. DVDs or flash drives.

Gabriel told him that safes are either in very ordinary places accessed by a pinhole catch, like he has for his closet, or something that's out of place. One the wall behind the loveseat is a large antique map of New Jersey. It doesn't fit with the room. Joel goes over to the map, seeing the subtlety in the glass front that covers it. He runs his hand on top of the picture and finds a wire that's out of place. He can't pull it. He reaches into his pocket where he has the switchblade, and uses that to pull out the wire.

The map opens like a cabinet. Shelves are built inside the wall. A line of DVD cases are on the shelves.

"Damn good search," Meese comments. "He has everything here. We can take them."

Joel notes that Meese has put the gun away in his jacket pocket. But he has to check the DVDs now. It's too important.

"I need to be sure these are what we're looking for."

Joel's hands are shaking as he pulls a DVD out from the shelf. On the case is written "Trenton 2001."

He takes it to the computer and turns on the TV; it's already connected to the computer. He puts the DVD in the computer tray and loads it.

The video starts abruptly. It has a POV perspective, likely from the glasses-camera. A man in his forties is talking to the camera in a friendly way. No sound, but Joel hasn't turned on the speakers. The man is walking outside some house into a backyard. He turns to point to something in the distance.

From the POV an arm lifts--its size says it's Cody, with a thin metal pipe. The arm slams on the back of the man's head. The man falls to the grass. The POV perspective goes back through the house to a car outside. Joel recognizes it as Cody's. Cody retrieves a black bag and walks back through the house to the backyard.

The man is crawling away. In no particular hurry, Cody talks a larger object, a crowbar, from the bag, and casually hits the man several times, splattering blood. He then rolls the man over. The man is still conscious. Cody takes out a straight razor and slices the man's throat.

Joel gasps and steps back as the blood flows on screen. Cody continues to slice the blade through the man's clothes. Joel fast-forwards through Cody leaving and going to a vantage point to watch the police arrive and being the investigation. Then the video goes blank.

Joel fumbles with the mouse to eject the DVD. He leans on the table breathing hard, shaking.

"I never understood how he stayed with the Jersey mob," Meese says conversationally. "Maybe he has something on someone. His fetish is just dangerous. They should have wacked him long ago."

Joel looks at him for a second, but he's afraid his thoughts will show on his face. He goes back to the DVD cabinet.

Were these in some kind of order?

"We should pack these up and get out. There's things I want to do..."

"One more to check."

Joel reads the covers of the first and the last DVD. The last one says "Wayne 2011." Feeling cold, he puts that DVD in.

And sees his father's face talking to him. To the camera. To Cody. Like the other video, Cody is wearing the camera in his glasses. Joel turns on the speakers.

"...Just get this over with."

Then nothing but the dining room. The sound of Gabriel arriving and talking, then whispering to Ken. The camera's on the move--through to the living room and the entrance to the hall. Catching Gabriel by surprise. Trying to cut him. Gabriel grappling with him long enough to get the knife away. Ken chasing after Gabriel and yelling for Cody to call it off.

Cody then follows them into the living room and snatches the shotgun off the cabinet. Cody cocks the shotgun and Gabriel looks back, horrified and startled at once. Then Cody shoots. Joel sees Ken jerk forward, and at the same time, the blood from the exit wound splattering on Gabriel.

Joel grabs the table, breathing heavy. He stares at the large screen, showing Gabriel suddenly falling in the hallway entrance. Pounding on the front door, and John Dell's voice.

Meese telling Cody to leave.

You fucking bastard. Breathing heavy, he ejects the disc and quickly puts it back in the plastic case, then slipping the case inside his shirt.

"You shouldn't have watched that, Joel. But it's good that this is all over."

It's all over now.

He turns and punches Meese in the face as hard as he can.

Meese staggers back and falls over. Joel now must get the gun away from him. He grabs the iron desk lamp next to the chair and yanks it free from the plug in the wall, then slams Meese in the head with it.

Meese does not go out like Ty did. He grabs Joel and pulls him down with him. For a moment, they struggle. Even injured, Meese's decades of training is overpowering. Meese's arm goes around Joel's neck in a classic police chokehold. "If you don't go with me...I'll do what I didn't want to have to do..."

Starting to see stars, Joel reaches for his jeans pocket. A snicking sound, and suddenly Meese screams in pain. Joel has stuck him in the leg with his switchblade.

Meese rolls away from Joel, scrambling to get his footing. He jerks the knife out with a grunt, and throws it across the room.

Joel picks up the lamp and swings it at his head. Meese blocks with his arm, backing up toward the doorway.

A voice behind Meese says, "I thought you were dead in the explosion."

Cody is standing in the doorway. In his hand is a giant knife, the other knife he had with him in Ken's house. The Bark River Bravo III.

Meese whirls around. He yanks the gun out of his pocket and fires at Cody. But the gun doesn't go off. It just clicks.

Meese quickly does a tap, rack, bang to his weapon, but it doesn't fire again.

Cody shakes his head. "You got a squib load there. Probably the powder got wet underwater. You should have heard the click and stopped firing. That can take your hand off if it blows up."

Meese stares at his gun barrel, which bulges slightly. The squib has damaged it.

Cody twists the gun out of Meese's hand. "This is better," Cody says. He draws the knife across Meese's throat.

Meese tries to speak, putting his hands to his throat as blood begins flow. Joel moves away from them both, toward his knife on the far side of the room.

Cody says, "You won't bleed out from that. This, though, will do it."

He shoves the knife in Meese's abdomen and slices up. Blood streams from the gaping hole in his torso.

"Save the coroner some trouble." Cody jams the knife in Meese's chest and yanks it sideways.

Meese falls backward on the floor. His blood has splattered Cody, and the immediate area of the room.

Joel has recovered his switchblade. Much smaller than the knife Cody has, but he's prepared to throw it at Cody, who's blocking the door.

Cody, finished with Meese, regards Joel. "I don't really know you. I have nothing against you. But I can't let you leave."

They hear a pistol being cocked behind Cody.

Gabriel's voice: "What you'll *do* is get on your fucking knees, and drop that fucking thing. Or you'll get to see your own brains explode out your head."

Inundated with relief, Joel watches Cody look over his shoulder at Gabriel, then at the knife in his hand. He drops the knife on the floor.

"Back up," Gabriel says.

Cody carefully steps back. His gaze falls, seemingly regretfully, to his knife.

"Get down."

When Cody hesitates, Zest says, "I suggest you comply with the request."

Cody slowly gets to his knees. Now Joel can see Gabriel holding the gun out in front of him.

Zest moves around Cody, keeping his own gun trained on him.

"You need to put your hands on top of your head."

"The professional. I don't suppose you still have professional courtesy?"

Zest moves further into the other room. "Not this time."

Cody puts his hands on his head and glances at Meese's body. Zest walks over and looks at Meese long enough to determine his status.

"He's dead."

"Joel," Gabriel says, "Come out here."

Joel walks out the room, giving Cody a wide berth. Cody is still looking at Meese's body. Maybe savoring the memory.

Next to Gabriel, Joel can see the absolute tenseness he has in watching Cody.

Gabriel asks, "Is there anything we need to know about?"

"Nothing that I could see, but I couldn't search too long."

As Zest is remaining in front of Cody with his own gun, Gabriel turns to Joel. "Go outside and wait for us."

From Gabriel's tone, Cody looks over his shoulder at him.

Joel just shakes his head. Gabriel and Joel stare at each other, communications not said out loud.

Joel sees what Gabriel is feeling, almost like he can read Gabriel's thoughts. Gabriel might have killed Meese, had not Cody done so. Now Cody stands in as a substitute for Meese. The man who killed Joel's father, who helped Meese. And who certainly was going to kill Joel had not Gabriel and Zest shown up.

Although Gabriel must be on at the pinnacle of adrenaline from his efforts to get here to save Joel, he appears calm...really, he's gone cold.

Joel has his own reasons to feel in a rage about Cody, who is now watching the two of them with his bloody hands on top of his head. Cody killing his father, trying to kill Gabriel, trying to kill him. While Joel cannot possibly process that emotionally now, he knows he doesn't want Gabriel to go further. He stopped Gabriel going over the line before...while he's gone over that line himself. Why does it make a difference?

Seconds tick by; Zest waits impassively, not taking sides either way.

Because Joel's afraid of how far Gabriel could go. How much he could lose. Whereas Gabriel was afraid for Joel's physical safety, Joel is almost afraid for Gabriel's soul.

He shakes his head again. And Gabriel, watching him, almost imperceptibly changes his posture.

Whatever might have happened doesn't happen.

The sound of the car on the gravel road.

"Dell," Gabriel finally says. "I told him about the cabin." He turns to Zest. "You need to leave."

Zest leaves the room and heads for the kitchen to go out the back door. "Your bag is outside here."

A few seconds later, a pounding on the door. "Police!"

Joel goes to the door and says through it, "It's me, Joel. I'm opening it."

He unlocks the door carefully. Dell enters with his service weapon drawn and quickly checking the room.

Gabriel is holding the gun up on his fingers, not pointing it anymore.

Dell approaches them swiftly. "Gabriel."

Gabriel hands over the gun, grip-first. Dell puts it in his pocket. "Is that him?"

"Stephen Cody. Hit man. He tried to kill me, and I saw him kill Ken McFadden."

"I have more than that," Joel adds.

"Meese is in the other room. He's dead. Cody killed him, too."

Cody is impassive through all this.

Dell says to Cody, "I need you to put your hands behind your back. Lean forward, toes out."

Upon Cody's compliance, Dell puts cuffs on him, then pats him down. Dell then checks the other rooms.

He comes back out and makes Cody get up. "Anyone else here?"

Gabriel answers, "No."

"You two need to come with me. We should have backup coming soon."

∞

Once Dell packs Cody in the back seat of his car, I tell him, "I would like to retrieve my belongings from the back of the house."

"I can't let you do that. You're considered absconded from custody."

"I'm not running away."

Dell shakes his head.

Joel says, "Let me get them. I'm not in custody, am I?"

Dell looks at him. "Just hold on. No one's going anywhere right now. You said you had "more than that." What did you mean?"

"I witnessed Cody trying to kill Meese back at his house. Meese kidnapped me and held me at gun point while I was here. But I have a bag with his computer and some other records, in my car. I saw Cody kill Meese here. I found Cody's collection of videos; I suppose his hits for the mob. I found the one where he killed my father."

I add to what Joel is saying. "I have a laptop in my bag in the back. You can see what's on that video right now."

"Just wait. We'll sort this out."

"I'm calling my lawyer, then."

"You can do that."

Irritated, I take out my phone and call Michaela. As I'm talking to her, I see Joel is staring at Cody.

"He's doing something."

Dell looks in the back-seat window. "You need to stop moving."

They all hear a snap. And then amazingly, Cody brings his hands around to his front. His left hand, out of the handcuffs, is bent at an unnatural angle.

Dell's eyes go wide. "He broke his hand." He draws his weapon. "Stop. Right now!"

Cody shows no sign of pain or distress. He reaches his right hand down to his shoe, and takes a small black square device from inside the shoe under his foot. He presses a button on it.

"Drop that, right now!" Dell starts to open the car door.

A strange sizzling sound emanates from the house.

I pull Joel with me to the other side of the car, away from the house. "He has it wired! Get back!"

Dell joins us on the other side, but has to dive as something in the house explodes. I already have Joel and myself down on the ground.

We hear a thud inside the car, and a crash. The door on the other side of the car slams open.

Dell calls out, "Stay where you are..."

More booms from inside the house, and then one final explosion, where we can hear bits of the house flying off. The pieces drop around us and on us.

Dell is on his knees, aiming at Cody. Cody's running for the woods behind the cabin. But with the debris and smoke, Dell can't get a hit.

After a few seconds, we get up cautiously. A large piece of the house frame has dented the car.

The house is destroyed but the frame is mostly standing. Tiny fires are visible inside.

My phone is still on, with Michaela still there. I quickly let her know what is going on. Dell runs for the woods to see if he can catch Cody.

Michaela asks, "Why would Cody blow up the place?"

Joel says, "His DVDs were in there. Of his murders."

He takes a case from under his shirt. "But I took the one that counts." He turns to me and buries his head in my shoulder.

I tell Michaela, "I imagine he had an escape plan all along."

Taking advantage of the opportunity, I go around the back to search for my knapsack. It's under some rubble but intact.

Dell comes back alone, as a couple of police cars arrive. Dell starts arranging a search for Cody, as I take my laptop out and set it on the trunk of his car and start it up.

I tell Dell, "Ms. Connor is on her way." I hold my hand out to Joel. He hands me the plastic case. I load the DVD.

Dell is still hyper over Cody's escape, but watches the screen with me. Joel walks away to avoid seeing it again.

I'm extremely disturbed to see Cody's point of view like some Eighties horror movie, of him chasing Ken and I, and shooting Ken. And then Meese hitting me in the head.

I see Dell staring at the screen, his cop's passiveness temporarily disrupted by the ugliness he's watching.

"Fuck this shit," I say to Dell. "Have I managed to demonstrate my point?"

"Yes, that's a given." Dell then goes with Joel to get Meese's stuff out of Joel's car.

Michaela arrives not long after this. But I can't leave with Joel or Michaela. I technically absconded from custody. Dell takes me with him back to the Wayne police station. Joel follows to give a statement. Michaela calls the Passaic County prosecutor, and then heads back to her office to type a motion for my release.

It's about fucking time.

∞

DÉNOUEMENT

Alan Moore (in V for Vendetta) said, "The past can't hurt you anymore, not unless you let it."

∞

Friday, June 11, 2011
Broadway, 11:30 pm

JOEL PAUSES OUTSIDE the diner on Broadway to light a cigarette. He exhales slowly, watching the smoke dissipate.

He's just come back Churchill's estate in Alpine, New Jersey. Churchill had requested he come over that evening. Joel figured it was to arrange when he'd collect on the favor.

Instead...Churchill was regretful.

"*What happened to you...all I can see is a line back to that man. The man who hurt you. I asked myself if Jan would have asked you to do this. And he wouldn't. I shouldn't have asked you to either.*"

A man turns a corner and smiles when he sees Joel. Harry. They hug each other. Then go inside the diner and sit at a booth.

After giving their order to the waitperson, Harry says, "How are things going? About all the stuff you mentioned last week?"

Joel toys with his Coke straw. "I guess it's all going pretty well. Uh, Gabriel is going to pursue an action against the jail. And I'm keeping on with mine."

Harry nods gravely. "That's brave of you."

"The other victims who joined the suit...I want it to work out for them. Whatever money Meese may have had, the government might take it. But if it's settled, I'll give it to the Milk Center. I was trying to think of some kind of thing to do there anyway. Something meaningful for the kids..."

Harry touches Joel's hand briefly. "You have a lot to share. You can help them, because you were there."

"Yeah...So, remember Churchill?" He tells Harry about what happened that evening.

"That was an interesting turn. Did your boyfriend know about this arrangement?"

"I told him. Keeping something like that secret wouldn't work. Gabriel told me whatever I had to do didn't mean anything between he and I, that we would always be good with each other."

"I'm glad. He treats you right, then."

"He does. We treat each other right. We see that every day. When we got back together, it was a little strange. But going through this--it was important to have his support. We take care of each other. I think we're stronger for it. We've been taking time off. A weekend here and there to just be together and connect and talk."

"Your favorite thing--talking." Harry smiles again. "How about your mom?"

"Uh, well. It doesn't look like the feds are going to go after her for anything. So that's good. Um, it's not easy to have this relationship with her. She's sorry, I know that. I'm trying the best I can."

"I can imagine how that is."

Joel nods. "I appreciate that you're able to meet me at the last minute. Gabriel is on a job tonight. It seemed like a good opportunity."

"No problem. I have some information. You were right about what you were thinking."

Joel shrugs. "I'm not surprised. I have something for you. I remember that you liked these guys." He hands over to Harry a gift bag that has a baseball glove wrapped in tissue paper. The paper bag also contains $10,000 wrapped like a parcel.

Harry unwraps the glove. "Vintage. Signed. Mantle. That's a prize for sure."

"It's yours."

Harry looks up at him.

"I know some people who can get things. I was looking for something for Gabriel. Some pitcher he likes. Guidry."

"Ron Guidry. The Gator. The 18 strikeouts man."

"So I've *heard,* believe me. Anyway, since I was searching for that guy, I got this offered as well."

"You didn't have to do that; the cash was enough," Harry says. But he's clearly pleased with the old glove and touches it gently. "So...let me tell you what I found out. This Andreas guy, like you figured, also deals in child porn. On the darknet. Not a lot of material, but I guess he made the kids do the porn, or he had someone else make them, before he sold them. Just to make the extra money."

"That's why I need the advice. I don't know how to handle getting him arrested, and that's what I want to do. I'm not killing anyone, or sending someone in undercover for this."

"What were you thinking--I mean, what would you want to happen?"

"If this material with the kids is absolutely, for sure, *his* doing, it needs to be found on his computer."

Harry contemplates things for a moment, as a waiter brings them their orders. "I know you, and how good you are with computers. Angela used to yell for you all the time: *Joel, how do you do this? How do you do that?* You probably know how to set this up. And your boyfriend, he's a private investigator. Wouldn't he be willing to help out?"

"I could set it up, but I prefer to pay for some plausible deniability. As for Gabriel, there's things he's willing to do, but let's just say there's things I don't *want* him to do. He doesn't know about this. It has nothing to do with our relationship, so he doesn't have to know about this."

Harry leans forward. "These people who deal in child porn live in an entirely different world. They think different, they rationalize different. They play dirty, so taking them down dirty...I don't care about the ethics--if there are ethics to consider in this case."

"I know. I don't care either."

"And it's not fake stuff being put on his computer. It's not like some ransomware scheme to extort money from people. With this guy Andreas, it's his own work, his own crime."

"Harry...all I can say is that Gabriel has crossed lines for me already. I don't have to ask him about this, and I'm not going to. For me, it's different. This particular situation and how to handle it doesn't bother me. I just wanted to be sure about if it was actually Andreas's stuff, and I trust you on that."

The two of them discuss some details. From there, they go on to talk of other, more pleasant things.

Joel asks, "Retired from the agency?"

"Clean break. I'm looking to have a peaceful life. Angela would probably love to hear from you."

"Maybe. Right now isn't a good time."

Harry smiles at Joel. "Maybe. Things changed. Big time. Something you should be proud of."

Something catches Joel's eye outside the diner's window. Rain is starting to fall, and people are walking closer to the buildings to catch cover from awnings and overhangs.

For a second, Joel sees Jan in an open raincoat, smiling. He's holding a cigarette. He then starts to walk down Broadway.

Does that mean it's over? I don't see you again?

In his head he hears Jan saying, *Life is never over. There's always something to keep with you. But the past has to move on.*

You need to move on. It's time.

∞

CODA

From The *New York Scene's* Thin Blue Line column, by Carl Mankiewitz
September 1, 2011

More fallout is happening in Queens, with the Andreas Trakas case. Trakas is facing indictment on several charges involving possession of child pornography. A source in the Queens County DA's office tells us the office received an anonymous tip that led to the discovery Trakas has been running a child trafficking operation. The trafficking appears to be in conjunction with the child porn operation. That tip also led to the arrest of one of Trakas's alleged associates, Sean Lewis.

The case first hit the news a month ago, after Trakas brought his laptop into a computer repair service, complaining of a virus. The tech working on the laptop found hundreds of files of children in sexual situations, and immediately reported it to law enforcement.

Meanwhile, the federal investigation continues in the New Jersey state government scandal. The murder case of Division of Development chief procurement and land use officer Ken McFadden opened up a web of fraudulent schemes, including deals made with known organized crime figures, bid rigging, false work orders and vouchers, and bribery. *The Scene's* favorite unruly private eye, Gabriel Ross, was arrested for but later cleared of any involvement in McFadden's murder. Through Ross's and Joel McFadden's (Ken McFadden's son) work with Wayne NJ police detective John Dell, the prime suspect in that murder and several other mob-related murders was identified as Stephen Cody, an alleged hit man for the New Jersey families and collaborator with Ken McFadden. Cody is also accused of murdering Passaic County undersheriff Lawrence Meese, another conspirator in the corruption schemes. Cody escaped custody in May, and is the target of an ongoing federal manhunt.

Recently, the State of New Jersey offered Ross a settlement regarding his claim of abuse and excessive force while being held in the Passaic County Jail. Joel McFadden, Ross's significant other, had a positive turn of events in his own difficult legal matter. McFadden and three other victims are suing his father's cohort Lawrence Meese for sexual abuse committed when McFadden was a teenager. A recent hearing allowed the lawsuit against Meese's estate to proceed, despite some allegations being over 17 years old...

THE END OF THE BOOK OF JOEL

GABRIEL AND JOEL WILL RETURN IN DEAD
FOR NOW.

AUTHOR'S NOTE

Once again, this book is dedicated to survivors, who rise above being victims and do not let the past define who they are today. From one survivor of sexual abuse and sexual assault to others--it's not you, it's them.

The *Gabriel's World* website features a LGBTQIA+ resources page, with links to articles and websites on the topics in the books, including sex work and sexual assault, as well as other articles of interest and recommendation. You can find the resource page by going to GabrielsWorld.com. Recommendations for sites are welcome.

While the streets of New York City had little to offer teens like Joel at the time he was thrown out, that has changed. In New York and other cities, programs and shelters are available for LGBTQIA+ teens and young adults, giving a measure of protection unavailable in other shelters (which hold potential for abuse or violence). If you ever deem a charity worth a donation, I recommend an LGBTQIA+ youth shelter. The *Gabriel's World* resources page has a growing list.

--Alex Fiano

GABRIEL'S WORLD EXTRAS:
PREVIEW OF THE NEXT GABRIEL'S WORLD STORY, DEAD FOR NOW

Brilliant and provocative New York City private investigator Gabriel Ross has a feeling he's being watched. His paranoia is justified--a rogue faction from the sinister Tertullian Society is stalking him. Psyops master Damon Clement has dangerous plans for Gabriel. Gabriel tries to protect his friend and business partner Veronica and his boyfriend Joel, while still secretly exposing the Society's misdeeds. His work in uncovering the conspiracy has sparked a viral protest movement which agitates for answers even as Gabriel and the Society head toward a final confrontation.

INTRODUCTION: UNKNOWN KNOWNS

∞

From the YouTube Channel "Tom Paine Events," in a video entitled: <Unknown Knowns and Raising the Right Question>

Transcript: "In an article, philosopher Slavoj Žižek discussed the concept of 'unknown knowns'--those events which we do not or pretend not to know about, although these events determine action and form policy. Žižek said, "...philosophy as the 'public use of reason' is not to solve problems, but to redefine them; not to answer questions, but to raise the proper question."

Perhaps the dead are the ultimate 'unknown knowns.' They were present and real at one time, but then faded from consciousness. Yet their death may determine other actions and form policy. Some deaths are ignored. Some are reconstructed to a different truth, although the original truth of the death still exists. In their death, they become a symbol: emotion, love, pride, justice, sorrow, evil.

Some deaths are questionable--they are metadiegetic in that their death is a story within a story. Their death does not answer questions, but raises questions about society and what we choose to know. In videos to follow on this channel, aside from information and documentation of conspiracies going back over several decades, I will also have a philosophical take on mysterious deaths that have that metadiegetic quality. Are all these deaths conspiracies? Perhaps not. But in a sense the definite misdeeds of government, corporations, and evil interests create a hyperreality in which an actual conspiracy doesn't matter--what matters is raising the questions about an official story. Any official story."

∞

PRELUDE

"But it is just the truth that cannot be known of the multitude, for truth is revolutionary." *--From a 1912 pro-women's suffrage periodical called "The Vote: The Organ of the Women's Freedom League."*

According to Garson O'Toole (QuoteInvestigator.com), this quote is a possible origin of another alleged quote: "In a time of universal deceit, telling the truth is a revolutionary act," which ironically is universally attributed to George Orwell, despite no evidence of his having written or said this.

However, as Ioan Culianu and Umberto Eco have suggested, a misinterpretation can create a reality greater than the truth. Perhaps Orwell would be pleased to own the quote that didn't happen.

∞

Transcript: "Litvinenko was a dissident whistleblower and former Lt. Colonel in the Russian FSB, living in London. In November 2006 he became severely ill and died from poisoning by polonium-210. When he was in the FSB, he had targeted the Russian mafia. As a dissident, Litvinenko had publicly alleged Russian government-sponsored assassinations of journalists and bombings in Chechnya, and he also alleged corruption within the FSB itself. Litvinenko had told acquaintances of threats made to his life shortly before he was poisoned. He died horribly of organ failure due to the radioactive compound. Whistleblowers, as we've seen in the US and other countries, have not fared well. Speaking out--bringing light to abuse, injustice, and crimes--leads to persecution and death. Those who are guilty are unknown knowns. Litvinenko's death raises the question of how can society better protect and listen to whistleblowers?"

∞

Saturday, August 6, 2011
Warinanco Park, New Jersey 1:10 pm

A SONG IS PLAYING. Lush, moody, a hit in the Eighties. Joel McFadden sinks in the luxury of the leather seats in his leased Nissan Rogue, although he doesn't turn the music up as he's on his iPhone, using FaceTime.

"You really want this project to happen," Travis Churchill comments on the on the other end of the call.

Joel makes his voice firm. "Yes. It's what I want. I don't care if you pay me for the mural; I want the Milk Center project funded."

Churchill chuckles. "Joel, you know you're getting both. My corporate offices here and in New York are going to be even more provocative and energetic with your murals--imagine if...who was it who tried to paint in Lincoln Center? Picasso? If his work hadn't been censored or something."

"Diego Rivera," Joel responds mildly, although he rolls his eyes. "His mural in the Rockefeller Center. *Man at the Crossroads.* Our former governor Nelson Rockefeller ordered it destroyed because it appeared anti-capitalist."

"I know I'm annoying you and I like seeing your face--even annoyed you're beautiful."

Joel glances over at the basketball court to check that Gabriel isn't close enough to hear that. No. He looks back at the screen. Churchill, a nice-looking super-fit white guy in his late forties with wavy brown hair, smiles at him.

"Just so you know, I have it stipulated in the contract your work will not be destroyed--even if it's nothing but dicks. I hope it's more than just dicks, but still. If something happens to me and the board takes over and wants it gone, you can decide what to do with it. *And* I'm making a donation through my foundation to the Milk Center, to enrich your art project with the kids. Soon."

"How soon?" Joel can be blunt with him. He's earned the right.

"Monday. I have to twist the arm of the board, but I'll be picturing you glaring at me impatiently the whole time. They'll do it. I'll call your friend Juanita at the Center to set it up."

"And the donation for basic necessities. Don't forget that."

"Yes, your kids should be able to shower as needed."

"And eat."

"Spartan Foundation is known for its community service, Joel. Look at our rating on Charity Navigator." Spartan Foundation is the philanthropic offshoot of Spartan, the software/app company Churchill designed, founded, and which made him a billionaire. He had just started the company when he first hired Joel as an escort, back in 2001.

Churchill sighs. "Hold on a sec, one of my five other phones is going off."

While on hold, Joel turns up the Breathe song and glances outside at the court again. By extra-sensory perception, Gabriel Ross in turn looks over his shoulder back at Joel. Even at a distance, Gabriel's feelings are clear and Joel smiles faintly. Joel will probably have to fly overseas again soon, and so *Hands to Heaven* fits in with his feelings about leaving Gabriel for a week or so, alone and--

Then Gabriel's close friend Bob Jarvey charges and slams into Gabriel, snatching the basketball out of his hands.

Joel can hear Gabriel's "*What the fuck?*" even in his closed car. Bob is triumphant. "*Too slow, my man. I'm like Wilt in two ways. Only one is on the court.*"

"*Because you cheat, you dick.*" They go back to their strange one-on-one that seems to involve a lot of rough physical contact, like two dogs play-fighting. Both men are white, muscular and of dark Irish descent. Bob is more than ten years older than Gabriel's 37, and at around 6'1, 4 inches taller, but they are evenly matched on the court.

Churchill returns and goes into boring but important details of times, dates, and whatnot.

Gabriel and Bob suddenly bounce into the side of the SUV; the two of them have somehow traveled the ball all the way to the edge of the court and into the parking lot.

Travis looks quizzical. "What's that noise? Are you at some kind of sporting event?"

"I'm at a park in Jersey."

"I bet I know who with. I remember Gabriel at that softball game a few weeks ago. What I like about Gabriel is his confidence. He keeps all eyes on him and he knows it."

And true, a few stragglers have come up to the fence to watch Gabriel and Bob's little show, *Gladiator Basketball.*

For whatever reason, Joel feels a little uncomfortable when Churchill discusses Gabriel. Churchill hasn't tried to come on to Joel sexually since an attack of conscience a couple months ago. But he also seems to have sublimated his desire into sponsoring Joel's art.

"Swing by and pick up the contract," Churchill says. "Or do you need Isabella?"

"No, this is different than my gallery work."

"Good. Come on by."

Churchill could just email it, but Joel knows he wants to see Joel in person and talk. Joel can handle that. Joel wraps up the call, feeling that whatever Churchill's kinks may be, it's worth it for what he can do to help the homeless kids. He opens his window, and skips songs on his sound system, considering what he would play while working on Churchill's murals.

Bob raps on the driver's side window. Joel lowers it.

"Hey Joel," Bob says. "Why you gots to be all business? Give your man a break. He's trying to show off for you. He's *never* this good."

"If I don't react, he tries harder. I like to see how far I can make him go."

"You're mean," Bob responds, laughing. "Are women that mean? I guess so, but I can ignore it for the trim. Gabriel just turns into a helpless fool with the puppy dog eyes."

"Don't hate the player, hate the game." Joel lights one of his clove cigarettes and coolly watches the men go back to the court. True enough, his demeanor makes Gabriel work harder to make an impression on him. Gabriel is fast on his feet and has excellent shooting abilities.

"Now who's too slow, trash-talker," Gabriel says to Bob after making an elegant jump shot.

"I let you do that," Bob retorts. "I didn't want you to look bad in front of your arm candy and not get any tonight."

"You're jealous of my skills." Gabriel looks back at Joel again, and this time, Joel allows a smile that gets all of Gabriel's attention. Impulsively, Joel crooks his finger at Gabriel, who immediately drops the ball and starts towards the car.

"Oh Jesus, this again," Bob complains mockingly. "Time-out for foreplay."

Ignoring him, Gabriel comes up to the window and leans on it. "Hey baby. What's going on?"

Joel meets Gabriel's dark brown eyes with his own blue-gray ones and moves his head closer. "I need to do some things. Can you get back on your own?"

"Too difficult being a sports husband?"

"If you were actually playing something instead of fucking around, I could take an interest. No, I'm kidding you. I really do have to take care of some stuff in order to be free later. You'll reap the rewards."

Gabriel takes Joel's hand and raises it to his mouth, touching the index finger knuckle with his tongue. He bites softly, erotically. Joel pretends this doesn't do anything to him, flicking his cigarette in the ashtray casually.

"I could mug you for that damn thing," Gabriel says, still holding Joel's hand. "The desire for it never ends."

Joel leans forward so he's almost speaking against Gabriel's lips. "Humn. If you behave yourself, I'll let you watch me smoke it later."

Gabriel smiles. "You really want that ass-kicking, don't you? Keep working that smart mouth, see what happens."

"I know exactly what will happen." Joel smiles back. "I can leave you in such a way now that you'll be unable to play any more fake basketball. Unfortunately, you'll only have Bob for company. No relief there unless you turn him out."

Gabriel kisses Joel's hand again. "I can do the same to you...unfortunately, if you're going to see Isabella, she'll notice for sure and offer to take care of it for you. Probably film it too for whatever Jeff Koons-type thing she has in mind..."

Joel never fails to be irritated at any mention of Koons. He says, changing his tone, "I'm going to see Travis."

"Jesus Christ, same situation. I can't win."

"You've already won. Remember whom I'm coming home to."

"Archie. You're coming home to Archie--you're his fun dad. I'm just the sucker dad who buys his food and catnip."

"I can be your fun dad too."

"*Uhhh.*" Gabriel straightens up. "That's it, lost the erection. Don't ever use the word '*dad*' in a sexual way. I need to go to my happy place now."

But he leans back in to kiss Joel on the mouth. Joel smiles and drives away, waving at Bob.

∞

And then the hairs on the back of my neck go up. Various incidents over the past couple years have left me extraordinarily sensitive to things around me being off. Yeah, people are watching Bob and I play the fools. Yeah, a couple look uncomfortable when I kiss Joel. That isn't what I'm feeling.

More like someone's there who shouldn't be. And that I'm under observation. I turn our one on one into boring practice shooting hoops to get the stragglers to lose interest. Then I pace the court with the ball, scanning all directions. An SUV is at the far end of the parking lot; it is dark with tinted windows. Something about it doesn't sit right with me.

When Bob and I are done, we head for his Cherokee in the lot. He's going to drop me at the train station to go back to NYC. I have him stop the Cherokee near the SUV and act like we need to check under the hood.

I pretend to look at the engine. "Can you set your alarm off?"

Bob does, with his remote. I lift my head to watch the SUV. When the alarm screeches, I see a hint of movement inside, and a subtle shift in the frame of the car. More than one person is inside. I nod at Bob and he slams the hood down. As I get in the passenger side of the Cherokee, I notice the SUV has extra antennas. Not obvious--the wires run with the chrome trim of the back window.

Bob asks, "Who do you think your new friends are?"

"Hard to say. As far as I know, neither the feds nor locals have a reason to be on my ass."

Bob laughs. "It has to be *you*, though. I try to stay out of trouble these days. The city of Paterson sure isn't fond of you. I thought those might be agents from the Passaic County Sheriff's office."

"I think they'd be more open about pulling us over and beating the shit of me. Like they did in the jail."

I keep watch as we head to the station, but I don't see anyone following us. I find hard to believe that any official agency would spring for a multiple-car tail. Granted someone could have put a tracer on Bob's car so they could stay out of sight. But why? I'm not important.

My paranoia doesn't get better on the PATH train to downtown New York. I surreptitiously scrutinize the people in my car. Most are summer tourists. But one short-haired man in a suit stands out.

A quote from the Nero Wolfe story *The Doorbell Rang* comes to mind, when Archie Goodwin catches a couple of FBI agents tailing him. "*They were not-looking at me, the way they are trained to not-look in Washington.*"

That describes this guy. He has an iPad held awkwardly in front of him and is studiously not-looking. For fun, I get up and wander over closer to him, as if I want to be near the door. Then I lean over him and rudely look at his iPad. I catch a glimpse of the subway car on the screen--he's using some camera device to help him not-look.

He clutches the iPad to his chest. "Excuse me?" He has a faux-outraged tone.

I look him in the eye. "Technology is wonderful. But has technology helped you find Jesus?"

The two people next to him glance at me warily, in case I'm going to proselytize. But my man drops his eyes to his lap, frowning.

I laugh to myself as I get off the train at the World Trade Center stop. This could all be coincidence. I could be the crazy one. After all, nothing I'm doing is worthy of consideration from intelligence agencies.

∞

In an unknown area of New York, two US intelligence personnel [*REAPER and MORTEM*] send a secure message to their supervisor [*KISMET*].

[SCRAMBLE MESSAGE]
ypW0TgsssP vmtu0mKzOt A7149YE3KB 3SkosB2LTc qSjfFAhwBz
[Unscramble] ENIGMA Project/Eyes Only

From REAPER and MORTEM, to KISMET

This is a follow-up on our collective information regarding subject [*Redacted: Gabriel Ross*] Codename MAGICIAN, DOB 2/15/1974, who is worthy of consideration by our agency lately. Our asset ETERNITY has told us his colleague BEDEVIL is still maintaining surveillance of MAGICIAN. Because of BEDEVIL's interest, we checked on ETERNITY's information regarding MAGICIAN and we are adding to it from our own investigation.

As background, MAGICIAN has few family members. He doesn't appear to be close to his father JEFFREY ROSS, Lt. Col. US ARMY. [See File Appendix] He has a half-sister he does not speak to. His mother KATERINA SHEEHAN ROSS is deceased from cancer, DOD 12/01/2003. MAGICIAN was very close to her and her younger brother DOMINIC SHEEHAN. SHEEHAN lived in the apartment MAGICIAN lives in now on Avenue A in the East Village. SHEEHAN died 09/12/2004. MAGICIAN started his own business with the insurance proceeds from their deaths. SHEEHAN's death was due officially to being caught in a 'freak accident' construction collapse on the CUNY Midtown campus. [SEE File 8745-S/D re: PARADISE]

ABOUT THE AUTHOR

Alex Fiano is a bi/genderqueer writer, teacher, artist, and LGBTQ+ advocate (particularly for youth) living in New York City.

The books in the *Gabriel's World* Series are:

The Hanged Man
Two-Faced Woman
The Book of Joel
Dead for Now
Hardcore (2019)

[Cover images in part from dead_brushes/brusheezy.com]

www.ingramcontent.com/pod-product-compliance
Lightning Source LLC
Chambersburg PA
CBHW072107250626
47159CB00007B/2340